PONDERED IN HER HEART

PONDERED IN HER HEART

K. ORME

Illustrated by
JESSICA MCKENDRY

TEA NOTES
PRESS

First paperback edition June 2021

Illustrations Copyright © 2021 Jessica McKendry

Cover Illustration and Design Copyright © Alyiesha Harris

Author Photograph Copyright © Abigail Bankes

ISBN 978-1-7372-0040-6 (paperback)

ISBN 978-1-7372-0042-0 (hardcover)

ISBN 978-1-7372-0041-3 (ebook)

www.teanotespress.com

Printed in the U.S.A.

To Brooke, Tori, Hannah, Nora, and Jess.

Brooke. You are the fearless captain. If you hadn't created the writing group for all of us in the Enchanted Lair, I never would have picked this project back up. You are incredibly strong. I admire you greatly.

Tori. My dude. 3 AM convos while we wrote and agonized over forgetting words, calling refrigerators "chilly bois." You have been my #1 hype woman and I am forever grateful for your input and advice.

Hannah. You are my INFJ sister. We are on the same wavelength. With this dedication page, you have the high ground. I believe you joined the writer's group the session I drafted this book and were thrown into my fangirling antics but still decided that I was cool enough to play D&D with.

Nora. You are like the little sister I never had because I only have one brother in real life. (Hi, Bobby.) I see so much of myself in you when I was your age, and I am so blessed that I get to call you "friend." When we end up in Narnia together, we'll be queens at the same time. I promise.

Jess. Every time I remember how we met, over an internet forum concerning art and a certain Henry Moore from this very book, I start to cry a little because of how fortuitous that event was. We spent early morning hours fangirling about historical fiction boys afterward, and I remember thinking "wow. I found somebody like me. Somebody who 'gets it.'" Thank you. Thank you for being you and befriending me. I am grateful for you and your immense art talent.

I hold you all in the highest regard, as sisters and fellow authors.

CONTENTS

LIST OF ILLUSTRATIONS

I

Felicia loved it when her husband played the violin. She loved the way his long, pale fingers traipsed over the neck of the instrument, the way his dark brows furrowed in concentration, the way he swayed to the music as it spilled from his hands. She'd sit and listen to him with a sigh, while he gave her small smiles and secret glances, chin against the rest.

But wars and violins tended not to mix, and there wasn't much music at the Hawkings estate as of late, nor much by the way of gaiety since the massacre in Boston. Most assuredly, the soldiers had won their case, and tensions alleviated if only a mere fraction for the king's soldiers, but with the Tea Party and the events at Lexington and Concord, there could be no more denying that a war had started. Now, Major Thomas Hawkings was more likely to pour over correspondence letters in his office, door closed, than to play the violin.

Felicia pushed one of the high-backed velvet chairs from the front sitting room down the hallway to the office door. She tucked a stray chocolate-colored lock of hair behind her ear and under her mobcap, upon the chair, and pressed her supple pale cheek against the door, fingertips splayed on the wood, listening for him, trying to hear his voice if he thought aloud, but she could only perceive the scratch of his quill on parchment. She pulled a folded paper from her pocket, bit her lip, and slid it partially under the door.

Can't you just play one song?

The quiet sound of writing stopped, replaced by the creak of heavy boots on wooden floorboards. The paper disappeared, and she held her breath. She heard a low hum then the sound of scratching up against the door. A new note appeared in its place.

If I give you my purse, will you go to town and entertain yourself?

"Tom!" She squealed, her voice mixed with excitement and petulance.

Thomas laughed, the soft, warm laugh he reserved only for her. She leaned against the door, pressing her cheek against it, hoping he was leaning against the other side.

"Felicia." His voice, low and crisp, held a hint of teasing that softened the edge of his London tone.

She sucked in a breath. His voice—and face, if he'd open the door and let her see it—still sent shivers down her spine and filled her with joy, even after a year of courting and four years of marriage.

"It's warm out, and I don't want to go to town. I want to see you." Her voice cracked as she tried her best not to whine. "Can't you just open the door, and let me see your face?"

The door opened, and Thomas leaned against the frame. Felicia's eyes flickered over him. His weskit was undone, and his ribbon clung loosely in his dark-blond hair. A fire blazed within her as she gazed over her husband. She reached up, took the ribbon from his hair, and handed it to him.

"Now you have seen me." He curled his finger under her chin, tilting her face up toward his. His features were drawn and tired but softened while he searched her eyes. He pressed a kiss to her forehead. "Might I get back to work?"

"No." Felicia crossed her arms and frowned up at him, and he stood stalwart under her narrowed gaze. "Tell me, love. When was the last time you ate?"

Thomas glanced to the side, and his fingers twitched as if he counted in his head.

Felicia twisted her lips into disapproving pout. "Too long." She reached for his hands, intertwining her fingers with his. "I worry for you, love. You work too hard with so few breaks. Come and see if there's something left in the kitchen."

"I don't have the time," Thomas protested as Felicia led him through the house. "I need to finish my letter."

"Tom, please you must take care of yourself. If you can't take care of yourself, how will you care for our little family?"

"I will rest when I'm finished with the letter."

"Perhaps I should bring you something instead?"

"No, I must concentrate." He took her dainty hand and gave it a light squeeze. "But you may sit with me. I'm nearly finished." He rarely allowed Felicia to sit in the office with him while he read through his letters, but she knew if she just tilted her head just so, and pouted her lips just right, he might give in to her requests. While she couldn't say she got exactly what she wanted in the moment, Thomas had granted her access to himself, and with the times, it was more than she could ask for.

Thomas sat at his desk in the center of the room while she sat in the chair by the window, his violin in her lap, plucking at the E string. With every pluck her husband's shoulders tensed. He tapped the quill and set it upon his blotting paper.

"What is it you wish?" Thomas asked, rubbing at the bridge of his nose.

Felicia scooted her chair closer to him and pressed her cheek against his arm. She closed her eyes, breathing in his scent, then slid the violin onto his lap.

He glanced down and drew in a heavy breath. "I must finish this correspondence. Perhaps then."

"I'd rather see rosin on your fingers than ink splotches," Felicia said, taking his hand. She pressed kisses on his fingers and his palm. "The rosin smells nicer."

"If I play one tune, one little tune, will you let me finish up? And then I promise I am yours."

"Yes," Felicia said, drawing out the word, bouncing on her seat.

Thomas smiled. "There are days when you seem much younger than four and twenty, Lissie."

Felicia rolled her eyes and then nudged his arm. "Music is the food of love."

"I suddenly feel inclined to oblige you." He leaned down and kissed her cheek, a gleam returning to his eye.

"You haven't played in so long." She wrapped her arms about his waist. "Are you sure you remember?"

"I think I may recall a tune or two." He rummaged through his desk drawers, pulling out a box of rosin. Felicia retrieved the bow from the case, and she plunked down beside him once more.

He drew the bow across the violin, then fiddled with the pegs, tuning the strings. He leaned back in his chair, adjusting the instrument on his shoulder and chin.

"What does my dearest wish to hear?" he asked, and Felicia tapped her fingers together, closing her eyes, trying to recall a tune for him to play. "Vivaldi?"

"Yes, but I always ask for it."

"Because you like it," Thomas said, and he played the opening notes to Vivaldi's *Winter Concerto in F Minor*.

"I do so like it," Felicia said with a hum. Her eyes halfway closed, and she listened as Thomas played the quick notes with a regimented urgency. She peeked under her lashes, watching his fingers fly over the neck, to hit each note, watching the bow waving over the strings. Almost as quickly as he had started, the piece was over. He rose from his chair, pressed a tender kiss to Felicia's forehead, then strode to his case to stow the instrument away. Felicia's gaze flickered from him to his desk, to the letters shrouded in the red tape. She walked her fingers over to a letter and picked it up.

To Major Thomas Hawkings

She slid a nail under the seal, trying hard not to break the wax and the initials, those of General Gage, and started to slide the letter out.

"What are you doing?"

Felicia dropped the letter back to the table with a startled gasp and swiveled around to Thomas. "I'm sorry—"

"Felicia! You know you're not supposed to—did you read it?"

"I didn't!" Felicia said. "I just saw your name and thought—"

"It has red tape." He paced to his desk, clasped his hands together, and pressed his thumbs to his lips. "You know you're not supposed to touch those! If Moore finds out you've—"

"I wanted to help!" Felicia covered her face with her hands. A choked sob escaped her throat. "Thomas, forgive me. I didn't take note of the tape."

Thomas set the violin on his desk and leaned forward, rubbing at his eyes. "You didn't read anything?"

"No."

"I suppose there is no true harm in it if you didn't read anything. But don't let Colonel Moore know you touched it."

Felicia shook her head back and forth but kept her face covered. For a moment, she heard nothing but the quiet rustling of his clothes as he breathed. When she lowered her hands, he took the envelope, turned it over in his hands, and slid the letter out with a hum.

"Perhaps I will let you know part of it... you should know after all." He handed her the letter and waited as she read over it.

He massaged her neck and shoulders to quell her shivering as she perused the letter. Felicia leaned back against him, nearly forgetting she was supposed to be reading, but when she finished it, she let out a small squeak and raised her head, eyes wide, mouth agape. He pulled his chair from around his desk and sat beside her. His lips twitched downwards, and his gaze fell to his lap.

Felicia read over the letter again, then slid it back into the envelope. "Oh, Thomas!"

"It was bound to happen soon enough, my dearest."

Felicia waved the letter in the air. The red tape caught him on his nose, but he didn't flinch. She pushed the letter from her as far away as she could and pressed her fingers to her temple, closing her eyes. "You're being called away? To Massachusetts? I can't just leave my family! How long will this be for? When were you going to give us notice? What will we do?"

He only watched her, a tender smile on his lips, and gently took the letter from the desk. "My men—and Colonel Moore's—are needed there after the events of Lexington. You know the colonials forced us back to Boston. But it is only temporary. You will stay here."

"But..." She reached toward him, and her lips and hands trembled as she gripped his arms. "But why do *you* need to go? Can't another regiment go? Why do you think me not coming with you is a good thing? How long have you known?"

"One question at a time." Thomas placed the letter from General Gage in a drawer. He strode to the window in the room and studied the yard. "There has been some correspondence since March, but nothing set till recently. Lissie, I am a part of my men. I am called to go. I thought you liked having a major for a husband."

"I did!" Felicia crossed the room and tugged at his sleeve. He glanced over his shoulder at her, raising a brow, and she drew a shaky breath. "I mean, I do. But I think I like the idea more than the actual thing. An idea doesn't have to go to war. One that can stay home with his family. We've waited so long for this and now—"

Thomas turned to face her, his features soft and gentle. The small curve of his smile nearly masked the regret in his eyes. "Oh, sweet Lissie. I like the idea better, too. But I'm not an idea, am I? I'm a soldier, and you knew that when you married me. Nonetheless, it won't be a long engagement. After we show our force in Boston, I'll be back to you. Besides, it's only over a week's travel. I could return or send for you easily." He paused a moment, frowning. "In truth, I don't think I could come back all too easily lest they think me a deserter."

Felicia wiped her damp lashes with the back of her hand and took in a deep breath, "When do you leave?"

He pulled out his handkerchief and dabbed at her cheeks. "This Friday. Four days."

"I'd rather you didn't," Felicia said with a heavy sigh. "Why not Monday?"

"I'd rather not as well, my dearest one. But that's my job. It's my job to go, and your job to look pretty. Think of how this Christmastide will be all the sweeter." He quirked a smile, bending to place a chaste kiss on her lips.

Felicia took his face in her hands, gazing into his pale blue eyes. He blinked at her, then gave her another peck.

"Can I propose an idea?" Felicia asked after he stepped back from her.

"What sort of an idea?"

She wrapped her arms about him and pressed her face into his chest. He ran a hand over her hair and sighed.

"Thomas, when have we last had a party?"

He hummed. "I don't know... Last Christmas?"

"Let's have one before you leave. It's only Monday. Let's have a party Thursday with dancing and music, and then you can leave, but we'll have the happy memory of the party in our minds as you go off. Say let's do it, Thomas. Say we'll have one last party before you go? Let me wear a fine silk gown and feathers, and you can wear your uniform, and we can dance all night."

Thomas intertwined his fingers with hers and brought her hands to his lips. He peered down at her over his nose, his features softened and pensive. "Is that what you'd like?"

She nodded.

"I fear you may overtax yourself, my love. You're in no condition for commotion."

"Nonsense, a little minuet never hurt anyone. We could invite those of us who are leaving Friday, our families, our friends, everyone we know, really."

Thomas stood straight, clearing his throat. "It is short notice. I'll have to rush an order for wine barrels."

She nodded more fervently. "We can have madeira and port, and..."

"And I can play my violin." Thomas grinned. "Go tell Selah and Amos to start preparing. Write your invitations. It'll be a grand party."

2

F elicia churned out invitation after invitation as she sat across Thomas at his desk, holding his right hand with her left as they worked quietly together.

A wave of nausea swept over her, and she let out a small moan, dropping the quill on the table as she covered her mouth pressed her lips tightly together.

Thomas glanced up from his ledger, brows furrowing. "Again?"

Felicia gently shook her head. "I'm sorry. I didn't mean to disturb you."

His fingers tightened around hers. "Are you sure it isn't too much for you? You've been feeling ill frequently of late. We can cancel—"

"No! Please. It has passed. Rose tells me it's normal."

Thomas eased back, but kissed her hand, then returned to his ledger, and she resumed writing invitations, sprinkling each paper and envelope with orange oil before she set it aside in a shallow basket.

She finished the last one and pressed Thomas's cool knuckle to her cheek. "I'll give these to Rose to post as soon as possible.

He nodded and extricated his hand from her grasp.

Felicia smoothed her skirts, set the basket in the crook of her arm, and pressed a kiss to his temple, before leaving the office and closing the door behind her.

Rose was sweeping the kitchen. Felicia picked up the front of her skirts in her other hand and rushed across the oak floors, her face beaming.

"Rose, please don't mind the sweeping right now. I need you to take these to the post, so they are delivered on time."

The older woman bobbed a shaky curtsey, her long gray hair falling loose from her cap, set the broom against the stone wall, took the basket in her aged brown hands. Felicia handed her two half-crowns.

"Thank you, ma'am. Yes ma'am." Rose paused at the back door and glanced back at Felicia. "It's to be some party, ain't it?"

Felicia tugged on a brown curl that hung over her shoulder, twirling it in her fingers. "I hope so! The last before the Major leaves. Please hurry now before the post closes."

"Yes, ma'am. Of course, ma'am."

Felicia closed the door behind Rose, then spun around to make her way to Thomas's office, but paused in her steps as another wave of sickness passed over her. She wrinkled her nose and shifted on her feet, bringing her hands to her head. If only it wouldn't interfere with the party for that Thursday.

FELICIA HUNG garlands of evergreen and columbine and on the sconces on the walls and the staircase with Rose, while Selah and her young daughter prepared the night's food. Felicia fidgeted while she decorated, smoothing the taffeta on her skirts and stomacher, tugging on her hair, and fiddling with the boughs, breaking up some of the pine needles in her fingers they turned quite sticky with sap. On the bright side, the whole house smelled of fresh pine.

"Ma'am, what's troubling you?" Rose asked, placing a hand on Felicia's shoulder.

Felicia jumped turning around to face her. "I haven't seen Thomas all day, and I wanted to spend time with him before the party."

"He's a hardworking man, ma'am."

"I know, and I love him for it. But of all the days! Rose, he is leaving tomorrow."

Felicia left her decorating and paced from room to room in the house, muttering to herself. "When is the tea to be ready, where are those barrels we ordered, and Rose! Could you fetch my embroidered fichu, please? I'd be very happy indeed!"

A hollowness echoed in her chest already without Thomas and was not sure how she could manage without him while he was away. If only he could write out in great detail all she needed to do to care for the manor, she'd feel more at ease, if only a little. She wrung her hands on her plain kerchief, ridding her fingers of the pine sap lest she ruin her taffeta gown. Oh, what a time for him to be leaving. She tried to console herself with the thought of Christmastide, but it was too far off.

"I really need you, Tom..."

Amos stopped cleaning the stained glass on the front doors and bowed, adjusting his wig as he straightened. "If it pleases you, ma'am. Major Hawkings went into his office this morning."

"He said he wasn't going to do work today!"

Amos shrugged his wiry shoulders and bowed again. "Selah will have tea ready in a moment, but I couldn't tell you where the barrels are, ma'am."

"Why, thank you, Amos," Felicia said, her voice softening as she calmed down. She dug her hand into the layers of her skirt, the taffeta crinkling as she rummaged for her pocket and pulled out a shiny silver half-crown. "There you are for answering me so quickly."

"Thank you, ma'am."

Felicia strode over to Thomas's office door and rapped her knuckles on the dark mahogany door. "Thomas, I know you're in there. Please let me in."

There was no response, but before Felicia tried again, a knock sounded at the front door. She huffed, spun around, and flounced down the hall. Amos threw open the dark, heavy doors, just as she reached him.

A tall, tan man, stood on her front porch. "Mrs. Hawkings?"

"Aye," Felicia said, tapping her foot under her skirts. Amos stood silently behind her, waiting to be called upon.

The cooper motioned toward the two large, wooden barrels at his side. "I have the Major's order."

"Ah, yes! We've been wondering when you'd arrive." She glanced behind her for her husband. "You'll have to forgive us our haste." She craned her head to look up at Amos. "Please find my husband?"

The thin man bowed. "Of course, ma'am."

For several arduously awkward moments, she and the cooper stood at the door, silent. Felicia crossed her arms as she waited, but the cooper stayed stalwart. Amos returned and shook his head, then pushed his glasses further up on his nose. She let out resigned sigh.

"I am terribly sorry for the delay," she said and stuck her hand her pocket, "The Major is incredibly busy today. How much will the order cost?"

"He paid upfront."

Felicia rubbed at the inner corners of her eyes but plastered a smile on her face. "All right. Carry them down this hallway and to your left if you will. Amos can help you."

"Thank you, ma'am."

The cooper tossed a long lock of his dark hair to the back of his neck, took up one of the barrels on his brawny shoulder, then started into the hallway. Felicia motioned for Amos to help with the other barrel. Once they had disappeared down the hall to the kitchen, she returned to the office and pressed her face against the door.

"Thomas, my mother and father will be here shortly. Could you at least be ready to greet them?"

"They're about five hours early."

Felicia let out an exasperated sigh. "Thomas, they will be here for both of us. Could you *please* open the door? I want to see you as much as I can before you leave." She jiggled the handle. "Thomas..."

Selah brought the tea cart, but Felicia took the cart from her, eyes pleading for forgiveness. Selah bowed her head with a gentle smile and returned to the kitchen. She pressed her forehead against the door.

"Don't knock again unless it's tea," Thomas's tired voice came from the other side of the door.

"It's tea."

Heavy boot steps plodded closer to Felicia, and the lock clicked. The boot steps plodded away.

Felicia pushed the tea cart into the room and closed the door behind her. As she unloaded the contents of the cart to Thomas's desk, Thomas glanced up at her, and drew in a deep breath, then let it out slowly, pressing his lips together.

"What are you doing?"

"Serving you tea." Felicia pointed to the sugar and the cream. He shook his head, so she poured the tea from the silver teapot into a china cup, and the earthy, rich smell of black tea wafted up on the steam from the golden-brown liquid. Thomas picked it up with a sigh and brought it toward his lips.

Thomas sipped his tea, a bemused expression on his face. "I see you have taken over Selah's work."

"It was my only way to see you before the party." Felicia poured herself a cup. "Now, what has you cooped up in your office mere hours before a dance?"

Thomas set his cup down on the saucer and waved a hand dismissively in the air. "Correspondence. Colonel Moore has given me letters to read before they head to their intended owners." He stood and began to pace. "With times like these, you can't be too careful not to find spies."

"Mmm," Felicia said, picking up an open letter, glancing at the handwriting. "It's lavender-scented. Look at the handwriting, love. It's filigree. This is no spy work. This is gossipy woman. I don't need to read her letter to know that. *I am one.*"

Thomas tilted his head toward her with a grin on his face. He took the letter back.

"Would a spy use lavender scented stationary?" she asked.

"You never know."

"I think it's rotten to read other people's letters."

"I don't retain a word they say," Thomas said and took her chin in his fingers. His grin faded to a gentle smile. "The recipient will receive the letter just as they are meant."

Felicia rose to her feet and wrapped her arms about his shoulders, pressing a kiss to his head, tugging on his braided queue. "Now, why don't you take a break for family."

"I don't have time right now," Thomas said. "If I'm to be done by the party, I'll need to work for another hour or so."

"Can't you make time?" Felicia grasped his arm with both hands. "It's for your family." She pressed his hand just at the edge of her stays. He stared down at his hand on her embroidered stomacher.

"Lissie, I want to. The sooner you let me go the sooner you'll see me again."

"We waited so long, Thomas. And now you have to leave me."

"It's only for a little while, my love."

She watched his face as he focused on his hand and what was underneath his palm.

Felicia brought her hand from his sleeve to press over his fingers, still holding onto his arm with the other.

He flicked his eyes up toward her, a toothy beam growing on his face. "Perhaps we should tell them today."

Felicia fidgeted. "I don't know, Tom. I don't know if we should yet. They'll find out soon enough, I suppose. I fear we may jynx it."

Thomas straightened and cocked his head. "You're such a little orchid, I'd rather people know now so someone can watch over you while I'm gone."

Felicia couldn't argue with his logic. She nodded, her curls bouncing. "I suppose with all the sensitivities..."

"It would put me at ease if others knew, if only to protect you when I cannot." He took her in his arms, pressing her in a secure hug. "It hurts to know I won't be here for most of it. But where I cannot be, I will protect you from afar."

Felicia clutched onto him, pressing her cheek against his chest. "If it'll put you at ease, then I'll be at ease," she murmured. "I can just feel the beginnings the life in me. It's so new and exciting."

Thomas let out a deep rumbling laugh. "After four years of marriage, you'd think we'd have at least three or four little ones."

"One would think." Felicia pulled away from him to study his face. She drew in a deep breath and closed her eyes, quieting her voice. "But better to have one late, than many lost, or none at all."

"True, my sweet Lissie," Thomas said, his voice too dropped low. He raised his eyes to see her face. "But that is not our plight now, is it?" He stroked her jaw with the back of his hand. "You and the baby will be protected. I'll see to that. And when I come home, we'll be able to hold him in our arms."

Thomas brought Felicia in close again. "Oh, my Lissie," he murmured into her hair. "I want to be here, too. What else can I say?"

"You could say that you love me." Felicia tilted her face toward him.

"I love you, Felicia." He whispered into her ear, then pressed his lips to the crook of her neck. "I love you more than life itself."

She gasped, grasping onto his shoulders. "I should leave you to finish your work, my love, so I may spend time with you before you must leave me."

"Of course," he said and fit his hands at her waist, gazing down at her stomacher, then back at her face. "I'll be there in a moment. Lissie?"

She spun around, her long skirts swirls of silk. "Hmm?"

"Shall we announce it before or after the dancing?"

Felicia turned to him once again. He puffed out his chest, his face radiating pure joy from his gleaming blue eyes to his bright smile. It was the happiest she had seen him in a long time.

Felicia flashed a grin at him. "Whenever you wish, my love."

3

The string quartet played from the parlor's back corner, and their music poured over the guests' laughter and chatter. Selah and Rose bustled in and out with trays of hors d'oeuvres, making sure everyone stayed fed, while Amos kept the wine and rum punch flowing. The crisp scent from the pine boughs mingled with the men's musk, and the women's floral powders mixed wonderfully with the sweet and tangy aroma of the raspberry wine brought up from Williamsburg, courtesy of Colonel Moore's brother, Henry Moore. And though it was nearly too strong for Felicia's delicate sensibilities, she was glad to have the familiarity of gaiety about her home once more. The glistening gowns and the sparkling diamantes on brocade and jewelry gave Felicia a hope for the future, that all would go back to the way it was before Lexington and Concord. But the buttons and gold tassels on the gentlemen's uniforms and overcoats competed for dominance in Felicia's mind, the overcoats reminding her of the haven of normalcy while the tassels and uniforms reinforced the unknown of war. But nevertheless, the scintillating party caused delicately rouged faces beam to see their soldier partners relaxed, even joyful. They laughed when the wide panniers of dresses collided and they bumped into each other during jigs, or any given dance. Couples made arches with their arms while others wound through.

Candles in the wall sconces cast an orange ethereal glow on the parlor, where the chairs had been pushed to the perimeter to make room for dancing. It reminded Felicia of an early fall night. A cool breeze blew in from the window, causing the flames to flicker, casting eerie shadows, but she thrived on that feeling. It was haunting, almost as if ghosts danced among the living. Men and women faced each other in lines and Felicia wondered if the departed stood with them. But Thomas never believed in ghosts, and no matter during how many parties she brought it up to him, he brushed her off, and pointed to his thick family Bible saying, "It's not possible."

Nevertheless, as Thomas had her sit out every other dance, Felicia studied her guests, observing Mother dancing with Father and Colonel Moore with his daughter, but she couldn't help wondering if the breeze that pushed Henry Moore's gilded green overcoat was really the wind, or the passing pannier of a departed loved one. She hoped the reason Mrs. Haddock's hair feather kept flopping in front of her eyes was because some vindictive spirit despised that stringy ostrich plume as much as she did.

The dancers indented the carpet with their intricate weaving, and the fast-paced music kept everyone bouncy, clapping, and smiling. Three-quarters of the men would leave early the next morning, but there were no frowns or teary eyes. It wasn't as though the party absolved the *aide memoire* that the men would be leaving for Boston, but it provided a welcome escape to already war-weary minds.

Felicia loved to dance the minuet with her Thomas, but she preferred when they were not partnered up for dances like the Haymakers, which required dancers to switch partners far too often for her liking. She barely would touch her partner's hand before moving to the next person.

No, Felicia needed more time to dance with solely her husband, although she enjoyed the thrill of the happenstance when she found herself matched up with Thomas during a dance. His hands were made to hold hers, and there was something indefinable about the way his pale blue eyes twinkled at her in the candlelight and softened when he had the pleasure of spending even those next, fleeting moments with her. But though the dances spun her about, it was when Thomas held her that Felicia felt the dizziest.

"Perhaps it best you sit, Lissie," Thomas said. "You haven't stopped in three sets."

"I'm perfectly fine so long as it's not a jig." Felicia drew in a breath and waved a hand laconically. "Let's continue!"

"And why shouldn't she be?" Mrs. Haddock, the general's wife, said, her nasally voice piercing the music. "She's young. Let her have her dances with you before you leave."

"Age has nothing of the sort to do with it," Thomas said, leading her to the wooden chairs lined up by the fireplace, and sitting beside her, legs outstretched. Felicia pressed kisses to his palm, whispering between each kiss, and Thomas's eyes glimmered. He hummed a laugh, pulling his hand away from her. "Soon, my love," he murmured.

"Regardless, I think we've had enough dancing, haven't we?" Mrs. Haddock lowered herself into a high-backed chair next to them, fanning herself with her large pink ostrich plumed fan. She sighed and brushed an errant powdered-gray curl over her shoulder.

"Oh, I second that." Colonel Moore smoothed back his thick blond hair, tightening the ribbon holding it. "I'm far too old for this anymore. Tom, tell the quartet to take a break, will you?"

Thomas motioned to Amos and the quartet. When the men set their instruments down, Amos brought them each a glass of port.

Felicia took a hold of Thomas's arm. "Play, now," she whispered once more, gently playing with his fingers. "Before the night is out."

"Very well." Thomas gave her a playful eye roll and crossed the room to the mantle where the maple instrument lay. He cleared his throat, gathering everyone's attention. "It seems to be the custom that I play when people are over."

"It's the only reason we come," Victoria Moore said. The Colonel's daughter, who was a pleasant girl, with a soft face and dark, silken hair, and large, bright, hazel eyes perched herself delicately on a settee by the mantle and gave Felicia a roguish grin. She patted the space beside her, but the Colonel shook his stately head. Her dark-haired uncle took the offer instead, and Victoria rested her head on his shoulder.

"Oh, of course." Felicia wagged her fan toward her young friend. "I thought you came to escape the men in your house!"

"The men of her house aren't so bad." Colonel Moore's long, elegant nose wrinkled ever so slightly, not even marring his vulpine features. "We're a fine sort."

"Ha! A fine sort we are, indeed." Henry Moore's brown hair had come loose from its queue while he danced and now framed his face in limp curls. He blinked tired eyes, leaned back on the settee, and brought a glass of wine to his lips. "I'd give us both a toast if this were our party."

"Oh, dear Henry, that better not have been the last of the good wine you brought up from Williamsburg," Felicia said, her voice a mix of gentleness and humor.

Henry quirked a side smile as he twirled the empty glass in his fingers. "'Twas good while it did last..."

Victoria leaned up against his side. "I had hoped you'd save some for me."

He pressed his pointer finger to her nose and kissed her forehead. "It was too strong for you."

Thomas finished tuning his violin. He cleared his throat and glanced at Felicia, a shy boyish air about him. "Shall we say it now or when the music is over?"

"Say what now?" Henry asked, running his finger along the rim of his glass.

"Indeed, Thomas." Mother tapped her fingers together. "What do you need to say?"

Felicia flashed Thomas a smile, and he nodded back.

"Let me dedicate this song then—" Thomas ran his bow across the *A* string of the violin. "Let me dedicate this to my beautiful wife, who I know loves the winter." He started playing the opening notes to Vivaldi's *Winter*, then paused. "I suppose that's when the baby is to come, isn't it?" He continued only a moment before pausing again and grinning at her.

The whole room gasped.

Father opened his mouth to speak, but Mother cut him off.

"Ah!" Mother clapped her hands together. "Finally!"

Thomas drew the bow over the strings again, and the murmurs quieted down as he played.

The sound of his violin filled the house, from the floors to the rafters, from the kitchen to the bedrooms. He played so fully that not only the servants could hear, but Felicia imagined even passersby on their nightly stroll stopped to listen.

Felicia wanted to soak in the sight of him, to keep as much of him as she could before he left in the morning. Her eyes flitted over him till they fixed on his hands as he played her favorite piece Standing there in his blood-red uniform with a cream cravat at his throat, holding the mahogany violin against his chin, Thomas looked as if he were straight out of a master's painting. The golden tassels on his shoulders shook as he moved his bow and fingers over the strings, and he swayed to the haunting melody.

But the music had to end, and when it did, Felicia stood and breezed over to her husband, taking the violin from him to set back on the mantle. She wrapped an arm about his waist, and he gave her a small, tired smile.

"You do have such a gift." Colonel Moore stood up. "I haven't heard anyone play like that in the colonies. You should be back in England, playing there."

"Well, once we're able to get the colonials back to the status quo"—Thomas glanced down at Felicia— "and after the child is born, I think moving back home would be wonderful."

"Good G-d! A child at last!" Felicia's father turned his face away and wiped at his eyes with the lace on his sleeve. "You've waited so long..."

"Indeed, we have." Felicia gave her father's arm a light squeeze. "But we are finally starting our family, and the Major has even more to come home to now."

Shortly afterward, the guests left, and Thomas and Felicia stood in the foyer to bid them each farewell. Colonel Moore tarried a little longer, chatting with both Thomas's and Felicia's parents, but once almost everyone else had left, he made his way to Thomas and stared intently at him. Thomas stood erect, clasping his hands behind his back. Felicia stepped closer to Thomas's side, holding onto his arm.

Thomas plays the violin

"The letters have been read?"

"All are good," Thomas said.

Amos handed the Colonel his hat.

"Bring them with you in the morning, and we'll have them sent as we head out." Colonel Moore tipped his hat to Thomas and then took Felicia's hand, pressing a small kiss to her knuckles. "And you, dear Felicia. I'll get him back to you just as you see him leave. I promise."

"See that you do," she said, and eased her clutch, only to link her arm with her husband's but flashed a smile at the Colonel. "He means the world to me."

"My Martha would have said the same thing about me, and I wouldn't want to disappoint her memory, now, would I?" He took her free hand and pressed another gallant kiss on her fingers before facing her husband. "Goodnight, Thomas. I'll see you early."

"Goodnight to you, William."

Colonel Moore tipped his hat once again and strode out the front doors. Felicia and Thomas were alone in the foyer.

"So... I guess since our guests are gone." Thomas rested his arm over Felicia's shoulders. "I could have you to myself."

"They're not all gone." Felicia pursed her lips and silently pointed behind Thomas, where her father glared at him. He wasn't much taller than Felicia, but his glare made up where his stature lacked. "Father," Felicia said quietly, as her mother joined them in the foyer, "stop trying to kill Thomas with your eyes. Your act has worn out years ago and now he has to help raise your grandchild."

Her father's glare melted, his face radiating pride and joy. "The Colonel is right. You have a gift. It was a marvelous piece you played."

"Thank you, sir."

"You should know by now to call me John."

"Yes, but your glares demand that I call you 'sir'," Thomas said with a short laugh.

Her father patted Thomas's arm and then hugged his daughter. "And you, my sweet girl. A mother. I'm sure this means you'll be calling on us a little more now?"

"Only if you'll allow it," Felicia said.

Felicia's mother hugged them both, too teary to talk, and when their carriage pulled up to the front door.

"Our guests are gone." Felicia wrapped her arms around Thomas's waist, and he glanced down at her, a soft smile on his lips.

"And now?" he asked.

"Now I think we need to rest. Tomorrow is a big day for you."

Thomas took her hand and led her up the stairs. "I will only be a week away—six days at the earliest—and you can write to me all you like."

"I'll write you three times a day." Felicia paused on the landing and began unpinning the purple silk gown from her stays. "Here, hold these..."

Thomas held his hand out for the straight pins, and she slid sideways into their bedroom, the front of her dress hanging open to reveal her stays. Thomas followed her in, dropping the pins into a small china dish which rested on her toilette stand in the room's back corner.

"It is a wonder," he said.

Felicia craned her neck around, raising a brow at him as she stripped each layer off her body to place back in the wardrobe or laundry basket.

"It's a wonder how many layers you have." He made a great show of putting each item into basket.

"You know there are more in the winter," she said flatly and slid out of her petticoats and pannier, till she stood in nothing but her stockings and chemise while Thomas took off his coat and set it aside for the morning. She gave him a quick kiss before undoing her hair from its curled height, then perched on the bed so Thomas could untie the ribbons at her knees.

"Tom, when do you think you'll be home?"

Thomas cocked his head toward her, tender resignation etching his tired features. "Perhaps a few months. If we show the colonials our force, they may back down, and we won't need to worry about a full-blown war."

"That would be preferable." Felicia flipped back the cover, watching as her husband loosen his hair from its braided queue. It tumbled over his shoulders, and her breath caught in her throat. She pressed her lips together. "Hurry up."

"I'm going as fast as I can," he said with a laugh. He hissed slightly as he sank into the mattress, tilting his head against the pillow.

Felicia pulled the blanket over his chest and smoothed it out, sidling up against him. "Thomas, don't leave me."

"I won't be gone long." He kissed her forehead. "I promise."

Felicia drew in a shaky breath. "What'll I do when you're gone?"

Thomas lay quiet for a moment, then leaned on one arm and rested a hand on her middle. "I suppose you could start getting ready for this one to come," he said, running his hand over the small curve of her belly.

Felicia rested her hand atop his. "Even the baby doesn't want you to go. *I* don't want you to go."

Thomas leaned down, his face close to Felicia's belly. "I promise, little one, that I'll be back sooner than you'll realize. I'm sure of it." He pressed a kiss to the top of Felicia's belly, then straightened to kiss her lips. "Lissie, I love you more than life itself."

Felicia held his face close to hers and whispered, "I love you, too, Tom."

4

Felicia's mother already had taken to giving her advice, mostly of not straining oneself with too much exertion. Yet, Felicia decided a walk about town with Victoria would be just the level of exercise needed. Thank goodness Penchester was a small halfway sort of town, just a simple stop for travelers heading to Philadelphia or New York. Although most of the soldiers' wives and the upper-class families rode in carriages to visit or attend parties, when the shopping needed to be done, walking sufficed. Saturday was warm with a lovely breeze, which mixed scents of fresh breads from ovens and flowers from gardens, and a stroll, was certainly in order. Besides, Thomas would want her to stay healthy and in good condition for their baby. And perhaps, the merchant store might have received a shipment of tea. Felicia needed daily pots of tea to calm her nerves, but they had been out of stock lately, a matter which distressed her to no end.

"So, tell me, you've been keeping in contact, yes? I can't stand to be away from a loved one for so long. I make Uncle Henry write to me five times a day when he's away for business," Victoria said as she and Felicia strolled through Penchester's main thoroughfare. "I couldn't fathom what it must be like to be away from a husband."

"It's left a hole in my heart, to be sure." Felicia inclined her head toward the tavern, then to her friend. "But he'll be back soon enough and if I keep looking forward, Thomas will be with me once again. Did you want to stop at the tavern?"

Victoria shook her head. "No time," she said. "I have etiquette lessons soon."

"I do miss those." Felicia closed her eyes and drew in a deep breath, letting it out slowly. "Learning to dance. To serve tea. I believe it's how I won Thomas over." She winced. "I'm not boring you with my talk of him, am I?"

"No!" Victoria laughed. "The way you talk of him gives me hope that I'll find a love as strong."

The two continued ambling down the road, past the blacksmith and apothecary.

"Are you picking up an instrument soon?" Felicia asked, glancing at her reflection in window. She fixed an errant curl, then focused on Victoria.

"What did you learn?"

"I sang."

"Mm. I've yet to choose." Victoria kicked at the dirt. "Father isn't so keen on music in the house when there isn't a party, but he might allow singing."

Felicia twisted her lips. "He doesn't like music?"

"At parties and orchestras, surely, but not when he's working or resting."

"What a shame," Felicia said.

"Good ladies! Buy some fresh flowers!"

The woman's call brought Felicity and Victoria to a halt. Baskets of flowers lay at her side, each overflowing with lavender and peonies. Felicia glanced to Victoria and inclined her head toward the woman.

"Some lavender is always nice to have around the house," Victoria said. "I hear it's supposed to calm you."

"Well, since tea is becoming scarce, I suppose I'll make do with lavender," Felicia said and reached into her pockets. She pulled out a few coins and exchanged the money for the flowers, then rejoined Victoria in walking down the road, handing her companion a small bouquet.

"So, about your husband," Victoria said, bringing the lavender up to her delicate nose. "Has he sent any messages back yet?"

"Thomas will send me a letter as soon as he reaches Boston," Felicia said. "As of right now, he should still be en route. I have written three letters already. They are waiting to be—"

"Watch your step!"

A rogue barrel rolled out in front of Victoria and Felicia. They jumped back, nearly tripping over their petticoats, as the cooper chased it down.

The barrel secured, he glanced over to them. "Ma'am! Sorry." He tipped his tricorn hat. "It fell off the stand."

"Try to be more careful." Victoria wrinkled her nose, but her expression softened. "She's carrying something far more precious than your barrels."

Felicia pursed her lips toward her friend, then bobbed a curtsey toward the cooper. "I'm perfectly fine, Victoria."

The cooper tipped his hat again. "Please accept my sincerest apologies. My apprentice must learn not to push the wares. He'll be reprimanded. If you have any orders in the future, either of you, I can give you a percentage off."

"I'm sure it'll all be well." Felicia offered him a small smile. "That is kind of you, but I'm sure it won't be needed—"

"Not so fast," Victoria interrupted. "I'd quite like a bucket for our kitchen."

Felicia tilted her head and raised her eyebrows, blinking her eyes. "Why would you need that?"

"Father hates Colonial craftsmanship." With a wink, Victoria fitted her hands on her hips. "Let me take this opportunity to annoy him when he returns."

The cooper rumbled out a laugh. "It can be done."

Felicia nodded to him. "Be kind to your apprentice. I'm sure he meant well."

He grinned. "As you wish."

She gathered her skirts and turned to Victoria. "Come on. It's getting hotter out, and I'd like to go home and rest. We can talk more there before your lessons."

"Of course." Victoria tucked her arm through Felicia's. "Goodness knows I'd want to be out of the heat if I was carrying a child."

Felicia and Victoria walked the long dirt path back up to Hawkings Manor, talking idly from subject to subject, taking in the breeze on their skin.

"How much longer before they arrive in Boston?" Victoria asked as they neared the estate's wooden fence. "Father barely uttered a word about anything."

"They left yesterday, so I'd say a week from today, or perhaps from Sunday. But either way, I shouldn't get his first letter till sometime after—"

"Mrs. Hawkings! Ma'am!" Rose ran the front path to the house, waving a dish towel. "Mrs. Hawkings!"

Felicia pushed open the gate, her heart dropping into her stomach. "What is it, Rose?"

"I don't know. The Colonel is in the parlor and is asking for you. I just left to find you."

"The Colonel? Colonel Moore? But he is on his way to Boston!" Her lungs constricted, and a cough caught in her throat as Felicia glanced to Victoria, then back to Rose.

Victoria wrung her hands. "Should I come? What's he doing home early? Is he asking for me, too?"

"Oh, no, miss." Rose frowned and shook her head. "He only asked to see Mrs. Hawkings. He hasn't mentioned you."

"Perhaps you should go find your uncle." Felicia shifted her weight from foot to foot. "This could be official business."

Victoria rolled her shoulders and brought her arms close to her chest. She let out a shaky breath, her lips trembling. "God be with you in whatever this is." She curtseyed and started off down the road for her home.

Felicia gathered up her skirts and scurried into the house, Rose following closely.

"Don't you hurry, ma'am. Don't go rushing for the sake of your baby."

Felicia refused to heed Rose's advice and skidded to a halt in the foyer. She took a deep breath, smoothed her skirts, and arranged the curls hanging over her shoulder. Rose closed the front door as Felicia breezed into the parlor. The Colonel and two of his officers stood in front of the sofa, where something lay, covered with a dark sheet of fabric. She entered the room, and they straightened then nodded curtly to her.

"Colonel Moore, what do I have the pleasure of—" she started, but the Colonel held his hand out to stop her.

"Felicia Hawkings, this is not a visit of pleasure." His face was severe, lips drawn tightly together. His slanted features seemed sharper in the afternoon sun's waning light. "We had to turn around. Our supplies were ambushed."

Felicia furrowed her brows. "I'm not sure I understand why this means you—"

"Last night was very dark. Trees covered most of the stars and all of the moon," one of the officers stepped forward and took her hand, leading her to a chair. Once she was seated, the officer fell silent.

The Colonel continued. "The colonials stole our weapons and ammunition as we neared the Pennsylvania border. Shots were fired."

Felicia shook her head. "I don't—"

"My dear Felicia," Colonial Moore said, his voice dropping low, "Thomas was hit." He knelt in front of her and tried to take her hands, but she pulled them away.

"Hit? Where? Is he all right? Where was he hit? Where is he?" Her breathing quickened, and she tried to avert her eyes from the dark sheeted figure lying on the sofa. She forced herself to look at Moore.

The closest officer rested a hand on her shoulder. "I'm sorry, Mrs. Hawkings."

"What are you sorry for?" Felicia attempted to laugh, but coughs bubbled up in her throat. "I'm sure you have done nothing wrong. Where is my husband? How badly was he hit?" Her voice rose, and she had to remind herself the decorum of being a major's wife. She willed herself to sit still,

"Felicia," the Colonel said again. "He didn't make it home."

She lost all decorum as her voice grew louder and more frantic, and she rose to her feet. "Where is my husband?"

Colonel Moore took her hands in his, gently shushing her and drew in a deep breath. "Felicia, he's here. But you must calm yourself for your child's sake." Slowly, he turned her to face the sofa and its dark sheet.

Felicia swallowed and stepped toward it. She gently held the edge of the fabric in trembling hands. She shook her head, raking in ragged breaths. "I can't."

Colonel Moore took the fabric from her fingers and pulled it back.

Thomas.

No.

But he lay there, his eyes closed, and the coloring had fled his cheeks. A pained frown pinched his lips. His chest neither rose nor fell.

"He's sleeping," Felicia protested. She turned to the officers. "Wake him up."

The Colonel started, "Lissie—"

"Only my husband may call me that." Her voice cracked, and throwing him a fierce stare, she shook her head so fiercely that more curls slipped loose. She cleared her throat and set her jaw. "You're the Colonel. Wake him up."

"You know I can't," he said quietly.

Her eyes sought any sign of life in her husband's still face.

"I don't understand." She gritted her teeth, clenching her fists and fighting the scream that welled up in her throat, and tears started to stream down her cheeks. "I don't understand. Why is he sleeping? Colonel Moore, *wake him up*! You said you'd bring him back to me as he was!"

"The ball hit him in his back," was the Colonel's only answer. He stepped past her to drape the cloth back over Thomas. "I realized we had no choice but to turn around to get him to a proper surgeon. He died this morning, Lissie. Only an hour ago."

Felicia shoved Colonel Moore aside and threw back the sheet. "No, he's only sleeping. He must be only sleeping. Tom! You're home. Come on, now, wake up! Wake up! I don't understand, Tom! You said you'd stay safe!"

"Surprise attacks happen all the time, ma'am," the third officer said.

She glanced up to see him extending his hand. She wrinkled her nose at him, lips curled and flashed a glare to Colonel Moore before turning back to Thomas's body and pressing kisses to his cold forehead. "Thomas, please for the love of God, wake up!"

The second officer stepped closer and placed his hand on her back.

She shrugged him off and slipped her arms under Thomas's neck, pulling him up against her chest. His head lolled backward, and Felicia let out a cry. He was so pale. Her tears plashed onto his crimson jacket, and she tilted her head to heaven and ground out through her tears, "Oh, dear God, they say You've raised the dead before. Give him back to me, oh my God, please... Please... Give him back to me. What's makes Thomas different from Lazarus? Thomas has only been gone for an hour, and the other four days. This would take far less of a miracle —oh please, God!"

"Mrs. Hawkings." The officer's voice sounded choked. He cleared his throat and grasped ahold of Felicia's arms, gently pulling her from Thomas's body. She stood frozen in place while he held her. "We did everything in our power to get him the care he needed and to bring him home. I was with him."

She fell limp in the officer's arms, her head and heart throbbing. "When he... Did he say anything?"

"'Let her know.'" He shook his head. "He probably wanted to let you know he loved you."

He guided Felicia to a chair. As she sat, she inclined her head to face Colonel Moore, her eyes burning, her cheeks sticky with tears.

"You!" Her voice was hoarse and shook. "You promised me! He isn't as he left me! What have you done?"

"Westall is right," Colonel Moore said. "Surprise attacks and ambushes happen. You know as well as any soldier's wife that we can't leave formation."

"I know as well as anybody that a man of honor must keep his promise." Fresh tears welled up in her eyes, and she let out a choked sob, threw herself atop Thomas's chest, and pressed tear-stained kisses on his face.

Colonel Moore gently pried Felicia off her husband's body and covered him back up. "Is there anything I can do while I'm here? Anyone whom I can tell to save you that pain?"

Felicia sat stiffly on a high-backed chair, her back to the dark sheet. Her body ached with exhaustion and the numbness that came with sobbing.

"No. Just give me his things. His rifle and bayonet, his flask. Give me his things."

Colonel Moore shook his head, frowning. "His rifle and bayonet are missing. The rebels probably stole it in the raid after they shot him. His flask is on his person."

Felicia swallowed a cry and straightened her back. She remembered her decorum and would no longer sob in front of the Colonel. She would no longer cry. She was a soldier's wife. She would be strong. "I need nothing."

Colonel Moore bowed to Felicia, and his officers followed suit. Quickly, they marched out of the house. When the door shut behind them, Rose and Selah poked their heads into the parlor. Their eyes flickered between the dark sheet and Felicia.

"Ma'am?" Selah asked, gently, carefully.

Felicia tilted her head up and the tears began again as she said in a barely audible whisper, "Call on my parents." She took in a staggered breath. "There's work to be done."

5

There would be no more violin music at Hawkings Manor. The only music was the sound of the rain against the roof.

Felicia was the wife—no, now a widow—of a major, and she sat straight while friends and relations came to bid their farewells.

Thomas was laid out in the parlor in front of the fireplace, dressed in full regalia, and Felicia sat beside him in a high-backed chair, the chair and her stays the only things enabling her to sit upright. Thomas's maple violin rested on his chest, hands clasped over the neck of the instrument. Felicia had tried so many times to turn his lips upright, so he didn't look so pained, but the corners of his mouth were permanently frozen in that hurting frown. His casket was plain, but she had insisted on an inscription on the lid, which was propped up next to him for all to read:

Non est musicam morte.

Felicia wore a simple black, cotton gown, and while Rose had attempted to style her hair, Felicia couldn't be bothered to sit still long enough for the curls to set. In the end, Rose had simply piled her hair atop her head and covered it with a mob cap.

Mother walked quietly into the parlor and pulled up a chair beside Felicia. She stroked the side of Felicia's face, then took her cold, pale hands in her delicate, wrinkled ones. "Don't get yourself too worked up, my dear."

Felicia regarded her wearily.

Her mother frowned gently. "You don't want to work yourself up for the sake of the child. You are being put through the fire, that much is true. But we can weather this. You will make it through all the stronger."

Felicia heaved a heavy sigh. "What would you know? You've never had the strings pulled from your heart." Her voice cracked, and she rubbed at her eyes, then glanced at her husband's still form. "The strings he used to play to the tune of Vivaldi have been severed."

"I—"

"My G-d, it hurts." She clenched her teeth together and forced her eyes shut. "It hurts so much. What did I do to deserve losing my husband?"

Mother said nothing, just tightened her grip on Felicia's chilled knuckles, but Felicia gazed at her husband's body, tears squeezing out of her eyes. She sniffed and wiped her face with her handkerchief.

"I'm sorry," she said through a gasp, then ran from the room and down the hall, searching for solace in the kitchen where Selah rolled out the dough for pastries for after the burial.

Her wracking sobs startled Selah, who brought her apron up to wipe at damp eyes. "Ma'am, shall I leave you?"

Felicia shook her head, motioning for her to stay where she worked, drew a shuddering breath, and fought a rising wail. "No, I'm sorry. Please keep going. The guests can't go without."

Selah wiped her hands and brought her a wooden chair, and Felicia promptly fell onto it. She hid her face in her hands.

The sound of tapping against the floor echoed in the kitchen. After the tap-tapping stopped, Felicia felt a hand on her knee. She looked up and cocked her head toward her mother, who handed her a handkerchief.

"My dear, my sweet little Lissie. You're right—I don't know what it's like."

Felicia wiped at her eyes and dabbed at her nose. "It's as if a snake has coiled its way around my neck and chest and is slowly squeezing me to death." She slowly took in a rasping breath. "I'm afraid. I'm scared. Mama, kill that snake."

"Oh, my child, I would if I could." Her mother scooted closer, and Felicia leaned into her mother's arms, resting her head in the crook of her neck.

"He's just in the other room, lying there. He's physically there, but a hollow emptiness fills my core when I look at his face."

"His soul is in a better place, you know." Mother ran a hand over her hair. "His soul is with his Lord, and he's happier for it. He has no colonials to tame. He has—"

"No wife or child to greet him."

"No, he doesn't. But the Good Book says that 'The Lord calls all times soon,' and we must think of that. Perhaps Thomas need not wait long for you to join him, though you will live on for years and years more."

Felicia took a long sniff in and nodded, but the heaviness from her tears kept her head lowered.

Her mother took her face in her hands and pressed a kiss to her forehead. "And he'll be your guardian, watching over you from heaven."

"I wish he was watching over me on earth."

Selah picked up a tray of pastries and carried it over to her. "Go on and have a taste, ma'am. I think you'll like it." She offered the hint of a smile. "I know this was his favorite."

Felicia pinched off a piece of pastry. Her mouth flickered upright ever so slightly. "Thank you, Selah."

"It is no problem, ma'am."

"Do you feel a little better?" Mother rubbed her hand over Felicia's shoulder blades. "Have you gotten your tears out?"

Felicia took in another shaky breath, leaning against her mother's arm. "For now."

"You are allowed to cry. It's only natural. Thomas's death wasn't natural, and tears should be shed over him."

"I should have been prepared," Felicia said. She ran her hands down her face. "I was a soldier's wife, and we are never guaranteed, never promised... We cannot be sure we have the next day with our husbands."

"I know." Her mother pressed another tender kiss to her forehead. "But even the most prepared are never ready."

Felicia dried her eyes then straightened in her chair. "It's past noon. We should bury him."

"Yes, I believe so. Are you well enough? Do you need me to have your father bring a chair for you?"

"That would be preferable, actually." Felicia rested a hand on her stomacher. "I'm sure the babe isn't taking to my emotions very well."

Her mother stood and helped her to her feet. "I'll walk with you. Lean on my arm. There you are."

She took her daughter's arm and guided her gently back through the halls to the parlor. Thomas hadn't been moved yet, but Officer Westall was removing the violin from his hands. He walked over to Felicia and bowed curtly. She took the violin and bow from his hands and held them close to her chest while Westall moved to place the lid on top of the box.

"Wait."

Felicia held her hands out and the officers paused. She went up to the casket, and they slid the lid back off for her. She cupped his cheek and gently pressed a kiss to his lips.

"You are still my world," she whispered. She backed up from his body and nodded to the officers, who slid the lid back on and closed Thomas away forever.

They carried Thomas outside into the backyard. In the rain, the mourners' faces were gray and wet. Their hair clung to their heads, hat brims filled with water; tears mixed with the rain. The garden was overly green, the lavender buds not yet open. Father had a chair ready and held onto Felicia's umbrella for her.

They gathered around the plot, and the officers lowered the casket. The parson read from the Book of Common Prayer, then prayed a simple prayer and offered those closest to Thomas the opportunity to say a few words.

Colonel Moore strode to the front and slicked back his long blond hair before replacing his hat on his head. The rain dripped from his nose, but he made no attempt to wipe his face dry.

"Major Thomas Theodore Hawkings was a damn good soldier. But more than that, he was a damn good man. He was a man who'd be at training at five in the morning, alert and ready for the day even while other officers struggled to keep their eyes open, and at the end of the day, he would still host a party with his beautiful wife. And he'd never say no to playing his violin. The man was gifted, and now that talent will be lost to us forever. He would been better suited as a first chair violinist for His Majesty rather than a major for his army. I will miss him dearly. Felicia, dear girl, may you find solace knowing that your husband was the best soldier of us all."

Felicia bowed her head.

"Did you wish to say anything, dear?" the parson asked, turning to Felicia.

Felicia sighed. "He would have been a wonderful father," she said, her voice low and tired. She cleared her throat.

An officer handed her a shovel, and she gave him a disgusted glare. He winced before turning back to his companions. The parson opened the Book of Common Prayer once more.

"In sure and certain hope of the resurrection to eternal life through our Lord Jesus Christ, we commend to Almighty God our brother Thomas Theodore Hawkings, and we commit his body to the ground;
earth to earth, ashes to ashes, dust to dust. The Lord bless him and keep him, the Lord make his face to shine upon him and be gracious to him, the Lord lift up his countenance upon him and give him peace. Amen."

Together, they shoveled the earth over the wooden box with the engraving on the lid, then packed it down tightly. A stone marker was placed at the head of the grave.

Major Thomas Theodore Hawkings.
Soldier. Son. Husband. Father.
May 25th, 1745- June 1775

The small crowd was silent as they stood in the rain. Felicia kept her head bowed low and her face covered. She may have been a soldier's wife, but she was no soldier herself. She was a widow. She couldn't keep her head up any longer.

Her father cleared his throat. "On behalf of Felicia, ourselves, and the Major's family in England, I would like to thank you all for paying your respects to the Major. If you wish to linger on, there will be some light faire in the dining room."

The mourners filtered into the house, but Felicia stayed seated by the grave outside. Father knelt beside her.

"Dear Felicia." His voice sounded strained and broken. "What would you like me to do for you?"

"I suppose I don't know." Felicia took the umbrella from her father. "It's seems like ten thousand years since he died."

"And it'll feel like ten thousand more till you can see him again." Felicia's father said tenderly. Felicia covered her eyes, tilted her head back, and lowered the umbrella, letting the rain wash over her face. Father set the umbrella right again, then wiped Felicia's face with his handkerchief. "To feel such heavy pain is a grief observed. A great man once said that it's easy for somebody to say that his tooth aches, but to say that his heart is broken? It's a much harder affair. You are far stronger than you'll know, Lissie. But for now, let's mourn and rest."

Felicia stood, walked to Thomas's grave, and ran her hand over the cold, unfeeling tombstone. "Something vexes me... what am I to do with his things? When will the estate come in?"

"Let us not think of that right now. There will be storage needed, and you'll receive the letter in a few weeks, but give yourself time, my dear. Now, let's get inside before the rain soaks us."

The two joined the others inside where Selah had created a simple but delicious spread of pastries and cold meats for the guests, and yet Felicia couldn't bring herself to take a bite. She had no stomach for food. Leaving the others, she wandered through the house to the parlor and sat silently by front window, watching the rain create muddy puddles in the road, holding tightly to the violin as she stared outside.

There would be no more violin music at Hawkings Manor. No more dark brows furrowed in concentration. No more strong hands and fingers creating sound. No more swaying and bobbing to the tune. No more secret glances and smiles. No more music.

No more Thomas.

❧ 6 ❧

I t rained through a fortnight, but the smell of rain was overwhelmed by the scent of roses, a nauseating romance that made Felicia want to wretch.

If she received another bouquet of flowers from some church acquaintance expressing their condolences or well wishes for the babe, she was going to scream. She hid in Thomas's office, the only place that didn't smell like a lover's bouquet. There, the fading of his pipe tobacco lingered with the hint of gunpowder from his rifle, the fresh cotton of his shirts, and the clove pomade in his hair.

Felicia sat at his desk, pouring over his paperwork with bloodshot eyes, finally setting the stacks of paper aside, and resting her head against the cold dark wood. Arms stretched out before her, she rubbed at her eyes and heaved a sigh.

She'd received a letter from a Mr. Arthur Bach Esq. from the Philadelphia branch of London's Bach Trust, stating that Thomas's will was being reviewed at their office and would be sent to her at the nearest convenience. He had perished in June and now it was the end of July, but who knew what "nearest convenience" meant during a war.

Mrs. Hawkings,

Considering the circumstances, we tried to rush this letter as soon as possible.

I wish I were not writing this. I am completely and utterly gutted. Major Hawkings was a good man, and I will miss him. Please accept all my condolences. We are reviewing your husband's estate and will send it to you as soon as we are able. Once again, please accept any condolences and don't hesitate to write to us if you need anything.

~Arthur Bach Esq.

She pushed the seat back away from the desk and bent forward, arms over her head. A knock sounded at the door. She gave a pathetic groan.

"It's tea, ma'am."

She gave another pathetic groan.

Rose bustled in with the tea cart and set out the cup and saucer on the table, pouring the freshly steeped tea into the china. "Cream or sugar, ma'am?"

"Both today."

Rose slid the prepared teacup to her. "There you are ma'am."

Felicia slowly lifted her head, using a finger to pull the cup and saucer closer. "My thanks."

"Will that be all?"

"I think so," Felicia said, then cleared her throat. She rubbed at her eyes with the back of her hand and took a drink of the tea.

Rose bowed her head and curtseyed, then started to leave, but as she passed through the door, she murmured, "It's not the same around here anymore."

"What's that?" Felicia asked.

Rose froze. She turned slowly on her heel. "I—"

"You may speak your mind," Felicia said. "It's not the same?"

Rose shook her head. "I'm sorry, ma'am. After the Major left and never came home—"

Felicia flicked her pained gaze up toward Rose, gritting her teeth, and fighting back fresh tears. "He did come home, just not as he left."

Rose shook her head, then bowed it. "It's just so quiet around here."

"Well, that's about to change, at least for today." Felicia swallowed the tea and then cupped the china in her hands, thrumming her fingers along the sides.

"Ma'am?"

"I have asked for the cooper to call this afternoon discuss storage." Felicia glanced out the window. "A month has been long enough to put this off. He should be here after noon."

"Shall I boil a fresh pot of tea for when he comes?"

"I think that would be pleasant." Felicia sniffed and cleared her throat. "You know..." Her hand came up over her stomacher, and she intertwined her fingers in the laces.

"Ma'am?" Rose asked again.

"I must confide in you..."

"Of course."

Felicia gestured toward the door. "I keep thinking he's going to walk in. I keep thinking he's going to come in here, put his rifle aside and go back to his paperwork like he does. I keep thinking he's going to come down from upstairs, in just his shirt and trousers, hair out of the bow, just to play his violin." Felicia wobbled, and the housekeeper scooted the chair behind her mistress. Felicia sat down hard. "I can hear them, Rose, those notes he plays. They echo through the house, playing in my mind. And I look for him here or in the parlor when I hear those phantom strains. I don't understand, Rose. I don't understand. He didn't even make it to battle."

Rose stayed silent for a moment, then handed her a fresh cup of tea. Felicia gave her a weary, heavy smile, but brought the china to her lips.

"Ma'am, I don't know why bad things happen to good people. He was a good man, and you're a good woman. What happened was a very bad thing. But I think, if what I hear at the back of the meeting hall is right, it could work for good."

"I just don't know how it could."

"I don't think we're meant to know how. I s'pose God likes to keep certain things mysteries."

Felicia finished her second cup of tea and set it down on Thomas's desk. "Well, I don't care for mysteries or surprises."

"I don't think many do ma'am."

As Felicia opened her mouth to speak, a loud rap at the door echoed through the hallway. She cocked her head toward the foyer. "That should be the cooper."

Rose put the cup and saucer back on the cart and curtseyed. "I'll freshen the tea." She wheeled the small cart toward the kitchen.

Felicia took a deep breath in to collect herself. She smoothed out her skirts, then walked to the door, reaching if before Amos did. She stood face to chest once again with the cooper. He was drenched, his long black hair falling from its queue, clinging to his tan face. His hands were clasped behind his back, and a satchel hung from his shoulder.

"I don't normally make house calls, Mrs. Hawkings." He wrung his floppy farmer's hat out on the front porch and slapped it back on his head.

Felicia quirked a brow at him. "Do you need to shake yourself off?"

The cooper let out a low hum and crossed his arms.

Felicia winced. "I didn't mean that how it sounded."

He let his arms fall to his sides as his shoulders loosened.

"I'll be fine."

Felicia motioned for him to come in. He took his hat off as he stepped into the house. She led him through the hall to the small sitting room.

The cooper paused at the threshold and peered around at omnipresent vases of roses and the floral-patterned chairs, which had been wedding gifts from Colonel Moore, the game table near the windows, with the wooden chairs on either side of it. Felicia had always hated those chairs. Something about the way the grain looked in the drizzly, gray light made her want to weep. She wrenched her gaze from the gaming table, only to have the fireplace grab her attention, but above the mantle, two portraits hung, one of Thomas in his uniform and of Felicia in a gown made to be a facsimile of a shepherdess. Felicia glared toward the two of them. How dared she look so happy? How dared she look so in love? What gave her the right to smile?

The cooper's voice drew her attention back. "Quite a nice place, this is."

She sat on a floral-patterned chair and said flatly, "We have an important matter of storage to discuss."

The cooper sat across from Felicia in the other floral chair, long legs sprawled out in front of him, and pulled out a small brown leather notebook from his coat pocket. "What sort of storage? Wet or dry?"

"I need to store my husband's things away," Felicia said. "Whatever you'd use to store dry goods, I suppose. Definitely one watertight barrel to send back to London."

The cooper flicked his eyes from his notebook toward Felicia and frowned. "The Major?"

Felicia cleared her throat. "The Major is dead. I don't want his things rotting where they are."

The cooper parted his lips, then frowned, eyebrows drawn into a dark line. "My condolences for you and your family. Is this a good time? I can come back in a few weeks or months."

"No, I've put this off long enough." Felicia gritted her teeth, then cleared her throat and softened her jaw. "In a few months, I won't be able to care for his things like I want."

"I understand," the cooper said, his voice soft.

"I don't think you do." Felicia ran her fingers through the curls hanging over her shoulder and closed her squeezed her eyes shut. "But I appreciate the sympathy." She stood and began to pace the room, head bowed low, eyes to floor.

"How many barrels will you need?" he asked, eyes following her as she paced.

Felicia threw her hands into the air. "I hoped you could tell me." She leaned on the floral seat's tall back, scrutinizing over the cooper. "I don't know where to start with this sort of thing. It's for clothes and personal items."

"How many things did he have?"

Felicia plunked down in the chair again, tapping her hands to her temples. "His wardrobe is nearly full. I suppose I won't need to keep all of it. I might give some of his uniforms back to Colonel Moore to reuse, though I don't know if I can. I want to keep his toilette, his pipe, and his violin."

"I wouldn't pack away the violin, ma'am. The notes will turn sour if kept away in an airtight space for so long."

"What do you propose I do with a violin?"

The cooper glanced up at her and shrugged. "I'd play it."

"I don't know how. I just sang along."

His eyes flicked between the violin on the mantle and Felicia. "Keep it where it's at in its case? As a momentum?"

Felicia pressed her lips together tightly, narrowing her eyes, but not in anger. She took in a deep, though shaky, breath and closed her eyes. "I can't look at it without hearing it," she whispered.

Silence permeated the air, and the cooper stretched his long legs and continued to write in his notebook. Felicia rested an elbow on the arm of the chair, propping her face up with her fist, watching him. The seconds ticked by with an agonizing trepidation, the only sound in the room the scratching of his pencil on the paper, and the foundation creaking.

Rose came in with the freshened pot of tea on the silver cart, setting things on the table between Felicia and the cooper. When Rose bobbed a curtsy and left, Felicia assumed the tea duties.

"Master Cooper." She cleared her throat. "May I offer you a cup of tea?"

He paused mid-scribble, glanced up at her, then went back to writing. "No, thank you."

"Do you not like tea?"

"I don't drink tea. I cannot afford it."

"I don't charge my guests to use my china," Felicia said, pouring a cup of tea. She gave him a mirthless smile. "I don't think I'd have that many guests that way."

"I don't think I'd have many customers if I drank tea," he said, his voice cool and even regarding her through half-lidded eyes and resumed his writing.

"What are you?" Felicia asked, nose wrinkling lightly. "A rebel?"

He set the short pencil down and narrowed his eyes. "If that's what you wish to call me. Some people say patriot, and others just don't care." He stood up and shoved his book into his coat pocket before she could answer.

Her mouth fell open, and her cheeks heated.

He crossed his legs, his shoulders loosening. "Ma'am"—his voice softened— "I calculate you'll need at least two thirty-gallon barrels and one watertight fifteen-gallon. I can get them to you in about a month and a half, two months' time."

Felicia closed her mouth and put the teapot back on the tray. She counted on her fingers on one hand, the other hand absentmindedly coming up to the laces over her stomacher. Her cheeks grew even warmer. "Could you get them done sooner?"

The cooper's eyes flicked down to her hand and up to her face again. "I could," he said slowly. "How soon do you need them?"

"Preferably before my child makes himself prominent," she said. "I don't want to be packing his belongings while... with a kicking child."

"Is three weeks to a month better?"

"Yes." Felicia sat down in the chair again and tilted her head toward the cooper. "How much will the total be?"

He sat crossed his legs, slid his notebook back out of his coat, and resumed writing. "How much are you willing to pay?"

"Whatever the market demands."

He glanced up at her, then back down again. "How are you?"

"I'm fine." Felicia smoothed her skirts and adjusted her paniers on the chair with a dignified huff. "What's that got to do with anything?"

"Your husband died. Are you able to make payments? I don't want you to struggle just to put your husband's memories away."

Felicia raised her head to stare at the cooper, and her eyebrows furrowed. She pouted slightly while she mulled over his words. It ought to have been completely evident she was more than capable of paying for a simple barrel or two, what with the grandeur of her house, and most of all, tea set. Nobody else had a tea set like hers: fine cream china with the gold edging. The cooper glanced up at her prolonged silence.

"I—I'm fine," she said. "I have an estate."

"Will this number do?" he asked, turning the book to her.

She leaned forward and squinted at his handwriting. "Aye."

"And I suppose that, in your state, you'll need somebody to help you move them around?"

"Just to deliver them. I only have one man, and I don't wish for him to break his back picking them up from town."

"Very good." He stood up and held out his hand out to her.

Felicia stood and took his tanned hand. His palm was rough, calloused by his trade. He started to squeeze her hand to shake, but stopped, as if suddenly remembering a lost item. He loosened his grip on her fingers and brought her hand to his lips, pressing a kiss to her knuckle.

If Felicia were being honest, she'd have admitted she found his lips softer than she thought they'd be.

He dropped her hand, bowing curtly at his waist. "I'll have them ready at a month at the latest."

"Thank you, master cooper."

"Nathaniel Poe," he said. "Saying 'master cooper' does tend to get tedious."

"Thank you, Master Poe." Felicia gave him a small curtsy. "Now, if you'll wait here so I can fetch the pocketbook, I'd be more than happy to pay you upfront."

He offered her a short nod, and Felicia left him in the room for only a few moments, before returning with a black leather wrapped pouch. She handed him some paper bills and coins.

The cooper counted the money. "I believe you overpaid."

Felicia closed his hand around the money. "And I believe you under-charged. I recently read our ledger, and there was a different price for the last two we ordered for the party last month..."

Nathaniel Poe stood silently for a few moments. "Exactly my reason for my price this time." He slid the change back into her palm. "You don't need any extra charges in a time like this."

Felicia tilted her head to study his face, his hand still holding the money against her palm. She stifled a gasp. Though the man was a Native to North America, against his tan skin, and in contrast to his black hair, brows, and lashes, pale blue eyes stared back at her, so like the pale blue eyes that glanced at her while playing his violin. How could he have the same pale blue eyes that softened whenever he heard the words, "I love you."

She blinked and shook herself. "I'm sorry," she said, pulling her hand from his.

The cooper—Master Poe—slid the notebook back into his coat pocket. "Will that be all for you then?"

She opened her mouth to speak, but nothing quite came out. She mustered a small nod.

He picked up her hand and kissed her knuckles again. "God be with ye."

"Oh—ah—let me walk you back to the door," Felicia stammered. "I'm terribly sorry. My mind has drifted. It's prone to doing that lately."

"As it does with many a woman in your state," Nathaniel Poe said as Felicia led him back through the house.

She opened the door for him and curtseyed, the hint of a smile coming back to her lips. "Your wife is with child as well?"

"I'm not married." He put his hat back on his head, and her smile faded. He raised a brow at her. "I meant to allude to the sorrow you're facing. But I suppose being with child would aid in that fog. Good day to you. And please do accept all my sympathies."

The cooper tipped his hat and started down the path away from the house.

Felicia stood alone in the doorway, lips lightly parted. She closed the door and leaned against it, completely and utterly flummoxed by those pale blue eyes in someone else's face.

"Ma'am?" Rose came from the sitting room, pushing the tea cart in front of her. "Is everything all right? You barely touched your tea."

"I—well—he didn't take any," Felicia said, glancing toward the door. She cleared her throat and hummed. "I suppose you'd better warm it up for me. I'll take it in the Major's office."

"Yes, ma'am."

Felicia dragged her feet toward Thomas's office. It would be a long month before the storage arrived. She ran her hand over the light cover of her stomacher.

"But when will it go back to normal?" she whispered under her breath as she closed the office door behind her. "When will things seem right again?" She glanced up. "Thomas. When will things feel right again?"

The familiarity was fading by the day. The tobacco and clove pomade were nearly a memory. The office was still the only haven she could find, but even it was starting its solace was starting to slip from her grasp. Everything was so still, and it seemed that even the dust particles stayed floating in stasis. It was unnatural and unnerving.

The click of shoes echoed down the hall, and Felicia sank lower in Thomas's office chair. The door whooshed open with a gust of air and the scent of roses, and Mother asked, "How many bouquets does this one make?"

"I don't know. Close the door," Felicia said with a moan, wrapping her arms around her head.

"What a sight you are." Mother settled into the chair across from her. "And what are you doing in here? Haven't you gone over every scrap of paper he kept?"

"I have, but I'm still waiting on his will. It's August now. I want to have everything in order before my time comes."

"I'm sure the letter will come soon enough," Mother said. "Has any of the estate come in yet?"

"Yes. I am receiving a yearly allowance and it's enough for a while. It is not the whole thing I am due, but it will last."

Mother peered over Felicia, studying her appearance. She stood and walked around the desk and picked up her arm, inspecting the skin at her wrists. "Oh, my dear girl, you are so very pale."

"I'm always pale, Mother."

"But even more so now. You have such dark circles under your eyes. Has the child drained you so?"

Felicia let out a loud, longsuffering sigh. "I'm fatigued, but well. Except for the flowers. They need to leave."

Mother took Felicia's face in her hands, a concerned frown marring her graceful features. "Oh, if I could take the pain from you!"

Felicia took her mother's hands from her face and flopped back down on the desk. "Leave me be."

"Felicia, we need to have a talk," Mother said.

Silence permeated the room for several moments, then Felicia her cheek on the desk to narrow her eyes at her mother. "What sort of talk?"

"*The* talk."

Felicia sat up slowly, eyeing her mother warily. She wagged her head. "I'm with child. I don't need that talk."

Felicia's mother breathed out a long breath through her nose and leaned on the desk. "You know what talk I mean."

Felicia plugged her ears and stood to pace the room. "I don't want to hear it. I didn't like it the first time."

"Felicia, you're nearly halfway to your time." Mother's voice grew harried, and she drew in a breath. "Think of the child, Felicia."

Felicia stopped pacing and spun to face her mother, petticoats, and apron swishing. She fitted her hands at her hips and frowned.

"No one will be able to fill Thomas's shoes, Mother, nor do I want them to."

"Your father and I worked very hard arrange an advantageous marriage the first time." Felicia's mother took her hands. "And when Thomas proposed to you, we expected our job to be over."

"Your job *is* over," Felicia said, narrowing her eyes. "I'm still Mrs. Thomas Hawkings."

"Yes, yes. But you must think about the baby. Do you really want your child to be born without a father?"

Felicia tugged on her hair and sat back down on Thomas's chair. She pressed a hand to her stays, pressed her mouth closed, and shut her eyes. She took in a deep breath through her nose and let it out in a shaky exhalation. "I don't want my baby to be without his natural father. But I can't have what I want."

"No. And it is the baby's fault that you can't just go out to find a suitable replacement for Thomas, either."

Felicia wrinkled her nose and huffed, disgusted. "Suitable replacement, indeed. Not my baby's fault, indeed." She glared up at her mother. "I don't like that term, and I wish not to use it. If I marry again, whoever he is wouldn't be replacing anything but the bullet-shaped hole in my heart, and even then, it would be but a leaky patch."

Mother offered her a consoling smile and squeezed her hands. "Of course not, my dear. It's not nearly enough time to grieve and your time is less than most widows'. You need to think about marriage again."

Felicia chewed at her lip. *Widow.* The word had a cruel sting to it, and she didn't like the way it clung to her. Most of the widows in the church were old women whose children took care of them. There were a few younger women, but none of them twenty-four. She certainly didn't want to be known as Widow Hawkings.

She despised that name. She despised it vehemently. For so many reasons...

"What do you propose I do?" Felicia lowered her voice. "Most men would not want to marry a woman carrying another man's child."

"There are good men, my dear, ones who'd be willing to raise the child and give you a good home once again. They may not be Thomas, but they'd provide for you both."

"Thomas is still providing for me, Mother! Once I get word from Bach, I'll be set. I should get regular installments. Thomas wasn't stupid. I know he has provided for me... for his family should... should *this* happen."

"Yes, yes, of course. But it isn't right that you remain unmarried."

"What do you plan to do, Mother?" Felicia scoffed. "Throw me another coming out party?"

A large smirk grew on Mother's lips, and Felicia let out a gasp and jabbed a finger at her. "No."

"A dinner with some suitors could be an excellent idea, dear."

"No!"

"Oh, it would be suitable for your age and station, preferable even since you're carrying the child. Meeting a suitor in this manner—calm, collected, and at home, not at some play or opera is a grand idea."

"What part of no is not in your lexicon? I don't want to, and it's *my* life we're discussing here!"

Mother reached out and patted her hand against the small curve of Felicia's stomacher. "But this is not only your life we're discussing, is it?"

Felicia peeled off her mother's hand. "That life is in me. I have the say on whether or not that life has to endure a dinner full of suitors."

"What's that? Here, Felicia, step closer." Her mother leaned in close and pressed her ear to Felicia's stomacher.

"Mother!"

"Shh... I see." Felicia's mother sat back again. "The child says that he would love to have a father again."

Felicia narrowed her eyes, drew in a deep breath, and pinched the bridge of her nose. Stepping back from her mother, she said, "I'm not going to be seated at a table full of males and be made a spectacle."

FELICIA WRIGGLED on the chair in front of her toilette.

"Come now, ma'am," Rose said. "I have to set the curls right. Please sit still."

"You're pulling on my head."

"You have to look nice for the dinner tonight. You don't want to seem like a ragamuffin, all in disarray. Don't you want to be pretty for your guests?"

"Not particularly, no."

"I'm sure you don't mean that ma'am." Rose pinned the lock

against the back of Felicia's head and curled the loose tendrils of hair hanging loosely at the base of the intricate and lofty coiffure. She arranged several curls over Felicia's pale shoulder, then stepped back and surveyed her work, before nodding once.

Felicia groaned, stretching her neck. "I think you underestimate my distaste for this venture."

Rose moved to rummage through her wardrobe. She pulled out a cream dress with a large floral print and proceeded to layer it onto Felicia. "There now," Rose said as she adjusted the silks. "You can barely tell there's a new life in you with the way this dress fits."

"Perhaps," Felicia said, "to the outside eye it may not appear so. But I feel larger... and given the nature of the dinner, I don't want to lure any suitor with the false promise of a pretty little maid."

"I'm sure your guests are aware of your situation, ma'am."

"I'm afraid of that too. I don't want pity. It's a cycle of logic I cannot win. They don't know I'm with child and leave disgusted, or they know and pity the poor girl."

Rose gave Felicia a reassuring pat on your shoulder. "I wish I could console you further. I would trust your parents. They are good people."

Felicia craned her neck to look at Rose. "I suppose so. Thank you." She offered a trembling smile. "If you will, please go set up for dinner."

While Rose curtseyed and scurried from the room, a wave of resignation with a hint of indignation, swept over Felicia and she trilled her lips. "I better go see if my parents have arrived with the bulls then." She pushed herself to her feet and muttered under her breath, but as she reached the base of the stairs, a knock sounded at the door. Amos was nowhere in sight, so she rolled her eyes, brushed at her skirts, and opened the door.

Felicia stared for a few moments at the tall man on her porch. His thick brown hair was pulled back into a loose queue at the nape of his neck and curled up at his ears, and his midnight blue eyes seemed almost black.

She frowned lightly and stepped back a pace. "Henry?"

"Ah, yes, I'm afraid it's I." Henry Moore removed his tricorn hat, a small smile on his thin lips, bowed at the waist, then shrugged his shoulders. "I was told you were hosting a dinner, and if I wanted to come, I should. In fact, I think your mother meant me to be here." He kept his hands and hat clasped behind his back as he stood in the doorway. "May I come in?"

"Oh, of course." Felicia led him to the sitting room and offered him a seat. "I have to admit I really did none of the planning for tonight. You could call me a guest in my own house."

"I had a feeling you might not have had much to do with it," Henry said.

Felicia sat beside him. Rose was right to tell her not to worry. Henry knew very well of her situation. But did he know this was meant to be a supper to find her a suitor? Somebody to marry and to raise Thomas's child? She exhaled slowly, her shoulders sagging. At least she could be franker and more open with him at the supper.

"And what did my mother say to lure you over to this entrapment dinner?"

"Is that what this is?" Henry gave a short, stilted laugh. "She just said that I should stop by if I found myself unoccupied and had the time. I found the time, and behold, I am unoccupied."

Felicia rested her cheek in her palm and exhaled. "How fortuitous that you should be able to stumble upon a free dinner."

Henry offered her a good-natured grin. "Well, if you know me, then you know I'm not one to turn down a free dinner." He brought a hand to his slight paunch. "No matter the circumstances."

"Well, of course." Felicia tilted her face away from him and grew silent. "Who would be so very unwise to turn away a meal?"

Felicia heard Henry shift in his chair.

"How are you doing?" His voice was soft and low. "It's been some time since—well—and you seem to be holding together very well."

Felicia looked back and upon seeing his sad frown, offered him a small smile. "I do try. It's been hard... especially since the little one is growing every day, and there's been so much to do. I'll get to a better state eventually, but I don't like to talk about me or that event. How are you doing? Is the business well?"

"As well as I can manage it from here." Henry stretched out his legs in front of him, his frown melting into nonchalance, and waved a hand in the air. "The colonials have blocked my ships from their harbors, though they know full well it's cloth and lace, not tea. It's a difficult time for any mercantile. If they want to create their own scratchy stiff lace, so be it. They won't have mine to give them the refinement they lack."

"I've given up on the colonials," Felicia said with a dignified sniff. "It's increasingly harder to find good tea, and my stash is getting exceptionally low. Do you think you could procure some?"

Henry gave a bellowing laugh that echoed down the hall. "I'll do my best."

Another knock at the door startled Felicia, and she stood up again. Henry stood with her.

"If you'll excuse me, dear Henry, that's probably the one who organized all of this."

Henry motioned broadly and sat back down as Felicia left the room. She stiffened her shoulders and opened the door. This time her parents stood on the step.

Felicia peered around them. "Are you it?"

"Are you displeased?" her father asked.

"I expected other guests with you," Felicia said. "Only Henry Moore has arrived."

"Oh, wonderful." Mother stepped around Felicia, while her father took off his hat and pressed a kiss to her cheek as he entered the house.

"It proved rather hard to find somebody who could be suitable for you." Mother paused to fix her hair in the mirror hanging on the entryway wall. "Most men would be a step down for you. Henry would be a level step. Isn't that what you want? A level step?"

"I want some lavender water." Felicia rolled her eyes. "You're giving me a headache."

"She gives me headaches as well," her father said with a small smirk. Her mother hit his arm, and he chortled under his breath.

"Oh, bother it all," Felicia said, motioning for them to move to the sitting room. "Come into the sitting room and wait with Henry while I see if the first course is ready."

Felicia's parents adjourned into the sitting room with Henry, and their idle chatter seemed to follow her as she started down the hall to the dining room where four place settings were ready for the diners.

Even my help knew the number of guests before I did.

She sniffed in again and glanced toward the kitchen. Selah came toward the dining room with a crock, the handles balanced on her forearms.

"Oh, ma'am. Supper is ready," she said, setting the crock at one end of the table. "May I call for your guests?"

Felicia shook her head. "I'll call them in. It'll make me feel useful. Thank you, Selah."

The warm smell of bone broth, beef, and cooked late summer vegetables radiated from the pot and wafted from the kitchen, and Felicia breathed in the delicious scent, relishing it, before returning to the sitting room. She looked from Henry to her parents.

"If you wish to sit at the table, that would be quite all right."

"Felicia, are you quite all right?" Henry asked, standing up. "You seem pale. Surely you could have had one of the servants call us in."

"It's no problem. I am well, thank you. Exhausting work it is, creating life," she said, but Henry held onto her arms, keeping her steady.

"It may be best to have you seated." Henry guided her down the hall. He lowered her down in the chair and settled her at the table, before sitting across from her, while her mother sat to her right and her father to her left.

Selah and Amos filtered back into the dining room. Selah set a silver platter with a fish surrounded by fresh greens on the table while Amos filled the glasses with blackberry wine and Rose ladled the rich soup into their bowls. The tempting aroma gave Felicia cause to close her eyes and inhale.

"Is that better?" Henry asked.

Felicia bowed her head toward him, smiling lightly. Lord knew she loved a dinner or a party, but without Thomas... it was just so foreign and unnatural. There was an empty chair at the table that she knew Thomas would no longer occupy. It pained her to know she had to traverse menial conversation without him... and she knew how it would go...

How is your business? How are the ships? How is your dog? I'm so glad that he's doing better, I know he's like a second child to you. You were in Boston last fall, weren't you? Is it really as bad as the colonials say? I didn't think so. They tend to exaggerate the truth, don't they? Have you gotten any word from your sister in South London? Oh, she had a little boy? Congratulations. The weather has been rather wet this summer; don't you think?

Thomas used to praise her timely *of courses* and *yeses*. He'd been amused by her ability to tune out the humdrum but be able to recite the entire conversation when someone addressed her.

Felicia's eyes flitted from her soup to Henry, taking care to be discreet with her gaze. When he grinned, his eyes didn't crease the way Thomas's had. He didn't pull his lips back into Thomas's soft curve. She watched him smile mid-word and listened to how he made anything he said sound so elegant with his clear pronunciation, his accent light, but genteel. While he and her father discussed the ever-growing textile trade and the need for further expansion, Henry's chest puffed with pride, and he spoke calmly but powerfully on any topic.

But unfortunately, he was the only subject at the table of any interest to her, and even then, he still less interesting than her actual supper.

Another knock at the door echoed down the hall, and Felicia startled again.

"Who could that be?" Felicia's mother asked, the sound of her foot tapping against the wooden panels grating on Felicia's nerves.

"I wouldn't know," Felicia said. "I haven't called on anybody."

Amos, who had been setting the used plates onto the china cabinet to be taken back to the kitchen, said, "I'll answer the door, ma'am."

Felicia shifted uncomfortably while the table fell silent. Amos's voice and another man's came muffled from the foyer, but Felicia couldn't many out any words till footsteps started back up the hallway.

Amos said, "Come this way, I s'pose." He reappeared in the entryway to the dining room. "Nathaniel Poe here to see you, ma'am."

"I'm busy." Felicia motioned to her parents and Henry. "Couldn't this have waited till tomorrow?"

"I don't think so. He has three large barrels with him."

Felicia drew in a deep breath and lolled her head to the side, exhaling loudly. "Oh." Her gaze flickered between Henry and her parents, then she cleared her throat. "I'm terribly sorry. I won't be but a minute."

Henry scooted her chair back from the table, and she thanked him as she stood. She clasped his hand in hers, then left the dining room.

Master Poe waited in the foyer, sitting on one of the barrels. He tapped his hands rhythmically against his knees, glancing up as her footsteps clicked against the wooden floor. He slid off the barrel erect, hands clasped behind his back.

"This really isn't the best of times for a delivery," Felicia said, motioning between Poe and the barrels.

He bowed. "I'm sorry, Mrs. Hawkings. I just won't have the time after tonight to deliver them to you. I figured now would be better than much later."

"I suppose so." Felicia peered inside them, inspecting the crafts- manship. "This will suffice."

"Very good."

Felicia stood silently for a few moments, staring at the empty barrels in her foyer.

"Where would you like me to set them?" he asked.

Felicia winced. "The parlor. I suppose that would be best. It's down the hall on the right, the long room with the blue wallpaper." She started to move the smaller watertight barrel toward the side of the entry hall, but the cooper took her hands.

"I don't think you should be moving something so heavy in your state," he said, gently removing her hands from the barrel. "I'll be able to move these myself."

Felicia looked up into his eyes, then her gaze fell to his hands on her wrists. "Might you let go?"

He dropped her hands and picked up one of the barrels. "You have guests to get back to, Mrs. Hawkings."

Felicia gave him a curtsy, then hurried on back down the hall to the dining room. Henry stood when she reentered, then helped her back into the chair.

"What business does the cooper have here at this hour?" her father asked.

"I placed an order a few weeks back," Felicia murmured as Henry slid her chair closer to the table and gave her shoulder a gentle pat, trailing his fingers down her arm. She offered him a simple, mirthless smile. "I suppose I—"

A loud crash interrupted her. Felicia, her parents, and Henry all jumped and swiveled toward the source of the sound, which seemed to have emanated from outside the parlor, just across from the dining room. Through the doorway, she saw Nathaniel Poe staring down the hall, setting his jaw, resting his hand on his hips.

Her father started from his chair. "Is everything all right out there? Good G–d, man, you could wake the dead with your racket."

"My apologies," the cooper called, from the hallway. "The damn thing slipped."

Another round of silence. While a scowl starting to form on Henry's face, and Felicia's parents heaved a disgusted sigh, Felicia covered her face in her hands to hide a large grin beneath her fingers. She coughed, but the cough bubbled over into a full-blown cacophony of giggles and unladylike cackles. She pressed her hands over her mouth as her parents, Henry, and even the cooper all stopped and stared, but she couldn't stop laughing. She didn't want to. It was the first time since Thomas had left that happiness of any sort had taken hold.

Henry's scowl transformed into a warm grin. "Felicia, whatever is so funny?"

"'The damn thing slipped,'" she repeated through her laughter.

She snuck a peek from Henry to the cooper, who gave her a closed mouth grin then rolled the barrel into the parlor and stood it up right before leaving to retrieve the second one. The excitement for the night ended there. Nathaniel Poe rolled the second barrel in, tipped his hat toward Felicia and her guests, and left without another word.

But the cooper's quirked grin played in Felicia's mind, through dessert, and then tea and brandy in the sitting room. She could see him in her mind's eye, glancing at her from around Henry, giving her that sideways smile, and so she sat in relative silence for the rest of the night, her cheeks flushing at the memory.

Finally, Henry stood up. "I must thank you for having me over for dinner. The change of scenery and company did me some good."

"I enjoyed having you over," Felicia said. Her mother nudged her arm, motioning with her head for her daughter to follow him. Felicia sighed. "Let me walk you outside."

Henry smiled courteously, the corners of his eyes creasing ever so slightly. Felicia walked with him through the foyer.

"I really did enjoy your company." Henry's voice was hushed. He held his hand up, tentatively reaching it toward her hair then slowly wound his fingers through the curls that draped over her shoulder.

"And I yours," Felicia said, glancing down toward his hand. She pressed her lips together. "It was good fortune that you came."

"I'd say so as well. Would... would it be too bold to ask if I may see you again, perhaps without the eyes of your parents?" Henry dropped his hand to pick up Felicia's. "I don't want you to say yes just to please your mother, but I don't really want you to say no, either. I'm not so young, nor am I a replacement, but—"

Felicia took a deep breath through her nose and slowly released it. "Do not refer to yourself as a replacement for no one could replace the man I have lost. Do not think that I would say yes to appease my mother, for she knows that I am no longer hers to play as a pawn."

Henry nodded, and Felicia took in another deep breath. She gazed up into Henry's face, studying him. She studied the creases about his eyes and the way his lips turned neither up nor down. She studied the way his eyes studied her back, probably wondering why she was taking so long to answer him.

He was older than Thomas by five years, but with age came a sense of wisdom and stability. At least... that was what she thought about most of the soldiers Thomas brought into their home. The younger the officer, the more reckless he tended to be. But the older the officer, the more astute they appeared, opting to observe silently rather than to disrupt and cause disorder. She shouldn't care about age... As long as he was younger than her dear father, it ought to be all right.

Besides, a man, no matter the age, who situated himself in the textile industry wasn't likely to be called to aid in some battle in another colony and return with a bullet in his back.

He could provide for her well and perhaps... affection could follow...

But before that night he had only been a friend. Seeing him as more was new for her. Felicia couldn't make a judgement call so quickly. It might be good to court him further. After all... she *did* need to be remarried soon and he was so situated in life.

At length, Felicia said, "I'll see you again. Without my parents' eyes."

A smile curved his lips, and Henry's inky blue eyes glinted in the candlelight. He took her hand and brought it close to his lips, pressing a kiss to her fingertips. "Perhaps then I will call on you in two days' time."

"Yes... Saturday would be a pleasant day. If you would like, I could have Selah make for us a picnic lunch."

"I would like that very much."

Felicia paused again, cocking her head slightly, before giving him half a smile. "I am in eager anticipation for Saturday."

Henry pressed another kiss to her fingertips and released her hand. "I shall see you then. Thank you, dear Felicia, once again for a lovely meal."

He set his tricorn hat on his head, bowed toward her, and left down the path away from Hawkings' manor. With a relieved sigh, Felicia closed the door behind him and slunk back toward the sitting room, where her father played solitaire at the gaming table and her mother sat, hand cupped around her ear.

Felicia raised an eyebrow. "You can be at ease. He's gone, and I'm going to bed."

"You cannot leave me without the knowledge of what's to happen next," her mother said.

"Leave her alone, Abby." Father glanced up from his card game. "She'll decide what to do with her life."

"I told him I'd see him again." Felicia sighed and fell into the floral chair, resting a hand on her stomacher. "Oh, what I'd give for this whole ordeal to be over."

Mother crossed the room and took her hand. "I know, my dear, but if there is anything you need, anything at all, my love, please. Bother your father. He'll give you anything you want." She offered Felicia a glowing smile.

Father scoffed, muttering under his breath.

"I don't think Father could give me what I truly want." Felicia closed her eyes and took a deep breath. "But if I need advice, perhaps I could spare some time out of my day to come to you."

"We'd love that," Mother said, taking Felicia's other hand as well, giving both a squeeze, swaying them back and forth. "How wonderful it was to hear you laugh again."

The cooper's face flashed in her mind and Felicia bowed her head to hide her curved lips. She tapped her heel to the ground, trying to stamp it out. "I'm glad to laugh again."

Her father stood up from his game and came over to the two of them, and gently pressed a kiss to the top of her head.

"Now, my dear. We should get back home. If you'd like, we can return tomorrow to help you with the barrels."

"Yes. I'd like to have somebody near when I go through his things."

"Of course." Father curled a knuckle under her chin.

"And then Saturday, your life will begin again." Her mother grasped her daughter's arm and squeezed it gently. "It'll be well. I promise."

"I think so too," Felicia said. "At the very least, I hope so."

✣ 8 ✣

Felicia packed away everything of Thomas's except his violin. It remained on the mantle, where Thomas had displayed it during parties and suppers. She reasoned with herself that she kept it there as a *memento mori*, but if she were honest, she feared she would no longer be able to hear the strains of music in her memory should it be backed away.

For Thomas's mother, Felicia packed his pipe, and various sundry bits of his toiletries, as well as a lock of his hair preserved in a golden locket. Her letter had stated that she wished for Felicia to keep most of his things, telling her that while she still loved him, he belonged to Felicia's heart.

Thomas's things fit neatly in the two barrels with little room to spare. Felicia kept one of his shirts to sew into a pillow. The scent of musk and pomade still lingered in the cloth, and she wished to keep it with her as long as she could. She neared the middle of her fifth month that coming week, and though Selah and Rose claimed she had a particular glow about her, she didn't feel it. She felt rather like a tuber, a tuber with roots attached, and on top of that, her hair had become an uncontrollable mess that even her lavender pomade couldn't fix. Her back ached; her head was dizzy; she hated the smell of eggs; and most of all, she couldn't wear her favorite cream floral dress—the stomacher wasn't wide enough. She had to loosen her stays to fit into anything.

But alas, one cannot avoid the inevitable marching on of the days and weeks, and Saturday came upon Felicia all too quickly.

She had been dreading Saturday, but nevertheless, she sat at her toilette as Rose fixed up her hair, aged hands working on delicate curls.

"Rose, I don't even remember how to go about being courted. What do I do?"

The older woman brushed back a stray strand of her white hair, then continued to tend to Felicia. "I wouldn't know Ma'am. I never courted. My first mistress picked my husband, God rest his soul."

"I don't know what is worse. To choose for oneself or somebody else." Felicia wiggled in her seat away from Rose, wincing, as the woman attempted to tame the wild beast that was her hair. "There is a part of me that wishes someone would just pick for me, which I suppose my parents did with Henry."

"But you have the chance for love with their plan. You loved the Major, didn't you?"

"More than life itself..." Felicia's voice trailed off. She shifted away from Rose again, but Rose held her in place with one hand. "I met him at a dinner, you know. Not a contrived dinner, like this past one. My parents and I were invited to a dinner at Colonel Moore's house, when his wife was still alive. Thomas was twenty-five. I was nineteen."

Rose powdered the pomade to calm down Felicia's hair. "And was he smitten with you?"

"Like one of those fairy tales from England," Felicia whispered. Her lips transitioned between a smile and a frown, and she closed her eyes to stop the oncoming tears. "He sat two chairs down across from me. He kept asking for the potatoes because they were in front of me, and that evening, he asked my father for permission to have lunch with me in the court building gardens the next day. We were married a year to the day later."

"He really was a good man, ma'am. I miss him very much."

"Will there ever be a time when I won't miss him?" Felicia craned her neck to see the older woman. "There will be, right? I'll move past all this like waking from a terrible nightmare, right?"

Rose paused setting Felicia's hair and took in a deep breath. "Ma'am, if you ask me for my honest answer, I don't think you will move past him. I think there's always going to be a place in your heart where the Major is." She used a wooden roller stick to set the last few curls in place in buckles above Felicia's ears. "But don't underestimate how big a heart can be. I lost my husband after many years of marriage. You lost him young. Your heart has far more room than mine could ever hope to have." She tied a ribbon at the base of Felicia's hair, grouping the remaining curls into a low queue. "There. Your hair is tamed, and I dare say it's beautiful."

Felicia rose and peered at herself in the mirror, turning her head this way and that, flouncing her skirts. "How do I look? Not too round?"

Rose studied at her mistress and pressed her mouth closed. "I wouldn't say round..."

"Oh, Rose, no..." Felicia moaned and squinted at her reflection. She glared down at herself, pressing her hands to the growing curve of her skirts under her stays. "Stop growing! How will I find you a suitable father if I look like I'm smuggling a gourd under my skirts?"

"You'll want that baby to grow and move," Rose said softly, stashing away the brushes and rollers into the toilette drawers. "You know the baby is well when you feel that baby grow. The day you stop feeling that baby move is something scary."

Felicia spun around, brows furrowed, mouth agape. "You... you stopped feeling your baby move?"

Rose bowed her head.

Tears welled up in Felicia's eyes, the first tears that hadn't been for Thomas or herself. "Oh, Rose. I'm sorry."

"It's no matter, I s'pose. She's with her daddy now, so they get to be together while I'm here on earth with the boy. He's grown. Has a family living in Boston. Heard he got a job for the Boston Observer. So proud of him, I am."

A moment of silence passed between them, then Felicia strode over and hugged Rose, who stood there, unmoving.

"Ma'am? Ma'am, what are you doing?"

"I'm thanking you. You've been a wonderful companion and help to me."

Rose slowly wrapped her arms around Felicia's back. "You're welcome."

Felicia peeled herself off Rose and stood straight, but before she could say anything else, a knock at the bedroom door disturbed their thoughts.

"Ma'am? Mr. Henry Moore is at the door for you," Amos said from the hallway. "I have him in the sitting room, if that pleases you."

"I'll be right there." Felicia glanced up at Rose, brushing at her eyes with the back of her finger. "Thank you, Rose. You really are wise."

Rose bobbed a curtsey and gave Felicia a weathered smile. "Yes, ma'am. Now, go down before he starts wondering where you are."

Felicia picked up her skirts and made her way down the stairs.

Amos greeted her at the bottom step with a good-natured grin and handed her a large wooden basket. "Here, Miss. Selah made this up for you."

She took the basket with both hands and thanked him, making her way for the sitting room.

Henry stood as she came in, smiling brightly. "There you are. I thought you'd forgotten about our engagement today." He took the basket from Felicia and looped the handle over his forearm. Taking one of her hands in his free one, he pressed a kiss to the tips of her fingers.

"Of course, I didn't," Felicia said, bringing their intertwined hands closer to her mouth. She brushed a hesitant kiss to Henry's red signet ring. "I just wanted to make sure I'm presentable."

They started out of the house and down the path toward the edge of her property.

Henry offered her his arm. "You could wear what one of the colonials wears and still be absolutely beautiful."

"You're too kind." Felicia took her fan from her pocket, covering her face behind the delicate wooden slats. "It took me far too long to look halfway decent. Have you decided where to stop for the picnic?"

Henry cocked his head toward. "I'm thinking about the court

building gardens. They really are lovely this time of year, what with all the rain keeping them well watered."

Felicia nodded wordlessly, then clicked her tongue, and cast her eyes toward the road away. "Yes, the gardens are lovely."

Henry paused, gazing at her features. A frown crossed his face. "Is something wrong with the gardens?"

"No." Felicia rested her free hand on her stomacher. "It's just... that's where Thomas took me when we first courted."

Henry hummed, and squeezed her hand, and his frown melted into a consoling smile. "We don't have to go there. There is a nice field behind the milliner's shop. No tables, but it is a decent picnicking spot."

"I suppose so," Felicia said, but glanced down at her hand. "But it isn't as if Thomas owned a monopoly on the gardens. I'm sure many other people have gone there as well. Besides, I think the child would rather I sit in a chair than on the ground."

While Henry still smiled, concern lingered in his eyes. "Are you sure?"

"I really don't mind. The idea of sitting on the ground and attempting to get back up is already quite taxing." She leaned into his arm, and they continued walking.

THE GARDENS WERE lovely in late August. She loved the rose bushes, though the smell still nauseated her. She could still appreciate the beauty of the flowers and the ivy which crept up the stone court building and the trellis against the brick wall. It was a place that stayed in stasis and normalcy. The magistrate's wife had placed a table and two chairs in front of the trellis for visitors. The small mill, which didn't offer much more than an aesthetically pleasing view, still churned water along on the left side of the courtyard.

Felicia began to unload the basket's contents, while Henry supervised. He tried to have her sit while he set the table, but she insisted that she had to do something other than rest for a change. A heavy silence filled the air between the two that the watermill and birds tried to fill to no avail.

Soon, they both sat at the table, talking over the packed lunch of beef sandwiches and ginger beer.

"Have you been able to get your ships into the harbor safely?" Felicia asked. "It would be terrible if they dumped all your good textiles into the murky Delaware River just because you fly a Union Jack."

"Mmm... that would be a tragedy," Henry said, then took a bite of his sandwich. "They wouldn't get away with it like they did with that tea. Let the siblings learn from the other's mistakes. Philadelphia cannot want to be as heavily guarded as Boston is now."

"One would hope, but they've already staged raids." She stiffened her jaw so hard it clicked. She clenched her fists till her nails indented her palms. "I don't see why they wouldn't take matters into their own hands elsewhere."

Henry gently pried open her hands, massaging them in his large warm ones. They were soft, but not so smooth. He had old calluses on his left hand's fingers, and on the balls and heels of both palms, which took Felicia by surprise. "I suppose anything could happen. They are doing a fine job of blocking my trade. If they persist in keeping my ships at bay, I don't know what I'll do."

She relaxed her jaw and started to smirk but a little. "Stage a coup of your own?"

"I don't quite have the brains to stage a coup. Perhaps I should get William to help me." He started to smirk back. Felicia started packing their things back into the basket. "Enough of me. How are you?" Henry took the basket from her and set it on the table, peering at Felicia from over the handles. "Any news from the trust? Is Thomas's family doing well?"

"I'm not thrilled to be months removed from the horrid event, while still having no closure to the estate. They said they'd be back to me at their earliest convenience and that was back in July. It's nearing the end of August," Felicia said with huff. "But other than that, things are as fine as fine gets. I do worry for the future... Henry, I'm afraid this delay will leave me a pauper with a babe. Do you think they're trying to get me married faster so I lose money and they can keep it? It's forcing my hand and all so vexing. My nerves are veritably frayed."

Henry opened his mouth to speak, but closed it again, his eyes softening. "I—"

"Oh..." Felicia brought a hand over her mouth, eyes widening. "Am I too bold in saying that? Don't think me forward. Please accept my apologies."

"I don't think of you as forward, Felicia." Henry stood. "It is, after all, security you are aiming for. I am... I am honored you'd trust me enough to ask me such a question. And honestly, I can't answer you. I'd hope they wouldn't. Do they know of your predicament? Not that a child is a predicament."

"I believe I know what you mean," Felicia said. He picked up the basket and held his hand out for her. She stood and linked arms with him. "You don't seem very much the type to consider a child a predicament."

"No..."

They started back out for the main road through town.

"It's exactly a matter of security." Felicia glanced up at Henry as they ambled back up the road, past the shops and the women sitting on their stoops, flowers, and small wares in shallow baskets beside them. "Being married to a major did provide me with financial security, but there was always the chance of him being killed. I don't want to do that again. I frightened by the idea my future husband might leave me too early as well."

"Well, if I may say this—" Henry stopped along the side of the road — "it's rather hard to get killed when you're in the textile industry."

Felicia pursed her lips. "Yes," she said slowly.

Henry stepped closer to her. "And the textile industry is fairly lucrative."

She kept her eyes and head cast down. "Yes."

Henry curled his finger under her chin and tilted her face up toward his. Felicia tried not to look him in the eye.

"If I was bold, I wouldn't ask you for a kiss," he said.

Felicia squinted, screwing up her lips. "Are you bold?"

"I might be."

Henry bent to her level and pressed a kiss to her lips.

Felicia's eyes flew open, and she braced her hands against Henry's shoulders, fingers spread wide. His mouth worked against hers, but she pinched her lips closed, holding her breath as he kissed her. Eyes still open wide, she saw someone in a shop window, staring directly at the two of them—kissing! —by the side of the road. Henry kept a grip on her waist, still with his lips plastered against hers.

Mortified, Felicia strained to identify who saw them through that window. She could just make out the sign over the door, a crude wooden sign with painted letters.

Nathaniel Poe: Cooper.

Felicia's stomach flopped, and she pulled away from Henry with a gasp. She covered her mouth, eyes wide.

"Was I too bold?" Out of breath, Henry gazed intently into her eyes, concern furrowing at his brow.

"Perhaps a little," Felicia said from behind her hands, glancing around Henry. The cooper had moved away from the window.

A tightness manifested in her middle but couldn't tell if the child moved in her or a snake wound its way around her stomach.

"I should get back home," Felicia said, sliding the basket off Henry's arm. He watched her as she adjusted the basket steadying it on her hip. "I suppose I shall see you?"

Henry winced. He stepped away from her, clasping his hands behind him. "Are we to see each other again?"

"Ah, I suppose... maybe," Felicia said, keeping a hand over her mouth. "We live in the same town and attend the same church. I really do have to go. The babe is turning over in me. You understand..."

She gave Henry a quick curtsey and leaving him standing on the side of the road, hurried back up to her house.

Felicia searched the kitchen, looking through the cabinets and under the large sink by the window. She could feel Selah watching her, but she couldn't care.

Finally, Selah asked, "What are you trying to find, ma'am?"

"Butter churn," Felicia said.

Selah stepped to her side and pulled the little wooden churn from the cabinet beside the stove.

"Thanks." Felicia grabbed the churn by the handle, then, promptly whacked the defenseless wooden thing against the edge of the island table.

"Ma'am! What are you doing?" Selah cried, holding her hands out as Felicia beat the churn to its inevitable demise.

Turning the battered butter churn over in her hands and inspecting the jagged crack down the side, Felicia said, "Oh, dear. It broke." She handed the broken wood to Selah. "I suppose we'll need to call on the cooper to make us a new one."

Selah cradled the dead churn in her hands. She squeaked quietly, looking woefully up at Felicia. "Why did you go and break a perfectly good butter churn? It was a fine churn."

"It was old. It was bound to break." Felicia motioned with her hand, stuttering. "Ah. It was too small? Oh, just have Amos call on the cooper to come over to talk about a new churn."

"Wouldn't it be easier to have him just order it while he's there?"

"No!" She paused and pressed her lips together, then twisted them into a frown, adding more quietly, "I mean, no. This is a specific request. He needs to make sure he gets the dimensions correct, and I need it in a... in a certain color. I will wait in the parlor."

Felicia started out of the kitchen, but then glimpsed back over her shoulder at Selah, who still stared down at the slain churn. Felicia gently pried it out of Selah's hands. "Selah, perhaps, if it's not too much to ask, if you could make up some more sandwiches?"

"MRS. HAWKINGS, I meant it when I said I don't normally make house calls," Nathaniel Poe said as Amos showed him into the parlor.

"It's a specific request." Felicia gestured for him to sit in a red velvet chair. "I was just in town earlier, and this happened so soon after I got back that I just couldn't go into town again."

"What is it?" The cooper rolled his eyes and took out his small notebook.

"The butter churn gave up the ghost."

Nathaniel stopped writing and looked up at face her. "The butter churn... died?"

"Very tragically." Felicia picked up the broken wood to show him. "Split right down the middle."

"How on earth did you manage to ruin a decent churn down the middle?" Nathaniel asked, turning it over in his hands.

Felicia propped her face up in her palm. "We put too much cream in it, and the butter broke it."

Nathaniel glanced over at Felicia, who only gave him a broad grin and a shrug. He leaned back in the chair. "So, you need a new one?"

"Yes."

"Same size?"

"Yes."

"Same color?"

"Yes."

"Mrs. Hawkings—"

"Felicia."

Nathaniel stared at her and Felicia locked eyes with him. She kept her grin on her face, crossing her hands on her lap.

He took a deep breath. "Felicia, then. Why did you have me called out of my storefront just to order a replica of this broken churn? I haven't eaten dinner yet, you know. I sure ain't your damn lackey."

"Have you not?" Felicia asked, rising to her feet.

Nathaniel watched her, eyes flickering over her face.

"Well, that won't do." Felicia motioned for him to follow her. "You likely won't make this order in time if I keep you from your dinner."

He huffed and stood. "Mrs. Hawkings. I have two orders for wine barrels that need to be finished by tonight and if—"

"Felicia."

Nathaniel heaved a sigh. "Felicia, they are for Colonel Moore, and if I don't have them for him by tonight, I can assure you that I will not be alive to make you that butter churn in the morning."

"I know the Colonel." Felicia waved a hand dismissively, leading him down the hallway and to the kitchen. "I'm sure he won't kill you."

"I know the Colonel, too," Nathaniel said. "Granted, I'm not out kissing his brother."

Felicia groaned under her breath, keeping her back to Nathaniel. "I didn't kiss him. He kissed me."

Selah had laid out more beef sandwiches on the kitchen table. Felicia pointed from Nathaniel to the table but kept her face just out of his line of vision. She heard him step up to the table to take one of the sandwiches and risked a peek. He was watching her.

"Did you call on me to fix a butter churn... in order to have me over for dinner?"

"No." Felicia spun toward Nathaniel.

He leaned against the table, chewing on the sandwich. He seemed amused, as she wrinkled and unwrinkled her nose at him. Nathaniel swallowed a mouthful of sandwich.

"It seems to me that you did."

She threw her arms into the air. "I need a new butter churn."

"Aye."

"And you are the cooper."

"Aye."

"And I just so happen to have left over sandwiches from when I went out earlier."

"Indeed."

"And you haven't eaten yet."

"Indeed."

"It's not my fault the butter churn broke."

"Was broken," Nathaniel said calmly as he reached for another sandwich.

Felicia gawked, unable to speak coherently.

He nodded. "I made that first one, you know. There's no way too much butter could split that churn."

"You did?"

He dusted off his hands and showed her the underside of the churn. There, etched into the bottom, were the initials: *N. B. P. Cooper*. And below that, his insignia: a bow and arrow.

"Oh..."

Nathaniel snickered at her under his breath, his mouth full. He swallowed the last bite of sandwich and wiped his hand on his shirt-front, then crossed his arms. "How'd you do it?"

Felicia mumbled, hiding her face from him.

"Oh, come on. I'll build you the new one for free if you tell me how you broke this one."

Felicia stared down toward her feet and muttered. "I banged it repeatedly on the edge of the table, much to the chagrin of my cook."

Nathaniel let out a loud, melodic laugh, full-bodied and full of real mirth. He set the broken churn on the island table and held his sides, his voice echoing through the hallways and rooms of the house.

That snake started coiling around Felicia's middle again, and she pressed her hands to her stomacher. As the snake tightened around her, the child moved. The mix of trepidation and new life did not set well in her. She let out a small gasp, then pressed her lips together.

She hated that feeling. She hated feeling helpless to that snake, but the frightened tightness consuming her body overwhelmed her. She missed the butterflies of a childish love. But they'd flown away after Thomas died and this... this was no love. This was fear.

How dare you feel this way toward the cooper? How dare you? And he'll be torn from you just as Thomas was. All because you feel this way. The snake tormented her, transforming into a rock in the bottom of her stomach.

She pinched the bridge of her nose, rubbing at the inner corners of her eyes till a few eyelashes came loose, and rocked back and forth on her feet.

Nathaniel's laughter ebbed, and he cleared his throat. "Maybe coming here wasn't so much a waste as I thought." He winked, grabbed another sandwich, and started back up the hall. "I'm afraid, since this particular project is a gift, it will take a little longer for me to complete. I must get the paid orders in first. But don't worry, it'll be well within your time." He stopped and the front door and leaned against the frame while he waited for Felicia to catch up to him. "Is that all right with you?"

"Yes, of course," Felicia said. "But, for the sake of my sanity and lack of butter, how long?"

"About a month."

Felicia bobbed her head and gave him a short curtsey, holding her hand out for him to shake. He wiped his hands on his shirtfront again and took her hand, but as she gave his hand a light squeeze, he raised it to his lips and pressed a kiss over her fingers.

"God be with ye," he said, gazing down into her eyes.

She averted her gaze.

Amos came in from the hallway and handed him his hat, and Nathaniel bowed to Felicia and started toward town. Felicia stood in the doorway, watching him leave.

"Ma'am?" Amos said. "There are too many flies out. Should I close the door?"

Felicia wordlessly backed away from the threshold, moving to the window in the sitting room, watching as Nathaniel disappeared down the road.

❧ 10 ❧

Felicia roamed Thomas's office. The office didn't seem much like his anymore now his books were packed away, and his last letters sent off to their recipients. There was no trace of him left in the office, but still, she could sense him in there. She sat in his chair, leaning against the back as she swiveled toward the window, delighting in melancholy over the grandeur of early autumn and a lingering Michaelmas Summer, then closed her eyes, letting the light flood her face.

Strains of Vivaldi's *Winter* played in her ears. She could almost see him, standing in his uniform, violin tucked under his chin, back to her as he played the notes ringing in her head. A breeze blew in from the window, caressing Felicia's cheek. She sucked in a breath, memories of parties and flickering candlelight dancing through her head. It was nearly that haunting season of autumn.

"It's not possible," Thomas said, pointing to the family Bible.

But she had to ask.

"Thomas?" she murmured, her eyes still closed. "Thomas, what am I to do?"

He stopped playing, stepped closer, and sat on the edge of his desk.

"I don't know what I'm feeling, but I don't care for it. I don't want to move on from you."

Thomas said nothing, but Felicia held out her hand. He leaned back.

"Thomas, please," she said. "Would it be all right to marry again? You've only been gone three months though it feels like years."

She tried reaching for him again, but, again, he moved away.

"Your child kicks me constantly." Tears escaped her closed eyes. "He's making me quite large already. I suppose he's to take after you."

At that, Thomas beamed, flashing his teeth.

"Oh, Thomas, say something. Say *anything*," Felicia said. She opened her eyes.

Thomas wasn't in the room. She knew he couldn't have been, but she had seen him so clearly, heard his violin so distinctly.

She stood up with an exhausted huff. "Oh, just because you can kick me doesn't mean you should so hard," she said, running her hand over the growing curve under her skirt. "Don't hurt your mother."

A knock sounded on the office door, and Selah said, "Ma'am? Your parents are here for tea. Shall I seat them in the parlor or sitting room?"

"The parlor if you please. I'll be right there."

"Very good, ma'am."

Felicia closed her eyes again. Thomas stood once more before her. She lunged toward him, grabbing at his arm—and touched him so distinctly that she let out a gasp. "Oh—!"

Her eyes snapped open. He staggered toward her, but he didn't frown. They stared at each other. She pulled back slightly, not letting go of him. The fabric had an icy stiffness to it, as if he had been marching in snow for over a day. His eyes were darkened, with black marks around the sockets. No earthly color remained in his face, but he did not have the waxy pallor she remembered. Instead, his skin was thin and pale, like the gray of the sky during a snowstorm, and just as cold.

He shook his head, avoiding her gaze.

"Thomas?" she whispered, tentatively holding a hand to his frigid cheek. He closed his eyes and leaned into her touch.

Perhaps Thomas was wrong to deny the existence of ghosts

"Aye."

"Are you really here?"

"Not so much..."

"I can feel you..."

"I know."

She placed his hand over her skirts, squeezing her eyes shut as tight as they would go.

"Can you feel him?" she asked. "Oh, say something."

"The child is going to need a father," he said. *"And if I'm not there, you know to do what's best."*

"That's not what I wanted to hear," Felicia murmured, letting go of his arm. She opened her eyes. Thomas was gone, once more. She spun frantically, looking for him, but it was no use. She rubbed her eyes with the heels of her palm. She exhaled and left the office, joining her parents in the parlor.

The tea caddy waited, and a desert tier on the side table was filled with black current and rosewater scones.

"There you are." Her mother greeted her with a large beaming grin. She moved over a space and patted the seat and poured Felicia a cup of tea and added a sugar cube and a splash of milk. "We'd surmised you'd gone back to England for a moment."

She kissed her father on his round cheek and embraced her mother before sitting. "Forgive me, I was just thinking in the office." Felicia's hand shook as she reached for a scone. "I've been thinking a lot since last month."

"Oh?" her father asked, eyeing her shaking hands. "And have you seen much of Henry recently?"

"At three times a week since that entrapment dinner." She took a bite of the scone, then cleared her throat. "We've had an ongoing game of chess. I think we've exhausted our conversation topics, but we still see each other. But—"

"But what?" Mother sighed, her eyebrows knitted in concern. "My dear, you need to get married again, and preferably before your time."

"Do you think Thomas would understand me marrying again so soon?"

"Dear, I don't think Thomas exactly has a choice," Father said.

Felicia regarded him, askance.

"I mean—oh—damn it, Felicia," Father sputtered. "You know what I mean."

"Yes, I know." Felicia took a sip of tea. She stared into the creamy brown liquid, swirling it in her cup. "I could have sworn he was here just now. I could have sworn I felt his arm, touched his sleeve. He said to find the child a father." She finished her tea and her mother poured her another cup. "I just don't know if Henry would make a proper father."

"He'd keep you safe." Her father leaned back, crossing his legs, and tilted his head toward Felicia. "He'd keep you warm. Has he mentioned the child at all?"

"He wants to provide a secure home for him"—she gestured to her belly— "but he wants at least five of his own. In all honesty, the thought of becoming with child again doesn't sit well while I carry this one."

"It's only natural that a man wants his own children," Father said, and he ran his fingers through the loose hair hanging down Felicia's shoulder. He glanced over to his wife. "How many times did I mentioned to you, love, that I wanted four sons?"

"For years, you told me once a day, starting the week before you proposed."

Felicia set her cup and saucer on the tea cart and glanced between her parents. "There is a difference between your intended telling you of the future and being a widow with child and having a second suitor mention more babies. Not that I suppose I can begrudge him for saying as much, but it sits ill with me."

Mother cocked her head to the side then brushed some wisps of hair back from Felicia's forehead. "What is wrong with Henry?"

"I don't believe she said anything is wrong with him," Father stated.

"I don't know—that's just it." Felicia counted on her fingers. "He's secure. He's safe. He has a good business. I'm sure he could get me beautiful fabrics to turn into the best dresses. He isn't bad looking... actually, he's quite handsome. He's tall. He's eloquent. And most of all, he isn't a soldier! He won't go off and get himself killed. He won't deal with spies. He won't be near a rifle. He won't die before he gets to meet his children."

"Sounds like the ideal man," Mother said. "I don't understand, then. Speak your feelings, my dear. Why, if he seems ideal, are you not secure?"

"You're not wrong," Felicia said. "He's nearly perfect. But I just don't know. I don't think I love him."

"Ah." Mother took her hands and gave them a squeeze. Felicia looked into her face, bracing herself for whatever her mother had to say. Her mother pressed her lips together in a sad reminiscence. "Felicia, love is a luxury that most can't afford."

Felicia wriggled her hands from her mother's and backed away. "You love Father, don't you?"

"Yes."

"And you loved him when you married him?"

Mother bowed her head. Felicia peered back at her father, who also nodded.

"I loved Thomas when I married him. Why can't I be able to love again? What if I—" She cut herself off, biting her bottom lip and breathed in deeply, eyes drifting off toward the mantle at the back of the room.

Her father eyed her. "What if you what, my dear?"

Felicia glanced toward the ceiling, saying a silent prayer. "What if I do have feelings for another?"

"Feelings are fickle creatures." Father tapped his hand on his knee. He frowned, though not angrily, then tucked his fingers under her chin and tilted Felicia's face up to see his. "But this is an important turn of events. What makes you think that these feelings are the same as love?"

"Well, I don't know, entirely." Felicia huffed and placed her hand atop her belly. She wrinkled her nose. "Oh, this child."

"Your child is taking your side, I see. Kicking you hard enough to change subjects," her mother said. "May I?" Felicia guided her hand to where the child moved. Mother smiled warmly toward their hands, then reached for a scone and searched around on the tier and cart. "Where is the butter?"

Felicia turned red, wiggling out from her father's arms, pinching at the bridge of her nose.

"The churn broke. I'm having a new one made."

"How on earth do you break a butter churn?" her father asked. "Good G-d, that must have been quite a cow to produce cream so strong."

"Hmmm, yes. It was a strong cow."

Felicia stood up and moved to the mantle, where the violin still rested. She picked it up, strumming the strings with her fingernails.

"Henry is a very good man," Felicia said slowly, plucking at the *E* string in a steady rhythm. Even she could tell the instrument was out of tune.

"Do you love him, Lissie?" Father asked.

Felicia stopped picking the string and set the violin back on the mantle. "My child needs to be safe. Henry would take good care of me and the child."

Her father walked up behind her and gently set his hands on her shoulders. "If he came over this instant and asked you to marry him, would you?"

Felicia hummed under her breath, then grimaced.

"Felicia, would you spend the rest of your life with him?"

"Mother is right," Felicia said. "I'm having a baby. Who am I to put my feelings over the safety of my child?"

Father took her arms, turning her to look into her eyes, his face full of love and concern. "If the man you have feelings for proposed, would you accept?"

Felicia's eyes widened. She opened her mouth to speak, but nothing came out.

Father raised a brow.

She crossed her arms, glancing down over her skirts. "He doesn't know how I feel. I barely know the man. I simply—I fancy him is all."

Her father walked her back to the settee and helped her to sit, then lowered himself beside her. "Do you remember what you said after meeting Thomas for the first time?"

"Father, I'd be hard pressed to tell you what I said the day I married him other than 'I do'."

"You said, as we rode back home, that you were intent on marrying him."

"I did?" Embarrassment crept over her. "Was I really so intent?"

"You were," he said.

Felicia glanced over to her mother who waved a hand in the air. She grimaced and muttered, "I'm sure I didn't mean it."

Her mother poured the last bit of tea into her cup. "Oh, you did."

"Why are you reminding me of my foolish mouth?"

"You knew the day you met Thomas that you were to marry him," her father said. "That's what I'm meaning to say. So, if you knew then, why not now?"

"Because I'm older and wiser and a mother now. That's why not now." She sniffed and tapped her foot on the wooden floor. "I'm not going to marry that man. Besides, I'm certain he doesn't feel anything toward me other than annoyance. Henry is a good man."

"Oh, so is the town cooper," her mother said.

Felicia coughed, covering her mouth with one hand, and grasped at her skirt as she nearly heaved up her lungs. Mother frowned, raising a brow at her, while Father patted her back and laughed.

"Are you all right, dear?" Mother swatted at Father. "John, stop laughing!"

"I'm very well," Felicia said and cleared her throat. "Please, continue."

Mother waved a hand broadly, then brought it daintily back to her lap. "But being a good man doesn't necessarily make him marriageable."

"Henry is a great man and as far as I'm concerned could be marriageable," Felicia said, catching her breath. She caught her reflection in the silver of the teapot, her face as red as a ripe strawberry in the heat of the summer. "What do you have to say to that?"

"So, you've made up your mind then?" her father asked. "If Henry were to propose, you'd agree?"

Felicia stretched her neck from side to side and shifted in her seat. "I'd have to think about it. He hasn't proposed yet, although he knows he'd have to do so quickly, if he wants to get the banns in before my time."

Mother took Felicia's left hand, inspecting her ring finger. "When do you see him again? Perhaps he'll propose sooner than later, and you'll have the last couple months to settle and make a new life."

"Tomorrow." Felicia stood and crossed to the window, glancing outside down the road toward town. She sighed, then moved a pawn to knight-four on the game table.

And it might have been her mind, or perhaps a trick of the light, but it seemed as though the bishop moved to capture her pawn. She shook her head, then returned to her parents, leaning over the edge of the settee.

"He might propose to me then," she said. "He might propose to me next week. As long as he does within the next month, my child will never know life without a father." She gave her parents a shaky grin. "See? Surely, I know how to listen to reason, and I know how to pick the right man with whom to spend the rest of my life."

II

I t was a blustery sort of day where Felicia had to bend over to walk at all. The leaves, mix of spotted greens, oranges, and some full vibrant crimson, blew about her, whipping past her hair and face. October may have been her favorite month, but she'd rather have been home with a nice hot cup of tea by a fire. Though it was still early in the month, the cold wind tore through her clothes, and the child within her kicked fiercely.

The faint smell of clam chowder drifted from the tavern, the warm scent wafting toward her, battling the wind. But it won the battle, lingering in the air as she fought her way up the road to the Colonel's manor.

The will had not delivered yet. She did find it odd that it was not in her hands, considering the branch was in Philadelphia, and Mr. Bach Esq. did say it would be with her at everyone's earliest convenience. That was in July and it was October. She didn't pretend to know what it was like to go over wills and estates, but she knew what it was like to be without closure. If Thomas had been there, he would have walked in the wind to fetch it, but his absence was the reason she needed the will. She'd thought about having Amos run over to check, but she couldn't stand to be cooped up in her home any longer. Besides, it wasn't a long walk, but she hadn't slept well the night before.

She clambered up the stairs to Colonel Moore's manor and leaned against the railing while she knocked at the door with her foot, silver buckle glimmering in the gray morning light.

A small boy with dark skin and a white powdered wig opened the door. He stared wide eyed up at Felicia, then bowed. "Can I help you, ma'am?"

"Is the Colonel home? I must speak with him."

"Not as of the moment." The boy peeked around her. "But I think he'll be here soon. Please come in."

Felicia bowed her head toward the boy and shuffled into the foyer.

The boy checked behind Felicia once more, then turned back around. "Do you need to sit?"

"Very much," Felicia said.

The boy pulled his face into a grimace, then bowed to her, and left to search for a suitable place for her to sit. He returned a few moments later to usher Felicia into the office and offered her a chair in front of the Colonel's desk. Felicia surveyed the tidy stacks of envelopes with their pretty red tape, blue wax stamps, and black wax stamps. Quills were lined on one edge of the desk, one whittled and ready to go, and two more freshly plucked. There was nary a spot of ink on the desk, save for a droplet near the inkwell.

Felicia leaned over to get a better look at the mail, but the boy let out a small squeak and grabbed her hands. "Please don't touch those!"

Felicia sat back, a small frown on her lips. "I'm only seeing if my mail is in it."

"He'll think I touched it, ma'am! I don't want that!"

"Of course." Felicia frowned and furrowed her brows, clasping her hands in her lap.

With that, the boy left the office.

Alone in the office with her thoughts, Felicia sniffed to hide a rush of emotion. The poor boy left her with an ache in her heart. He had looked so frightened. Why would he be so afraid of William Moore? She had known the Colonel for five years, and he never gave her reason to be afraid. He was a congenial man, stern but good-natured, though not as jovial as his brother.

The sound of the violin pricked at her ears. She closed her eyes and held out her hands. "Are you there, Tom? Do you know where your will is?"

She couldn't see him, trying as she might, but she let out a sigh. A smile came to her lips. "So," she whispered breathlessly, "you are here?"

Still, she received no answer. She rolled her shoulders, opening her eyes, but unlike before, the violin didn't fade. She tiptoed to the door, to listen better. The sweet tune filled the house, flowing into the hallway and office.

"Victoria?" Felicia grinned broadly and called, "Victoria! You finally chose an instrument!"

The music didn't stop, but played on, its sweet tune growing and swelling around her. Oh, the girl had talent! She filled the house with the sweet tune of a great love, perhaps the greatest love of all, whatever that may be. Felicia stood transfixed, and the child moved within her. She rubbed at her belly and moved out of the office, down the hall and to the parlor, stepping in time with the melody. The parlor doors were closed, but the tune flowed from soft pianissimos to soaring fortes, imbuing such an emotion in each note. Felicia leaned against the door, relishing every moment.

Dare she go in and interrupt the girl in her lesson? But she had to hear better.

Felicia opened the doors and stopped on the threshold. The Colonel's daughter was not in the room.

Instead, a man stood, his back turned to her. Brown hair tumbled over his shoulders in a wild mass, as if it couldn't decide if it wanted to be wavy or curly. He wore only his shirt and breeches, not even his stockings and shoes. His right sleeve billowed as the bow danced gracefully over the strings. He swayed lightly to the music, and though she couldn't see his face, she could feel the emotions he poured into the tune.

Papers littered the floor where he stood, and every so often, he'd flick a new sheet to the ground from the stand in front of him.

The music wrapped around her, the notes trapped her, and Felicia found herself unable to move from her spot. Her stomach tightened as her gaze riveted on the man. That wasn't... it couldn't have been... *Oh dear... oh...* A blush heated her face, but... it was his home after all... if that was...

"Henry?"

The music stopped abruptly, and the man spun around. He was, indeed, Henry Moore, and he stood there, violin still on his shoulder, the bow still poised mid-air, his hair falling all about his face. He squinted at her through small round glasses perched on the edge of his nose, opened his mouth to speak, then closed it again.

Felicia motioned to speak, blinking her eyes. "Henry, I—"

"Felicia?" He cleared his throat and adjusted his glasses. "What are you doing here?"

"I'm here to talk with your brother." She stepped toward him, her head cocked to the side.

He staggered back a pace from her, shaking his head. His cheeks and nose flushed pink, and he turned from her, packing up the violin, gathering the broadsides from the floor.

Felicia let out a little cry. "Oh, no, Henry. Don't stop!"

He stilled but didn't turn back around.

"Play more," Felicia pleaded, stepping closer to him again. She rested her hand on his shoulder, and his muscles tightened under her touch. "Won't you?"

He glanced down at her, his hair in his eyes. His voice rasped, "What would you have me play?"

Felicia hesitated, gnawing at the inside of her cheek. "*Winter*?"

Henry let out a low, rumbling laugh, one far different than the laugh she'd heard months ago at the dinner. It was a quiet sort of laugh, unassuming. She drew in a breath as he pushed the case from the chair and flopped down into it, bringing the instrument to his chin once more. He glanced up toward her, a tired, gentle smile playing on his lips. Though his lips smiled, there was a sort of melancholy about his eyes. He began Vivaldi's piece, and the notes swelled and shivered.

He didn't play like Thomas at all. His *Winter* was slower, more subdued.

Henry plays music in secret

Thomas played a frantic and driving variation, but Henry's took its time, hitting all the notes with a grace and poise that matched his demeanor.

She studied his features, his unruly hair and unkempt outfit. It was almost sinful to see him in such a state, playing the violin. It seemed forbidden, like she stumbled onto a faerie circle and didn't know if she should look away and wait in the office after all or listen to the extemporaneous concert.

But the music ended, and Henry lowered the violin to his lap, leaning back with heavy yawn. He titled his head toward her.

"I didn't know you played." Felicia's voice wavered, and she cleared her throat, picking at the lace on her bodice.

Henry shrugged. "Not many people do." He stretched his arms high above his head and let out a tired breath. "I don't play often, and I certainly don't play if William is around."

"Why not? You're good. I'd say as good as Thomas—"

"People liked Thomas's playing." Henry shrugged again, absently plucking at the strings. "I don't aim to be like that. I don't play for people."

"Who do you play for?" Her gaze flickered from the violin on his knees and his face.

Henry thumbed toward his chest, then shrugged. "And occasionally Victoria."

Felicia lowered herself onto the chair before him. "Would you play for me?"

He tilted his head toward her, his hair flopping in front of his face, and smile creasing the corners of his eyes. Henry took her hand and pressed a kiss to her knuckles. "I suppose I'll have to."

He brushed his hair away from his face, blowing up toward his forehead, then rested the violin once more on his shoulder, setting his chin upon the rest.

Then, he closed eyes and began a different song. There was a sorrow about it, a pleading song that only asked for a simple favor.

Felicia watched him again, studying how his fingers wavered over the dark fingerboard, how he drew the bow across the strings, the red glint of his signet ring sparkling with every bow stroke. His brow furrowed in concentration as he played, though nothing took away from the softness of the song. Henry hummed with the music, low and smooth. It seemed like such a simple song, the notes, long and vibrating through the house, and when married with his humming, stirred a most frightful and wistful longing in Felicia's chest.

"Aye!" Colonel Moore's voice bellowed through the hallway. "What's that god-awful noise?"

Henry stopped mid-song, his bow screeching. He shoved his violin and bow back into the case and kicked it beneath his chair. Felicia gasped, her mouth agape as she glanced between Henry and the case.

The Colonel poked his head into the parlor, and Henry sat back, crossing his legs, folding his hands over his chest.

He puffed out a breath, then grinned over toward his brother. "Felicia's here to see you."

Colonel Moore stepped back, smoothing his hair, straightening at the waist. He glanced askance at Henry. "Why aren't you dressed? It's nearly eleven!"

"Late night."

"Isn't it always," Moore said flatly, but he held his hand out toward Felicia, who still sat in a state of dismay at the stopped music. "Felicia! What a pleasant surprise! What have you come here for?"

Felicia eased out of the chair, wobbling on her feet. Henry reached up and rested his hand on her back to steady her. She glanced down toward him, and he withdrew his hand, bringing it back to his chest.

"Ah, actually I came here to talk about the mail."

The Colonel let out a dignified, snorting laugh. "What a boring subject! Well, now that you're here, you might as well stay for dinner, too."

"Oh, I don't think I could. I really only meant to stay a little, but..." She glanced at Henry and he shook his head. "But I got to talking with Henry. I'm just wondering if you have any mail for me that perhaps fell through the cracks? That is, I mean, I'm still waiting for Thomas's will from Mr. A. L. Bach, and I'm starting to worry."

Colonel Moore strode toward Felicia and sat her down once more, taking her hands. "Don't fret, dear Felicia. When it comes in, I'll let you know." He offered her a soothing smile, as he took her chin between his thumb and pointer finger.

She shook her head and leaned back, though her frown melted slowly. "Of course, but with the little one growing and my time coming ever closer, you can understand my worry."

"Of course," he said, and Henry cleared his throat. The Colonel turned to his brother. "Did you have anything to say?"

"Oh, no." He waved a hand lazily in the air. "Just thinking, I suppose."

William Moore gave Felicia's hands a squeeze. "Are you sure you can't stay for dinner? It would be no imposition, and I'm sure Victoria would love to have the feminine company."

"I don't.... I really should be getting back," Felicia said, and he let go of her hands.

Henry shifted in his seat and murmured under his breath.

"Did you say something?" Felicia asked.

He shook his head.

Felicia stood again, and when she wobbled Henry steadied her.

"Will you be needing help getting home?" the Colonel asked.

Felicia wrung her hands, eyeing the window. "Has the wind died down?"

"It's calmer, but it still whistles."

"Hmm, I should be able to make it back home."

Colonel Moore bowed toward Felicia. "Well, then, if you will allow me. I must get some work done before dinner."

"Of course." Fear of toppling rendered Felicia only able to bob a shallow curtsey when William Moore left the room. She started to address Henry but caught him grinning at her behind his hand. She quirked a brow for just a second, and he dropped his hand and the smile. Her voice just above a whisper, she said, "Thank you."

He waved his hand in the air, then brushed his hair away from his face. He opened his mouth, but before he could get a word out, his brother's voice thundered down the hallway.

"Henry! Go get dressed, for the love of G-d! You won't sit at my table if you think you can stay dressed like that!"

Henry closed his mouth, rolling his eyes, and stood with a faint sigh. "I suppose it best we both be going." He quirked a smile and brought his hand to his middle. "That is, I do if I want to eat. And I do want to eat." He leaned toward her and pressed a kiss to her cheek.

Felicia inclined her face toward his. "I suppose so."

He gazed at her through half-lidded eyes, glasses fogging, breathing softly, his lips hovering dangerously close to hers.

Felicia drew in a breath and averted her gaze from his. "I'll see you tomorrow, perhaps?" She took his hand and began to bring it to her lips but stilled. She shook her head and dropped his hand.

He froze, lips slightly parted, eyes wide and brows furrowed, but she scarcely registered the expression. "I'll see you tomorrow."

She spun on her heel, but paused a moment in the foyer, her hand on the gilded doorknob, and waited, hoping to hear the strains of the violin again, but the music had ended.

The floorboards creaked, and she glanced over her shoulder to see Henry make his way upstairs, case in hand.

Felicia let out a soft breath and opened the door. There'd always be other days for music.

W hen Henry arrived at Hawkings' Manor the next day to take Felicia on a walk-through town as usual, she offered him a happy grin, but instead of the soft quirked smile she was growing accustomed to, he simply gave her a modest smile in return, eyes toward the ground. She frowned lightly as she studied his face, searching for the reason for his quietude. Bags hung under his eyes, his forehead was etched with lines, and his skin appeared sallow. She tugged on a curl that hung over her shoulder, twirling it around her finger. Perhaps it wasn't so much quietude as it was exhaustion. Nonetheless, she linked arms with him, and they walked down the road to town.

Several moments of quiet passed, and Felicia grew restless. "How are you today? You seem tired, dear Henry."

"It was a very late night," he said.

"Were you at the harbor negotiating for your ships?"

"One could say that, yes," Henry said slowly then cleared his throat.

"Have they finally docked?"

Henry shook his head.

"You must tell me when they do." Felicia rubbed her free hand along his arm. "I pray nightly for your dealings in that beastly business."

"To be frank, Felicia, they aren't going to dock." Henry sniffed in. "I lost the ship meant for Philadelphia and all the cargo therein."

Felicia gasped and pulled them to a halt on the side of the road. Her eyes widened, and she reached up and gently swiped a loose tendril of his thick light brown hair away from his face. "How did that happen? The rebels? But you are insured, correct? They cannot get away with this act of theft."

"Aye." Henry nodded curtly. "Unfortunately, the lot is lost for good, and there's nothing I can do about it."

"All the textiles? The crates?"

"Down to the flag."

"Have your brother force the rebels to give it back." Felicia took both of Henry's hands and squeezed till Henry pulled his hands away and shook them out. She pulled a face and muttered an apology.

He gave her a small smile. "I... it isn't that simple." He cleared his throat and picked up his pace as they entered the market square. "I'm sending word to the office in London. I'm sure I'll make up for it, eventually."

"I'm sure you will too"—she drew in a shallow breath as she tried to keep up— "You are an excellent businessman. But, oh, Henry, how awful. Are you sure there can't be anything done about it?"

Henry shook his head slowed his pace, and relinked his arm with hers, offering her a conciliatory smile. "Don't worry for me, Felicia. I'll end up fine."

"Shall I add it to my prayers?"

"If you so wish."

"I will."

They walked through the town, not pausing to inspect windows or farmer's stalls, but ambled, slow, and steady. Whenever Felicia needed to rest, Henry stopped so she could lean against his arm.

The cool air chilled Felicia, even as it brought the crisp scents of dying leaves and autumn spices over the wind. The wafting smell of the tavern's vegetable soup called to Felicia, and she was half-inclined to ask Henry to stop there but decided against it at the last minute. It might have been a rather poor decision, since she was rather hungry, but she was more afraid of being an imposition than she was concerned with eating. She sighed slightly as they left the tavern behind, but she rubbed at her nose and tried to ignore the scent of the soup.

Henry, it seemed, wasn't as unobservant as perhaps Felicia thought. He cocked his head toward her, nudging her arm. He broke the silence between them. "Are you faring well with the child? Do you need me to get you anything?"

Felicia leaned heavily into his side, letting out a long breath. "The child is restless, but the midwife says he's doing well. I feel as well as I can. You needn't get me anything." Felicia squeezed his hand, finding comfort in holding a hand again. She kept her grip, wrapping her fingers around his. But something was different... She frowned and lifted his hand up to inspect it. The glint of red on his left middle finger was indeed missing. "Where is your ring?"

Henry glanced down. "I suppose I left it on my dresser."

"How do you forget your signet ring? What if you need that?"

"I told you I had a late night, but that's unimportant." He stopped along the side of a wooden fence by a long stretch of green pastureland and curled his finger under her chin. "Truly, now, my dear, how are you feeling?"

Felicia shook her head, lowering his hand from her chin, then resting her own over the curve in her skirts. "I think I'm fine. The fresh air does me and the child good. But oh, this child. I swear. Every time I get comfortable, he starts up."

"I can walk you back home if you'd like," Henry said. "Perhaps we have gone too far? Have I been inconsiderate? I have an engagement later so if you want to go home early, I wouldn't mind."

She gave him a tired smile. "Of course not. You are never so inconsiderate. But it may be best if I rest a moment." Felicia rested against the upper rung of the fence tilting her head back as she let the cool air naturally rouge her face. "What kind of engagement?"

Henry waved his hand in the air. "Oh, it's no large matter. I just play cards with him."

"Cards? What games?"

"Nonsense games," Henry said.

Felicia let out a long breath, then tightened the ribbons on her bergère so it wouldn't fall off her head. "Maybe you could teach me to play. I always wanted to; you know."

"The games I play aren't exactly ladies' games." Henry let out a laugh under his breath. "But I'm sure, if you wished, I could teach you twenty-one."

"Oh, I would like that." Felicia gave his arm a squeeze, then giggled. Henry's face warmed at seeing her delight. She patted his hand. "Here, give me your hand."

"My hand?" Henry asked.

Felicia took his hand and placed it atop her skirts. He stared at his hand.

"Can you feel?" she asked, pressing her hand atop his.

Henry only stared silently at his hand as the child moved underneath his touch. His mouth twitched, and his brows furrowed, but still he stayed silent.

The corners of Felicia's mouth curved up gently.

"He just kicked you."

Henry opened his mouth to say something but closed it again. He hummed. "It's been a long time since I've felt an unborn child kick."

"Well, now you are up to date," Felicia said, gazing up at him. She reached up, tentatively, and placed a hand on his cheek, but he didn't move, eyes still fixed on his hand, his mouth flicking between nothing and a frown.

Before Henry could reply, a man's voice called out, and a loud volley of musket fire sounded from the pasture behind them. Felicia startled and stumbled forward at the sound and Henry lunged to steady her. Her hat slipped down in the confusion, her fichu fell awry over her neck and décolletage. She spun around to the source of the sound, gasping in a quick breath.

"Are you all right?" Henry adjusted her hat and settled her fichu over her dress. "The child isn't hurt, is he?"

"The child was just as startled as I, but we're well." Felicia brought her hand up to her heaving chest spying out over a line of colonials lined up to face the trees.

A row of dummies stood limp in front of them. Felicia stared, unable to pry her gaze away. It was as if someone had tacked her through the grass and dirt, down to the core of the earth.

"On my count," a man's voice rang out, walking from the flank to join them in the line. "One. Two. Fire!"

The men fired. The blast rang through the village green, and a spray of cloth, straw, and feathers erupted from the dummies.

"What are they firing for?" Henry asked. "They know it won't amount to anything."

The blood rushed from her face. "I hate it," she said, voice trembling.

She stared out among the men, the Minute Men, as they fired their muskets into the dummies again, and a shudder took her. She squeezed her eyes shut and, turning toward Henry, pressed her face into his chest, wrapping her arms around him. "One of the last sounds Thomas heard was that firing."

"William said he died in town," Henry murmured. He placed one palm atop her hat and set the other against her back. "Perhaps... the sound he last heard had a more familiar ring than that of a musket."

Felicia rested against Henry for a moment. He brought nothing to the hug but a warm body and the soft cotton of his shirt. His hand on her head only provided pressure, not comfort. Although he had kissed her with a passion before, this time, he remained still in the hug, and his touch was disconcerting. The only comfort she gleaned was how his soft belly moved against her as he breathed. She wrinkled her nose against the buttons of his weskit. She could smell his scent of musky tobacco, mulled spices, and fresh pressed cotton, but it overwhelmed her sensitive nerves.

She pushed away, her attention pulled back to the Minute Men. They drew her focus, as if she were watching a highwayman hold up a carriage. There was nothing to say or do but to watch helplessly.

Their leader left his spot in line, stepping further to the side to survey the scarecrow carnage. "What are you men doing? Half of you are missing your targets! Shoot with both eyes open. You'll see twice as well. And for goodness's sake, stand your ground! Don't recoil when you shoot!"

Felicia let out a gasp, stepping away from Henry toward the fence. She leaned up against it, bracing her hands on the topmost rung. "It can't be!"

"Felicia?" Henry asked and moved next to her. "What do you see?"

She only let out a moan.

Nathaniel Poe's words echoed dimly in Felicia's ears. "The kickback is fierce. Stand your ground." He fired.

An explosion of hay erupted where the dummy's head once was.

The feeling that had tormented her when Thomas had been called to Boston—that crushing, constricting snake that had wound its way around Felicia's stomach when Colonel Moore had thrown the cloth from Thomas's body—that fear squeezed her again till the pain gave her reason to cough. She backed away from the fence, rasping and coughing as the tightness in her stomach rose through her chest and into her throat.

Nathaniel led these makeshift soldiers?

"Felicia? What is wrong?"

Henry's voice rang through her head, but she couldn't answer. She bent in half, coughing until her lungs and back ached, her arms around her middle, squeezing her eyes shut. Pain rose through her throat and neck. She tried stretching her jaw, but she couldn't seem to find a way to open her mouth wide enough to ease the tension through all the coughing.

The firing ceased in the background.

"Felicia! Felicia! What is wrong?" Henry called, his voice frantic and harried. He grasped hold of her arms to steady her.

Tension rose from her mouth and jaw and into her eyes. Henry's face flickered in her vision, and she blinked to keep him in focus.

"Felicia?" a different voice called out, warped, and distorted in her ears.

Out of the corner of her eye, she saw one of the men jogging from his spot on the green, but as the sounds around her grew faint, she crumbled to the ground. She lay on the grass by the fence, the coughs finally gone from her throat, and her vision completely vanished.

～

NATHANIEL POE HOPPED THE FENCE, next to the fallen Felicia and the confused man in the emerald coat, holding her in his arms. He bent beside them and turned toward the man—Henry Moore. The Colonel's brother. His focus shifted to Felicia's belly, and hurriedly, he knelt beside them.

"What happened?"

Henry Moore only shook his head. "I wouldn't know." He held Felicia closer to his chest, cradling her head. "She saw your men, started coughing, then she fainted."

Nathaniel looked Henry in the eye. "Lay her on the ground. Turn her onto her side."

"Don't tell me what to do," Moore spat. "She needs comfort." He adjusted Felicia in his arms.

She uttered no sound, her head lolling against the crook of his neck.

Nathaniel shook his head. "Moore—" The man sneered, seemingly disgusted. "Mr. Moore! She needs to breathe." Nathaniel made his voice steely and stern. "Turn her onto her side. I'm only here to help."

Nathaniel began to slid Felicia out of Henry's arms, but Henry recoiled, clasping her tightly.

"Don't you take her!" Henry snapped, baring his teeth. "You think I don't know how to care for her?"

"Then for G-d's sake, man, turn her on her side!"

Henry yielded Felicia from his grasp, and Nathaniel quickly turned her onto her side. "There," he said and ran his hand over Felicia's back. "What caused this? What happened?"

"Your men caused her to faint." Henry shoved Nathaniel's hand away and rubbed Felicia's back. "Goodness knows your men killed her husband during that raid." His voice trailed off, and he looked tenderly down at Felicia. "She's been through too much to have had this reminder of that horrific even."

"I know nothing about a raid." Nathaniel tried to look into Felicia's eyes. "I can't tell you anything about *that*. I want to know what happened *now*. She needs go get home."

"Aye—"

"You go into town."

Henry sat back on his heels, the disgusted look returning to his features. He set his jaw, glaring at Nathaniel. "*You* go—"

"You know the loyalist midwife."

"I don—"

"You know somebody who'll take care of her. I don't. Go into town. Take care of business." Nathaniel stared Moore down and pointed toward town. "I'll take her home."

Henry tilted his chin up, narrowing his eyes at him.

Henry glared at Nathaniel. "I can—"

"The child may be in danger," Nathaniel said. "Please, for the sake of the child—"

A terror passed over Henry's face and he nodded, rising to his feet. Without a word, he turned on his heel, jogging back down the road.

Nathaniel picked Felicia up, adjusting her weight in his arms. Her head lolled against his chest, and she let out a small moan.

He pressed his lips together, then muttered, "God save you, girl. You deserve none of this."

And with that, he started toward her home, moving as quickly as he could.

✻ 13 ✻

Felicia awoke in her bed, with Rose holding a damp cloth to her forehead. She sat up, blinking slowly. The room spun around her, and she pressed back into her pillows with a moan.

"Don't speak," Rose said, gently pressing the cloth to Felicia's cheeks. "You fainted away something fierce."

"How'd—where is Henry?"

"Henry Moore came in with Doctor Merriman two hours past, ma'am. He just left not too long ago."

Felicia blinked again, a slight moan escaping her lips. "How did I—" She felt the blood rush from her face. She pressed her hands to her sides and sucked in a gasp. "The baby?"

"I said not to say nothing." Rose held onto Felicia's shoulders, keeping her secure in bed. "You fainted dead away after a terrible coughing fit. The town cooper carried you back home while Henry fetched the doctor. He stayed till Henry came back. The baby is fine," Rose added. "Kicked the entire time. The cooper said he had trouble carrying you for all the kicks he received."

At that, Felicia brought the covers over her head, moaning loudly. *Oh, of all the people to carry her. Why him? Where was Henry?*

"Don't get yourself all worked up." Rose peeled back the blanket. "You should be happy that the cooper brought you back."

Felicia shook her head, her mouth trembling. She whimpered, "No."

"Ma'am. What is the matter? You're fine now."

"He's a soldier," Felicia said, and then bit back a sob. "I can't do that again!"

"Who's a soldier?" Rose asked. "Child, you're going to—"

"Nathaniel! He can't be a soldier," Felicia cried. She pulled a pillow over her head and sobbed into it. "He simply cannot be a soldier! I can't do it again. I can't love a soldier again."

"Who's to say you have to love him?" Rose asked quietly, running her hand over Felicia's hair.

"Everything in my body says so! Every time I think of him, my stomach tightens. I close my eyes, and I can picture that grin he gave me the night of the dinner. The wink he gave me after he said he'd make a new butter churn. I can't love a soldier."

"The last time I checked, he didn't wear a red coat," Rose said. "What makes you so sure he's a soldier?"

"That's the rub! He's part of the colonial militia. He's their rag tag leader. Rose! This simply cannot be. I cannot love a colonial!"

Felicia attempted to dart from the bed, but Rose kept a firm grip on her. "Ma'am, you're getting yourself all worked up over nothing. You need to breathe in and calm your nerves."

"My nerves are as calm as they are going to get!"

"I think they could be a tad calmer." Rose smoothed her hands over Felicia's hair. "Settle yourself, or your baby'll get all worked up, and he'll kick you till you bruise."

Felicia puffed a breath of air from her nose.

"Nobody says you have to love a colonial militia soldier." Rose kept her voice low and tender. "Nobody says you can't love him, either. But, ma'am, what of Henry Moore?"

"Oh, what of Henry?" Felicia asked, her voice tired and drawn out.

"He's been a courting you for a month or so now. Haven't you feelings toward him?"

Felicia's mouth pulled down into a sad pout. "He kisses without warning and hugs without feeling. The only thing he could offer me is safety and music and at this point, I'm going to have to take it should he offer it." She pulled a pillow back over her head. "I can't marry a soldier, Rose. Not again. He'll get himself killed, and I don't know what I'll do if that happens."

"You talk as if he asked you to marry him when all the man did was carry you back home after you fainted."

Felicia let out a cry into the pillow. She heard Rose's feet shuffling on the floor. The sound of rustling cotton pricked her ears, and she felt the presence of something over her face.

"Here."

Felicia sat, propping herself with a pillow.

Rose held out a fresh sprig. "I cut this from the garden earlier. Take it and breathe it in deeply."

Felicia took it, and tears dropped onto the tiny flowers in her hands. "Lavender," she said, her voice shaking.

"Take a breath in."

Felicia inhaled the bud's mellow, soothing scent.

"Better?" Rose asked, trailing her aged fingers down Felicia's jaw.

"Aye."

Rose took the lavender back and crushed up the buds in her hand, sprinkling them over Felicia's pillow. "That scent will linger a while longer. It should help you calm down. I want you to rest. I'll have Selah bring your dinner. Would you like me to call on your parents?"

"I think this is an event my mother needs not know about," Felicia said slowly, her breath hitching in her throat. "The last thing I want is for her to become anxious over me. Because then I'll become anxious. The seasons are changing, and that's probably the only good cut of lavender left. I can't have it be overworked."

Rose smoothed Felicia's hair back, smiling warmly, the wrinkles on her face deepening. "Of course. Can I get you anything? Tea?"

Felicia hummed, tapping her fingers together. "How much do we have left?"

"Not much, ma'am. We have the one tin left. I could send Amos to find some tomorrow if you'd like."

She sighed. "The general store doesn't sell tea anymore. Let's hold off on the tea till the occasion cries for it."

"Very good, ma'am. Should I see if we have any scones in the kitchen? Perhaps Selah could make something special?"

Felicia tapped her fingers on the blanket's hem, contemplating her choice. "I really liked those black currant rose scones."

"I'll have her bring some up for you," Rose said. "Doctor Merriman said to stay in bed till the morning. So, you just rest, and don't you worry about a thing. I left a bell on your nightstand." She turned to leave, then turned back. "Is there anybody I should let in in case they come? Mr. Moore? Your parents?"

"I suppose... let Henry in if he wishes to see me. Did he say anything before he left?"

"He waited by your side as long as he could when he returned with the doctor. He left about an hour before you woke, saying he had an engagement with a colleague. Told me to tell him to keep him abreast of the situation."

"I'll see him tomorrow most likely, then." Felicia slumped back into the pillows, shoulders sagging, and sighed. "Perhaps this episode will have him propose sooner than later."

Rose moved around the room, softly, lighting the candles on the windowsill and on the toilette. "Will that be all then?"

"I think so."

Rose bobbed a curtsey, then left the room, closing the door with a quiet click.

The soft, orange, candlelight made her things cast eerie, dark shadows on the wall. She breathed in the scent of the crushed lavender buds to calm her fraying nerves.

"He'd better propose sooner than later," she said under her breath and rolled over onto her side. "For the sake of my sanity and my child." She closed her eyes, heaving another tired sigh.

A strain of Vivaldi piqued her ears, and she opened her eyes, looking around the room.

"Thomas... are you there? Can't you give me advice?"

"Close your eyes, Lissie."

Thomas sat at her vanity. He cocked his head toward her and gave her a shrug. *"I'm dead, sweet Lissie. What advice could I give you?"*

"Tell me what to do."

"It doesn't matter very much what I think." He stepped over, boots creaking against the floor, to sit on the edge of her bed. The mattress dipped lightly. *"What say would I have?"*

"You could come back to me."

"We both know that's not possible."

Felicia, eyes still closed, still laying on her side, reached out for Thomas, wiggling her fingers at his spectral form. He drew no closer, only wiggled his fingers back at her.

"Go to sleep, sweet Lissie. Go to sleep and don't think of me anymore. Think of your future. I would only hold you back."

"Don't leave me," she whispered.

"I have to."

Thomas slowly faded from her vision. He smiled, regret filling his features, then completely disappeared.

"I'll be with you always," she heard his voice say. *"I may not be there in person, and I can't be the one you grow old with. But I'll be in your heart always, my dear Lissie."*

Felicia jerked upright, looking around frantically, drawing in a gasping breath. The phantom violin strains quieted down in her ears. Soon, nothing but the crickets sang outside her window.

❧ 14 ❧

Felicia sat amongst the fading ivy at the iron wrought table in her garden, staring at the tombstone in the far corner of the yard. She breathed in the fresh air and autumnal scents, letting the mid-October sun warm her face, moved the brim of her hat down, shielding her vision from the golden rays.

The child moved within her, garnering a glowing brightness within her soul. She rested her palm atop her belly, sensing the movement against her hand. Her mind wandered into the future, imagining her child's face: his pale blue eyes and little button nose, his pouty toddler lips. She imagined him playing in the garden. She imagined kissing his little face. Tousling his dark blond hair.

Most of all, she imagined naming him after his father.

"Ma'am?"

Felicia craned her neck back toward the house. Amos stood at the door to the kitchen, waving his hand to her.

"What is it, Amos?"

"The cooper is here. He says he has a delivery for you."

The snake started coiling its way around her stomach again. Oh, how she wished she wished to live without the sense of trepidation every time she heard his name. She never felt such a tightness around Thomas. But then, she hadn't lost Thomas yet.

"Mm." She pushed herself to her feet but kept her head bowed. It would do no good for Amos to see her gray with fear and even less to let Nathaniel see it. "Where is he?"

"He's still at the front door, ma'am."

Felicia huffed and started back into the house. She regarded him wearily. "Oh, you could have let him in, you know."

"He said he needed to speak with you first."

The fear came slithering back and tightened around her. She tilted her head toward Amos and hurried past him through the halls to the foyer. Behind the stained glass, she could just see Nathaniel's silhouette. Drawing in a deep breath, Felicia smoothed out her skirts, and opened the door.

Nathaniel grinned at her and held the new butter churn. "I told you it would be finished in a month."

Felicia quietly took the churn and turned it over in her hands. "Will that be all, then?"

Nathaniel's eyes flickered down. "No. I'm hoping to talk with you. May I come in?"

Felicia raised her eyebrows. "Of course."

She stepped aside and motioned for him to come in, then led him down to the parlor, where he sat in one of the velvet-backed chairs, clasping his hands on his lap. He shifted uncomfortably for a moment and let out a long breath.

Felicia eased into the chair beside him. "What is it you wished to talk about?" She puffed out a breath and closed her eyes. "I'm afraid I don't have anything else I've broken."

"Oh, it's not about that," Nathaniel said. "I suppose... I'll start by asking if you are feeling well."

Felicia cracked open her eyes and tilted her head toward him. "You mean about yesterday? I'm not sure what happened myself. But I am feeling well, thank you."

Nathaniel hummed and clasped his hands, his gaze wandering about the room. His eyes fell on the violin on the mantle. "That's a lovely violin."

"It was Thomas's. He could play just about anything on it."

"Could I look at it?"

"Did you come over just to look at the violin?"

"No," he said slowly.

"Well, go ahead, see it, then say what you want." She pressed her lips together. Her chest constricted, and her throat tightened. She swallowed down her fear and cleared her throat. "If you don't mind..."

Nathaniel moved to the mantle and picked up the violin and bow. He twisted it in his hand, this way and that, inspecting it, before setting it against his chin. He started playing a few notes, then adjusted the tuning pegs and ran the bow over the strings, beginning a rustic melody.

Felicia turned fully around in her chair. "What are you doing?"

Nathaniel halted mid-note and set the bow and violin back on the mantle. "I haven't played a good one before." He clasped his hands behind his back. "I had thought you meant—"

"I thought you just wanted to see it." Felicia's voice shook. "I—I didn't know you played the violin."

"I'd use the term fiddle, but, yes, I have been known to play."

Felicia closed her eyes. "You lead a regiment. You play the violin. Is there anything you can't do, Nathaniel?"

"I can think of one thing," Nathaniel said. "And I prefer it if you called me Natty."

Felicia brought her hand to her throat, then grazed her trembling fingers along her skin till her hand rested on her chest. "Natty..." She inhaled, then said, "Could you just tell me why you came to deliver the churn if you don't make house calls?"

He gave a curt bow of his head and looked into her eyes. The intensity of his stare drilled into her face. "Felicia, I have feelings for you."

Felicia said kept silent. She scooted to the edge of the chair and struggled to her feet, pressing her hand to the small of her back to steady herself. "I think I've heard enough."

Nathaniel frowned. "You've heard enough?"

"Nathaniel—Natty. Master Cooper. Whatever I'm supposed to call you. Why are you telling me this?"

"I think it's the custom, that when you have strong feelings for another person, that you tell them."

"Well…"

"And since I harbor strong feelings for you—"

"Stop," Felicia said. "You cannot harbor feelings for me." She slowly sat down again, pressing her face into her palm. "Oh, you can't…"

It was a weak protestation, almost resigned, and she knew it.

The chair scooted closer to her and the sound of the wood scraping against the floor grated in her ears. "Does it have to do with my position concerning the war?"

Felicia shook her head.

"Is it because I am not of the same station as you?"

Her shoulders sagged. "Of course not."

"Then why can't I have feelings for you, especially since I'm sure they are reciprocated."

Felicia froze. Lips pressed tightly together, she lowered her hand from her face and narrowed her eyes. "What makes you so sure they are reciprocated?"

Nathaniel quirked a soft side smile and wordlessly pointed to the churn by her foot. She grimaced at the wooden object.

"So, tell me. Tell me why I can't have feelings for you?"

"For the same reason that violin is without its owner," Felicia said, motioning toward the mantle. "For the same reason I'm a widow. I will not be entangled with a soldier again. I need safety, and you cannot provide me with what I crave the most."

Nathaniel bowed his head, staring at his lap. They sat in silence for a few moments, moments that seemed like hours.

Finally, Felicia spoke. "Have you had dinner?"

"No." Nathaniel shook his head. "I left before I did."

She stood slowly again, staggering as her center of balance shifted. She attempted to bend down to pick up the butter churn, struggling to reach it over the curve of her belly.

Nathaniel handed her the churn, and she pursed her lips and tucked it under her arm. Cocking her head for him to follow, she led him down to the kitchens again where a plate of cold chicken and beef sandwiches sat on the center table. Felicia set the churn down next to the platter.

"Before you leave, please do have lunch," she said, her voice low.

Natty took a sandwich and leaned his hip against the table. "Felicia, I need to know if you do have feelings for me as well. And if you do, what we're supposed to do with them."

Felicia crossed her arms over her chest. "There are things about you that I'm drawn to. Your eyes are similar to Thomas's if I can say that. You have strong convictions. You even play the violin. But how am I to know I'm not simply imposing my past love onto you? And how am I supposed to keep sane, knowing you could be called away to war? To the other side! I can't live like that again. I can't fathom your fighting for the men who killed my love..."

Nathaniel watched her, eyes flickering over her features. "Felicia—"

"You want to know why I coughed myself half to death?" Her eyes welled up with tears, but she tried to blink them away. "I saw you. I saw you leading the rebel militia. I saw you firing your long musket at those dummies. And I wasn't afraid of you fighting against the King's army. I'm afraid of you getting killed in the fight."

She could no longer stifle her tears. Nathaniel wiped his hands on his shirt and reached into his jacket pocket, pulling out a scrap of white cloth. He handed it to her, and she wiped at her eyes. She sniffed in, and handed the cloth back to him, before continuing.

"Do you know what that's like?" Felicia pleaded, hoping he'd understand. "You wake up every day wondering when your love is to be called to join the fight, there is *nothing* you can do. And then you can't help but wonder if he's going to return home in a box or alive and smiling." She paused her voice catching in her throat. "And when that day comes, that he does return, and you find out he's not alive and smiling..." She studied his face but couldn't ascertain what he was feeling. He only watched her, half-amused, half somber and concerned. She threw her hands up into the air, resigned, exasperated with herself. "What if you go to war? What if you don't return alive? What would that look like for me? Fear feels like a snake, a long winding snake that wraps itself around my stomach and squeezes till the pain reaches my head. I felt it whenever Thomas went with his men to practice. When

I saw you on the green, the snake squeezed me till I couldn't handle it. It is no flighty feeling of young love I feel toward you, Nathaniel. I am terrified."

Nathaniel waited a moment, then drew in a deep breath and held his hands for her. Gently, he took a hold of her forearms and guided her to the chair by the back door and sat her down. He crouched low before her, elbow on one knee as he rubbed at the bridge of his nose. He reached out and took her hand with his free one.

"We're never guaranteed tomorrow, though I know you know that all too well. I can't promise you that security you want. No one can. It doesn't exist. But I can try my best while on this earth to protect you. I'll do what God wills me to do."

Felicia took in a staggered breath, and Nathaniel lowered his hand from his face and took both of hers, giving them a squeeze. He continued. "Truly, I do not know what you are going through, Felicia. I can't offer you much other than my business. I'm not some textile merchant, and I'm not a lawyer. But I'm not necessarily called to battle the same way your husband was. I can't be hung for desertion. You see, I'm not in the militia. I'm a volunteer. If my wife needed me at home, I could stay with her. If my country needed me to protect it. I could protect her. It's not a definite security, Felicia. But it's more than I think you imagined. You see a musket and red flashes before your eyes, and rightfully so. But I can protect you. I can keep you safe. We only are ready at a minute's notice, and we can leave to come back home after a battle is over."

Felicia's brows knitted. "You're a soldier, but not—"

"I'm not officially called to war. I feel I have to go, but I don't need to go."

Felicia pressed her lips together, but her tears had ceased falling. "So... you're safe?"

"I wouldn't know exactly how safe, compared to Henry Moore," he said, drawing out Henry's name, wrinkling his nose. "I don't think I'm quite as boring as he. But I can provide you with a roof for your head, food for your table, warmth in the winter. With your permission, I'd like court you."

Felicia lowered her eyes to the floor. "I've a feeling that Henry is going to propose."

"Has he?"

"Not as of yet."

"I see. But you think he will?"

"We've been seeing each other for two since August. It'll be soon. It's something our families desire."

"But you—"

"Do not."

"Then let me court you. And say no to that contented fop."

Felicia fought her lips as they tried to curve upward. "He isn't a fop..."

"He certainly can't stand on his own two feet."

Felicia let out a breath and looked at Nathaniel, her eyes aching, but not wet. "Would you really have a widow with a child?"

He nodded, face tender. His lips turned up into a soft smile and he pressed a kiss to her hands. "You and the child come together, and I'm more than willing to take you and the child on."

"You'd have my child as your own?"

"Yes." He pressed a kiss to both her palms. "If you let me."

Felicia bit the inside of her cheek and stared into his intense eyes. "There's another problem."

Natty furrowed his brows, squeezing her hands tighter in his.

"I'm still very concerned about our ideals..."

She started to stand, and he helped her to her feet. Felicia motioned for him to come with her back through the foyer.

"What is so different about our ideals?" Nathaniel asked as they reached the front door.

"You must..." She paused, trying to collect her thoughts. "You're on the other side. And the other side killed my husband."

Natty shook his head. "We had nothing to do with any raid or whatever your Henry mentioned."

"He isn't my Henry," Felicia snapped.

He stood tall in front of her. His brows furrowed, though he seemed slightly hurt. "I lead the Minute Men of this town." A sadness tinged his voice. "You think I would try to see you knowing that one of my men or I could have killed your husband? Do you think so little of me that I would try to steal your affection for the sake of his blood?"

Felicia opened her mouth to speak, but Nathaniel held his hand up. "I do not respect a man who tries to rule colonies—a whole new country from over a vast sea—without representing us in his court. I do not respect a man who has sent his armies to control the people of those colonies, to threaten and cajole them into submission."

"Are you saying my husband threatened this town?"

"Certainly not," Nathaniel said. "My quarrel is with the king, not his people."

Felicia blushed and stared down at the floorboards, scuffing the toe of her shoe along the dark wood grain.

He curled his finger under her chin, tilting her face up to his, and offered her a soft smile. "With more men like the Major, I'm sure this war could have been over before it started."

"I thank you," she said, unable to fully look him in the eye.

Nathaniel brushed an errant tear away from her cheek. "I don't expect you to think the way I do about the colonies. I really don't expect you ever change your mind. No matter the outcome of this war, I want you to know that I'll respect your ideologies, if you understand mine."

Felicia took in a deep breath. "My husband died for the sake of my ideals."

"Your husband died in a raid and was killed by a coward," Nathaniel said. His words were dipped in venom, though not toward her, or the late Major. "And I swear to you he will be avenged in time."

Felicia brought her hand to her belly, closing her eyes for a moment. She was silent as she led him back to the foyer but paused before him at the door, looking up into his resolute face. "Natty, I'll admit to you plainly. I do have feelings for you. I have since you dropped that barrel in the hallway. But I can't tell you right away what I think we should do about those mutual feelings. I still want to see you, but I don't know if I should. I can't tell you much of anything." She traced her fingers on the door's stained glass. "You tell me that you'll take my child in. You tell me you're safe and secure. You even respect my Thomas. You call the rebel scoundrel who killed him a coward, yet you, too, could be considered a rebel scoundrel."

They stared into each other's faces, gazes lingering over eyes and lips.

Felicia blinked. "How long would you wait for me to give you an answer?"

"Considering you don't have much time to think"—Nathaniel glanced down at her belly— "I think I could wait a while."

Felicia wrinkled her nose, bringing her hands to her middle. "I have but a few short months till my time comes. I can give you a full answer within the week."

Nathaniel beamed. "You have a faster turnaround time than I do for my woodwork."

"Well, I would consider this particular instance a rush order," Felicia said with a slight smirk.

Nathaniel huffed a low laugh under his breath. He picked up one of her hands in his, massaging his fingers into her palm. He brought her hand up to his lips, kissing her knuckles and tips of her fingers, then started out the door.

"Natty, wait." She grabbed his arm as he left.

He paused, one foot past the threshold. "Yes?"

"Should I send my man to call you here once I've made up my mind?" she asked, gazing up at him. He glanced to the side, thinking a moment.

"I think maybe I could start making house calls," he said. He stepped back toward her and pressed a kiss to her forehead. "But only for you. Just don't break the new butter churn to bring me back. I did work hard on it."

Felicia bit her lip, glancing aside. "It did work the first time, though."

He held a hand up tentatively, and she gave a nod of her head. He cupped the side of her face, then kissed her forehead again. "Do it a second time, and you won't ever be able to make butter again." He took up both her hands and kissed them both. "God be with ye." He dropped her hands and left.

Felicia watched him as he disappeared down the road back to town.

She closed the door and leaned back against the stained-glass windowpanes. And then, she smiled. The child kicked, causing her to gasp.

"Listen here, little Thomas," Felicia said, glancing down to her skirts. "You really have to learn to not kick my ribs. It's very rude, and I can't concentrate when Natty is talking. It hurts, you know."

She received another kick as a response.

"Oh, you have your father's stubbornness. Can you hear my voice? Is that why you won't stop kicking?"

She gently rubbed her fingers in small circles over her skirts. She turned and pressed her forehead to the cool glass, whispering to herself, "Maybe things really are starting to turn around."

While Felicia missed the days of broken wax seals on invitations, the look of pride on Thomas's face as she came down the stairs in her taffeta gowns, and dancing minuets and reels, she did not miss the self-righteous officers and their equally pompous peacocks of wives. But with Thomas, and his ever so subtle mockery, his dry wit that could cut like a knife and often flew clear over the heads of those he derided, Felicia was at ease.

And at least, she was going to Colonel Moore's house accompanied, for if she were to flounder, she would have Henry. He was pleasant and good company at parties, though she had not been to one with him since the dinner at her house, and she was glad for his companionship.

Henry walked with her in the dark autumn night down to his brother's manor. He wrapped an arm around her shoulders, keeping her close to his side.

"Felicia, smile, my dear. This is the first event we are attending as a couple."

Felicia's stomach flopped over. "I think that's why I'm nervous." She glanced up at him. The torches that lined the walkway cast an eerie, orange glow over his face, and she crossed her arms over her chest. "It has been a long time since I've gone to such an event like this. And unmarried, no less."

"Well, perhaps... Perhaps you never will need to weather another event unmarried ever again."

Felicia's heart leapt into her throat, and she stumbled on the path. Henry caught her arm.

"Oh?" she asked.

Henry hummed and led Felicia up the long path to Colonel Moore's house, then helped her onto the porch and rapped on the door.

A young servant answered and motioning silently for them to enter. Felicia regarded the boy with a warm smile. Henry handed him his hat.

"Ah, Henry, there you are. Felicia, it's so good to see you," Colonel Moore said, coming from the parlor to the side of the door. "How are you doing?"

"I've been well," Felicia said. "Thank you. And how is everything on the front?"

The Colonel led them into the parlor, where the rest of the guests gathered for hors d'oeuvres and small talk. "The regiment has been told to stay here till further notice. We may join troops in New Jersey soon, though."

"What good could come from New Jersey," Felicia said, wincing as she sat down in an armchair. Henry stood beside her, smirking at her comment. She winced and tilted her head up to him. "Oh... I don't mean your acreage."

"Oh, I know. Besides. I'm not from New Jersey. I just live there from time to time." Henry waved a hand lazily in the air. "Quite frankly, the only thing New Jersey has going for it is the fact that William Franklin is still a royal governor. Other than that? Nothing much, is there?"

"Not with the way the people are acting in that so called Royal Colony," Colonel Moore said with a curl of his lip.

And it was true after all. There was unrest in grew all over, and it was getting no better with the passing days. William Franklin seemed the only thing in New Jersey that held to the King's orders, and Henry had worried about it the other day on their walk. Henry's estate was in

New Jersey, and should the colony turn against the king, like Massachusetts had, what would that mean for him? For the rest of the good Loyalists? He lived near the town that was providing weaponry for George Washington's army, not that Henry talked too much about it. Felicia didn't press him concerning the matter. If Henry didn't outwardly express any concern, she thought it best not to bother him with her cares, but still, she had a gnawing feeling that his estate might be in jeopardy.

"You don't think they'd become like Massachusetts, do you? Stage raids?"

"Don't fret, Felicia." Henry laughed abruptly, then nudged his brother's arm, who only gave a disgusted click of his tongue. "They are nothing like those Boston radicals. In fact, they're rather boring."

He scanned the room, catching the eyes of his card playing companions. He bent to her level and gazed into her eyes. "You will be all right if I step away?"

She smiled gently, motioning for him to join his friends. He curled a finger under her chin, then strode off, head held high.

"Oh, why Felicia Hawkings, is that you?"

Felicia winced.

A familiar plump, woman with powder gray hair, accompanied by her husband, strode into the room.

"Hello, Mrs. Haddock."

"How have you been? You look very well," Mrs. Haddock said, abandoning her husband to talk with Colonel Moore. Her eyes flickered over Felicia, and she pursed her lips. "Very well, indeed. How is the Major?"

"Dead."

Mrs. Haddock stared blankly at Felicia. "How terribly dull of me to say so. It seems like forever ago the raid happened... and in all truth, it slipped my mind."

"I don't expect people to remember," Felicia said flatly, the corners of her eyes burning. She blinked, then performed a dignified sniff. "But it would be pleasant to have a bit more curtesy shown." She waved her hand in the air, then brought it to rest on her belly. "So, I suppose he's well in heaven, but he certainly isn't well on earth."

"Oh, my dear. I suppose it just wasn't God's will that you stay married."

Felicia pressed her lips together tightly. She glanced over at Henry, who was unfortunately still engrossed in the conversation with his poker companions. She let out another long breath. "I don't think God wills that we lose our loved ones before we think it should be their time, but I've been told it'll work together for good."

"That's the way to see it. And besides, he left you with his memory." Mrs. Haddock reached down to rub Felicia's middle. Felicia stepped back from her, but the older woman patted her stomach regardless. "We were all wondering when you were to give the Major a child, you know. It's too bad that you couldn't have given him a child sooner, so he could have been a living father."

"Henry!" Felicia called. Henry glanced over toward Felicia, then gestured to his group, and turned back to their conversation.

Would Natty leave me to weather Mrs. Haddock? If I hear another double-edged compliment, I may turn feral. Child, do I have permission to blame you for any actions I might take against Mrs. Haddock?

A kick.

I shall take that as a yes. Thank you.

A stately, pale woman with blazing red hair under her mobcap stepped into the parlor, calling for supper to be served, her eyes toward the floor. O, blessed day. She adjourned to the dining room without answering Mrs. Haddock's obnoxious statement that she should have conceived at a more opportune time.

Henry took Felicia's arm as they walked to the dining room, then helped her into her seat, gently scooting her in before sitting across from her.

Mrs. Haddock sat on Felicia's right, across from her husband. Victoria Moore sat to Felicia's left, across from her father.

"Oh, would you look at that," Mrs. Haddock said, leaning to Felicia. "A thorn between two roses."

Felicia took in a deep breath, closing her eyes.

Bite your tongue, Felicia. Bite your tongue and keep your thoughts in your brain.

"Thomas, why can't you be here with your witty retorts," she whispered under the din of the guests. "*You* could get away with saying them."

She could hear Thomas's snickering.

"But you are the better to prick her with, my dear Lissie."

Felicia grinned at the little secret in her heart, opening her eyes again.

While the dinner was delicious—fish and rabbit, crawfish and potatoes, peas, and finally cream pastries and sugared fruit—the conversation was bland. Although no one quipped witty retorts or make silly discreet faces at her, she appreciated that Henry, to his credit, kept giving her secret glances and smiles throughout the meal.

Although she was glad to be seated next to Victoria who was sweet as always, and although no one except Mrs. brought up Thomas or the unfortunate instance that took his life, the talk around her was drivel. She rarely uttered a word unless directly addressed, and an incredible sinking feeling filled her chest as the conversations swirled around her. Dread crept up each time anyone opened their mouth—what if they might be addressing her? Suppers and parties seemed dull, anymore, without Thomas.

But Henry, despite having ignored her earlier with Mrs. Haddock, seemed to take note of her unease. Even though she could very well speak for herself—and she knew that Henry thought so as well—he responded frequently on her behalf. But incredible exhaustion overwhelmed her, and he seemed to understand.

"The child," Mrs. Haddock said loudly. "When is the child to come?"

Felicia glanced wearily to Henry.

"She thinks the child is to come in December," Henry said. "Though I believe I have said so seven times prior."

"And what of the estate?" Mrs. Haddock asked.

Felicia let out a small moan, unheard by the dinner guests.

"There has been no word from A. L. Bach's office in London," Henry said. "The mail comes through here first and I've yet to see it."

"And how shall you christen the child?" Mrs. Haddock pressed on, either unaware of Felicia's growing discomfort, or ignoring it completely.

A sly look crossed Victoria's face, and she leaned forward, beating her uncle to an answer. "Indeed, how are we to christen a child before it is born, especially under dear Mrs. Hawking's present circumstances?"

Bemused, Felicia looked to Henry, but he was pinching the bridge of his nose.

"Victoria..." Henry started, and he glanced at his brother who was busy laughing with the Lieutenant. "Victoria, not tonight."

Victoria grinned, her features looking a little more hellion than cherubic. "Mrs. Haddock"—the woman peered around Felicia— "how are you christening *your* child?"

"My children are grown," Mrs. Haddock stammered.

Henry moaned. "Victoria, I will give you two pounds ten to cease talking."

Growing evermore nonplussed, Felicia faced Henry's niece, who was obviously contemplating the worth of the two pounds ten for being quiet against continuing with her thought. The diplomatic look of bargaining was plain on Victoria's face.

"Make it three," she said. "And a song."

"Thank you, sunflower," Henry said, leaning back in his chair. "You'll be paid in the morning."

Victoria hummed and adjusted herself in her chair, a happy little smug smirk on her face. "It's just funny because I thought I saw the general toting a small child with him when he was about town."

All conversation at the table died. Felicia brought up her kerchief, coughing into it. At least she hoped those giggles sounded like coughs.

"You have lost the song and the three pounds," Henry stated, glaring daggers at his niece.

She grinned at him.

Mrs. Haddock opened and closed her mouth, looking just like her namesake.

"That, that was his... granddaughter," she stuttered.

"Of course," Victoria said, forking the cake on her plate. She leaned over to Felicia and whispered in her ear, "The child just seemed too old to be a granddaughter and too young to be christened."

Felicia held her hand out, hissing a soft hush. "Shh, you'll get us into trouble if we laugh."

After dinner, the guests met in the parlor for games and drinks. Felicia watched the women titter, and the men discuss current events. The children could be heard in the hallway, playing with tabletop ninepins and Jacob's ladders. The Lieutenant's child sneaked into the parlor and gave her his Jacob's ladder to play with, and thus she stayed occupied for the next half an hour, rolling each block down over each other, twisting her wrist back and forth.

Felicia sagged in the high-backed chair. The child had started up kicking with a fury after the supper, and she was just in no condition, in both mind and body, to give her attention to much else. Her eyes flitted from one cluster of people to the next, and her ears caught snippets of conversations. Henry and his companions moved to the center of the parlor, their voices pitched low.

Suddenly, Henry stepped away from his group and cleared his throat, clapping his hands.

"If you all please," he called, "I have something that must be done."

Felicia raised her brows and blinked at him as the room quieted down. Henry came over to her, kneeled to her level, and took her hands.

"Henry, what are you doing?" Felicia asked. She shifted in her seat, digging her heels into the floor. She sat stiffly upright in the chair.

"My dear Felicia," he said. "We've been courting for a while now."

"Indeed, we have," she said slowly, a little afraid of what he might say next.

"And I suppose that, if we want to get the banns in before your time, I should probably propose to you now." His face was soft, though etched with an air of nervousness.

Felicia stared at him, trying to understand the words coming from his mouth. Her mind failed her, drawing blanks every time she tried to string his words together.

"Felicia?" Henry asked, giving her hands a squeeze.

"I'm sorry... what are you asking me?" She sucked in a breath, holding it. Her eyes widened, and she could feel the blood rushing to her cheeks. This was exactly what she had been waiting for...

"Would you do me the honor of becoming my wife?" Henry let go of one of her hands to reach into his coat and pulled out a ring from the inside pocket. The ring—a large diamond set in the center of the gold band—glittered in the candlelight in the room. He turned the ring this way and that in his fingers, so the diamond caught the light.

Felicia stared wide-eyed at the ring in Henry's fingers. The guests held their breath in a rapt silence, watching Henry on his knee and Felicia. She could only assume she was staring like a fish at Henry and the ring.

"I—"

"I know I'll never take the place in your heart that the Major had," Henry said, taking Felicia's left hand. He gently folded both hands over hers. "But I will do my best to take care of you and his child."

"I—"

"I will provide you with security and safety. You wouldn't need to worry about anything."

Felicia opened her mouth and closed it again, then tried to speak, but no words came out. This is what she waited for, after all. He owned ten acres of land in New Jersey, had disposable income, a confidence about his person, and knew what the next days would bring.

She should be happy. She would be married before her time, and her child would have a father who would keep them both safe and secure.

So, why couldn't she answer him?

She glanced down at the ring on her finger, wondering when exactly he had put it there, then back at Henry.

"Henry, this is really..."

He brought her left hand close to his lips.

She bit her lips together and breathed out through her nose. When Thomas proposed, he had done so in a quiet manner, alone, in the garden where he was now buried. No one bore them witness to the proposal. Here, nearly all of Colonel Moore's commanding officers and their wives had seen it. And Mrs. Haddock.

"Henry," she said slowly. "Henry this is—well, it's not sudden. But —ah—I don't know how to quite answer you."

"Answer, 'yes,'" Henry's inky blue eyes were soft in the candlelight, and his lips turned up into a warm curve. He leaned in a little closer to her, lips nearly against her ear and lowered his voice to a whisper. "I'll play for you every night. *Winter*, folk tunes, anything." His lips grazed over her cheek. "Please, make me the happiest man in the world and say yes."

But in the back of Felicia's mind, she could see the tan cooper, smiling at her. She imaged his pale blue eyes, glinting in the candlelight. She could see him with his musket, practicing on the green with his volunteer soldiers. She envisioned him playing Thomas's violin, taking the sting the bow strokes.

"Oh, Henry. I just... it's so much for me to think about."

Henry let go of her hand, hovering his palm over her swell under her skirts. She nodded to him, and he gently rested his hand against her belly. "I know you want to do right by your child. And I know this must all be so taxing to your emotions. It's not natural that you should have to marry so soon. But I promise I will take care of you."

"Henry, I can't take this matter so lightly." Felicia brought her hand up tentatively, then smoothed a lock of his hair over his ear and sighed. "Henry, you must give me some time to answer you properly... perhaps more privately."

"Of course," Henry said, his smile flickering for only a moment. But while his smile stayed on his lips, a look of trepidation played in his eyes, marring the sparkling joy that filled them a moment before. "But wear the ring while you think. When can you answer me? When can you make me happy?"

Felicia winced at the ring on her finger, then gazed upon Henry. "Are you sure you want me to wear it?"

He covered his mouth with her palm, pressing kisses to her hand, his eyes glinting.

"Wear it while you think. Perhaps it will help you reach your decision sooner rather than later."

Wearing the glittering rock on her hand wouldn't help her to decide faster. She was sure she had made up her mind on the subject, but it was a difficult thing to say, "I'd rather not; I'm in love with the town cooper," in front of everyone.

Besides, would she rather not? Was she really in love with the cooper?

Natty cropped up in her mind, his pale blue eyes staring intently back at her.

Oh, why can't Thomas be alive? This wouldn't need to happen if only he could still be here!

Felicia shook herself and glanced around the room at the guests, who only stared in rapt attention. Finally, she tilted her head toward Henry, barely pressing her forehead to his. "I'll wear it as I come to my decision."

Henry beamed, took her hand, and pressed a kiss to her fingers and palm. "Of course. Take the time you need. It's a big decision, and one that affects more than just you, I know it." He pressed his hand to her skirts again, and the child moved against his touch. Felicia placed her hand atop his.

"I'll be as quick as I can."

"Oh, just say yes to him," Mrs. Haddock brayed. "Oh, just say yes! He's such a fine catch. He'd be so good for you. Elevate you."

There wasn't much left to the party after that. Shortly after Henry stood up again, most of the guests started filtering out.

Henry brought Felicia her red wool cloak. They bade the others farewell and left.

The night air blew crisp, and the sky was blanketed in an inky darkness with barely a star visible on the walk home. She shivered, and he drew her in close, shielding her from the cold October air.

Finally, Felicia glanced up at Henry. "I hope I didn't embarrass you."

"Why would you embarrass me?"

"I didn't exactly give you a definite answer, did I? And there were so many people there expecting me to say something more than I did."

"Well, my dear," Henry said, pushing open the gate to Felicia's front yard. "I wanted them to bear us witness, but you're not obligated to answer me. I wish you had, but it is a big decision, and one that I'm sorry you must make... I wish the major hadn't... but what more is there to do now?"

Felicia shook her head, clicking her tongue, while he helped her up onto her porch. "Thank you, Henry. I really do appreciate you giving me the time. It really is all so much for me to think about." She pressed her hand to her belly. "And it isn't just my life I'm making decisions for."

Henry tilted her face to his. "Of course. Such a precious life to think about. Goodnight, my dear Felicia. I'll call on you soon."

"Tomorrow at one?"

Henry frowned and shook his head. "I've just been called on business to Philadelphia. But when I come back, I'll call on you. And I hope for an answer then."

"How long will you be gone?"

"A week."

She could give Nathaniel her answer while Henry tended to his business and still have enough to try to figure out just how to word her answer to both. "I should definitely give you an answer by then."

"Then I will wait in eager anticipation until I return." He leaned forward, and Felicia braced herself into the kiss. She kept a grip on his arms as he kissed her, otherwise still as Henry set his arms around her waist. For the first time, she was quite glad for her size. The child caused a respectable distance between them as he bent low to kiss her.

Finally, he broke the kiss and stepped away. "Goodnight, my dear."

"Do stay safe," she said. She squeezed his arm gently, offering him an exhausted smile.

He gave her a grin. He picked up her hand and pressed one last kiss to her knuckle before started back to the road for town. Felicia waited on the porch till he was out of sight, then spun around and pushed open the front door, pausing as she noticed the glimmering ring on her left hand.

"Oh, Henry, why'd you wait this long?" she muttered under her breath as she came in from the cold. She wrinkled her nose. "Not that it would have very much mattered, I suppose."

She fell back upon the door as it closed behind her, resigning herself to the ring on her finger. The diamond set in the center mocked her, a reminder that she'd eventually have to tell Henry her definite answer.

At least she had a week to think about how to do it...

❧ 16 ❧

"This isn't how I thought I'd be spending the first few hours of my day." Felicia sat on the edge of her bed, struggling to slip on her stockings, but her large mid-section made bending over impossible. She tried twisting her leg up onto the bed next to her, but alas, she still couldn't reach down to get the stocking onto her foot. "*Rose!*"

A scurrying sound echoed through the hallway. Rose threw the door open.

"Are you all right, ma'am?" she asked, breathlessly, but when her gaze fell upon the Felicia, her leg twisted awkwardly to the side on the bed, the stocking hanging on to one toe, and the ribbon clenched between her teeth, Rose let out a peal of laughter.

"Stop laughing and help me," Felicia grumbled against the satin ribbon.

Rose didn't obey the first order, but she walked over to the bed, took the stocking, and slid it on Felicia's leg, tied it with the ribbon, and repeated the process to her other leg. "Will you be needing help with the shoes?"

Felicia narrowed her eyes. "Probably."

Rose slid Felicia's crystal buckled shoes onto her feet.

"And probably the stays as well," Felicia said, sliding off the bed.

"What's the fancy buckles for, ma'am?" Rose asked, tying up the sides to Felicia's stays, loosening them the further down she laced.

"I'm—ah—I don't know if you need to know that." Felicia took her stomacher off the mattress, then began pinning it in place. "I suppose you could say I'm meeting a friend."

Rose caught a glimpse of the glimmering ring on Felicia's finger. "Ma'am, I don't remember seeing you wear that ring before."

"Henry." Felicia held out her hand to inspect the diamond inset and the little clusters of stones in the band. "He gave it to me a few days ago."

"You're betrothed to Mr. Moore?"

"No?" Felicia said, wrinkling her nose. She held her arms out, and Rose slid on the dress's robe, then began pinning it to the stomacher. "He proposed, yes, but I didn't exactly answer him. Told me to keep wearing the ring till he returned from Philadelphia."

"Very good, ma'am," Rose said.

"*You* think so." Felicia settled her bergère hat atop her head and tied it under her chin. She turned about in her mirror, inspecting her outfit.

Rose adjusted Felicia's skirt. "I don't think it matters much what I think."

"Go on."

"I don't know, ma'am. It's really not my place to say."

"Please," Felicia asked. "I really want to hear it."

Rose sighed and tilted her face away from Felicia, staring at the door. "I just can't imagine you and Mr. Moore being married, is all. You say he's a good man, and I'm not doubting it, but he just doesn't seem like *your* man. Your man was the Major, and Henry Moore just isn't... Am I making myself clear?"

"I think so. So, if I, oh, say, started seeing somebody else," Felicia said, making her way to the door. She paused and winced, rubbing her hand over her belly. She let out a long sigh. "Would you see that person as 'my man' or however you say it?"

"Depends on the man," Rose said. "I might say so. But don't let my thoughts get in the way of your love."

"I cannot foster any love toward Henry," Felicia said, turning to face Rose. "I appreciate him. But I do not love him."

Rose picked off a piece of lint from Felicia's shoulder, then spoke lowly. "Then why do you keep seeing him?"

Felicia wrinkled her nose again, bringing her hands to her belly. "I need security; he seemed to be the only option, and I thought maybe affection could grow between us. I believed love to be a luxury I couldn't afford, what with the baby."

"But you do love?"

"With that," Felicia said, turning back to the door. "I have business in town."

"That cooper talks loud, ma'am. I picked up everything he said when he came over to drop off the churn."

Felicia froze.

"I know he said he wanted to court you."

"I never answered him either," Felicia said, pressing her lips together. She glanced back over her shoulder at Rose. "I'm about to do so now."

"Very good, ma'am."

"I'd pray for me if I were you." Felicia stopped at the head of the stairs, peered down them, and gave an already tired sigh. "Oh, this child."

Rose came up beside Felicia, laying a hand on her shoulder. "Here, let me help you."

She wrapped an arm around Felicia's back, steadying her mistress as they walked down together.

"Thank you, Rose," Felicia said with a puff of air as they reached the foyer. She glanced out the window, watching the trees blow in the cool early November wind. "I'm not going to like this."

"You have my prayers." Rose ushered Felicia to the door. "Go on, ma'am. It'll be well."

"I'm glad one of us thinks so," Felicia muttered and took her cloak from Amos and wrapped it tightly around her shoulders.

THE AIR CHILLED Felicia to the bone. She shivered, wrapping her cloak tighter around her as she walked up the road to town, past the colonials' houses. Her child did not take the journey very well, kicking and moving about against the cold weather and Felicia's steps.

"Oh, stop it," Felicia chided. "I'll be resting shortly."

Finally, against the babe's protests, she reached the town center, waddling along the sidewalk till she spied her destination.

Nathaniel Poe: Cooper.

Felicia glanced through the foggy, thick, glass window, rubbing it with the edge of her sleeve to get a better peek inside. Nathaniel stood over a small bucket, sliding a metal ring down the wooden blocks to keep them in place. She reached up to pull on the doorbell.

Nathaniel started up at the sudden ringing of the bell, and he left the bucket to open the door. "Felicia?"

"Aye."

"Come in," he said, stepping aside. "What are you doing out?"

"I know it's early, but I need to talk with you." She leaned against his worktable and glanced around. "Henry's away till Saturday, and this must be said now."

She had never actually been in his shop before. Thomas had either sent Amos to create an order or had gone there himself, and Felicia had only met Nathaniel when he came to drop off orders or made house calls. His shop was relatively dark, with wood shavings nearly ankle-deep where Nathaniel worked. The scent of cedar filled the store, and she breathed it in deeply. The scent brought her back to her young childhood making Christmas decorations with her parents back in England.

"I suppose I have some time to talk," Nathaniel wiped his brow and nodded curtly. "Do you need a seat?"

"Please."

He moved a barrel from his workspace near the back of the shop up to Felicia and motioned for her to sit. She tried to slide herself onto it, but after two attempts, Nathaniel picked her up and set her on the barrel. His eye caught the sparkle from the ring glimmering on her left hand. Nathaniel set his jaw, eyes fixed on her ring.

"Is this what you came to tell me?" He took her hand in his, turning it this way and that to examine the ring.

Felicia blushed and pulled her hand away, shoving it into the opening in her skirt. "No."

"Then what is that?" Nathaniel asked, eyes steely, voice cool and even. "It sure looks like a betrothal ring to me."

Felicia's lips parted, eyebrows knitted, and a dismayed low bleat escaped her throat. "That's exactly what it is. Henry *did* propose to me a few nights ago."

Nathaniel crossed his arms, closing his mouth tightly. He drew in a deep breath, exhaling slowly through his nose. "I see."

"I never answered him," Felicia continued. "He gave me the ring, but I never said yes."

"Then why wear the ring?"

"I told him I'd think about it," Felicia said. "He proposed in front of friends and family. I didn't wish to humiliate him after."

Nathaniel shrugged, moving back to the bucket he was finishing, and sat on a small stool as he fit a second ring onto the bucket form. He started hammering the bottom in. Felicia slid off the barrel and walked through the wood chips to his side.

"Nathaniel, don't ignore me," she said. "There is a certain decorum I have to keep up at parties, you know. Besides, Mrs. Haddock was there, and do you know what she's like? I would have been branded an ungrateful wench forever for saying a straight answer no."

"Actually, yes. I do know what Mrs. Haddock is like." Nathaniel pointed to the bucket. "For her."

Felicia scooted the bucket away from him with her foot. He tilted his head up toward her, unamused. "Mrs. Hawkings, if you don't mind. I do need to get back to work."

He brought the bucket back, but Felicia scooted it away again. Nathaniel grumbled. "What is it you want from me?"

Felicia attempted to crouch down to his level, holding onto the workbench for balance. She plopped to the floor.

"I came here with every thought in my mind tumbling around like leaves in the wind. But when I close my eyes, I don't see Henry. I see you. I really don't care if you're a patriot, and I really don't care if you're a soldier. But I don't want Henry. I don't even want to wear this ring anymore." She wriggled the band off her finger and tossed it into the bucket. "Henry is the man that my parents would want. He's the one that they found to help me because he is the secure choice."

The child kicked, and Felicia brought her hands to her belly with a grimace. Nathaniel reached into the bucket, then handed her the ring back. She shoved it into her pocket, exhaustion creeping up on her.

"But sometimes, the secure choice isn't the right choice." Felicia stared into his eyes, her gaze fiery and intense, unwavering. For the first time, she looked at him without the fear of that snake tightening around her stomach. And oh, how she loved it. "You don't get called to join the war. You only go at a moment's notice if needed. Natty, please, don't make me go away because I had a ring that barely fit my finger."

"Aye, I suppose I do," Nathaniel said, then stood up. Felicia reached up to him, and he lifted her to her feet. "I'm not going to make you leave the store. But if you came all this way in your state, what did you have to tell me?"

"I think I just told you," she said a little exasperated.

"You told me that Henry wasn't the right choice." He crossed his arms, staring back at her with the same passion she showed him. "You didn't answer my question."

"I want to see you," Felicia said, breathlessly. "I want you to court me."

Nathaniel paused a moment, then picked the bucket up, setting it on a table of unfinished projects. He turned back to her and leaned on the table, studying Felicia intently. Felicia tried to make sense of him for a moment, lips parted in a light frown, then made her way back to the barrel and, pulled a bucket over, then stepped up and onto her seat. She grimaced, bringing her hand to her skirts, pressing her hand against her stays.

"Oh, this child," she said with a hum.

Nathaniel stopped gathering wooden blocks for the next project and glanced over at her. "Are you all right?"

"The child moves like I've never known," she said under her breath.

She huffed and grimaced again, grasping her skirt in her fists. "Pain low and high. I've never heard of such things."

Nathaniel came over to her and stood there, watching her clench and unclench her fists. "Could I?"

"What would you know about babies?"

Nathaniel crouched before her, then leaned back on his haunches. "I raised sheep and horses before apprenticing as a cooper."

Felicia glanced up at him and nodded, albeit tentatively. He pressed a hand to her belly, feeling the child move beneath his palm.

Her tired eyes narrowed in a glare. "I'm neither an ewe nor mare."

"Of course not. But if you're contracting early, I might be able to tell. How far along are you?" He stood straight again, crossing his arms. He cocked his head to one side, looking gently upon her.

"My time is in December."

Nathaniel held his hand out for her. "You are overworked and need to rest. I'll walk with you back to your home. If you're feeling this way, I can't have you walking alone."

Felicia took his hand and slid off the barrel again. She glanced up at him through her lashes, the hint of a smile playing on her lips.

"You're the town cooper. You're the leader of the town's patriot volunteer soldiers. You play the violin. Is there anything you can't do?"

"Kiss you, apparently."

Felicia paused, and keeping a hold onto his hand, she turned to fully face him, taking his other hand. "Nothing is stopping you," she said in a whisper, the hint of a smile growing into a full beam, eyes half-lidded as she gazed upon his face.

He freed a hand from hers, and brought it up to her arm, running his fingers up and down her shoulder. He freed his other hand, setting it at her waist.

"May I?" he murmured, lips hovering over Felicia's.

"Please."

Nathaniel hesitated but a moment longer, then closed the distance between them and kissed her.

Felicia breathed him in, taking in his musky, oaky scent and threw her arms about his neck, and kissed him back. She untied his hair from the string that held it back, and it spilled down over his shoulders. Stepping closer she fished her hands through his long dark hair as he deepened the kiss. A vague earthiness lingered on his lips.

He kept a hand at the nape of her neck as he kissed her, causing her bergère to slip off her head. Pressing his other hand into the small of her back, gripping at the fabric of her dress, he moved his mouth in sync with hers.

The thrill of the kiss rushed through Felicia, sending her child into a whirl. The baby gave a forceful kick, and she pulled away from Nathaniel with a gasp.

"I think your child wishes me to slow down," Nathaniel said with a small smirk.

"The child may wish it, but I don't!"

Nathaniel hummed a deep throaty laugh under his breath. "Shall I walk you home now?"

"You'd better, I'd think," Felicia said, rubbing over her skirts with a sigh. "The child is worked up now and is giving me pain again."

Nathaniel grinned and set her bergère right on her head, then tightened the ribbon.

Out of the corner of her eye, Felicia saw a shadow pass outside the window. "Did you see that?"

"See what?"

"The shadow?"

He furrowed his brows but shook his head, then opened the door and shrugged. "Just a passerby." He held his hand and helped her out of the shop, and together they made their way back up the road.

Felicia glanced back over her shoulder and caught a glimpse of someone in a green brocade overcoat walking away from Nathaniel's storefront. She craned her neck to see better, but the man in the over-coat disappeared around a corner.

"Who or what did you see?" he asked. She shook her head and turned around, shrugging as they continued away from town.

"I couldn't see his face... but..."

Nathaniel quirked a brow, gazing down at her.

"I think it's Henry."

"Henry? You said... What is Henry doing back so soon?"

"I wouldn't know. But I don't like the feeling seeing that man gave me."

"He could very well have just been the bookkeeper as Henry," Nathaniel said with a shrug. "I wouldn't think too much of it."

He walked with her along the road, his arm around her back for stability. She leaned into his side, resting her head on his arm. She glanced up at him—how he stood tall and how straight he walked, much like a bonafide soldier. She leaned a bit heavier into his side.

"So then, you'll court me?" Felicia asked, her voice soft.

"Only if you'll let me," Nathaniel said, pushing open the gate at the end of the path to her house. He walked her up to her house, helping her onto the porch.

"I'll let you," Felicia said with a small grin. She wrapped her arms about his neck and stepped as close to him as possible given her current state. He wrapped his arms about her waist.

"Good," he said. He leaned down and placed a chaste kiss to her mouth, then pressed his forehead against hers. "But I'll come to you. I don't want you walking so far by yourself with the child giving you pains."

Felicia grinned against his lips. "Trust me, I don't think I'll be able to walk so far by myself soon if the child keeps growing the way he is."

Nathaniel stepped back and took one of her hands, pressing tiny kisses over her fingers and palm.

"God be with ye," he murmured, then turned to leave.

As Nathaniel started up the path and Felicia looked up to see him off, they both came face to face with Felicia's mother and father, who only stared at the cooper and their daughter, wide mouthed and eyed.

Felicia froze, like a carriage being stopped by a highwayman. She glanced up to Nathaniel, over to her parents, and back and forth again a few times. Their eyes flashed from Nathaniel to their daughter and back again. Mother's basket slipped from her hands while Nathaniel stood there, caught in the middle.

"Oh no," Felicia breathed.

"I think I'd better stay." Nathaniel hesitated. "You may need all the help you can get..."

"No..." Felicia murmured. She pressed his hand. "I think they want to talk with me alone."

"Are you sure?" Nathaniel whispered.

"She's sure," Felicia's father answered.

Nathaniel peered down at Felicia and pressed his lips together. "God be with ye," he said again. "I think you're really going to need it."

❧ 17 ❧

Felicia sat in her sitting room, with her parents sitting across from her, the distinct feeling of Déjà-vu crept over her. A heavy silence danced with dust particles in the air, the clock ticking acting as their metronome. The sun had shifted, casting severe shadows on her parents' faces that only assisted in unearthing that memory.

When she was nineteen, she snuck away one night to meet Thomas in secret behind the stables next to the court building. That night, he first played his violin for her, entrapping her ears and heart in his musical hands. Hour after hour, adagio after adagio, and kiss after passionate kiss between the pieces passed, and Thomas returned her home before they did anything further compromise the other, for despite this slight lapse, Major Thomas Hawkings was an honorable man. Fortunately, the townspeople were sleeping, and they didn't find out. Unfortunately, by the time they arrived at her parents' doorstep, the sun was rising over the pasture, and her father was waiting on a porch chair.

Felicia was positive the look on her father's face was the same as that night, if not strikingly similar.

"I really don't have any words to say on the matter." Felicia tugged on the lace on her sleeve. "I don't know what to say."

Mother said, thrumming her fingers on the arm of the chair. "I could say a few things."

"I could say a *lot* of things," Father added. He crossed his arms, tapping his shoe on the floor.

"Let me just start off, then, by saying that I am a grown woman now. And, any choice I make as an adult should be understood as such."

"You were in the arms of the half-breed *cooper*," Mother said. "When I said he's a good man, I didn't actually think you'd take it to heart."

"Whether or not the cooper is Native to these lands is not my concern, nor do I appreciate your calling him *that*." Felicia brought her hand to her belly and scrunched her face. She huffed, gripping the arm of her chair with her free hand, her knuckles turning white.

"What's wrong?" Mother asked.

"It's nothing." Felicia's grimace softened. "He's just like his father—exceptionally strong."

"I think your child knows how to distract the matter at hand," her mother said.

"I have trained him well."

Silence hung in the air for a few moments as Felicia waited for the pain in her ribs to subside. Selah brought in the tea cart silently and left with a small curtsey.

"But what about Henry?" her mother asked. "I thought he'd proposed."

Holding her breath, Felicia reached into her pocket and pulled out the diamond ring.

"He did propose," she said, handing the ring to her father. "But I didn't accept then, and I'm not going to."

Felicia flexed and unflexed her hands, tilting her head back.

"Are you sure you are all right?" Father asked, eyebrows knitted together into a dark line. "You look pale."

She kept her head bowed low but flicked tired eyes up at him.

"Father, I assure you, that I am merely with child—a stubborn child who enjoys butting heads with my ribs and kicking at my hips." She heaved sighed with relief when the babe slowed down. "It's better now."

"Felicia," her mother said, taking the ring from Father, "I just don't understand. Henry is a fine man! You said so yourself! Why not marry him? He shares your ideals. He's handsome. He'll protect you and keep you and your child safe, warm, and fed."

"I don't love Henry." Felicia pulled the teacart closer and poured herself a cup of tea with a sugar cube and some milk. "I never have. I tried to make myself feel some affection, but I just can't muster it. He's handsome. He has connections and is probably the safest option."

"But"—Father hesitated— "you don't love him."

Felicia stared into her teacup. "I can't imagine spending my life with him. I'm a fool, really. I love Natty."

"Natty?" they asked in unison.

"The cooper. Nathaniel Poe. He's a good man. He has a business, and he'll protect me. He may be a soldier, but—"

Mother held up her hand, cutting Felicia off. "He's a soldier?"

"Volunteer, actually. He won't get called to go and report for duty. He goes if the need arises. Safer than a major." She paused, looking down at her belly. "Though my Major should have been safe..."

Silence permeated the sitting room for several minutes. Felicia took up a small spoon and swirled it in her tea, then tapped it delicately on the edge of the cup. She glanced up at her parents, forcing a demure smile on her face.

Felicia sipped her tea, then murmured, "What can I say? I have a penchant for soldiers."

Her mother let out a long, drawn out moan. "If the cooper is a soldier, why doesn't he wear red?"

Felicia pressed her lips together and took in a deep breath through her nose.

"Because he's a rebel?" Father asked.

Mother turned to Father, though Felicia could still see her face. He cocked his head to her, quirking a brow.

"She loves a rebel," Mother mouthed.

Father shook his head.

"A rebel. Re-bel."

Father shrugged.

After a few moments, they both turned, staring at Felicia.

"You're in love with a colonial?" Mother whined, dismay tinting her voice. "Felicia! How could you?"

"I don't know how. Ask my heart! He has the same eyes that Thomas had," Felicia said, counting on her fingers. "He's quiet and stoic. He's gentle. He cares about me. I could go on."

"Please don't," Father said.

"He said he didn't care if I'm a loyalist, that as long as I respected his opinions, he'd respect mine. He said he'd avenge Thomas somehow. And I love him," she said, throwing her hands into the air. "I love him, and if he were to propose to me, I'd accept without hesitation. I love that rebel, and I don't care what you think."

She stood up to leave, but her father held his hand up. "For G-d's sake, Felicia, sit down."

She sat back down in a plush velvet cushioned chair.

"We're not here to interfere with your heart," he said.

Mother relaxed her face and calming her voice, said, "Well, it wasn't what we originally intended this afternoon."

"No, we're not." He sighed, looking intently at his daughter. "How long have you been seeing him?"

"Since the order for the barrels... the ones he dropped that night at the dinner. I've been seeing him quietly since then."

Mother gasped. "Behind Henry's back?"

"Henry and I never made attempts to be official if you will. He never asked me to solely court me, after his first inquiry after the supper."

"It was *implied*, Felicia! You could have mentioned that you didn't want to see him anymore."

Felicia slumped back into her chair, "I'm sure I should have. I just tried to find affection toward him! I thought, maybe, if I saw him enough, I could love him. But I don't. And I can't. I know that now.

Oh, I'm sure I should have never seen him after that butter churn. I tried to choose the right thing to do for my baby! But maybe the right man isn't the best one—oh, I'm rambling. I hate rambling." Felicia shook her head, and a buckle came loose from behind her ear, unfurling over her shoulder in a soft curl. She buried her head in her hands, letting out a small squeaking sound. "I don't want to hurt the man, but I just don't love him. I can't marry—and have children with—somebody I don't love. And knowing that he wants five kids makes me feel just terrible considering the way this one is going."

"Well, no," Father said. He leaned over toward Felicia and gently pried her hands away from her face. "You don't need to explain anything. I could tell a mile away you're not interested in him."

Mother quirked a brow. "You could?"

"Oh, the whole world could, Abby! Good G-d. Every time she sat next to him, she'd be as still and quiet as a dead mouse. He'd have his arm about her, and she'd sit there like this—Abby put your arm about me—there."

He sat there, sitting as straight and stiff as a signpost, with a vacant stare on his face.

"It was very disconcerting, to see you so... so..." Father tried to find the right words to say.

"Unaffectionate..." Her mother frowned and brought her pointer finger to her chin. "It's true, now that I think about it." She glanced between them. "I suppose I had hoped you acted so, Lissie, because he's not Thomas, and you weren't accustomed to courting. But as the time went on, you acted no different. But today... Seeing you in the cooper's arms... you—"

"In truth, are happy again," Father said.

"He's certainly not Thomas, but he's promised me security, and oh, how he acts toward me. He's a gentleman," Felicia said. "If a rebel. I think that's his only fault."

"It's a pretty big fault," her mother said slowly. "Are you sure you'd rather him over somebody so astute as Henry?"

Felicia breathed a puff of air, let out a longsuffering, drawn-out groan, and stood up to gaze out the window. "I can only see Henry as a friend. Somebody Thomas and I used to invite to parties. Colonel Moore's brother. He was doing his best to be gallant, I suppose, and I'll be grateful for what he intended."

Father tapped his fingers together. "But the cooper?"

Felicia pressed her fingertips to the cool class and peered out to town. "But Nathaniel? Natty piqued my curiosity. He's as much a mystery to me as Thomas when we had started courting. I'm a little pressed for time now... and things are moving faster than I would want. But... I do think I love him." Felicia closed her eyes and leaned back on her heels, hands still against the windowpane. "He plays the violin."

She stood there in silence, relishing in the warm light flooding her face.

"I still love my husband. But Natty? He helps to fill that bullet-shaped hole in my heart. I don't think it's nearly as leaky as I imagined it'd be."

A calm, warming weight pressed into her shoulders. Felicia turned around, coming face to face with her father.

"He'd take you, the widow of a 'redcoat' major? He doesn't care?"

"I think some part of him does, in all truth. But I'm running out of time," Felicia said, her voice cracking. "I'm nearing my time with every passing week, and I just can't wait any longer to be married. I couldn't care less about the estate at this point. I must give my babe a father. But I won't marry Henry. I can't marry him. I'm just praying that Nathaniel does indeed love me and will propose soon." She threw her arms about her father, and he simply held her, letting her soak his shoulder with her tears. "Daddy, I don't know how to feel. It's so foreign. It's all so strange."

"I know, my love," he said softly, stroking her head. "I know it's all different. But things never happen the same way twice. And though I have been most fortunate to have had the same woman by my side for twenty-five years, I could only imagine that trying to fall in love a second time would hurt more than the first time ever did."

"I want to do right by myself." Felicia bit back a sob. "I want to do right by the child I carry. But I also want to do right by Thomas, and I'm afraid he'd... he'd never be all right with all this." She clenched her eyes shut, the tears just squeezing out the corners of her eyes, and whispered under her breath, "Would you be?"

She lifted her head, and though her eyes remained shut—

Thomas stood behind her father. He gave her a regret-filled smile. His eyes glistened with tears, and he reached for her, straining his fingers, clenching his teeth, trying to keep a smile on his lips. He looked like a little boy lost, and he kept stating the same thing.

Felicia frowned and let go of her father, wiping her cheeks.

"No," Thomas said, struggling to speak. *"No more."*

"No more?" Felicia asked.

"No more what?" Father asked.

"No, not more, more!" Thomas's voice grew more frantic. *"More!"*

"More what?" Felicia asked.

Thomas let out a pained groan, gritting his teeth, but he disappeared before she could open her eyes. Felicia cried out, reached for the man who was no longer there.

"Felicia, what is this about?" Mother crossed the room to join them at the window. She frowned and gently took her daughter's chin in her hands.

"It seemed as if he was here in the room with us," Felicia stammered. "Sometimes, if I call his name and close my eyes, I can see him. I can see him clearly. I've felt him—so cold—nearby! He tried to tell me something."

"Who, Lissie?" Father asked.

"Thomas!" Her voice cracked and she searched the room with her eyes closed. "He was standing right behind you."

"It may very well be that your imagination has run away with you, my love." Mother goaded Felicia to a chair. "Women, when expecting, are prone to their minds wandering."

"No, Mother, it's real. He's here!"

Her parents glanced at each other, then led Felicia back to a chair and sat her down. Mother poured the last dram of tea into her cup and handed it to her.

"I'm sure he is here," she said, voice soft, resting a hand on Felicia's shoulder. "And I'm sure he said that it's all right for you to move on."

"Oh, he's said that before," Felicia said impatiently, sipping her tea and stealing glances about the room as she fidgeted in the chair. "But just now, he tried to tell me something else."

She finished the tea and held her cup out for more. Her mother shook her head.

Felicia sighed. Straightening, she called, "Selah!"

Presently, the sound of shoes on wooden floors came up to the front of the house from the back kitchen, and Selah appeared in the alcove to the sitting room.

"Ma'am?"

"More tea." Felicia held the teapot out for her, wiggling it lightly. The top rattled.

"There is no more tea," Selah said.

Felicia gasped, sinking low in the chair. She brought her hand to her chest, opening and closing her mouth like a freshly caught fish. "No more tea?"

"That's the last of it, ma'am."

"Send Amos to the store?" Felicia asked.

"No more tea at all, ma'am."

Felicia whimpered, slumping back in the chair, as far as her stays and growing belly would allow.

"How am I supposed to get through this ordeal by fire without tea? Oh, why must we have taxed their tea to the point where they *dumped it in the harbor?*"

"Shh, my dear," Mother said, gently running her hand over Felicia's arm. "You'll stress the baby."

"Stores boycott it." She kept her voice low and even. "They won't allow me to drink it. I bet you that damned continental Congress— those *considerate* men who sit around trying to defect from the king— drink their tea covertly!" She glared. "To whom can I write?"

"*Felicia!* Your language!" Mother cried, while Selah left to hide in the kitchen.

Felicia crossed her arms, wrinkling her nose.

"I don't think you can write to anybody," Father said.

Felicia puffed her cheeks out and clenched her fists shut. "I've gone through so much. Must I go on without tea?"

"Oh, good G-d! Abby, do we have any tea?"

Mother held up her hands. "Yes, we still have two tins. Felicia, don't give your father a case of apoplexy. Next time we come 'round, I'll remember to pack you the tea. You have gone through so much. And if you'd like, I'll ask the Continental Congress myself to send you their secret stores of tea."

Felicia rubbed her eyes. "It's one thing after another anymore."

❧ 18 ❧

The town slept that cold, November night. Henry held a dimly glowing lantern to light his way, and not a sound could be heard save the crunching of dead leaves under boot.

He brought up dust as with each passing step toward town the road. He held the lantern in front of his face to see better in the pitch black. Light cast awkward shadows across his face, highlighting only the tops of his cheeks and the tip of his nose.

Henry kept silent, air crystallizing and curling in front of his mouth as he breathed. He swallowed, glancing about the path. He was sure this wasn't his best or even second-best idea. But after what he had witnessed, he had little choice but to meet after hours outside his brother's home. Besides not wanting to risk waking Victoria, his throat ached for a drink.

Only one building's windows spilled light, the tavern at the edge of town. He stole up the stairs to the porch, he leaned into the door, and blew out his lantern before he entered.

Eerie quiet filled the usually bustling room. At this late hour, only three people were present—a man slumped over a mug in the back corner on the floor, a woman wiped down the tables and swept the floor, and a shrouded figure sat hidden at a table near the kitchen door.

"William," he whispered coarsely.

The shrouded man moved, his shoulders twitching slightly. He took in a deep breath and moved his long blond locks out of his eyes, pulling it back into a loose ponytail. "It's past midnight, you know," William Moore said, motioning to the empty chair across him. "You can't just expect me to meet at any hour. I have a family, Henry. Something *you* wouldn't understand."

Henry flinched, but set his jaw, narrowing his eyes. "I would if she'd answer me," he said, curling his lip. "But that's why I'm here."

"Felicia hasn't answered you yet?" William asked. "Why not?"

"She doesn't know I'm back," Henry said, waving at the woman.

She approached and exhaled a guttural sigh. "What'll it be?"

"Port," Henry breathed.

The woman gave another tired sigh dropped her broom and walked back to the kitchen.

"Then why are you complaining?" William asked.

"She's in the arms of the cooper."

William blinked, and his fingers tapped the table. "How do you know?"

Henry rubbed at his temples. "I saw her yesterday. She was at his shop. Didn't have the decency to move away from the window."

The woman handed Henry his port, and he drank it in one gulp, and handed the glass back for a refill.

"The cooper? I don't understand. Isn't he some lowly rebel? Why is she with him?"

"That would be the question of the hour," Henry muttered.

The woman came back with his filled glass and slammed it on the table. A bit of the port splashed Henry's sleeve, and he scowled at the woman. She clicked her tongue, thrusting him the decanter, only filled to about a third, and returned to her broom.

"I thought you both were in love," William said.

"Oh, what's love got to do with it," Henry said, his voice raspy as he drained the second cup. "There's no love involved, not on her part."

"Why take on Hawking's expectant wife if you don't love her?"

Henry paused a moment, taking in a deep breath only to let it out slowly, then glanced to the side and pressed port-stained lips together.

William leaned forward. "You don't love her... I am correct?"

Henry still stared, eyes vacant, toward the wall. "You and I both know quite well this isn't about how I feel." He offered William the decanter, but William held up his hand up. Henry poured himself another glass and grimaced as he drank it down. "I lost the ship in the harbor, Will."

William's face contorted in derision and disgust. "Damn rebels sank your ship?"

Henry swirled the port in the decanter, watching as it created a whirlpool. "No. It was a bad game of twenty-one."

"First your ring and now your ship. You were always a stupid boy"— William snatched the decanter from his brother's hand— "and you've never outgrown it."

"I was dealt a dirty hand," Henry said, reaching across the table for the port. "It was a rigged deck."

William held it away from him. "It's *always* a rigged deck, you ass. How are you paying for this?"

Henry scowled again, letting out a huff.

"That's what I thought," William said. "How much do you need?"

"I need Felicia." Henry pulled the decanter from his brother's hand, drank directly from it, then coughed into his sleeve. "I need her estate. I need her..."

"Then marry her in the morning. I'll get you the license and you can bypass the banns."

Henry clenched his teeth together. "Nathaniel Poe is in my way," he murmured and brought his hand to his chest, clutching the brocade. "He stole her heart before I could even hope to do so. She won't marry me if she's in love with someone else."

"Then make her fall out of love."

Henry paused, mid-drink. He set the decanter down, stifled a hiccough, and swallowed hard. "How could I possibly do that?"

A smirk crept across William's thin lips. He fixed the bow in his hair and leaned forward. Henry blinked at him, widening, then narrowing his eyes, trying to see him clearly.

"You tell me," William asked. "I'm merely a colonel who was caught in a raid. A raid that killed Felicia's husband."

"Yes, I know." With a drawn-out sigh, Henry leaned back in his chair, glancing toward the near empty decanter. He walked his fingers on the table to it, before inching it his way to drain the decanter of its contents. "An awful event. How does that help me?"

"Tell me"—William leaned forward and took Henry's arms, shaking him, while Henry sat there, dumfounded, swaying back and forth—"how Felicia would hate Nathaniel. Tell me how she would tear herself from his arms and into yours."

Henry shook off his brother's grasp and waved his hands at him, the lace on the cuffs of his sleeves whipping back and forth. "Oh, I don't know," he said with a moan. "Let me alone to think!"

"You don't think," William sneered. "Tell me how she would hate a rebel soldier."

"Let me think!"

"You never think even when you're not filled with port? It's a simple answer."

"He didn't kill her husband." Henry protectively brought his hands up over his weskit. "I can't think of a reason for her to hate him if she's kissing him like she was."

"How do you know he didn't kill her husband?" William asked, his voice flat, his face showing no emotion.

Henry frowned. "He said he didn't know about a raid."

"And you believed him? Come now, Henry. Be logical." William leaned around the table stabbed Henry in his stomach with his walking cane, while Henry waved his hands in vain protest. "Why would Felicia hate Nathaniel and come running to you?"

Henry glared down toward the table, wracking his brain for an answer. He snapped his fingers. "He'd have to have been at the raid. He'd have to have shot Thomas."

"And..."

Henry twisted his wet lips and leaned forward, running his hands through his thick hair, pulling it loose from its ribbon. "If we could prove Nathaniel killed Thomas, we could do more than just make Felicia hate him," Henry said slowly, his mind clearing for a moment. "We could have him hanged. Thomas would be avenged..."

"Aye," William said, spreading his hands on the table. He watched Henry intently, eyes boring into him as he waited for an answer.

"But how do we prove it?"

"Oh, Henry. He's a rebel soldier. They carried out that raid. If he was out of town that day, who's to say that he didn't organize a raid? We only need a jury to believe he's guilty."

Henry nodded, frowning, though impressed. "It would take care of my problem quite easily, wouldn't it?"

William folded his hands under his chin as he leaned on the table. "Felicia would be yours, and there'd be one less little rebel leader to worry about. Without him, those Yanks would falter and flail. Hang him, and the town's free for British occupation. Then New York, and then Philadelphia." A faraway look came into his eye. "I have great plans... wonderful plans. Henry, the things my regiment could do without the Yanks in this town."

"Like—what?"

A hardened smirk etched onto William's face, and his focus flickered back to Henry. William grabbed him by the cravat, pulling him close, whispering under his breath. "Get our men here, and we'll have a direct route to the congress. We could kill those men where they sit and end this war now. John Adams? John Dickinson? Ben Franklin and Thomas Jefferson? We could sneak in and have them all hanged if we take control of *this* town first. No congress. No traitors. My regiment would be hailed as heroes. And you, you contented fop, would never need to worry about your debts again."

Henry sat in silence a few moments, blinking. He leaned back in his chair, glancing aside while he mulled over William's. "If you're to be the one to end this war through a surprise attack—"

"Hush!"

"If you are to do what you intend..."

"Your debts will be paid."

"But I fear she won't love me even if Nathaniel is gone..."

"Why not?" William asked.

"She just doesn't show me warmth... I'd like to see her smile. Love to make her smile."

William laughed a couple of short, stunted breaths. "Henry, give her time. She lost her husband." He grinned, steepling his fingers together.

"She's had nearly half a year. I want to be respectful, but she has the child. Perhaps I should have proposed earlier, but she seemed so distant."

Henry scanned the table, eyes falling on the empty decanter. He huffed, and William rolled his eyes, snapping his fingers. The tavern maid brought over a frothy mug. While Henry had hoped for port or madeira, he was pleasantly surprised at the rich, smooth taste and sweet scent hot buttered rum.

"Satisfied?" William asked, and Henry, receding into himself as he drank, nodded. William scoffed, "Don't you know anything about women?"

Henry slid the mug back and forth on the table. "I like 'em."

William waved the maid back over, pointing to the empty mug. She heaved a thick sigh and brought a steaming pitcher from kitchen. Henry shook his head, his cheeks and nose blushed and hot. William waved at him and the tavern maid refilled his mug. Henry brought the mug to his lips and took in a long slow drink, slipping low into the chair. Then, Henry glanced up at him over the edge of his mug.

"Listen," William said. "It doesn't matter what she thinks."

Henry nursed the drink, eyes growing heavy. "It should."

"No, Henry. Women are like that. Distant. Fickle. They like to toy with us to make us work harder. But she's a beautiful young thing. She'll be worth the time you put in."

"A beautiful, young, heavily laden thing."

"And yet, you know, she's quite ravishing. You've seen her assets? It's a real wonder that she and Thomas didn't have more children. If she were mine, she'd have had at least four by now. Five even."

Henry curled his lip. "Oh, don't talk about her that way! Good Lord, William!" He rose from his seat, but William calmly motioned for him to sit again.

"I'm older, but I'm not blind," William said. "But I highly doubt Victoria would like a step-mother who is only five years her senior. Thomas's child will soon be born around Christmas. She'll be back to herself in no time. She's a beautiful little thing, Henry. Once we straighten this out, you keep her on your arm, show her off at events, and sire your children."

Henry tilted his head back, closing his eyes. "A family of my own," he said slowly, tightness filling his chest. He closed his mouth and slid the mug back and forth on the stained table.

"Then, once we can obtain proof that Nathaniel was at the raid and the one to kill Thomas, take her into the comfort of your arms."

"But she doesn't love me," Henry said, his voice cracking.

"After finding out Nathaniel killed Thomas, she certainly will. Besides, do you think I loved Martha when I married her? Very few people marry for love, Henry. You should know that by now. Unless you have some other reasons for being unwed at thirty-five." Henry glared at him, but William tutted and held his hands up defensively. "I know your intended ran off years ago. But that is over and done. And now you have Felicia. Don't hide your silly blush, little brother. Marry her. She's a pretty thing, and she already comes with an accessory you bring to parties to show off. It's probably nice, not needing to wait nearly a whole year before your accessory comes. You would need to wait a month or so."

"You talk of Felicia and her child as objects, and I abject—"

"All women are pieces of a chessboard," William said.

Henry lolled his head toward his brother heaving a sigh and hummed.

"Here's to our plan then!" William said and waved the maid over.

Henry shook his head, tipping his mug over. "Empty..."

"Can be remedied," William said. "When have you turned down a drink?"

"No... can't... I'm..."

The maid refilled Henry's mug and handed William a fresh one.

"Oh, just toast, Henry," William said.

Henry took up the mug with a trembling hand.

"To the plan."

Henry repeated William, muttering the words. He stared down into the mug, watching the golden liquid swirl about, then blinked his tired eyes. Tilting his head back, he drained the mug dry.

"I'm going to bed," he said, stumbling as he stood. "What do you need from me?"

"Just your patience."

Henry waved his hand toward William and picked up his lantern, lit it, and started out the door.

"Mr. Moore," the woman called as he put his hand on the door. "The drinks?"

"Put it on the Colonel's tab," Henry said with a grumble, bringing a hand to his head. He glanced back at William who only grinned toward him. "He'll take care of everything."

Desperate, Henry appeals to William for help winning Felicia's hand

19

F elicia stood beside Nathaniel, attempting to help him form a barrel. It was no easy work, for certain, even though she simply held wooden slats in place for him to slip the first ring onto the barrel.

"Just hold the wood for me," Nathaniel said. "There you go."

"How do you do this?"

"I have two other hands. Those hands are tiny and having lunch currently," Nathaniel said. "You'd be hard pressed to see him. He hides when customers come in."

"Tiny? A child? How old is he?" Felicia said, keeping the barrel steady.

"I'd say about four or so. His father died last year. His grandfather decided an early apprenticeship would be appropriate. I beg to differ."

"Why would you foist a baby on a cooper?"

"Better the cooper than the blacksmith. Oh, he mostly just plays in the shavings and holds things when I need him to. His mother works all day, and his grandfather is just too old to take care of a rambunctious little thing. If I can just tire him out before lunch, I'm usually set for the day."

Nathaniel finally slid the metal ring down over the wooden slats.

However, as he shifted the ring down, the wood shifted, pinching Felicia's hand. She backed up with a cry, pressing her palm to her mouth.

"What happened?" Nathaniel asked, sliding the second ring on. He straightened and pried Felicia's hand away from her mouth. "Hmm. That's a deep splinter."

"Take it out!" Felicia cried, pulling her hand back. She sucked on her palm. "I don't want workman hands!"

"Come on, you little orchid."

Felicia closed her mouth as Nathaniel led her to a barrel to sit on. He hoisted her up to sit on the lid, then examined her hand. With his fingernail, he began scraping at her palm. She cried again.

"It's going to pinch," he said. "But the sooner you let me help you, the sooner it'll be over with."

"It hurts!"

"I know, little orchid."

Felicia closed her mouth, glancing at her nearly non-existent lap. "Thomas used to call me that."

Nathaniel glanced up at Felicia, then back down at her hand. He clasped her hands in his and nodded. "I won't use it then..."

Felicia bowed her head, looking up at Nathaniel through her lashes. "Just because I'm dainty doesn't mean I'm fragile."

Nathaniel hummed and dug his fingernail into the fleshy part of her palm. She winced.

"Tell me," Nathaniel said. "Tell me, when is the baby due to come?"

"Christmas tide," Felicia said, resting her free hand on her belly. "It's not too long now. Maybe a little less than two months."

"And has the pain subsided in your ribs?"

"Not much, to be frank," Felicia said. "But I've just been hoping that the baby has his feet entangled in my ribs and not his head."

"Aye," Nathaniel said, gently rubbing her hand in his. "And yet, you find yourself still unwed, hmm?"

Her shoulders sagged. "It's been well past a week since I declined Henry's offer."

"Hmm. And how did he take it?"

"Not very well," Felicia said, frowning. "He seemed very distressed. But I told him that I couldn't marry a man I just didn't love more than a friend. I gave back the ring, he told me to keep it, and he left it at that. I haven't seen him much since."

"I should have told you of my feelings when you brought me over for that butter churn," he said. "Would have saved us all time and him the trouble of proposing."

"Well, nonetheless, I find myself utterly alone once more. I never had to decline a suitor in my life, and I don't like doing it. I was fortunate the first time. Sometimes, I wish I did love Henry just to make all our lives easier."

"Well, all lives except mine," Nathaniel said, kissing her hand.

"You got it out?"

"A while ago."

Felicia started to slide off the barrel, but Nathaniel kept her there, holding her shoulders. "No... wait."

Nathaniel held his hand out toward her, then went back to his workstation, rummaging through the drawers on his design table. He pulled an envelope out, then came back over to her.

"I wished we had spent more time together, just you and I," he said. He glanced down to her middle. "But your time is short, and I don't want you to worry when it comes."

Felicia furrowed her brows as she watched Nathaniel pull a simple silver ring from the envelope. He knelt in front of her.

"Gabriel Barnet, the blacksmith, is my friend. I could get these made overnight." He smiled lightly and took Felicia's left hand, showing her the ring in the other. "I will keep you safe. I'll take your child in as my own. Just let me prove to you that I can be a good husband. I know it's sudden, but we really didn't have much time to begin with."

Felicia's lips parted, trembling lightly "Natty..."

He reached up, cupping the side of her face in his strong palm gently massaging her cheek with his thumb.

This was what she was waiting for.

He had no great amount of land. He had no real disposable income. He didn't pretend to know what future held. But he had a good deal of self-assurance.

And she wouldn't have it any other way.

His smile wavered, and he continued. "Felicia, I'm asking you to marry me. Let me prove through the years how I love you. I don't want to replace the Major. I don't aim to replace him, but I do aim to keep you protected and loved."

Felicia took in a deep breath, closing her eyes. "You really will love a widow and her child?"

I already love the widow and her child. I'd do anything to keep you safe. I'd die to protect you." Nathaniel's smile returned. "But considering I don't think you want to be a widow again, I'll endeavor not to."

Felicia kicked at his knee, hiding a beaming smile behind her hand.

"We'll get the banns taken care of. Only four more Sundays of waiting. You won't need to worry about your child being fatherless."

"You don't need to explain," Felicia said. "I've made up my mind a while ago. A long while ago."

"Then you will marry me?"

"With the parts of my heart that aren't torn," she said. "But only if you help to mend those torn bits."

Nathaniel took her left hand, sliding the silver band onto her ring finger, then stood. He leaned over her, tilting her head up toward his face. She held her arms out, and he wrapped his arms about her waist while hers twined about his neck. He pressed a kiss to her mouth.

"Mr. Poe? Mr. Poe? I'm back. Mr. Poe?"

Nathaniel broke away from Felicia in a flash, turning to the sound of the small voice. There, the little four-year-old apprentice who had entered the shop stood with greasy hands greasy, his face flushed from the cold weather. Felicia's heart burst as she caught a glimpse him, his sandy blond hair mussed from the wind. He wiped his hands on his pudgy toddler tummy, and she slid off the barrel, waddling over toward him.

"Oh, look at you, you're all greasy and grimy. Your hands are sure to slip if you try to hold the slats in place. Here, let me see them."

The little boy held his hands out, and she crouched as best she could to his level. She took up the apron over her skirt and held it out for him, gently wiping his hands off. "You want to be a cooper? Well, you're going to have to clean your hands to have a good grip on things."

"Mr. Poe don't have clean hands."

"His hands are all dusty from the wood," Felicia said, attempting to stand again. Nathaniel helped her upright. She flashed him a smile. "But you have what seems to be cold sandwich hands. Hmm-mm... Yes, just as I thought."

The little boy gazed up at Nathaniel, a pout twisting up his chubby face, his eyes wide and sorrowful.

"Don't look to me for help," he said. "She's going to be my wife. I'll have to do everything she says too."

The little boy scrunched his face. "Pretty women stinketh," he grumbled, stomping back to the workspace to sit in a tall pile of cedar shavings.

Nathaniel grinned broadly, suppressing a snort. He glanced over to Felicia, who, in all honesty, was just as amused.

"Is he a package deal with you?" she asked, stepping toward Nathaniel, wrapping her arms about his waist. He shrugged a shoulder, quirking a half-grin.

"You come with a package deal," he said, pressing his hand to her belly. "I suppose I do to." He pressed a kiss to her forehead. "But only till I close up for the night."

"Ah, my package deal is year-round, all day, all night."

Nathaniel smirked lightly, shrugging his shoulder again. "And yet, knowing that, I proposed."

"Mr. Poe, what's next?" the little boy called.

"I think a butter churn," Nathaniel called back, still with his arms around Felicia. He threw a glance back over his shoulder at his little apprentice. "Go get me the hammer and an awl."

The boy got up from his pile of shavings and climbed onto the work desk, searching for the tools.

Nathaniel turned back to Felicia. "And with that, I go back to work."

"Would you mind terribly if I watched? The child is pressing, and I really don't want to walk home alone."

Nathaniel frowned. "Are you well?"

Felicia nodded and gave him a smile. "He's been doing pressing my bones on and off for the past week or so. I'm fine. Only tired." She leaned up to give him a kiss. "Don't mind me, Mr. Poe. I'll just wait by the window."

"I won't mind, soon-to-be Mrs. Poe. Just try not to distract my apprentice."

"Of course," she said, wrinkling her nose. She moved to the table by the window and hoisted herself onto it, scooting back to lean against the wall. Nathaniel went back to work, with his little apprentice helping him. She watched as he worked with the child, giving him light commands and orders, mostly just to hold still, or to keep a tight grip on the form. She watched as he picked out little splinters from tiny hands, watched as he let the child hammer down the base to buckets and barrels, watched as he taught the child the tools of the trade.

Felicia ran her hand over her belly, feeling her child kick within her. She closed her eyes and relished a smile, imagining her child working with Nathaniel, playing with him. She imagined Nathaniel helping her raise little Thomas, watching him grow before her eyes with Nathaniel by her side.

She could only have been happier if Thomas still stayed by her side. Nathaniel wouldn't replace Thomas in her heart. But he would satisfy the void Thomas left, and she was grateful. Perhaps *this* gratitude was what Rose meant when she said that the heart was bigger than imagined. Thomas remained in her, hiding within her heartstrings, tugging on them every so often. But Nathaniel had also moved in, and there was room enough for both.

20

Heedless of her dignity, Felicia sprawled on the chair Nathaniel had brought in the back of his workspace while he flipped through his notebook, reading off his ideas for their ceremony. Great with child and greatly uncomfortable, if the most comfortable position was a sprawl, then by heaven, that was what she was going to do.

Nathaniel scratched on the paper, smearing lead on the side of his hand. "We've had fifteen days and can't decide on a single thing for this wedding."

Felicia clicked her tongue. "It took near a year to plan with Thomas. Though we are pressed for time..."

He tapped the blunt cedar pencil against his thigh. "I do stand for tradition. I'm partial to being married at the blacksmiths."

"I didn't know Natives were normally married at smithies, at least... I believed you to be a Native." She paused, screwing her face in confusion. "I lost three friends over you for that."

"My father was Susquehannock. My mother was born to French immigrants and ran away with my father to Mount Terre." He set his notebook on his knee and rubbed Felicia's arm. "Terrible shame about your friends."

"And here you are, not only a rebel, but *French*. What else are you not telling, me, Natty? Are you actually sixty and a crack shot back-woodsman?"

"I'm thirty-three, thank you."

"Nevertheless, despite your being *French*—"

"What's wrong with that?"

Felicia glared at him and he grinned.

Felicia playfully rolled her eyes, then ran her hands over her face. "We need someone to marry us. What is wrong with my parson?"

"I'm not a part of the Church of England. What's wrong with my presbyterian minister?"

"I like music."

"So do I." Nathaniel picked up his notebook and twirled the pencil in his fingers. "Just not in worship."

"You were predestined to say that weren't you?"

Nathaniel let out a blasting laugh. "Probably. But let's do settle. It's mid-November." Nathaniel resumed pouring over his notes. "We could get married in your garden. We'd have the reception back at your manor."

"I don't want to be married to a new man where my former husband is buried."

Nathaniel grimaced. "That is true. What about the courthouse garden?"

"Thomas and Henry took me there when they first courted me."

Nathaniel drew a line in his notebook, heaving a sigh. "How about the green? Out in the field, under the sky. If you even dare to say, 'No, I don't want to be married in the open. You practice your firing drills there, and I just don't want to be near that,' then I will personally call off the wedding and ship you back to Henry."

Felicia rubbed her hand over the swell under her skirts. She lifted her head, twisted her lips, and sniffed in, then focused back on her belly. She cleared her throat. "You're going to have to help me up to ship me back to Henry."

Nathaniel threw the notebook aside and groaned. "Felicia, we don't have time to plan some outlandish grand wedding. We need to get married before your time, and at this rate, the child will be ready for apprenticeship before we're married."

Felicia shot a withering glare at Nathaniel. "I don't like the green. It makes my heart race, and I don't want to cough at the wedding."

Nathaniel took in a deep breath and let it out slowly. "Behind the milliner's shop."

"That's a good one..."

"Or perhaps the blacksmith."

"Answer me first. What has the blacksmith to do with this?" Felicia brought her hands to her sides and hissed, wincing. "Oh, why can't this child stop crunching my bones?" Nathaniel knelt before her and took her face in his hands while they waited for her breathing to return to normal. "Forgive me. Where were we?"

"Tradition," Nathaniel said. "My parents married at one. I suppose yours didn't."

"Of course not. They married at church in England by a parson, surrounded by friends and family. It was proper." She pulled an embarrassed face. "I'm sure for your family, that's proper, but I'm not used to it."

"And when you married Thomas?"

"In the church, just in the colonies." Felicia crossed her arms. "But you're not keen on the church."

"I'm keen on church. I'm just not keen on *that* church."

Felicia sagged into the chair with a sigh. "We're—*I'm* going to need to compromise, you know. We'll never get anywhere if I don't."

Nathaniel clicked his tongue against the roof of his mouth. He sat back on his haunches and took her hands, massaging them in his. "What are you thinking?"

"This is your first—and hopefully only—marriage," Felicia said, pressing her forehead against Nathaniel's. "Where would it make you happiest to get married?"

"If you really want my opinion—"

"I do."

"The blacksmith."

"I can guarantee you that my parson won't like officiating at a smithy," Felicia said softly. She lowered her eyes and drew in a deep breath.

Nathaniel cupped her face in his palm. "I figured as much."

"Natty, I've been married before, so let's compromise. You have your minister and the blacksmith. And I invite anybody I wish."

Nathaniel's face melted into a relieved grin. "Of course." He took her face in his calloused hands, then pressed a kiss to her forehead. "If you're going to compromise all of that for me, I can't begrudge you your guests."

"And we'll have the reception at my house. It'll hold everybody comfortably, though it won't be a big reception. I can't dance much in my state."

"It'd be quite humorous to see you try..."

"You can see me dance after the child comes." Felicia laughed, then braced herself on Nathaniel's shoulders to sit upright on the wooden chair. "I'll lose my balance if I even think about it."

Nathaniel kissed her again and stood, stretching his back. "How long will it take for you to have the reception prepared?"

"Two days."

"I can get the minister by then."

He reached out, and she braced her hands on his forearms as she wobbled to her feet, wincing as the child moved.

"The day this child is born is going to be like Christmas. Sweet, sweet deliverance."

Nathaniel snorted under his breath, then gazed at her through half-lidded eyes, a warm smile on his lips. "I promise, Felicia. I won't let your child go without. I won't let you go without. I vow you'll be safe with me."

Felicia pressed her lips together into a small hopeful smile. She wrapped her arms about him, breathing in his scent of cedar and smoke, then rested her head on his chest.

THE SMALL SERVING boy showed Felicia into Colonel Moore's sitting room, where Henry slumped in a chair, watching the cold wind carry brown dry leaves far down the road. He stood slowly, then offered her the opposite chair.

Quietness overtook her after she offered him a seat at the reception table—she couldn't just leave him out—and now she waited beside him, hands twisting on her disappearing lap. He offered her a glass of the sherry from the table beside him, and she shook her head, holding her hands up. He shrugged and poured himself some instead, tapping long fingers on the glass. She took his hand, and he startled and pulled his fingers free.

"I really would appreciate it if you'd come, dear Henry," she repeated, and he inclined his head toward her, a sleepy haze cast over darkened eyes. "Nathaniel said it would be all right if you did. You have been a good friend for such a long time. And I am incredibly grateful for your gallantry."

"I appreciate it..." Henry rubbed his face and offered her a small conciliatory smile. "I just don't think it a wise idea. There's no ill will. You've made your choice."

"Not even for a dinner? You did tell me once that you weren't one to pass up a free meal, no matter the consequences."

He shrugged again then drained the drink in his hand, set down the glass, and absently picked at the buttons on his weskit. "Maybe there are circumstances when I can. Have a blessed time, my dear. You don't want me hanging around." He leaned over and pressed a kiss to her forehead. "Here." He stood, and the glass tumbled from his lap to the hardwood floor with a clink. Ignoring the unbroken glass, he shuffled to the mantle and stooped low, picking up some papers from the hearth. He tapped them against his thigh in a vain attempt to organize them, then turned back to Felicia, hand and papers outstretched.

"Call it a wedding present," he said, handing her the papers, then flopped back down into his chair with a grunt and covered his face with one hand. He reached over, took up a second glass, and poured himself more sherry.

Felicia looked at the papers, squinting at the scrawled handwriting. "It's sheet music."

"You have the violin, don't you?"

"I don't play..."

"But you sing?"

"Well, sometimes. But there aren't any words..."

Henry drained the second glass of sherry then fingered his buttons again. Felicia gently extricated the glass from his hand, lest it fall to the same fate as its forgotten companion, and leaning over him, set it back on the table. He poured himself another glass, uncovering his face at last.

"It's just some music you may like," he finally said. He cleared his throat, waving a hand lazily about. "Do with it what you will." He tilted his head toward her, his features soft, though lips turned neither up nor down. "My wedding present to you."

Felicia took his hand and pressed a kiss to his knuckle. "Well, I thank you. I'll try to pick out notes when I can." She patted his hand. "Are you sure you don't need something else, Henry? You're so pale anymore; a meal will do you well."

He shook his head, a lock of hair falling in front of his eyes. "No. I'll be quite content here."

So she left, but the walk home seemed longer than usual.

MANY BRIDES PREFER A WARM, sunny day with barely a cloud in the sky, the birds chirping, and the fresh scent of growing leaves on the trees wafting in the breeze. Some brides might have considered a cold, dark, cloudy day, when the wind whistled, rustling skirts and petti-coats, when the scent that blew in with the wind was chowder and not fresh foliage, a foreboding portent.

Not Felicia.

She relished in the stark dichotomy between the day she married Thomas and present. If anyone were to say that things never happened consonantly twice, then this was the sign. And, oh, what a beautiful sign it was to her. Just as her first wedding day was different from her new one, so was Major Thomas Theodore Hawkings different from Nathaniel Burnard Poe.

It was as if her soul soared high above, allowing her to watch the events unfold, as if she were a spectator at her own wedding, both engrossed in the moment and removed from it.

The Presbyterian minister stood behind the anvil in the blacksmith's storefront. Nathaniel and Felicia held hands in front of the anvil, before the eyes of their friends and families.

Felicia's parents stood beside her, and Rose, Selah, Amos, and their little girl watched from afar. Gabriel Barnet and the blacksmith were Nathaniel's only guests, since his parents were long dead, and there hadn't been time to let his surviving family in Mount Terre know.

And Henry? Apparently, despite his earlier assertions, he truly could turn down a meal.

Colonel Moore and his daughter were present for the wedding and reception, both of them happy and pleasant. Victoria brought gifts for the couple and child, and Colonel Moore wore his uniform, with all his medals and tassels showing, as if Felicia were marrying Thomas all over again. It was almost as if life were back to normal. Most of those she loved stood with her in a moment of peace and gaiety once more.

Nathaniel dressed in his best clothes—a deep brown weskit and cream shirt, with worn, inky blue breeches, and a matching tricorn hat. He pulled his hair back away from his face into loose queue, but a few tendrils slipped free to cover his face. He smiled at her as if she were not as large as a house. Felicia's panniers sat awkwardly at her hips, but they tied on, and the deep red taffeta and brown silk dupioni sat elegantly over the panniers and her belly.

She could not forget Thomas in these moments, nor did she want to. She would always remember him, hear the strains of his violin, but she was in catharsis, like a butterfly breaking from its cocoon. Her heart no longer felt torn, but thoroughly stitched together like a warm patchwork quilt.

They exchanged plain silver rings while they pledged to love and protect for eternity or until death did they part. And finally, with a kiss, they were married in the eyes of their Lord and family.

The manor bustled with laughter almost as it had in early June. But while Felicia glowed with true and radiant happiness, she couldn't shake a cold presence among the guests. It didn't frighten or unnerve her, and instead provided a melancholy peace and wistful hope.

Chatting and conversation no longer seemed dull for Felicia, but maybe that was because Mrs. Haddock had decided not to show up for the festivities.

Dinner consisted of rolls and beef, rabbit stew, peas, salads, corn, carrots. Selah had made her delicious honey cake for the groom's cake. A myriad of other sugary treats, from scones to crème puffs flanked the cake.

After dinner, they convened in the parlor, and Felicia made her way to the mantle and took up Thomas's violin and bow. Her fingers clutched the neck of the instrument, and the strings dug into her palm. She held her breath, then wove through the small crowd to rejoin her husband. It was once again time for music in the manor.

Silently, she offered Nathaniel the violin and bow. He stared intently at Felicia, eyes flickering between her face and the instrument.

She thrust the violin toward him, her eyes never breaking away from his. "Natty, I don't have a dowry anymore. But I do still have this... Thomas's violin. If he were here—well, I wouldn't be married to you—but if he could have a say right now, I'm sure he'd hand this to you. Please, Natty. Take this as my wedding gift to you."

"I can't do that, Felicia." His laughter abated and held out his hands in protest, concern over his features. "That's far too meaningful a gift."

"You *can*," she said, still extending the violin. "He'd want you to have it. *I* want you to have it."

Nathaniel took the violin in his hands, turning the instrument over, admiring the mahogany. He plucked the strings over the fingerboard, then set the violin on his shoulder. Felicia clasped her hands together and held her breath as the room grew quiet. Nathaniel ran the bow over the strings a few times, then tuned the instrument and ran the bow again. Finally, closed his eyes and started to play.

The tune was foreign to Felicia's ears, not the refined Vivaldi she was used to, but a piece filled with the fervor of the backwoods. It repeated over and over again, growing more intense till it finally built into a sweeping crescendo of elongated high notes. His brows furrowed as the music swelled from his fingers. He swayed to the music as he played, creaking open his eyes to steal glances Felicia's way.

There will be music at the manner once more

Blue eyes glinted back at her in the candlelight—familiar, but also new and exciting. The color might have been nearly the same, but the sparkle was different. Finally, the violin fell quiet, and the song finished.

Silent tears spilled down Felicia's cheeks onto the red silk, and her lips rose into a smile. She sucked in a happy gasp, clasping her hands together.

"And I suppose then," he said, gripping the neck of the violin in his hand, "you can call that my gift to you."

Felicia beamed. "The most beautiful gift in the world."

As if Nathaniel's music had cued the guests to leave, they started filtering back to their homes. Gabriel and the blacksmith left first, then the minister, and third, Colonel Moore and his daughter.

The Colonel took Felicia's hands. "I'm so glad to see you so joyous again."

"I do hope we may continue correspondence. You were one of Thomas's closest confidants." Felicia glanced at Nathaniel, who nodded to her. "Thank you for coming. I'm sure Thomas is watching, and he would be happy to know that you were here."

Colonel Moore's lips twitched, his smile faltering for a split second. He sniffed, his distinguished nose flaring for but a moment, and he seemed to recover quickly. "Of course." He glanced down his nose over to his daughter. "Come, Victoria."

Victoria tied the satin ribbon to her woolen, hunter green cloak and gave Felicia a hug farewell. "And if you need anybody to help you with the baby after he's born, please let me know."

Felicia grinned. "Thank you. I will remember. I would be more than glad to have your help."

She and Nathaniel watched the Colonel's blood red uniform and Victoria's chocolate taffeta skirts disappear down the road. Victoria flourished her cape for good measure, and the Colonel swatted it back into place just as they left two left Felicia's field of vision.

Only her parents remained in the parlor.

Felicia leaned her head upon Nathaniel's shoulder, smiling softly up at him. "There's one more thing I must do before our new life begins."

Nathaniel quirked a brow.

"Amos! Selah! Rose!" Felicia called, then paused, her voice faltering. "Please come here!"

They could not have been far afield, for the three arrived in moments. "Ma'am?"

"We seem to have a slight problem," Felicia said. "I'm afraid my husband isn't so fond of my keeping servants."

Nathaniel's eyes widened as Felicia threw him under the proverbial carriage. He leaned down and whispered, "Felicia, I thought we'd talk about this later."

She gave him a cheerful smile, then turned back to Selah, Amos, and Rose. All three waited with baited breaths for her to continue, a sudden worry over their faces, but soon, Felicia held her arms out wide for them.

"That being said, I'm going to have to let you go... to your *own* work or whatever you wish to do."

The room grew so quiet, Felicia could hear the snapping of branches under a horse's hoof outside. Her parents stared at her, mouths agape, eyes the size of saucers. Nathaniel stood there, silently. He glanced to Felicia.

"Free, ma'am?" Amos's voice trembled. He looked to Selah, but his wife seemed to be in a state of silent shock.

Felicia bobbed her head, a beam radiating from her face. "Thomas told me a long time ago that it was his intent, should one of us die and remarry, or if the need for servants is gone, whether for financial reasons or just timing, to let you go free. I don't need to see his will to know that. And since I want to live by both my husbands' wishes, I'm going to do what Thomas wanted *and* what Nathaniel wishes me to do. We will talk more on this on the morrow." She clasped her hands together. Her cheeks hurt from her unfading smile. "It is my wedding gift to you."

Selah bit back a sob, covering her face in her hands, but happiness shone through her fingers. Without a word, she ran back toward the kitchen, but Amos stood, frozen in place, glancing between Felicia and the back of the house. Felicia nodded once, and Amos rushed after his wife.

Rose stood there a moment, then gave Felicia a large grin. "Thank you." She started down the hall.

Felicia broke away from Nathaniel's side to catch up with her. "You have been my most treasured confidant." Her smile faded as the reality of Rose leaving set in. "I will miss you, my dear Rose."

Rose pressed her lips shut. "You are a good woman, Felicia Poe. You have grown so much... I wish nothing but the best for you."

"No... this isn't about me." Felicia clasped Rose's weathered hands in hers. "It is about you. Take good care of yourself. Please."

The two women hugged, and when Rose left to her quarters, Felicia returned to Nathaniel, who pressed a kiss to her lips.

"You could have given me notice," he murmured against her mouth.

"I had to do it on my own, my love..."

They stood wrapped in each other's arms, their foreheads pressed together.

"And I think with that, we should leave you, as well," Father said. He stood from the wooden chair by the window and held out his arms to Felicia. She broke away from Nathaniel, and her father wrapped her in a hug. Father extended his hand to Nathaniel who shook it firmly. "Please take care of her."

"I will, sir."

"John."

"Your eyes demand me call you sir," Nathaniel said slowly.

Felicia grinned.

Mother stood as well. She attempted to smile, but tears spilled down her cheeks.

"My sweet Lissie—" Her face scrunched, and she stood on her tips of her toes to kiss Nathaniel on his cheek.

Father wrapped a dark blue woolen cloak around Mother, and they, too, left.

Nathaniel glanced to Felicia, a gentleness over his features. He heaved a relishing but exhausted sigh. "And now?"

"And now we rest." Felicia lowered herself into a velvet chair. "The child's been putting up a fight today."

"Well, I wouldn't have known it," Nathaniel settled next to her and rested his hand atop her belly. He leaned in, pressing a kiss to her cheek. "Come on, Felicia—"

"Lissie." She set her hand atop his. Oh, how sweet it would be to hear the name Lissie once again from the man she loved. "Please."

Nathaniel smiled warmly. "Come on, my Lissie. Let me help you to bed. You need your rest."

Felicia braced her hands on his forearms as Nathaniel helped her up the stairs. He wrapped an arm around her, and she rested her head against his arm.

"Will you play the violin often?" she whispered.

"Whenever I'm not working."

A contented smile blossomed on Felicia's face. After all, she loved it when her husband played the violin.

21

The air grew colder nearing the end of November, the sky a constant gray, and as late fall and early winter set in, town life ebbed. Bare branches scraped against the side of the house and the windows, and Nathaniel slipped from bed, feet hitting the woolen rug on the floor. He rocked back and forth on his feet and his muscles relaxed as there was no cold for him to brace himself against. After Selah and Amos left two nights before, the house had become increasingly silent. But it wasn't an empty silence as much as it was a patient one.

"Do you have to leave today?" Felicia said, her voice cracking with early morning grogginess. "It's too cold to soak barrels."

"Warp wood." Nathaniel leaned back over the bed and pressed a kiss to Felicia's head, then plodded to the wardrobe for his breeches. "I do have to go to the workshop today, yes," Nathaniel said, buttoning his breeches. "I don't want to miss an order. But I will be back soon enough." He glanced back to her as he slipped his weskit over his shirt. She shuddered as she pushed herself up in the bed, bringing the blanket up to her chest. "Felicia?"

She whimpered. Nathaniel moved to her side and smoothed her

hair away from her face. He ran the back of his hand over her forehead, then trailed his fingers along her jaw. "What is it?"

"He's just so large now." Felicia exhaled through her nose. "There's no room for him anymore so he constantly presses against my ribs and hips.

Nathaniel frowned and rested a hand on her large belly. "It is not an early delivery?"

"No. I'm not feeling any grinding pains. I ..." Felicia clenched her fists and squeezed her eyes shut. "I think he's quite content to stay warm inside me."

Nathaniel combed fingers through her hair at her temples. "How much pain are you in?"

"I think it is just when he stretches, but the pain lingers." She hid her face under the blanket. "It hurts, Natty."

Nathaniel frowned. "Do you think you might have the child today?"

The blanket rustled, and Felicia muttered, "No."

He stood, shrugged on his overcoat, and picked up his hat. "Felicia, what do you want me to do? Do you want me to fetch the midwife?"

"No, I am not laboring." Felicia waved an arm outside the blanket, searching blindly for Nathaniel. He took her hand, pressing kisses to her fingertips. "I don't want to be an imposition, but could you see if Rose is still here. Perhaps she will sit with me while you are at work."

"Of course." Nathaniel squeezed Felicia's hand then lowered the blanket, revealing her red face. "I'm sure she wouldn't leave without a proper farewell, my love. I'll bring her to you. I think it's best you stay in bed. You're resting till the child comes."

"But visitors—"

"Are not as important as your health."

"And what about you?"

"I'll go into town for a moment, just to check the shop, but come right back to make sure you're all right. Does that suit you?"

"More than I can ask," Felicia said, her voice cracking. "I'll probably be asleep by the time you get back."

"I hope you are. You tossed and turned all last night." He pressed a kiss to her head. "Do get some rest, Lissie."

~

"MYLES, WHAT ARE YOU DOING HERE?" Nathaniel asked, as he walked up the street to the storefront.

The four-year-old wiped his nose on his sleeve and glanced up at him, blinking his large brown eyes. "Work."

"Do you want to unlock the door?" Nathaniel asked, taking the ring of keys from his coat pocket.

Myles scrambled to his feet and stretched for the door handle. His fingers barely grazed the doorknob. "I've got it, Mr. Poe."

"I know you do. You're a fine apprentice."

Myles stood on his toes, then grasped the doorknob and turned the handle. "I've gotten it!"

Nathaniel pushed the door open Myles scampered around him and threw himself into a pile of shavings in the back.

"We aren't working long today," Nathaniel said, grabbing up his notebooks on his desk. He slid them into an inside pocket and turned to Myles. "You need to go home."

Myles peeked up from the pile, jutting out his bottom lip. "But I don't want to stay home. I want to help you work. Grandfather will make me hide away all day till Momma comes home."

The boy jumped to his feet and dragged a large metal hoop over to Nathaniel, turning up his chubby face and his eyes begging eyes for the chance to stay. "I can do this. You teach good. Please?"

Nathaniel smiled gently and crouched low next to the boy. "You are such a great help, Myles. But I'm only here to grab my note-book." Nathaniel took the hoop away from his apprentice's grubby hands.

"I could watch the store."

Nathaniel tapped his chin. "What if you get lonely?"

Myles sat down in the shavings again, crossing his arms. "I can take care of myself."

Nathaniel rolled the hoop back with the others along the back wall, then moved back over to the boy. "Well, I'm afraid you're going to have the leave today, one way or another."

Myles glared up at him, then went back to sulking.

Just as Nathaniel bent down to scoop Myles up under his arm, the bell atop the front door jangled.

"See, this is why you need me!" Myles scurried to the customer, who kept his back toward Nathaniel, browsing through the pre-made barrels and buckets along the wall. "Welcome to Mr. Poe's Cooper Store. I can help you."

The patron glanced down over his shoulder at the boy. "I'm just looking," he murmured and Myles pouted.

Nathaniel stepped up and ushered Myles back to the pile of wood shavings. "You must forgive me. I was just closing. Family business."

The patron only hummed a response. His dark green overcoat rustled as he held it closer in the cold November air.

Nathaniel waited a moment, as the man ran his hand over the shelves. "My wife is ill. I need to get home to her."

The man's shoulders stiffened, but he kept perusing through each of the shelves, inspecting each bucket and churn and barrel. "If I ask for a custom order, how long would it take?"

"Depends on the order," Nathaniel said. He scooped Myles up, carrying him like a sack of flour under his arm. The boy yelped in protest, but Nathaniel kept a tight grip on him to keep him from wriggling. "If you come back tomorrow, I'll go over that with you. I shouldn't be out much longer with the state my wife is in."

The patron finally turned around. He folded his arms across his chest, leaning to one side.

Nathaniel stiffened, holding his chin up. "Henry Moore."

Henry only raised his brows.

"If you know what you'd like to order, I can figure—"

"Where were you exactly around the tenth of June?" Henry asked.

"A rather unusual order." Nathaniel wrinkled his nose as he tried to remember a half a year earlier. He pointed at the squirming boy. "I must have been here with this thing."

"A toddler is your only alibi?" Henry tilted his head to get a better look at the child, who went limp under Nathaniel's arm. "He's a baby."

Myles craned his neck to see just who had insulted him. "I'm not a baby! I'm four!"

"My apologies." Henry said with a bow.

"Why the devil would I need an alibi?" Nathaniel asked. "I have to get home right now."

"So you've said." Henry shifted his weight to his other foot. "I'm afraid this is of upmost importance to Felicia's wellbeing."

Nathaniel tipped his hat toward Henry then started toward the door. He motioned for Henry to precede him. The Colonel's brother huffed, but came out of the shop, holding his coat tighter. Nathaniel locked up the store with Myles still hanging under his arm.

"Who is that anyway?" Henry asked.

"My apprentice," Nathaniel said, setting Myles down on the step, and the boy wrapped himself around Nathaniel's leg. Nathaniel reached down and ruffled the boy's hair, then staggered down the steps to the sidewalk, with the four-year-old sitting on his foot.

Henry stepped in front of him. "Would the boy remember if you were in town?"

"Of course not." Nathaniel pulled his notebook from his pocket and flipped through it, then held it out to Henry. "Written here. Took an order for Dr. Merriman. Why do you need to know?"

Henry scowled. "I'm doing Felicia a favor."

"You'd be doing her a better favor by letting me get home." Nathaniel glanced down at the child on his leg. "Oh, get up, Myles. You can come home with me till your mother gets back from work."

The boy extricated himself from Nathaniel's leg and reached up to take his hand. Peering back up at Henry, Myles stuck out his tongue, and when Henry mimicked him, he let out a squeak and scrambled around Nathaniel.

Nathaniel set him on his hip and shot a withering glare toward the merchant. "Mr. Moore, would you kindly act your age?"

A sheepish grimace flickered across Henry's face before he replaced it with a haughty smirk. He shrugged.

Making a noise of disgust, Nathaniel turned his back on Henry and took Myles back home to check on Felicia.

∽

HENRY'S FACE smirk melted as he watched Nathaniel Poe walk down the road toward the Hawkings manor. He bowed his head and uncrossed his arms and gripped his left hand, rubbing at his ring finger with his thumb. A small frown pulled at his lips.

A hand landed on his shoulder, and Henry spun around.

William nodded once. "I wondered where you were. I checked the tavern, but for once, you weren't there."

"He has an alibi for the raid," Henry said. "Showed me in his book."

"Facts and figures are easily made up. He was lying through his rebel teeth." William held up a long rifle with a bayonet attached.

Henry took it in his hands. "What is it?"

William pointed to the side of the brown wooden stock. "See for yourself."

Henry stared at the rifle in his hands, measuring the weight, turning it this way and that. He squinted at the gilded letters engraved in the wood: Major Thomas Theodore Hawkings. He tightened his jaw, a steeliness forming in his eyes.

"It's Thomas's rifle," William said. "Found amongst Nathaniel's possessions. Gone missing in the raid. That son-of-a-bitch has been practicing his shot with the dead Major's weapon. And who would take a murdered man's gun, except the one who killed him?"

Henry's eyes narrowed his eyes, and disgust clouded his features as he regarded brother. "When did you find this?" he asked, his voice hushed and low.

William tilted his chin up and a satisfied smirk formed on his face. "I had my men search his store in the night. Now we know that bastard's to blame for Thomas's death. We can have him hanged."

Henry's lips twitched as he nodded silently. Uneasiness twisted in his stomach, and he cleared his throat and smoothed down his weskit. "When are you going to make your move?"

"I'm about to take some men with me now to arrest him."

"No!"

William crossed his arms, quirking a brow. "Why not?"

Henry glanced back over his shoulder, then to the rifle in his hands. He handed the weapon back to William and shoved his hands into his coat pockets. "Nathaniel's apprentice is at his house, and he's only a toddler. You don't want to frighten the boy."

William shrugged with an air of nonchalance. "It'll teach the boy, won't it?"

"I suppose, but William, do have some humanity. He's just a toddler. He won't understand. And above that, Felicia is ill today. Do it tomorrow if you must."

"I must," William said, glaring toward Henry. "But I do want Felicia to see her husband being carted away if only to show her she decided wrongly. I'll go in the morning. Perhaps the weather won't be so miserable."

They started back up the road, but William paused, grabbing Henry's arm. "You'll be there, won't you?"

Henry cocked his head to the side, knitting his brows together. "Why should I?"

"It was your idea to find blame in him." William pushed Henry's face to the side with his knuckle. "We'd never have found the Major's rifle had you not suggested it."

Henry pressed his mouth closed, the unease in his stomach winding its way into his chest, then pounding in his head. He rolled his shoulders and crossed his arms. "I did?"

"Or were you too drunk to remember?" William reached out with the rifle, the bayonet just pricking at Henry's middle, loosening a button from his weskit. Henry stepped back from the blade's edge.

"I... I'm sure I must have helped with the idea," he muttered under his breath. "Did you want me to be there?"

"She'd be able to fall into your arms much easier if you're there to catch her."

Henry shifted and glanced aside. "I'll be there."

William nodded curtly. "I'll see you at seven tomorrow."

22

A cock crowed, waking Felicia before Nathaniel. She slowly rolled onto her side, grasping at the sheets on the bed to help turn herself over. The child stretched within her, and she groaned at the idea of another day of kicking and prodding, then sighed and rested her hand on her side. The babe had ceased jamming his little feet into her bones and Felicia was relieved with thought that the worst of it was over.

Nathaniel still slept, despite the cock growing ever louder. She studied him in the dim bedroom, watching him breathe deeply and how his eyelashes fluttered against his tan cheeks as he dreamed. The man had spent all yesterday chasing after and entertaining a four-year-old, while intermittently running up and down the stairs to check on her. He had been so patient. He had passed a hand over her forehead or helped her turn to her other side. Then, Myles's tiny voice would call out, and Nathaniel, with neither hesitation nor an annoyed huff would be back downstairs, chasing after his apprentice.

What did she do to deserve such a wonderful creature as Nathaniel Poe? He was kind and gentle, yet fiercely strong, ready to jump in to protect his beliefs or his wife at a moment's notice.

How could she show the man her love? She couldn't fathom which words to use to describe the intense burning in her chest. The snake that used to coil around her stomach, the fear and trepidation that had paralyzed her before had blossomed into a bright and burning fire she thought she'd never feel again.

He was no replacement flame. And it was the oddest sensation, knowing that she still loved Thomas, but carried the intense devotion for Nathaniel as well.

She leaned over, resting her chin on his shoulder, and pressing a kiss to his jaw. "Natty?"

He moaned.

"Natty, it's time to—"

Nathaniel started with a gasp and turned over onto his back so quickly he caught himself in his hair. "Is it your time?"

Felicia pursed her lips but smiled gently. "No, it's time to get up. I think Myles will be wondering where you are if you don't show up for work again."

"Oh, that child," Nathaniel said, a somnolent grin on his lips.

"What do you think, copying me?"

"I believe it is called humor, my love." Nathaniel stretched his arms, then scooped Felicia down against his chest, pressing a kiss to her cheek. "I'll get there after breakfast."

"You open your store later now that you're married to me," Felicia said. "Didn't you eat breakfast before?"

"Not so much, in truth—" Nathaniel yawned. "Are you feeling well today?"

She hummed, tilting her head toward him. "He's moving about. Uncomfortable, but not painful."

"I suppose that's good." He kissed her cheek again. "I'll be able to work without worrying for you."

Felicia hid her face in his chest. "You worry for me?" she asked, voice muffled by his shirt.

"Of course, I do." He ran his hand along her back. "You're my wife and are having a rough time with the child. I promised I'd keep you safe."

Felicia hummed a sigh, then took one of his hands and pressed it against her side. He glanced down at his hand, and the child nudged against his palm. He pressed a kiss to the top of her head, then leaned back against the backboard, keeping his hand on her middle.

In the distance, the steady beating of drums broke the morning quietude. The uncanny, repetitive, rolling beat echoed down the road, coming closer to the house.

Nathaniel and Felicia craned their necks toward the window. The drums grew louder with each passing second. Nathaniel shimmied himself out from under Felicia, slid out of bed, and moved to the window. He opened the curtains and peered out of the shutters, then froze, the muscles in his shoulders and back tightening.

"What is it?" Felicia asked.

"A group of redcoats."

"My soldiers?" she asked, furrowing her brows.

"Hmm."

Felicia scooted to the edge of the bed and hoisted herself up. She waddled over to the window, standing just behind Nathaniel. She cocked her head to one side, watching as the group of twelve British soldiers, led by an officer on horseback with two rifles in his hands, made their way up to her property. They were followed by a civilian in a green familiar overcoat.

"That looks like the Colonel on horseback," Felicia said.

"Hmm."

Nathaniel stayed still and firm while Felicia tried to pry him away from the window.

"Here, help me get dressed so I can see what he wants." Felicia shuffled over to her wardrobe, pulling out a yellow floral dress. Without a word, Nathaniel closed the shutters again, and help Felicia with the necessary layers. He set the mobcap on her head, then slipped into his own clothes, before helping her down the stairs. Felicia grabbed up her shawl from the coat tree in the foyer and wrapped it around her shoulders.

Nathaniel stepped out first, crossing his arms as he surveyed the uniformed men marching up to the front gate. He turned back to Felicia and held out his hand for her to join him.

She stepped out next to him, wrapping and arm about his waist.

Cold air dried her throat as soon as she breathed in, and she coughed. The soldiers advanced forward to the front porch.

Colonel Moore swung himself down from his horse, his face grim and taut, haughty concern in his eye. "Felicia, I have news for you."

Felicia scanned the small regiment before her. Through them, she could just about see Henry's figure in the back. She bit at her bottom lip and held her arms close. "The sun has only just risen. What sort of news requires twelve officers?"

"We found this recently, and I think you should have it back." Colonel Moore held out one of the rifles he carried.

She looked to Nathaniel. He shrugged, the pressed a kiss to her temple.

"Take whatever he has, my love," he said, resting a hand on her back. "You know the Colonel better than I."

Slowly, she stepped toward Moore and took the weapon. "You came here to give me a gun?"

"Read it, Felicia."

Felicia studied the stock, narrowing her eyes to read the inscription. Her head snapped back up, her eyes growing wide as she clasped the cold metal and wood over her heart.

"Where did you find this?" she asked, breathless.

Nathaniel stepped closer to her. Her breath caught in her throat, as she showed him the weapon. He took it and turned it over in his hands.

"'Major Thomas Theodore Hawkings'," he read aloud. He addressed the Colonel as well, narrowing his steely blue eyes. "Colonel Moore, what have you got the late Major's rifle and bayonet for?"

"Why don't you tell me, Master Cooper?" the Colonel demanded. "How did I find it?"

"I don't know," Nathaniel said, voice low. He squared his shoulders, planting his feet firmly on the ground. "You're the one who came over here with it."

Colonel Moore's eyes narrowed, and he lifted his hat ever so slightly from his head, smoothing back his long, blond hair. He reached out, grasping at Felicia's arm.

"We found it in the back of his store," he said in a near growl.

She yanked her arm from his grasp, spinning to gape at Nathaniel. "My husband's rifle was in your store?" she asked.

"I've never seen this rifle before," Nathaniel said, softly, handing the rifle back to her and taking her face in his hands. "And I'd think I'd remember seeing a weapon as fine as this. Lissie, wouldn't I tell you if I'd found Thomas's rifle?"

The Colonel broke into the conversation, a snarl on his thin lips. "Not if you were at the raid where he was killed."

Nathaniel bared his teeth at Colonel Moore. "Don't you dare accuse me of anything. I didn't know anything about the raid or that you were called away."

The Colonel glared at Nathaniel from over his long nose, then laughed under his breath. "You and your Yankees followed us when we left that Friday morning in June, and on the tenth, you fell on us from the trees, like animals. You figured out we were leaving after your delivery for the party."

"No," Nathaniel snapped. "I showed your brother my records. We practiced on the green, then I worked the rest of the day. Neither my men nor I knew you moved out. I knew Major Hawkings had some party the day before, but that's the extent of my knowledge. I'll be more than happy to show you my ledgers to prove it."

Felicia, caught in a dizzying confusion, turned from Colonel Moore to her husband.

Moore bared his teeth. "What was the Major's rifle doing in the back of your store, Nathaniel Poe?"

Her husband crossed his arms. "You tell me, William Moore."

"You want to know? Fine." The Colonel turned to Felicia, twisted sympathy etched into his sharp features. "My dear, he killed your husband. He killed him at the raid and stole his rifle."

"No—" Felicia gasped, bringing her hand to her belly. "He wouldn't have done that. He told me he would avenge Thomas."

"He *killed* Thomas, Felicia. There's no two ways about it. He killed him and used the dead man's rifle when he practiced on the green to kill more of us, just to propel his quixotical ideals of freedom. He'd kill to have freedom, and now he's with you, worming his way in, using you like a pawn on a chessboard."

Nathaniel set his jaw and glared at the Colonel. "I'd die before I hurt the woman I married."

"Oh, you will, Nathaniel Poe. You'll be hanged for this." The Colonel lunged forward and grabbed at his arm. Nathaniel reeled back but pushed Felicia toward the relative safety of the door, then sprung forward, striking Moore across his face. The Colonel stood rock solid, then ran the back of his hand along his jaw and mouth. Glancing down, he examined his hand and rubbed the speck of blood from his knuckle, then motioned to two officers in the front. The officers surged forward, captured Nathaniel's arms, and dragged him down the steps.

Felicia rushed towards Moore. "Let him go! He didn't do it! I know he wouldn't have! He couldn't have!"

Officer Westall held her back with a firm grip. "He has to be tried, Mrs. Hawkings—Mrs. Poe. Tried and found guilty." A note of tenderness crept into his voice, so much like his tone when they had arrived with Thomas's body. Felicia stared expectantly into Westall's face. He loosened his grip, ever so slightly. "Don't you care about Thomas? Don't you care to bring his murderer to justice? I'm so sorry Felicia. It must be done. Colonel Moore found his musket in the shop. We must try him."

"I care about who really killed him! You have the wrong man! Nathaniel wasn't there! I can go get Myles. I'll go find Myles. Just let him go!" Felicia's voice cracked.

"You think the word of a toddler apprentice will carry weight in court? Come now, Felicia, be reasonable," Moore said.

Nathaniel stood still while an officer bound his arms.

"Nathaniel, fight back! Do something!"

"What is there to be done?" He craned his neck back at her. "Nothing we say would convince them otherwise."

"Take him to jail, and guard him well." The Colonel swung himself back on his horse and peered down his nose at Felicia. "I'm disappointed in you, Lissie. You should have known never to entangle yourself with a rebel."

He kicked his heels into the horse's flanks and started back up the road, and his men started to lead Nathaniel away.

"Natty!" Felicia struggled down the steps. "Natty, say something! Do something!"

"Don't worry for me." He twisted around to see her. "It'll be sorted out in the end."

An officer shoved him forward.

Felicia watched helplessly as her soldiers—her beautiful, red-coated soldiers—took her husband away, leaving her alone in the yard... Alone, except for Henry.

Her eyes brimming with tears and her shoulders shaking, she pled, "Henry, you know Nathaniel wouldn't have killed Thomas, don't you?"

Henry folded his arms over his brocade weskit. "They found Thomas's rifle in Nathaniel's store, Felicia."

"Henry!" She reached out her palms to him. "You must help me!"

Henry held his arms out for her, eyes pleading for her to come to him. Her eyes widened as she looked him up and down, aghast at his outstretched arms. Her stomach flipped over, and she shook her head, backing away.

"Not like that," she stammered, then rushed into the manor, glancing back at him once inside the doors.

As Henry folded his arm back over his chest, discontent washed over his face. He frowned, his sadness turning to anger, and he shook his head.

Tears brimmed in her eyes as she disappeared into her house, Henry's voice in her ears.

"Damn you, William," he said with a growl. "And damn me, too."

❦ 23 ❦

As soon as Henry had disappeared up the road to town, Felicia stumbled out of her house again. She picked up her skirts in one hand, grasping the rifle in the other, while spying eyes from the neighboring houses watched her try to run, though the child seemed to resent every thundering step she took. Fear snaked around her stomach, working its way up to her chest and throat. Cold November morning air rushed over her face, bringing stinging tears to her eyes.

She reached her parents' home—a large white house with red gables, only a stone's throw from the militia green—threw open the gate to the front yard, staggered up the path to the porch, and banged on the front door.

"*Let me in! Help! Oh, God have mercy!*"

A young black man in a white powdered wig answered her knock. "Mrs. Poe?" he asked, his brows knitted in confusion. "What are you here for? Are you well?"

"Oh, God in Heaven, help me!" She gasped for air, wrapped her free arm around her middle, and grimaced.

He bowed quickly and brought her into the parlor off the door, where he lowered her onto a settee. "What can I get you?"

"My parents," she rasped. The rifle dug into her chest as she bent forward and pressed her hands into her hips, gritting her teeth, squinting against the pain.

"Right away, ma'am." He ran from the room, calling out, "Master Winthrop, come to the parlor! Mrs. Poe needs you and your wife."

Felicia felt as if she were floating out of the parlor, watching everything happen around her from outside of herself. She barely perceived the chair beneath her and could only just hear the servant's frantic voice, which brought bring her parents scrambling down from the second floor, still in their night clothes. "Lissie!" Mother threw herself onto the chair beside the settee and leaned over, reaching out to cup her gray face in her palms. "Lissie! My love! What's happened to bring you to such a state as this?"

"They took him, Mother!" Felicia's voice scraped from her throat, and she coughed. "They took him, and they're going to hang him! William Moore took him."

"Colonel Moore is going to hang whom?"

A sob racked her chest, and she covered her face as she wailed. "Natty! He took my Natty!"

Father knelt in front of Felicia, taking her shaking hands in his. "Good G-d! Calm yourself, my love. Why in the devil's name would William Moore take Nathaniel away?"

Felicia dropped the rifle from her arms to the floor next to her father, and the bayonet scraped the wooden boards. Father picked it up and studied the engraving. "Thomas's gun. But the Colonel said it was stolen."

"I know he did!" A coughing fit shook her, and Felicia tugged her hands from her father's and brought them to her burning, dry throat.

Mother's forehead wrinkled as she gently lowered Felicia's hands. "Where did they find the rifle, Lissie?"

Felicia fidgeted, wriggling away from her parents. "The shop. The back of the Natty's shop." She pressed her hand to her belly. "I don't understand how. I've been there so many times and have never seen it!"

A frown creased her Father's face, and he finished for her. "And I suppose he said the only way Nathaniel could have obtained it is if he killed Thomas himself at the raid."

The words stung, and Felicia turned very pale. Just hearing "Nathaniel killed Thomas," no matter how untrue it was, turned her stomach over and up into her chest.

Father shook his head, setting the rifle aside, then sat next to her on the edge of the settee.

"But he couldn't have done it," Felicia rasped in a ragged breath, bracing one hand on the arm of the settee and her other on her father's knee. "He was here, the whole time! And he has an apprentice, though he's only a little child, and Myles won't remember dates that long ago. And goodness knows, they won't listen to a child's witness—Colonel Moore would be sure to throw out anything he'd say." She moaned. "Just when I thought I could put Thomas's death behind me! Oh, I know he didn't do it! I know it!"

"First of all," Mother said, rubbing her hands along Felicia's arms, "you're going to take a deep breath and calm down before you work yourself into having the child early. Second, you don't need to tell us he wouldn't have done it. The man isn't a liar."

"And I'm sure if we tried, we could find people in town who could vouch for him," Father said. "If you say his apprentice worked with him that day, then certainly someone must have stopped by the store."

Felicia shook her head and hid her face in her hands. "Oh, it won't matter." She cleared her throat and took in a deep breath. "Colonel Moore will be sure to see Natty hanged before we could find any more witnesses."

"Why are you so sure about that?" Father asked, tapping his finger against his chin. "What makes you think he will breech law to hang Nathaniel early?"

"He hates rebels and would jump at the chance to hang one—we all know this. And now that they found the rifle in Natty's shop, there's no way that a jury, even those of rebels, would be able to find him not guilty. He'd be hanged for murder."

"And sedition," Mother added, and Father glared at her.

"We have to do something! I can't be a widow again!"

"Let me think a moment." Father steepled his hands under his chin and closed his eyes.

Felicia watched her father, her eyes burning and brimming with fresh tears. She pressed her mouth closed, wriggling her hands in her mother's grasp till her mother's wedding ring wore at her skin.

"He's able to have a lawyer, you know," Father finally said.

Felicia regarded him in complete exhaustion. "Daddy, we can't afford that till the estate closes."

Mother frowned. "It's been nearly half a year since Thomas died. That should be yours now."

"It must be tied up. I wrote to them five times since, explaining my situation, and they haven't responded. Thomas wouldn't have chosen a poor firm. It must be because of the insurrection."

Father nodded slowly, tapping his fingers together, and narrowed his eyes. "Yes... I see. But you know, there are some lawyers who work pro bono. They'll represent a client if they know he's in the right, and if they tend to be on the same ideological side. Say, for instance, a rebel lawyer helping a rebel."

Felicia paused a moment, running her hands over her belly, staring out the window. She glanced between her father and mother. "John Adams! He helped our soldiers during the massacre, and now he's in Philadelphia, representing the notions of freedom that Nathaniel believes."

"My dear, I think your sights are too high," Mother said. "Aim a little lower."

"You're asking a woman who has been married to a British soldier for four years and has only been in British society for her whole life up until the last few months to think of somebody who would represent a rebel?" Felicia demanded. "If you ask me to remember any rebel who is a lawyer other than John Adams, you're going to be in for a sorry surprise."

Father bowed his head and frowned, holding his hand up for silence and muttering, "What to do, what to do?"

"What to do, indeed," Felicia said, exasperated. "Oh, if only we could just escape!"

Her father's head suddenly snapped up. "That's it."

"What do you mean 'that's it'?"

But Father's face broke into a great toothy grin.

"John, I don't like that grin." Mother leaned away from him. "I never have."

"What if," he said, "he didn't make it to court."

Felicia and her mother exchanged glances. "How?"

∼

THE SOLDIERS HAD SHOVED Nathaniel into a dark damp cell with only one small window where the roof and wall connected. Only one cot—nothing but a low wooden table—had been placed by the wall. Straw lay scattered on the floor, and a ratty, blue cotton cloth had been thrown on the cot for a blanket. Nathaniel stretched out on the cot, idly tossing a tin cup up in one hand, the other arm behind his head as a pillow.

The walls were cold and damp, and a rat slept soundly under a pile of straw in the corner. Nathaniel was the only man imprisoned in the jail.

A young officer with hair as red as his coat strode up to Nathaniel's cell and rattled his ring of keys on the bars.

Nathaniel tipped his neck back to see the officer upside down. "Hmm?"

"Colonel Moore has set your trial for the morning."

Nathaniel rested his head on his arm and heaved a sigh.

The officer rattled his keys again. "But you do have a visitor. The Colonel is gracious enough to let you see one person before your trial."

Nathaniel sat up, swinging his long legs over the edge of the cot, and rested his elbows on his knees. Who would be visiting him? Surely, not his wife. He prayed it wasn't his wife. Felicia needed to stay home, away from all this foul air.

The officer waved to the side, motioning for the visitor to come forward. "You don't have long."

He stepped aside, letting the visitor come forward.

"Felicia?" Nathaniel rose from the cot, stepping toward the bars and frowned. "What are you doing here? Go home and rest."

Felicia shook her head, a faltering smile on her face, and reached through to grab his hands. "You think you're going to be rid of me so easily?"

Nathaniel clicked his tongue but took her hands through the bars. "Lissie... I'm going to be tried tomorrow. Please don't come to the court. I don't want you getting worked up. You shouldn't even be here now."

She leaned her forehead against the cold metal bars. Her face softened, and she let out a long breath. "No, Natty. I'd be worked up at home, wondering if they are treating you right."

"The Colonel put me here. I highly doubt he would treat a rebel well, but I'm faring well enough now." He kissed her forehead. "Don't cry, my dearest. How were we to know any of this would happen?"

Felicia squeezed his hands tighter and hid her face from him. "I'm scared, Natty."

Nathaniel let go of one of her hands and reached through the bars to gently cup her cheek, massaging his thumb into her skin. "Don't be. I told you I'd protect you. I won't let you become a widow again. I promise. I just need to figure out how."

Felicia leaned into his hand and whispered, "I know how."

"What?" Nathaniel frowned. He leaned forward and whispered back, "How?"

Felicia pressed a kiss into his palm, muffling her words from the spying ears of the officer. "My father has volunteered to do the night watch, having decided that you are no longer an acceptable husband for his daughter." She kissed his palm after every few words. "Then, Mother and I will have a horse and cart waiting behind the milliner's. Around the witching hour, I'll come in, while my father guards your cell. No one will suspect a woman so heavily laden with child to break her husband out of jail."

She kissed his palm again and gazed up at him. Her eyes glinted with a mischievousness he had never seen before, and the look set his soul on fire. Mouth slightly open, he watched her silently, and shook his head. He stepped back and paced a few steps, pressing his fingers to his temples. He turned back to her, pressing as close to the door as he could. "What is the cart for?"

"We're leaving. Going far away from here." Felicia's lips started to tremble. "We have to move, or Colonel Moore will kill you for no reason."

Nathaniel frowned. His wife would leave everything? For what? Him? Her first love was here, and her family... her friends. He couldn't dream of causing the woman anymore pain. But she stood before him, determination on her face. Still, he hoped there was another way, for her sake. He brushed a lock of hair behind her ear. "But your manor— Thomas is in the garden."

Felicia's delicate face scrunched. "I'm sure he'd understand." Her voice wavered, and she cleared her throat. "We don't have a choice if we want to be together."

Nathaniel closed his eyes. "Aye." He took a deep breath, letting it out slowly before saying, full voiced, "Then you need to do something for me."

"Anything." She took his face in her hands, gazing up at him through half-lidded eyes.

"Tell Gabriel Barnet what is to become of me," he said. "And tell him to look after what I have been doing." Then, he bent down and pressed kisses to her mouth, the rusty iron bars marring the taste of almonds on her lips. He whispered after every kiss. "Tell him to train the men. He'll know what to do. I can't leave this town knowing that those boys are without a leader. I'll need my store to be closed up. Myles needs to be apprenticed to Gabriel. He'd take him on."

"Of course." Felicia squeezed her eyes shut and pulled away from him with a gasp, pressed a hand to her belly, and let out a breath. "Oh, this child."

Nathaniel reached between the bars, placed his hand over hers, and offered her a smile. "My dear Lissie. It'll work out in the end."

Felicia flinched.

"Are you well?" Nathaniel asked, cocking his head to one side. He pressed his hand to her belly, frowning. "You're wincing."

She offered him a faint smile. "It's just some movement I'm unaccustomed to."

Nathaniel brought both hands up to cup her face. She stood there, face caught between his hands, blinking at him. He pressed another kiss to her cheek. "Now go home and get some rest. And pray, Lissie. Pray with everything you've got."

Felicia leaned in close to the bars, trying to worm her arms through the arm and around Nathaniel, then she picked up her skirts as she walked away from him, back toward the front office. The doors closed behind her. He was left alone with the sleeping rat once more. If he were a simple man, he would have been raring and fighting to break free. But his chest constricted, and a pounding ache formed in his skull. Nathaniel pressed his lips together and said a silent prayer. This plan that the Winthrops and his Felicia concocted would be his saving grace or his death, and that was enough to strike fear into his heart.

He had vowed to his wife to avenge Thomas Hawkings, and he'd brave any storm to keep that promise.

Felicia conspires with Nathaniel

THE CHARADE HAD BEGUN.

Father stood in front of Colonel Moore's desk, shouting about his distaste for Nathaniel. The Colonel kept still, a small smirk etched on his lips, and behind him, Henry read silently on a wooden chair.

"There you are, Lissie," her mother said, rising from a chair near the door. "You stayed far too long with that rebel. Let's take you home, and we can think of what to do with this mess later."

Felicia gave a solemn nod. "Of course. I just felt that it my duty to see him."

"You are a good wife. But he a terrible husband. Come, John. Stop your shouting and raving."

Father glanced back over his shoulder. "I always said that Felicia should have married Henry. Perhaps then it's not too late."

At that, Henry snapped his book shut, tuning into the conversation at hand. "I don—"

The Colonel flipped his walking cane up behind him, jabbing Henry's stomach. Henry pressed his mouth closed.

"I would like to think, once that miserable son-of-a-bitch is hanged, that perhaps Felicia would reconsider Henry's proposal," Colonel Moore said, glancing back over his shoulder at his brother, his eyes narrowed.

"I suppose we shall have to see," Felicia said. Henry caught her eyes and immediately turned away. "I really should be getting home. This child is lying heavily in me."

Colonel Moore gave her a simper, but then reached out. "Spare yourself the trouble of coming tomorrow for the trial. Goodness knows you don't need to be worked up over anything in your state."

Felicia gave a short curtsey, then gathered up her skirts, and left the prison. She stepped into the sun, closing her eyes, taking a deep breath in, breathing in the earthen scent of decaying leaves. Her parents joined her on the road, and the three of them walked back through the town.

"What are we to do now?" her mother asked, stopping along the side of the road.

"We need to get things ready." Felicia leaned against a wooden fence. "Father, find Gabriel Barnet and tell him to take over what Nathaniel used to do and to take Myles in as his apprentice. He'll know what you mean. Mother and I will go to Natty's store and close it. Myles will probably be hanging about the steps. Then, we wait."

She gritted her teeth, wincing slightly.

"I think it's better that we take you home first," Mother said. "You're looking awfully pale."

Felicia rested her hands on her lower back. She let out breath of air. "Perhaps that might be best."

"When that's done, I'll get the cart ready," Father said. "We'll start packing up your things. Are you certain you can travel in your condition?"

Felicia bobbed her head. "I'll be fine. The child is just stretching and pressing Lord-knows-what part of him into my bones." She wrinkled her nose and took a step forward, but the child pressed against her pelvis, and she froze as pain rippled across her lower belly and back.

"Lissie, love?" Mother said.

She hissed as she bent forward. "That's new..." She turned to her father. "You wouldn't be able to carry me, would you?"

"I could barely carry your mother over the threshold."

Felicia steadied herself on the upper rung, then took one step forward, but the rippling pain shot from her lower belly into her inner thighs. "I'm going to need help..."

"What do you need us to do?" Mother asked.

Footsteps sounded behind them, and they turned around quickly. Henry, eyes cast downward, arms across his chest. He pushed past Felicia's father, keeping his head down.

Felicia bit at her lower lip. She absolutely couldn't go on. "Henry."

He paused mid-step.

"Lissie," her mother hissed.

"I don't have time to talk," Henry said, his back toward her. "Nor do I think we should."

"Henry, I need your help." Felicia wrung her hands and glanced at her parents.

Father sighed resignedly, but Mother only shook her head, murmuring, "Oh, the impropriety."

Henry glanced over his shoulder. "What do you need?"

Felicia twisted her foot on the ground, wishing she hadn't needed to speak.

Her father huffed, then spoke up for her. "The child is causing her some pain. Would you please carry her home?"

Henry sighed, then walked back toward Felicia, who met her parents' eyes. They nodded and headed into town. Henry whistled lightly through his teeth, then bent at his waist, scooping her up into his arms.

She wrapped her arms about his neck, but remained stiff, trying to keep from looking at him.

"You know," Henry said, carrying her down the road toward the houses, "when you said you needed my help, I believed you meant concerning your husband."

Felicia narrowed her eyes. "What help could you give me concerning my husband?"

"I don't know how much weight my word truly carries, but I could see about delaying his trial, I suppose."

"I don't need his trial delayed," Felicia said. She wrinkled her nose, turning her face up toward his. She hummed lightly, softening her features, and tried to give him a smile. "But thank you, nonetheless."

"Least I could do, really," Henry said as he came up to her front gate. He pushed it open with his hip. "How far do you need me to take you?"

"Preferably to a chair. The child is giving me more pain than I bargained for."

"You're giving me some more pain than I bargained for too, you know. Left side of my chest if you must know." He lowered his eyes to hers, and she glared up at him. The man, a friend for so long, seemed nearly a foreigner to her. His brother had imprisoned her husband, yet Henry was still so gentle to her, helping her when she needed. A guilty pang filled her chest and her face softened. She started to speak, but he quirked a grin.

"Careful of what you say."

He carried her up the steps, then worked the door handle with his fingertips. Carrying Felicia into the sitting room, he gently set her down on a plush velvet chair.

She sighed, relief flooding over her body as she leaned back into the cushion, head resting against the edge, eyes closed. Henry gently set her mobcap straight on her head and tucked a stray hair behind her ear.

"Felicia, I'm sorry," he murmured, and turned to leave.

"Sorry?" Her eyes flew open. "Why are you sorry? You're not the one who found the rifle in Nathaniel's store." Felicia let a short breath out, then lolled her head toward him.

Henry pinched the bridge of his nose, then turned his back to her. "I knew it all."

Felicia struggled upright, nostrils flaring as she stared Henry down.

"I knew William was out to arrest your husband for a long time."

Felicia stared silently at Henry—the Colonel's brother—who only stood there. If she harbored any guilt for loving Nathaniel, it was buried. She narrowed her eyes, her breaths becoming labored. "You *knew*? How?"

"I was drunk. I was desperate. I don't remember half of what I said that night. William told me they wouldn't have been able to pin him without me—"

"I think you had better leave. Now," Felicia said slowly. She drew in a deep breath, and let it out slowly, and though she kept her voice even, she bared her teeth. A fire burned in her eyes, searing through Henry's soul. "Get out of my house."

He bowed his head. "I'm sorry," he said again. "I really am."

And with that, Henry Moore left Felicia alone in the house. No Rose. No Selah, Amos, and their little girl. No Thomas. No Nathaniel. Friendless. The manor's foundations didn't creak. The birds had flown South. The trees were barren, and no wind upset whatever leaves remained on the ground.

Felicia covered her face in her hands and bent forward, squeezing her eyes shut. "Thomas, why'd you leave me in such a mess?"

She rolled her head to the side. There was Thomas sitting in the chair beside hers.

"If I had known I was going to die, I would have just stayed home." He cocked his head. "But I could have gotten hanged for sedition. Nathaniel's right, my Lissie. It'll work out in the end."

Thomas strode to the mantle and picked up his violin, turning it over in his hands. "It's been making music once again," he murmured. He gathered up the bow and bent down to set them in the case. Then, he turned and handed it to Felicia, who clutched it to her chest.

Before she could open her eyes, Thomas disappeared from the room.

The one thing left to do was to wait for midnight. She closed her eyes, a few remnants of tears trickling down her cheeks.

T he sun wavered above the trees, threatening to set by the time Felicia's parents returned to her house. Felicia barely heard the door open as she slept in the chair where Henry had left her. The violin case was slipping from her grasp as she slipped further asleep. Father carefully pried the case from Felicia's hands and slipped it under his arms. Mother rested her hand upon Felicia's shoulder, kissing the top of her head.

Felicia stirred, blinking aching eyes. She rubbed the back of her hand over her face as she tried to sit up, but noticed she no longer had the violin.

She glanced about frantically, but Mother held her in the chair. Felicia struggled upright. "Where is it?"

"What, love?" Mother shushed her.

"The violin. Thomas packed it for me," she said, voice cracking from sleep. Her father, who had been on his way to the kitchen to gather food supplies, turned back for the sitting room, silent.

"You were holding this, Lissie." His voice was low. "You must have dreamt he packed this after you had."

"No, I haven't moved since the Colonel's brother brought me here," Felicia said. "I swear to you on my life—"

"Ah, now, I wouldn't swear on your life." Mother shooshed Felicia again. "Not so close to giving birth."

"But I would." Felicia was adamant. "I swear to you he packed it and handed it to me."

Father nodded, holding the case at arm's length. "Perhaps he did. But I suppose it is no matter. I'll tuck it into the cart. For now, we'll pack. You rest."

Felicia leaned back, her eyes closed. She didn't even tilt her head to the sound of her parents' bustling. "You had better be packing my teapot and favorite cup."

"Felicia, you will have no time to make tea," her mother began, but when Felicia opened her eyes and gave her an exhausted glare from the chair by the fireplace, she sighed. "I will pack the teapot."

Meanwhile, Father filled the cart with blankets and a few boxes, creating a space for Felicia to rest on the trip, if she should need to. There was little room for most of the things that Felicia wanted to bring. The cart was borrowed from Barnet, but the man only had a two-axel cart. With mother padding the seats and back with every quilt she could find, Felicia's teapot and favorite cup the only luxuries she could fit. The paintings stayed above the mantle in the sitting room. Felicia's fine velvet and silk brocade gowns remained in the wardrobe. The new butter churn remained under the kitchen sink. The barrels filled with Thomas's clothing and personal belongings stayed in his locked office. Nathaniel's larger tools were left behind, but her father wrapped the awls, bores, and a small handsaw in oiled cloths, then put them in a small barrel he pilfered from the shop.

Felicia tucked Thomas's rifle in with their things beside Nathaniel's musket between bundles of blankets and the swaddling clothes.

The sun lingered in the sky, before slowly inching down past the trees. Felicia skipped supper in favor of sleeping in the parlor, but Mother joined her, carrying a tray of small sandwiches.

"Come now, my love," she said, setting the tray on the side table by Felicia. She pulled over an armchair to sit beside her daughter. "It's time you had something to eat."

Felicia cracked open an eye, sighed, then closed her eye again. "I'm not hungry."

"Oh, nonsense. You have a child inside. You have to eat something." Mother patted Felicia's large belly. "And with the trip ahead of you, you really should keep up your strength."

"I am. I'm sleeping."

"Just one sandwich, my love. You haven't had anything to eat all day."

Felicia grimaced and sat up slowly in the chair, running her hands over her belly. "I really couldn't eat anything. The child is lying so heavily in me."

"It's nearly dark out, Lissie," her mother said. She pressed her hand to her hands over Felicia's. "Are you sure you can't eat something? You have no reason to worry. Nathaniel will be all right."

"I'm not worried." Felicia sighed. "Well, no, I am. But I just can't eat. I'm not hungry."

Father strode into the sitting room, his hat on his head. "I'll be starting the watch soon. I think it's best we get the cart behind the milliner's. Are you ready?"

Felicia took in a shaky breath, her lips trembling. "I suppose I'll have to be. Can I just walk around a moment?"

He helped her stand, and she winced when she took a step.

"I just want to see one room," she said, moving slowly out of the room and down the hall, her mother following closely behind. Felicia pulled a ring of keys from her pockets, and thumbed through the multiple keys, the metal rattling as she sorted through them. She pulled out a long silver key and stuck it in the lock to Thomas's office. The door opened with a click, and Felicia pushed the door open, stepping inside the office for the first time in months.

The room was dark, though moonlight shone in through the window, casting a gray light on Thomas's desk. Dusk particles floated through the beams. Other than the barrels of Thomas's belongings sat along the back wall, the room almost the same as Thomas had left it on June ninth.

Felicia walked around the office, smiling sadly, tilting her head back as the memories filled her head. *Days spent watching him correspond with generals. Bringing him his tea. Telling him of the child. Dancing slowly together while he hummed. Listening as he played the violin.*

Wrapping her arms around her waist, Felicia exited the room, closing the door behind her. She locked it once last time and then handed the keys to her mother.

"Will you take care of the manor?"

"As best as we can," Mother whispered, extending a blue woolen cloak.

Felicia slipped it over her shoulders and grabbed the case which held the violin and bow, and then they made their way out the kitchen door to the garden and joined Father. Felicia paused near the tombstone in the garden. She ran her hands over the cold stone.

"I won't forget you," she said. "You'll be with me forever."

She pressed a kiss to the top of the stone, then stood straight. But as she did, the rippling pain that had coursed in her body earlier in the day returned, starting in her belly, and moving to her back. She shuddered as she took pained steps to the cart. Her father helped her up onto the seat, then helped her mother up and handed her the reins.

"I'll walk," he said. "You get behind the store."

"How long will it take?" Felicia asked, rubbing circles on her skirts.

"If I'm the guard, maybe ten minutes, but if I'm longer, don't try to come and help me. We'll make it out in time."

Father patted the chestnut mare's rump, and Mother shook the reins. The cart started with a jolt, then rolled off down the road in the dark. No lanterns lit the way.

BRITISH SOLDIERS who built the prisons, Nathaniel decided, did so with the specific and systematic intent to drive a prisoner mad. The walls and ceiling leaked. The straw on the ground seemed more for the rats than for the prisoner. The scrap of cloth barely functioned as poor handkerchief let alone the blanket it was supposed to be. No candles lit in the hallway. The small window near the ceiling provided the only light in the cell and the immediate hallway, which was obscured by thick bars.

As the notion of the trial weighed on his mind, a knot formed in his stomach. Sure, he had an alibi in Myles and his logbooks, but he wished his alibi didn't rely on paper, which could easily be burned or falsified, and on an impressionable four-year-old who on more than once occasion called him "papa." Goodness knows, either William or Henry Moore would use Myles's words against him.

Nathaniel tossed his long hair over his shoulders, smoothing it back into a ponytail, though he had no ribbon which to tie it back. He ran his hands along the bars, then paced back and forth.

His mind traveled to the gallows, where he would be headed after the trial. And when the trial did occur, would he want Felicia there, or should he send her home?

His eyes narrowed at the shadows. If they killed him for the Major's death, he'd come back as a ghost and get in between any chance Henry had with Felicia. His father had warned him about the vindictiveness of the departed. No way in heaven or hell, he was going to let a Moore marry his widow.

The sound of the front office door opening jarred Nathaniel from his thoughts. He glanced down the hallway, squinting to see who had opened it.

"There's been a changing of the guards."

Was that John? Hadn't Felicia said that she was coming? Was she alright? The plan was supposed to rely on the thought that an expectant woman couldn't break a man out of jail.

"Is there any soldier in here?"

It was John. His breath caught in his throat, his chest tightening as waited for someone to answer.

"Yes, what for?" the redheaded soldier called back.

"You're released from duty. Go on to your home to sleep. I was told to watch Poe tonight."

"On who's orders?"

"Colonel Moore's."

"He hadn't told me as much," Red said, indignantly.

Nathaniel strained his ears. Papers rustled then came a moment of silence.

"Go take a break, man," John said, his voice jovial. "You've been here so long! You can check Moore's logbook. You'll see I'm slated. Go to the tavern and get yourself a well-earned drink."

If Nathaniel were a simpleton, that would be an offer he couldn't refuse. He only hoped that the red-headed solider were one.

"Very well," the officer said.

Psalm one-hundred and seventeen, verse one ran through Nathaniel's head as boots thudded against the stone floor, and the sound of the door opening, and closing dissipated down the hall. Quiet filled the jail again.

Nathaniel pressed up against the bars and whispered, "John? Is that you?"

"Aye, yes." The flicker of a small candle outlined of his father-in-law's hand. John stepped closer to the cell, his face becoming visible.

"What time is it?"

"It's near midnight now," John said. "Do you know what to do?"

"I think so. Is everything ready? I thought Lissie would be here."

"Change of plans. She's too exhausted. She's waiting now. Loaded up the cart with things to keep you satisfied for the trip," John said. He flashed a mirthless grin. "And the teapot."

Nathaniel smiled. He couldn't begrudge his wife a teapot if she was willing to escape everything she knew for his sake. But his smile faded, as "she's exhausted" ran through his mind. He gulped, shifting his weight on his feet. "Is she in good health? She didn't look well earlier."

"She's been complaining of the child lying heavily, but she slept most of the day."

Nathaniel let out a breath. "Good."

"Now, let's get you out of here."

John took a step back and eyed Nathaniel, eyeing him up and down, then studied the bars on the cell.

"Do you think you can slip through?" he asked.

Nathaniel bit back a snort. "I would have escaped earlier if I could. They're quite close together, and I'm not so thin."

John frowned. "If I simply unlock the door, Moore will know I let you out. We are family friends, but I wonder if he'd hang me to get answers from Abby."

"I'd rather you not be hung," Nathaniel grumbled, glaring. He wouldn't let Moore hurt his family. "I don't think Felicia would be very happy about that, either."

John narrowed his eyes and tapped his foot. Nathaniel grasped a hold of the bars, stepping back to stretch his arms.

"I think I have an idea," Nathaniel said. "And I don't think it would involve you getting hanged, nor would it involve me and your daughter getting tracked."

"Go on," John said.

"You unlock my cell. We'll make it look somebody knocked you out and freed me. Wait a few hours before telling Moore I'm gone. It'll look like I escaped. Do you very much like your clothes?"

John shrugged. "Well, I—"

Nathaniel reached through the bars and tore at John's overcoat, ripping the lace from the sleeves and the collar from the neck, then clawed at the cravat, ripping holes into the cotton. He caught a hold of one of John's shirt sleeves, ripping them from the shoulder seams and grabbed the buttons on his weskit, loosening the fabric.

"Take out your queue," Nathaniel said, handing him the buttons.

John pocketed the buttons, his mouth in an open frown, eyes boring holes into Nathaniel. "What in G-d's name was that for?"

"To look like you fought to keep me in jail. You don't want to Moore to suspect, do you?"

"I suppose not."

Nathaniel offered John a bit of lace. "My apologies to your wife for the darning she'll endure to fix what I broke."

A faint smile replaced his father-in-law's frown. He muttered, "I'm sure she'd think it a worthy cause. Come. We have to be quick now."

Nathaniel craned his neck to see John vanish down the hall and back into the office. After a soft clattering, he rushed back and stuck a key into the lock. It didn't fit. He tried two more neither of which worked. Fumbling with the keys, he picked one at random. It fit, and the lock clicked. When the cell door swung open, Nathaniel rushed out, then John led him back into the office.

"You broke the drawer," Nathaniel said as John shimmied it back into the desk.

"I had to do something."

"Isn't he going to know somebody broke into the desk to take the keys?" Nathaniel snapped his fingers. "But that's exactly it. My supposed accomplice would have searched for and found them."

"But something must be done to show you had a confidant," John said. "I may be ragged, but while I don't want to be suspected, I don't want to get your friends in trouble either."

Nathaniel frowned as he bounced on his feet. "We don't have time to create a scapegoat. You are ragged. Perhaps that is enough. Let's leave it to Divine Providence."

John and Nathaniel slunk out of the front door and down the side of the building and crept behind the shops until they reached the small alley between the buildings and the fence around the pastureland. The cold air tore through their clothes, the pale moonlight barely helping to light their way, but soon, the cart was visible the distance.

"How long should I wait before I alert the Colonel?" John whispered.

"Give us at least an hour, though longer would be better. If you can hold off, tell him before daybreak."

"Aye," John said.

They reached the cart. Abby sat upright, keeping a vigilant watch, but Felicia hunched forward. John pulled on the corner of Abby's skirt, and she stifled a gasp, nudged at Felicia's arm. Nathaniel's wife stirred and blinked her eyes when Abby pointed down to John and Nathaniel. Her face was pale, and dark circles shadowed her eyes.

"Nathaniel!" she squeaked. She held out her arms, a smile lighting her face.

John helped Abby down off the cart, and Nathaniel took her place, leaning into Felicia's arms.

"I'm here now," he whispered, kissing her forehead. "I won't leave you." Felicia took Nathaniel's face into her hands, but he pulled away and picked up the reins, saying gently, "Save the kiss for later, my love. When we are safe."

"How far is Mount Terre from here?" Abby whispered.

"About a full day's journey," he said. "Up in the Endless Mountains. We could get there by this time tomorrow if we switch the horses. If not, another day."

"Then you better get a move on," John said. He came around to

Felicia's side of the cart and reached up to her. She reached down, and he pressed a kiss to her knuckle. "Stay safe, my love. We are here if you need us."

Abby joined her husband. "Write to us once you get settled."

"Of course. Of course," Felicia said, her voice lacking her usual pep. "Thank you so much. You're—Father! Why are you all torn up?"

Abby eyed John, who peered down at himself and gave a weak snort of laughter.

"Your husband," he said and handed Abby a tattered bit of lace. "Needed to be done. Go." He threw the keys far off into the night.

Nathaniel flicked the reins, and the cart started down the road. He glanced back once. John wagged his head, pressing his lips together, and Abby wrapped her arms around her husband's waist. Their faces were pale in the moonlight, as they watched the cart carry their daughter out of sight.

Felicia turned, waving a good-bye to her parents as the cart turned the bend and the town disappeared.

Nathaniel kept his focus on the road ahead, and after passing the last house, urged the horse into a near gallop. Felicia leaned against Nathaniel's arm. They travelled under the stars, changing between a gallop and a trot whenever the horse's strength flagged.

Felicia stayed relatively quiet, though she shifted in her seat awkwardly, breathing rhythmically. Her unease set Nathaniel on edge.

"Were you worried?" she asked.

"Only for you," he said. "I won't have you left alone again."

The cart hit a bump in the road and bounced. Felicia let out a low moan, and her fingers clenched around the seat.

"Would you rather sit in the back?" Nathaniel asked. "I don't want you getting hurt."

"I'm fine," Felicia said through gritted teeth. "The child just doesn't care for the bumps. He pushes up against me with such a fierce strength."

"Pushing?"

A groan bubbled in her throat, but she nodded.

"Is that all?"

"With the push comes a sharp pain in my back, but that's more when I walk."

Nathaniel hummed. He slowed the horse down to a trot and wrapped his arm around Felicia's back.

"Let me know if you feel anything more." He pressed a kiss to the top of her head. "I don't like you saying 'pushing'."

Felicia leaned her head on his shoulder, her body stiff against him. "Hmm, so if I feel more of the pain?"

Nathaniel glanced down at her then back at the road. "Yes! If you feel pain, tell me."

She quieted, her moans miniscule. Nathaniel had seen her in a worse state before when the child was pressing into her ribs. She seemed nearly calm now, and that frightened him more than her carrying on. He couldn't gauge her level of pain. But there was something in her eyes... something different.

"Felicia, are you laboring?" he asked, voice shaking slightly. He cleared his throat, keeping a stern focus on the road.

Felicia groaned and rubbed her hands over her belly, then leaned against the backrest. "In truth... I think I am."

＊ 25 ＊

Nathaniel glanced back and forth from his wife to the darkness that shrouded behind them and shook the reins to urge the horse to gallop. "I thought the child was supposed to come around Christmas."

"It is nearly December. I'm either further along than previously believed"—she held her lower belly and leaned back against the hard wooden seat— "or I'm having this child early."

Nathaniel pulled the horse and cart to the side of the road, under a canopy of trees.

"We are currently in the middle of nowhere, two hours from town, Lissie. What do you want me to do? Will you be safer at home?"

"No!" Felicia braced herself on the seat. "I think it may have started earlier when you were in prison." She closed her eyes, then sucked in a breath.

Nathaniel glanced to her, seeing the outline of her scrunched face in the flickering starlight. "You didn't tell anyone?"

She let out her breath then continued. "The grinding pains were few and far between. I didn't think much of them. As of this moment, it isn't so terribly strong. The babe has kicked me worse." She stopped, grasped his shoulder, and bit back a moan. "Let that horse walk."

"Lissie. You are my wife, and I must put your wellbeing before mine." He adjusted himself on the seat to face her. He curled a finger against her cheek. "We will figure out what to do after you've given birth."

"You're a wanted man, Natty. And before you forget, you are my husband." She took his face in her hands. "These pains are not so regular yet. My waters have not broken. We will continue till we both are safe."

Nathaniel pressed a kiss to her forehead, then flicked the reins and called out. He wouldn't argue with her. Despite not knowing much about the fair sex, he had the inkling that to reason with one while she is in labor would be one of the worst decisions he could make in his life. He would stop and find the nearest shelter when needed, no matter where it was.

Felicia grabbed his arm abruptly, jarring him from his thoughts.

With one hand gripping the reins, he pulled Felicia against his side, rubbing her arm.

"Lean against, me, love," he murmured. "We'll stop at the first tavern we come across."

"I've never been with child before," Felicia whispered, then protectively ran her hands over the large swell of her belly. "And I don't quite like talking about how this is my only child..."

"Are you frightened?"

Perhaps it was a stupid question, but it was one that he had to ask. She had been so calm and quiet, which unnerved him.

"I'm terrified." She shuddered. "Am I simply to wait and bear down? How will I know when? What if I miss the signs?"

"Felicia, it may be best to—"

"If you say turn around, I'll drive the cart myself." Her breath caught in her throat, and she let out a small guttural cough. "Oh, how can I deliver myself of the babe?"

Nathaniel quirked his brow, cocking his head toward Felicia, though kept his eyes on the road. Perhaps after tending livestock for so many years, he came to know how nature took its course, but certainly he thought that women instinctively knew how to birth. Didn't that knowledge come ingrained in the female brain?

"What is it you need to know? Let nature take its course, Lissie."

Felicia glowered at him and he shrunk back a little. "I just don't know exactly how to get them out—" She broke off with a moan and leaned back again, bracing her hands on the seat. Her face scrunched, but when Nathaniel tried to brush her hair back, she swatted at his hand. She let out a breath then resumed her speech. "The midwife simply told me it's painful, and that bearing down is involved. I'm my parents' only child, and since I had not had children, it was never pertinent. Stating that 'Mrs. Wilcox has been delivered of a son,' doesn't exactly tell me *how* it happened."

"Well... ah... I suppose—" he started, but she tapped his arm. "Yes?"

She grinned, despite the pains, mischief glinting in her moonlit eyes. "I know how to make them."

Nathaniel pressed his fingers to the bridge of his nose. They were silent for a few moments before Felicia groped for his hand in the dark. He intertwined his fingers with hers, then brought them to his lips, pressing a kiss to her knuckle.

"Natty?" she asked.

He glanced to her, eyes heavy, and sighed. "Lissie?"

"Do you know?"

He nodded. "I told you I raised sheep and horses."

"I'm neither of those, Nathaniel, thank you very much," she snapped.

Nathaniel winced and held his hand up in defense. "No, no, Lissie. You are far more beautiful than an animal. I just have seen the birth of many lambs and foals and there's a look in the mother's eyes."

The burning pain of embarrassment stung his stomach. He'd been married for only a few weeks and already had made the grievous error of insulting his wife and while she was in labor, no less.

Unamused, Felicia glared at him. She tilted her head to him, the smoldering fury on her face dimming to only a glowing ember. "Then I don't look like a laboring sheep to you?"

Nathaniel held the reins in one hand and turned to fully study Felicia, then offered her a small smile. "No, my love. I just know what to do."

A bump in the road jolted the cart again and sent her into a fit of moaning. She wrapped her arms around her middle and bent forward.

The hot embarrassment doused and turned into icy fear. He ran his hand over her back, pressing the heel of his palm into her muscles. "It'll be over soon enough. Just hang on a little while longer."

"How much longer." Felicia panted, still bent over. "Tell me what I'm supposed to do."

"Once the grinding pains get closer and more regular, tell me. If your waters break, tell me. We'll stop around sunrise."

Felicia huffed out a breath. "How long?"

"Till sunrise? About four more hours. The child? As long as it needs to take."

She groaned and leaned back, running her hands through her hair, disordering her curls. Nathaniel pressed a kiss to the top of her head. "Try to close your eyes, love. Sunrise'll be here soon enough."

PENCHESTER AWOKE in the middle of the night to William's men sounding alarms. William, rifle in hand, ran toward the prison in only his nightshirt and breeches, hair loose, with John Winthrop trailing after him, his own clothes torn and mussed.

Throwing open the prison's front door, William burst into his office, eyes darting around the candle-lit room dashed to Poe's cell. The door was wide open, swinging in the breeze. William let out an exasperated growl and ran back to the office, where Winthrop stood.

William grabbed Winthrop's shoulders. "What happened, man?"

"Someone hit me on the head, and when I got up, the cooper had escaped," the shorter man said. "He took my daughter with him. God knows where he's gone."

With a curse, William turned to his desk, pulling open the drawers. The lower drawer on the left side stuck. He glared up at Winthrop. "So what you're saying," he said, lowering his voice, "is that somebody broke in and got him out."

"He must have gotten in while I changed positions with the officer." He gulped. "Must've hid. Then, when I was alone. I don't remember much else."

"You're telling me that a person or persons unknown broke into the office and broke Nathaniel Poe out of his cell, and then Poe made his way to Hawkings' Manor, stole a girl who is very great with child, and absconded into the night? And somehow, you come away, looking like you've been sent to France and back again?"

"Well, Felicia isn't in her bed. When I told Abby that he'd escaped, she ran to Lissie's house to check on her. No one's there."

"Told your wife, *when?*"

"I ran home to check—"

"Instead of coming to *me?*" William stalked over to John.

"I was knocked out," John said, narrowing his eyes. He stared up at William, unrelenting. "My first thought was to make sure my precious girl was alright. Wouldn't you want to check on your daughter if you thought she was in danger?"

"I have been trained to go to my commanding officer," William stated, keeping his voice cool and even.

"I'm not a soldier," John said, his own voice matching William's steely demeanor. "My first thought is to protect my family."

William set his jaw. "That makes sense Winthrop, but one thing doesn't." William squeezed the barrel of his rifle. "So. You said it happened during the changing of the guards. Did you see him leave or not?"

William raised his rifle, pointing it at John's chest. The man lowered his eyes to the barrel of the gun, then raised them to William, pressing his lips together tightly.

"Why do I have the distinct feeling you're lying to me?" William asked, poising his finger on the trigger.

Winthrop raised his square chin. "Why would I protect a rebel cooper?"

"You let your daughter marry him."

"Nothing I could say would change that girl's mind. Once it's made up, you can't sway her."

"And still..." Chest heaving, William bared his teeth. "It seems to me that you had always had a soft spot for the colonial scum. Why don't we go for a walk, outside, shall we?"

William turned John around, pressing the rifle into his back. He goaded John out of the building and into the cold night air.

"I think you know exactly where they went," William said, pressing the gun deeper into John's shoulder blades. "I think you know exactly how they're getting there and when."

"If I did, wouldn't I have gone with them?"

"I wasn't born yesterday, Winthrop. You expect me to believe that an accomplice came in under your nose?"

"I'm old, Colonel Moore. There's a lot that gets under my nose."

"Then why offer to watch the cooper in the night? Don't play stupid, Winthrop."

Felicia's lying father craned his neck back to William. "If you kill me over the loss of the cooper, Penchester will never forgive you."

"He killed your daughter's husband. Don't you care?"

"We both know that Nathaniel did nothing of the sort."

William scoffed. "Perhaps."

At that, Winthrop spun around, the gun pressing into his chest. He winced as the cool metal dug into his shirt. "Then why did you have him in custody?"

"Why shouldn't I? We found the gun in his store. He leads the town's Yankee militia. Why shouldn't I have him killed?"

"Because if you kill him, this town will rally against you and your family. You'd never make it out alive."

"I am not afraid of some provincial militia."

The sun's first rays glistened over the grass as William's finger tightened on the trigger.

"The mountains," John said, wincing.

William stopped. He furrowed his brows and lowered the pistol. "Be more specific, or I'll have you hanged for abetting a murderer."

"It's a guess, nothing more. All I know is that he came from the Endless Mountains." John pointed to the North, over the pastureland. He tilted his chin, defiance burning in his blue eyes, a smirk growing on his lips. "Wherever they are, they're a good deal away. I'd surmise they're well passed the Schuylkill River. The sun is up, Moore. What are you going to do?"

William turned toward the pastureland. The cold air stung his eyes, and his breath curled before him in a haze. He let out a roar and spun around, smashing the stock of the rifle into John's temple.

Winthrop collapsed, blood trickling down the side of his face an onto his neck.

The sun brightened in the sky, illuminating the frost on the grass and windowpanes. There was no time to waste.

With a cry of rage, William took off to house, calling for his men to assemble.

❧ 26 ❧

"The grinding pains are fifteen minutes apart." Nathaniel slid his watch into his vest pocket. Felicia squeezed his hand and let out a breath, only to hold the next one. He gave her cold fingers a squeeze. "How bad is it?"

"It's a biting fury." Felicia let out her breath. She pressed her free hand to her belly, arching her back. "Can we please rest now?"

"As soon as I can get us to a tavern," Nathaniel said. "Then a comfortable bed and a warm drink will be yours."

As streaks of blue and pink wove through the sky, the pains wracked her twice more by the time they arrived at the tavern. Though the road compacted from constant wear, the cart bumped along, jostling Felicia. He winced in sympathy, gritting his teeth against the chilly November morning air. With one hand, he tried to keep her steady while he stopped the cart under a large oak tree. He wrapped the reins around a low hanging branch, and the mare immediately plunked her face into a trough by the tree.

"Can you walk, my love?" His voice was tender and low, though there was an edge of hurry in his words. She wordlessly nodded. He went around the cart to her side. "Here. Lean on me."

He picked Felicia off her seat and set her on the ground, then leaned her against his side, supporting her as they hobbled as quickly as they could into the brick building towering before them in the clearing.

Nathaniel tried to peer into the windows, but they were frosted over. There was no way to see just how busy the tavern was, and he prayed there was a space for them. There was no more time. Felicia quivered against him, freezing despite the perspiration clinging to her forehead and arms. He pushed the chipped, wooden door open, and led Felicia into the dining room, just as natural light began to flood the room.

Felicia was quiet, her face flushed bright red, her breath hitching in her throat. Nathaniel glanced around for help. Though there were a half-score of tables, they each had at least one red-clad soldier seated. A sinking heaviness filled Nathaniel's body, as he scanned the crowd of British soldiers. He bowed his head low, steadying his own breathing, and focused on Felicia.

The keep, a weathered, old woman, came up to Nathaniel and Felicia, drying her hands on a towel. "What do you need?"

"We've been traveling all night and need a place to stay for a few hours. Not even the day," Nathaniel said. "She needs to rest."

The woman slung the towel over her shoulder and shook her head. "No room."

"Do you only allow loyalists? I am so loyal," Felicia said with a gasp, bending over at the waist, resting her hands on the back of a chair. "The child is loyal too. The child's father is loyal. We're so loyal."

Nathaniel pressed his mouth shut.

The woman frowned. "Try the Blackbird up the road."

Nathaniel ran his hand along Felicia's back, glancing to the keep. "How far is it?"

Felicia moaned under her breath.

"Only just up the way. You can leave your horse here if you'd like."

"Natty, I can't walk," Felicia moaned. "Oh, the child is pressing further and further."

Nathaniel scooped her up into his arms, breathing a thank you to the keep, and rushed Felicia out of the tavern and up the road.

It wasn't far, but Nathaniel wavered as the grinding pains hit Felicia in the time it took to reach the Blackbird. He pushed open the door and set Felicia down in a chair at one of the tables. The tavern's dining room had fewer British soldiers at the tables, and its apparent emptiness gave Nathaniel a hope that a bed would be available for his wife.

Another older woman came up to them, though less weathered than the first. "Can I help you?" she asked, glancing between Nathaniel and Felicia.

"She desperately needs a place to lie down for a while. Not even a full day, I don't think. We've been traveling all night." Nathaniel leaned against Felicia's chair. "It's been a long time."

Felicia suddenly grabbed Nathaniel's hand, digging her fingers into his palm. He shooshed her, running his fingers through her loose curls, combing them back from her face.

"Oh, this child," she moaned, and he caught her as she keeled over. "It's rippling through me. The pain is riding in waves all through me. Oh, help..."

"Oh, the dear." The woman pressed her hand against the large swell under Felicia's apron. "Oh, dear!" She peered up at Nathaniel, shaking her head. She frowned and the lines marred her careworn face. "I'm sorry. I have no beds available."

Felicia let out a cry. "Oh, please, let me lie down! I'll die!"

Nathaniel crouched low next to her, taking her red, tear-streaked face in his hands. He gazed into her eyes, a deep ache settling into his soul. "I won't let you die, Lissie."

"I'm afraid there just isn't any available space. I'm all boarded," the keep said, regret in her voice, but Nathaniel barely heard her speak.

"Where's the next tavern?" Nathaniel asked, keeping his focus on Felicia as she shuddered and clenched her teeth together. "At least tell me where there's a midwife."

"The next tavern is about thirty miles from here, heading toward New York. I don't know about any midwives."

"That's nowhere near Mount Terre," Felicia whimpered. "I'll die! I'm going to die."

"You're not going to die," Nathaniel said. He glanced over at the keep. She seemed almost as anxious as he felt. "Please. You must give us something," he said, starting to lose the feeling in his hands. He turned his eyes to the room of soldiers. "Or perhaps one of you is man enough to give his bed to a laboring woman?"

There was an uncomfortable quiet in the room as the soldiers shifted to look away from Nathaniel and Felicia. Nathaniel drew in a long breath, then stared back at the keep. "Give us anything. This child is not going to wait thirty miles."

The woman stayed quiet for a moment, then said, "There's the barn out back. It's warm enough, and the animals won't bother you. It's got plenty of straw and hay. I'm sure it'll be fairly comfortable."

"It'll have to do," Nathaniel said, scooped Felicia up off the chair.

"I can't have my baby in a barn!" she cried, struggling in his arms. "That's just not what's done!" She began to cry, burying her face in his neck.

"Hush, love. It's been done before," Nathaniel said, as gently as he could as carried her outside to the large wooden barn.

The keep rushed ahead of them, throwing open the doors. Nathaniel brought Felicia into an empty stall and set her down against a bale of hay.

"I'll come back with a blanket," the keep said, then closed the doors to the cold morning air.

Felicia squeezed her eyes shut, grabbing at his coat, holding her breath. They stayed like that for a minute, before Felicia eased her grasp and fell back, gasping. "Nathaniel, please don't tell me that I'm going to have to have my baby in this barn. Please tell me that we're going to go to Mount Terre and stay with your family, or at least at a tavern."

"The baby is pressing more frequently," Nathaniel said, hushed, kneeling next to her. He tapped at his pocket. "The watch doesn't lie, love."

She grimaced and Nathaniel smoothed her hair away from her face. He hadn't felt this burning before. Every fiber of his being was alight, and he fought to keep his demeanor cool and calm. He had to remain strong for Felicia. She was no ewe or mare. She was his wife. He pressed a warm kiss to her forehead. "Tell me what's happening."

"I'm fine—" Her face scrunched, and she held her breath, squeezing her hands into fists.

"Sounds perfectly fine to me," Nathaniel said, still hushed and gentle. He picked up her hand and kissed it. "Oh, my dear Lissie. What can I do to ease your pain?"

She shrugged, shaking her head. Fresh tears spilled down her cheeks.

The keep ran back into the barn with two blankets and handed them to Nathaniel, who nodded and whispered, "Thank you," trying not to disturb Felicia. The woman left again, and Nathaniel and Felicia were alone with the animals in the barn.

"Oh, get me out of these things," Felicia sputtered, and Nathaniel helped untie her skirts and stays. Then, he unpinned Felicia's overdress from her stomacher and the stomacher from her stays. Sticking the pins into the overdress, he shoved it and the stomacher aside and tucked the blankets over her.

"Would it help if you leaned forward?" he asked, and she tried, shaking, groping for something to hold onto. He braced his arm in front of her, and Felicia took hold of it. Slowly, he rubbed her back, pressing the heel of his palm into her shoulders.

"Lower," she murmured, and he obliged. She hissed a small sigh of relief, shuddering.

As her tension abated, he felt his own loosening. With one hand massaging her back and the other keeping her steady, her murmured against her hair, "I know this is no place for you to have your child. I know you'd rather be in a bed in your manor. And I'm sorry I've caused such a disturbance—"

"It was William who caused the disturbance," Felicia groaned, then leaned back against his chest. "I think the worst of it is over..."

Nathaniel hummed. "Felicia..."

"Don't tell me otherwise." Her eyes fluttered closed, her breathing evening out. "I just want to rest my eyes for a moment. Why don't you do the same?"

"I need to keep a watch over you," Nathaniel said, wrapping his arms about her.

"Rest your eyes. That's an order from you wife."

Nathaniel couldn't refuse his wife, even at a time like this. He leaned back against a bale of hay, trying to relax. Felicia's head lolled against his chest, and she sighed. He smiled lightly, holding her close.

"I said rest your eyes," she murmured.

"Yes, love."

~

NATHANIEL WOKE WITH A START, as Felicia's thin fingers dug into his arms. She tore away from him and let out a cry, cradling her belly in her hands.

"Natty!" she rasped out. "Natty—I think—"

"I'm here." He blinked against the light coming in from the window in the loft and immediately shifted onto his knees, kneeling over her.

"The waters have broken," she said, then drew in a hiss as her body stiffened. "I can feel the child truly pressing now. It's twisting me up inside."

Nathaniel moved in front of her and shifted the blankets trying to keep them away from the wet puddle on the floor and to keep Felicia warm.

"You're going to have to bear down," he said.

"I can't do this," Felicia said, shaking her head back and forth. "I can't have the child. I'm not ready."

"You're more than ready," Nathaniel said with a tender smile "You've waited nearly a year for this day. It's quite a natural process."

"Why does it hurt so much if it's so natural?"

"I think there's a verse in Genesis as to why," Nathaniel murmured, moving the blankets up over her chest.

"I didn't eat the apple! It shouldn't apply to me!"

"One would think, wouldn't they?" he said, removing her damp woolen petticoat and pockets. He busied himself, clearing the area, making sure she had enough cushion behind her as needed. He held his hands out for her and she took them, clamping down. "Bear down when you feel the need."

"How will I know—"

"You'll know. Trust me, Lissie. I'm right here."

Felicia's face turned bright red as she bore down. And time lagged as the pains came in crushing waves. As the sunlight crept across the barn floor, her whimpers became screams, and tears streamed down her face. Each cry tore Nathaniel up inside. An overwhelming need to take her pain away and let her rest in his arms came over him. If he could only take on her pain, he would bear it for her.

Someone came in to milk the cows, then hurried away, muttering about distressed cattle giving less milk, though the cows seemed far less distressed than Felicia as they chewed their cud without so much of a sound. No one else arrived, and Nathaniel began to wonder if he should check. After all, how different could a sheep be from a human? He looked under Felicia's chemise while she cried, flexing and unflexing her fingers.

It was profoundly different, apparently, and though the process might have been similar, the feeling it gave him struck a different chord. His arms and hands tingled as excitement surged through him.

He could see the beginnings of a new human being.

"Natty—It burns! Make it stop, please—I just want it to stop—I need to sleep..."

"My love! I know!" Nathaniel leaned up and brushed the soaked, matted hair away from her face. "You're so strong. I know you want to sleep. It will not be much longer. But you must press on. Do it for the child. For Thomas's child."

Felicia sobbed, "Help me through this!"

"The Lord and I are right here for you. Just keep doing what you're doing. I saw his head. You're nearly there."

Felicia let out a blood curdling cry, and Nathaniel winced in sympathetic pain, then lifted the blankets. He let out a small shout and shot her a beaming smile.

"His head is nearly out," Nathaniel crowed. "Bear down once more. He should be here soon!"

Felicia cried again, her voice hoarse. She coughed and pressed herself back into the hay, letting out choked sobs, then bore down, her face beet red. Her fists clenched the hay, and she flopped back down, panting heavily as the babe slipped into Nathaniel's hands. He flipped her soaked chemise and lifted the tiny, mewling baby.

Grabbing his overcoat, he quickly wrapping the infant against the cold, then leaned forward and placed the child on Felicia's chest.

"Calling her Little Thomas is not exactly going to work," he said, placing a kiss against her temple. "It's a girl, Felicia."

Felicia shuddered. "A little girl," she said, her voice cracking. She pressed a kiss to the baby's head. "A beautiful little girl. Oh, this child," she said through a whisper. "Very worth the pain she is."

The keep peeked into the barn to inquire after Felicia, then dashed to the house and returned with boiled water and soft rags. Nathaniel cleaned and swaddled the tiny girl.

Delivered and cleaned, mother and child fell asleep in the barn, and Nathaniel watched over them both, pride rising in his chest. It mattered nothing to him that the child was not his own. What mattered to him was that his wife had been delivered of a healthy daughter. So, he sat in the chilly barn, counting their sleeping breaths, kissing both their heads.

The sun passed its zenith, but before the shadows lengthened, Nathaniel returned to the other tavern, where some kind soul had blanketed and fed the horse. He kept his face hidden and, ignoring the redcoats who swarmed around the tavern and practiced formation in the field behind the inn, led the beast back up to the Blackbird and packed the soiled clothing. He pulled out another quilt and threw it over all three of them. But still, even in this peaceful moment, a sense of dread crept over him, filling his heart. Moore might have figured out where they were. Those soldiers might've been part of his regiment or had known of the flight. They could surround the barn at any moment and tear him away from Felicia and the babe.

But, no, he couldn't think of it any longer. He willed himself to think only of his wife and the new life that lain against her chest. Nathaniel stifled a yawn, then curled his finger under the newborn girl's soft chin. They'd resume their ride to Mount Terre in the morning.

They would be safe until then.

They had time.

27

An eerie silence had fallen over the Penchester when. Henry finally stumbled from the tavern into the early morning light and found John Winthrop bleeding on the cold ground in front of the jail. Henry's head pounded and though he tried to pick up the man himself, was unable to. The last rum did him in. He spied several young men of the town, called them over to help, and the men staggered out to carry Winthrop to his wife. The word spread like a brush fire. The prisoner had escaped. Silence broken, the buzz of gossip rippled out from Penchester to the nearby towns, and by the time Henry returned William's house, a score of horses waited, stamping their hooves, and huffing with their hot breaths curling out from their muzzles, tacked, in the Colonel's front yard. Weary, Henry slipped to the parlor, and idly watched his brother and the other officers gather, in full regalia, around the dining room table, pouring over a map, moving flags and figures about.

"If we leave at this moment, crossing the Schuylkill at this point, we can be in the Endless Mountains in just over a day," William said, jabbing a finger at the map. "My bet is on Mount Terre since that is where he's from. They couldn't be going fast, knowing her condition. We could overtake them if we travel fast."

"Overtake whom?"

Everyone turned to the doorway, where Victoria stood, one hand on the white framework.

William shot a glare at Henry, who crossed to his niece's side.

"Nathaniel Poe escaped in the middle of the night," William said. "He took Felicia with him."

Victoria gasped, her face losing its bright rosy color.

"I suppose you're going to go hunt down the man and his expectant wife, then?" Henry asked through gritted teeth.

"For the sake of justice, I'll do what has to be done." William turned to his men. "We leave now. Every man to his horse. We have to reach Mount Terre before they do."

While the officers filed out of his home, Henry guided the stunned Victoria to a chair in the sitting room. Meanwhile, William packed up his map and grabbed his pistol and rifle before pausing at the sitting room door, then strode over the wooden floors and crouched low next to his daughter.

He rested a hand on her shoulder, but she shrugged him away. "Why is it so important that you capture the cooper?" Her voice was clipped and harried, and a quiet insistence increased in her eyes.

"Because he killed the Major and needs to be tried for his crimes," William said. He pressed a kiss to her hair. "Watch the home for me while I'm gone."

"I suppose I'll have to." Victoria clicked her tongue and turned her face away from her father. "But it just seems so superfluous to send out a regiment to capture one runaway man."

Henry tapped his hand against his thigh and his voice rumbled out, dry and raspy. "Indeed. She's right, William. I can't see it necessary to take your men to find one man. Surely, there have been other escaped convicts."

"Ah." William pet Victoria's head, stroking her hair, but kept his focus on Henry. "But we have been known to find those who do belong in debtor's prison."

Henry flinched and Victoria grew silent, the insistence in her eyes turning into restrained rage.

"Don't worry for yourself, you great buffoon." He poked at Henry, who, without looking, swatted his hand away, shifting uncomfortably. William let out a laugh. "And I do mean great."

Victoria shot William a fiery glare. "Father, if you're only here to deride my uncle—"

"Of course not, pet." He gave Victoria's shoulder a squeeze.

"Then what *do* you have to say?" Henry muttered. Henry knew justice meant the word to his brother, no matter the cost. But to endanger the wife of his closest Major was not a cost he thought would be spent. While Nathaniel needed to be tried and found guilty of Thomas's murder, Henry couldn't make sense of hurting Felicia in the process. Why the regiment? There was a foulness in the air, and Henry slowly became certain that Nathaniel Poe may be the reason for his brother's behavior, but not for the murder of Major Thomas Hawkings.

William studied his daughter for a moment. But when his gaze drifted to Henry, he set his jaw, narrowing his eyes. He drew in a breath, then smoothed his hair back and inclined his head toward his daughter. "Victoria, step out for a moment."

"Very well." Victoria sighed and scooted out of the chair, then gave her father a kiss on his cheek. "Be safe, Papa."

After she had left the room, William closed the door and turned the key in the lock.

"What do you need to say that she can't hear?" Henry asked.

"Things that she doesn't need to know." He reached into his coat pocket, pulling out a piece of paper tied in a red ribbon, then untied the letter and handed it to Henry. A smirk wormed its way onto William's thin lips. "Somebody must know. It might as well be you. Read it."

Henry glanced down at the letter, then back up at his brother, then read.

To General Haddock:

You may have heard of the massacre near the border of New York in Pennsylvania, in which Major Thomas Hawkings was slain. Under the pretense of aiding Gage in Boston, which you heartily recommended, we ventured out. However, you may know that no rebel has taken part in the raid—

Henry jerked upright. Both fear and anger swirled in his chest. In courting Felicia, the duty he felt to care for his friend's wife merged with love. But with his stupidity, his addled, drunk brain, in trying to win her heart and estate, nearly condemned the man *she* loved. And if his original obligation was to protect her, he'd done a shoddy job. To be angry with one's brother happened nearly all the time. But this was no ordinary anger. This was despisal married with fear. Fear for Felicia, the child, and the man she loved. "What do you mean that no rebel took part in the raid?"

"It was not a raid, Henry. It had to be done to be rid of the rebel influence. Read on."

"As it stands, no raid existed, but was a mere ruse to aid us in ridding the rebel influence near the Schuylkill River. In doing this, we may overtake Philadelphia quickly, destroying—" Henry rolled the paper back up. His fingers twitched over the vellum and clenched his jaw. "So, who was responsible for the raid that killed Felicia's husband?"

"I took a calculated loss." Still smirking, William pried the letter from Henry's hand and tucked it back into his pocket. "It had to be taken. He had to die, Henry. If nobody died, it wouldn't look very much like a raid, would it? The rebels wouldn't look so terrible, would they?"

He glared at his brother. And then the union of fear and despisal in him brought forth a new emotion. Panic. This was no normal death. Thomas Hawkings was murdered. He gulped, and trembling, asked, "Then it's true that Nathaniel Poe was nowhere near when it happened?"

William shrugged.

"And yet you had Poe imprisoned."

A sneer etched lines into William's features then pushed at Henry's jaw with his gloved fist, shoving his face away. "It was your idea, Henry. Don't you remember? You said we could pin him to Thomas's death. That's how you'd be able to win Felicia back. Or were you too drunk to remember much of anything?"

Staring square into his brother's face, Henry growled, "Who *did* kill Thomas?"

William didn't answer, just shouldered past him, and made his way to the foyer and out the front door. Henry jogged after him and grabbed his brother's arm, but William pulled away when he reached his horse and set his foot in the stirrup.

"William," Henry all but shouted, "tell me who killed Thomas Hawkings."

"I told you. It was a calculated loss." William swung himself onto his horse. "It had to be, done, Henry. If we blame the rebels for the raid, we can take over this town and clear a path into Philadelphia. Can't you see it was for the best?"

Henry clutched William's calf, holding on with the grip of a sailor holding onto a mast. It all fit together. It all came together. His brother was capable of more than he ever thought possible. Oh, to go back and erase that night he conspired in the tavern. What he thought was a simple trick of winning Felicia was intertwined with a much deeper, much more sinister plan than he could ever hope to untangle himself from.

Though soldiers had mounted their horses and lined up to travel up towards the Endless Mountains, Henry stayed fixed on William, feet planted firmly on the ground. "You knew Thomas was going to die the night of that party." Henry bared his teeth. "Did you really get called to aid Gage in Boston? Did the general command this? Or did you suggest it?"

"Why on earth would we have been called to Boston? Massachusetts has enough soldiers."

"Then you brought your men out to die on June tenth!"

William's smirks faded into disgust as he curled his lip down at his brother. "Only a few and for the greater good."

"And you'd have me marry Felicia? You'd have me marry the woman you made a widow?" The words stung Henry's throat and lips.

"It would have been a match made in heaven, no less," William snarled. "A match which would have been as advantageous for me as it would have been for you."

Henry kept his voice clear and low. "You can't get away with this."

"To whom would you go? Haddock has gone to Virginia. Besides"— William leaned forward— "Australia is a wonderful place to pay off your debts, isn't it?"

Henry sucked in a breath as his head reeled. The corners of his eyes stung as they watered. His nose ached and he set his jaw, trying to keep himself steeled against his brother. But he had loosened his grip on William, and he gave Henry a swift kick in the chest. The blow sent shockwaves of pain through his body as it sent him to the ground.

William straightened in the saddle. "A soldier does what must be done."

He flicked the reins, sending his horse into a gallop, leaving Henry to scramble up the steps, where he sat and watched his brother disappear down the road. He rubbed his ribs where William's boot had left a bruise, and a heaviness formed in his chest, growing thicker, spreading up his throat, as if he has swallowed molasses. He struggled to breathe.

A woman, great with child, traveled at all hours with her husband, who was hunted for a crime he was wrongfully accused. And his own brother took off to track them down.

The woman—*Felicia*—was in danger. Felicia—the woman he loved, for whom he longed in a way he couldn't fully explain—was in the path of his rifle. And if that rifle had ended her first husband's life, who was to say that it couldn't end her life as well? Her life and her child's?

The feeling in Henry's chest expanded, filling his body like hot sand. He had to do something within his power to stop his brother. If no one knew but himself, Henry had to do something, despite any threat his brother gave. He gripped his hands into fists staggered to his feet and thundered into the house.

Papers scattered about the floor of William's office as Henry searched through the correspondence, hoping to secure Felicia's safety. *Protocol be damned. Red tape damned.* Somewhere in the desk there had to be something that could help her. He rifled through the desk drawers, turning each out onto the floor, then fell to his knees to sift through the contents.

"Damn the man," Henry growled.

A gasp at the door startled him, and he half-turned. Victoria stood in the doorway, her soft hand covering her mouth.

"Uncle Henry," she said, her gaze darting around the disordered room and her eyes widening, "who deserves damnation?"

Setting his jaw, Henry took a deep breath. "Your father."

Victoria's face paled as she stared at him as he where he knelt on the floor in the pile of papers. She swallowed and crossed to his side, and sinking to the floor beside him, whispered, "What has he done?"

"Far too much." Henry softened, gently taking hold of her arms. "I need you to describe him."

"Describe Father? I don't know, Uncle Henry. What do you want me to say? He's for King and country, that much is certain. I could say that he is a generous father who gave me the best gowns and has tried to set me up for an advantageous marriage. I could say that he has given me all the affection a daughter could ask for. I could ask for a pony, and he'd give me three. But..."

Henry moved his hands from her arms to cup her delicate face. "But what, my dear?"

"But I could say he's a secretive man, who has great ambitions. He won't tell me how he came upon the satins and taffetas and the ponies. I'm not stupid, you know. I know we don't bleed that sort of income." She leaned over to a pile of papers, sorting through the letters and the ribbons, then looked at Henry, her face darkening. "I could say that he was faithful to my mother, but we all know what he did on those long weekends in New Jersey."

Henry furrowed his brows, frowning up at Victoria. "Then why won't you say anything?"

"And what good will it do? I wouldn't have any say about my father for seeing women in the harbor."

Henry leaned over, grasping Victoria's shoulders, pulling her close. "That's not all he's done, Victoria."

"I'm sure he *has* done more," Victoria shrugged Henry's hands from her shoulders and hugged her arms close, hiding the pained grimace on her face. She milled over to her father's desk and picked up a few loose papers and envelopes from the desk, idly perusing them. "But I'm only his daughter. If I perhaps were his son—"

"But I'm his brother, and I—Victoria." He held his arms out, and she leaned into him. He rubbed his hand over her back, pressing her close to his heart. "I don't want to hurt you. I love you, my sweet sunflower."

"Perhaps you could do something... but as I've said, he's secretive. And I don't know what more you want from me." Victoria pulled away and sighed, but when she glanced down at the envelope clutched in her fist, a frown spread across her face. "Uncle Henry!"

"Yes?"

"How long does it take for letters to be checked for spy work?"

"Not long. Why?"

She handed it to him. "It's for Felicia. Dated this past July."

Henry tore the letter from the open envelope and scanned it. His gaze snapped up, eyes wide. "It's Thomas's estate. From the Bach Trust's Philadelphia branch."

Her voice trembled. "You don't think Father would withhold it, do you?" She reached out for Henry, who grasped her hands in his free one.

Henry tapped the vellum against his side, trilling his lips. "This must have arrived while I was courting her. I remember she asked about it some time ago. He had no reason to withhold it..." He read over the letter again, this time aloud. "It says here that should Felicia outlive him, be it a natural death or death in battle, that half of his yearly income should go to her, and the rest to Moore's regiment."

Henry and Victoria shared a glance.

Victoria chewed thoughtfully on her lower lip. "You don't mean to think that Father has been keeping Felicia's part of the estate, do you? He's crafty, but is he capable of theft?"

Henry's stomach lurched and he sat back on his heels, blinking in stunned silence. "I... I... it's more than that, Victoria. This is just icing on an Epiphany cake for him..." He shook his head. "I can't explain it all to you now. But Nathaniel was framed for something he didn't do."

Victoria's breath caught in her throat, and she grasped at Henry, her face white as a sheet, hazel eyes wide and brimming over with tears. "It's not... oh God in heaven don't tell me Thomas was murdered." Henry nodded solemnly and Victoria let out a wail. "Don't tell me anymore. If you love me, save me from knowing more."

"I love you with all my heart," Henry said and held his arms open for her. She fell into his arms with a sob. "Oh, my sweet niece. How could I hurt you this way?"

"How can I feel this way?" Victoria sobbed, clutching onto Henry.

"I can't hate him. He's my father. He was distant but still my father. Uncle Henry, please..."

Henry eased himself to the floor, and Victoria curled up in his lap, weeping quietly. He rocked her back and forth, murmured gently into her hair, "There, there, my sunflower. I'm sure our minds are making things far greater than they truly are in our minds." He knew it was a lie, but he had to heal her heart somehow. "Don't think of me too highly either. I've done wrong too."

"Not like him," Victoria ground out. "Never like him."

Henry tutted, running his hand over her head and down her back. He could keep that little girl in his arms forever, humming to her, playing her music whenever she asked. But time was short. He held Victoria tightly and pressed kisses over her hair. He had to leave as soon as he could to warn Felicia and her husband.

"I have to get to Felicia and Nathaniel before he can." Henry gently extricated himself from Victoria's grasp, studying her crimson, tear-stained face. "I must leave. I'll be back in a day or so."

Victoria protested weakly as Henry stood and shoved the letter back into the envelope. He stuffed it into his coat pocket jumped to his feet and ran back out into the hallway.

"Uncle Henry," Victoria called.

Henry paused on the front porch, turning around to face his niece.

"What are you going to do?" she asked, her voice cracking. Her face was screwing as she tried to stop crying.

"Ride as fast as I can. If somebody is to stop William, I'll be the one to do it."

He shook his head. "Your father says he needs to bring his men for what? For justice? No, I need to ride to correct *his* justice."

Her attempts to stop crying were futile, and tears streamed down her cheeks. "But if he's possibly killed Thomas—hurt Felicia—oh! Uncle Henry, are you in danger too?"

"I'm his brother." Henry heaved a sigh. "He may have done a lot, but I don't think he'd stoop so low as to kill me. But Felicia and her baby are in danger. I have to take that chance."

Victoria flew down the steps and threw her arms about him,

holding him tightly in a hug. She drew in a breath, voice shaking as she whispered into his weskit.

"Uncle Henry, I feel like I lost Father years ago. And if all if this is true, he's caused me to lose Felicia. Please don't leave me too."

Henry pressed a final kiss to the top of his niece's head, then knelt to one knee and took her hands, looking up into her face, taking in every detail.

"My sweet sunflower. You are blessed to inherit your mother's beauty as well as her disposition. You are Martha through and through. Don't worry for me, Victoria. I'll be quite all right in the end." He leaned up and pressed a kiss to her cheek, then handed her his handkerchief. "So, you watch out here. Find Abigail Winthrop if you feel anxious. But don't be anxious for me." He dug in his pocket, pulling out a few coins, then handed them to Victoria. "Go and buy some music. I'll play it for you when I return." Henry pressed a kiss to her cheek. "Do not fear for me."

And with that, he jogged down the steps toward the stables. He looked back once and saw Victoria still at the door, her arms crossed, a frown on her face. She raised one hand in farewell, then spun back into the house. Henry pulled his green overcoat tight against the chill and ran to the stables, calling for his horse.

28

Before the sun had risen, Nathaniel packed up the cart, setting a few of the boxes up with him to make more room for Felicia in the back. After he had finished strapping everything down and had nestled Felicia and the baby into the cart, the tavern keep emerged, her shawl wrapped tight about her.

"I can't say as I've had any babies born in my barn," she said. Her eyes sparkled, and she smiled, clapping her hands softly. "Of course we've had baby goats and chickens, but never a baby-baby! Let me see her again?"

The exhausted Felicia tilted the child toward the older woman who cooed at the little girl, wiggling her wrinkled fingers over her tiny nose. Felicia beamed. "She is such a good, quiet baby, only fussing when hungry or wet."

"She is so tiny," the keep said, eyes still on the babe.

"But a little greedy thing," Felicia added with pride. "Will grow strong."

Nathaniel readjusted a bundle of clothes behind Felicia, then brushed a stray lock of hair off her face. She was too flushed, and worry for her battled with relief over the babe. "She does seem to be keen on nursing."

She shivered a little despite the blankets he'd wrapped around them both, but she grinned up at him. "I defy even Mrs. Haddock herself to complete such a feat. *She* would not be able to have a perfect baby in a barn."

The tavern keep straightened, pulled a blanket from under her shawl and handed it to Nathaniel. "Had it near the fire to heat it up. Hard weather for traveling."

"Thank you," Felicia murmured, burrowing down, and pulling the baby closer.

He nodded a thanks at the keep, then slid a makeshift pillow behind her back and head.

Nathaniel hopped out of the back of the cart, wiping his hands on his pants, and turned to the keep. "How much do we owe you?"

"For staying in the barn? Why would I charge you for staying in that drafty old place?"

"For the blankets then," Nathaniel said.

"I think they're being put to a good use," the keep said. She crossed her arms and smiled gently at the two. However, her smile melted into a graver expression and she shooed them off. "But you best be off. I heard tell of an escaped convict from a neighbor. Don't want to be caught around that business."

Nathaniel froze, and Felicia sat up a little in the cart, grasping the child closer to her chest.

"What have you heard?" he asked.

"Just some convict Colonel Moore from Penchester is after. Gossip spreads faster than wild horses running, you know. They say he killed a man when he escaped."

Felicia let out a cry and clutched at the baby. "Who?" she spluttered. "Whom did he kill?"

"I couldn't say." The woman reached out to soothe Felicia. "Some local drunk found the night watch bleeding."

"The night watch?" Felicia whispered, tears gathering in her eyes.

Nathaniel grabbed her hand, squeezing to warn her to remain silent.

The keep nodded. "Colonel Moore should be here soon on his way to find the convict. I'd get a move on if you don't want to be caught in the war path. But keep an eye out for suspicious men."

Felicia and Nathaniel exchanged troubled glances. She rocked the child in her arms, staring wide-eyed at Nathaniel. Her pale face lost any semblance of color she had after her ordeal. He could almost see the fear coil around her middle, tightening its way up to her throat. She hid a dry cough behind her sleeve, wiping at her eyes.

The tavern keep must have noticed their reactions, for she frowned lightly. "You're wasting sunlight. It'll be nightfall by the time you reach Mount Terre, and both of these girls need to rest properly."

Nathaniel thanked her again, then hopped up onto the front seat and shook the reins. The mare whinnied and trotted down the road. He glanced back. The keep stood, watching, her shawl gathered tightly around her. They traveled in silence for perhaps twenty minutes when Felicia asked, "Don't you have to be convicted to be called a convict?"

He focused back up at the road. "One would think that, yes. But we don't have time to argue semantics."

"We don't have time at all! They're coming, Natty! What are we going to do? My father! My father might be—"

"Moore must have lied," Nathaniel said, shooshing her. "Don't wake the baby, my love. You know he was very well when we left. Besides, we don't have a town drunk."

"Then my father is well?" Felicia asked, her voice catching in her throat.

Nathaniel leaned back in the seat and lowered his free arm down to her. She grasped it, squeezing it tightly, then let it go to cradle the baby.

"I'm very sure he is. We're going to press on till we get to Mount Terre and Emerald Rock Lake." He kept his voice cool and even but drew in a shaky breath, letting it out slowly, fingers tapping the reins. "There's no way that Moore will find us there."

"But what if he does catch us?"

Nathaniel looked over his shoulder at his wife and the sleeping baby. The tavern had disappeared behind them, but his throat tightened. If Moore did overtake them, if he did stop them or find them in

Mount Terre, he'd be in for a resistance far greater than the dumping of tea into the Boston Harbor.

Attack his family, and Nathaniel would fight back with the strength of the backwoods and the raging fury of his ancestors.

He squared his shoulders and sat up stiffly on the driver's seat. "He won't. I won't let him. Trust me, Felicia." He offered her a smile and reached down, brushing his fingers against her cheek.

"I'm just so scared, Natty," she whispered. "I believed him a friend."

"I know."

She leaned her face into his open palm, and for a moment, there was peace. Then, he sent the mare into a gallop. Felicia groaned at the sudden jolt, and the baby let out a wail. He pulled his hand away and tugged back on the reins, slowing the horse down to a walk.

He turned on the seat, facing her. "How are you doing?"

"I'm feeling rather hollow," Felicia said. "She's been in me for so long. It just feels so different to actually see her after feeling her move about inside. But the pain is better."

Nathaniel reached back and pulled the blankets further up around Felicia and the child.

"I sometimes wonder if it really is too soon to name her." she said softly. She pressed a kiss to the child's head, then carefully swaddled her up against the cold.

The cart hit a rut and bounced. Felicia moaned, and Nathaniel turned forward in his seat. "No, you should name her. Have you picked one?"

"I'm not entirely sure." Felicia hissed in a breath, letting it out slowly. "But I certainly can't name her Thomas as I planned. When will we get to Mount Terre?"

"At this rate, perhaps within the next five or so hours," Nathaniel said. "It may be cold, but it's clear, and the mare is rested and watered."

"But are you?"

"Don't mind me," Nathaniel said.

Felicia clicked her tongue and sighed. "The horse isn't the only thing that needs to be watered, Natty."

"I had something this morning while you slept. I told you not to give me any mind. Just get rest, my love. I'll rest when we get to Mount Terre."

Felicia hummed in response, and soon Nathaniel heard nothing but the wheels on the dirt, the axels squeaking, the horse's hooves pounding, and Felicia's moans in her sleep. He checked his watch for a moment, then slid it back into his pocket. They would be more than safe. They were nearing his territory now.

FELICIA TOOK to counting the trees as the hours crawled by. Nathaniel drove the cart down the road, alternating between walking and cantering every ten or so minutes, trying to avoid the worst ruts and dips. In between feeding the child, and sleeping as she could, Felicia searched for unusual looking trees, like a triple knotted oak or a weeping willow with a thick branch bent so low, she could have stepped over it, had she been walking.

At least watching and counting the trees kept her mind off the dull ache radiating through her lower extremities, which was a far better pain than the stabbing and tightening she had experienced the previous night. Still, she wondered if she'd be able to sit upright ever again.

Felicia gazed down at the child in her arms, studying her little face as she slept, the way her eyelashes fluttered, the way she looked exactly like her father, down to the tip of her nose. She pressed a finger into the child's palm, counting her fingers as they wrapped around her nail. She had done it. Her baby was finally in her arms, sleeping soundly. Despite the growing discomfort, Felicia smiled.

Since Nathaniel kept focused on the road when he believed she rested peacefully from time after time she assured him she was well. When he insisted that she eat, she told him to eat instead. She truly wasn't hungry. Perhaps she should have been, but all she wanted was to sleep.

The sun still held its spot high in the sky when Nathaniel stopped the cart to freshen the mare, stretch his legs, and take a packed sandwich from the back of the cart. Felicia finally ate something, then nursed the child, and promptly fell asleep. By the time she woke, Nathaniel had already resumed the trip.

The horse plodded along, the cart bumping and jolting more as the roads became less refined. Felicia held the baby close, trying to keep her as still, warm, and comfortable as possible.

The last few hours of the trip put that horse and cart to the test as the road grew narrower and steeper, but they reached the Endless Mountains with no sign of British soldiers on their trail.

The sun dipped below the trees, and Nathaniel slowed the mare down to a near standstill as the forest darkened around them. He jumped from the seat, and the horse snorted, and the cart jerked forward at a crawl.

"Natty?" Felicia sat up and craned her neck around to look for Nathaniel. "Where are we?"

"I'm on foot," Nathaniel called. "We're nearly there. I want to guide the horse from through the pass."

To the left, the mountain rose above them, but to their right, the land seemed to disappear. Felicia peered over the edge. Rocks tumbled over the side of the trail, and she spied a lake glimmering at the bottom of the gorge, waning sunlight glinting on dark, deep, green water.

"Emerald Rock Lake?"

"Hm-mmm," he grunted an affirmative, not turning around.

She pulled back into the blankets, hugging the baby to her chest.

They reached the top of the gorge, where someone had chopped down the trees both to make a clearing and construct a barricade. A tall wooden fence separated the buildings from the gorge, protecting the residents from accidental falls.

Felicia shuddered, passing her hand over her daughter's downy head. Whose death had prompted the residents to erect the fence?

"Hallo!" Nathaniel called out, waving his arm broadly toward a two-story log house in the distance.

A deep, weathered voice boomed out, "Is that Nathaniel Poe all the way from the Schuylkill?"

Felicia squinted out into the clearing, searching for who had spoken.

"Aye," Nathaniel shouted. He turned back to nod at her, a relieved grin spreading over his face, then faced the log house. "But only if it be my brother who calls."

The man emerged from the shadows and approached the cart. He grasped hold of Nathaniel's arms, a large smile plastered on his face. "Natty!"

"It does seem to be, Jasper, doesn't it?" Nathaniel said, gripping the man in return.

"What brings you home, Natty?" Jasper asked, shaking at Nathaniel's shoulders. "What brings you all the way back up to Emerald Rock Lake?"

"My wife," Nathaniel said, nodding to the cart. He released his brother, turning to Felicia. "We've finally made it," he said quietly and leaned over, pressing a kiss to the top of her head. "We're safe."

Felicia glanced between Nathaniel and Jasper but said nothing.

"Safe," Nathaniel murmured again. "You don't need to be afraid now."

Felicia huddled lower into the blankets. As much as she was glad for being in Mount Terre, away from Colonel Moore and any ghost of the past, a new fear crept into her heart.

This was not like home, with its brick houses and parlors and sitting rooms. This was entirely different. She was out of place, out of time, out of sorts. Her head pounded, and eyes burned. She glanced wearily up at Nathaniel.

"Safe from what?" Jasper asked, a frown replacing his mirth. "What's going on?"

Nathaniel's smile, too, faded. "They say I killed her first husband. Got redcoats on our tail."

Jasper huffed. "Leave it to Natty to bring the British our way."

Her husband bristled. "She's British herself. They're not all terrible."

"Though the majority are saying you killed her husband." Jasper's voice was cold, any happiness he seemed to have seemed long gone. He exhaled loudly. "No matter. If you say she's good, then there must be at least two good Englishmen somewhere. How long have you been traveling?"

"Far too long," Nathaniel said. "Delivered the babe halfway here. Please tell me you have a bed for her here."

"For you too, Natty," Felicia murmured. Her vision was becoming hazy, and her body ached, but the man hadn't slept well either. And if he kept putting himself last, she was going to force him, to get the rest he not only needed, but deserved.

"Of course there's room." Jasper clasped Nathaniel's shoulder. "here's always space for you." He glanced down to Felicia and offered her a smile. "And your family."

"Oh, thank God." Felicia heaved a heavy sigh. "I don't think I could stay in this cart much longer."

"We'll probably be needing to see an actual midwife too," Nathaniel said.

Felicia nodded, reaching up, groping for Nathaniel's hand, intertwining her fingers with his.

Night blanketed the sky, and Felicia finally let her body relax. It seemed that the worst was behind them.

29

As she had anticipated, the bedroom had a vastly different style than the one Felicia left behind. The home had been built of logs, not quite gray yet, but not so dark brown either, and no wallpaper decorated the walls. No scrolled wardrobe held ornate gowns. One bowl and pitcher had been placed on a small stool that could be used for washing up, but there was no toilette where she could curl her hair.

But, while an orange glow from the fireplace in the corner of the room provided the only light, it was welcoming and warm, and the bed sunk beneath her, cradling her tired body. She was comfortable, clean, and finally warm and within arm's reach, the baby slept in an old cradle courtesy of Jasper and his wife, who no longer needed it for their own children.

Felicia wiggled into the bed, pressing into the pillow, relishing in being in a clean chemise, lying on fresh, cotton sheets. Nathaniel had changed his clothes after washing his face and had nearly nodded off, even though he sat in a stiff wooden chair by the bed. Felicia all but begged for him to be there with her after the journey they traversed, and the midwife allowed it but not without some hesitation.

The midwife arrived after they had settled, and she smiled warmly as she reached into the wooden cradle and picked up the baby.

"You say the child was early?" she asked, inspecting the child's little hands and arms, gently prodding at her feet, watching them as they curled reflexively.

"She wasn't supposed to come till closer to Christmas," Felicia said. "That's what my midwife at home told me."

"How was the birth?"

"About four hours of torture to deliver her, but worth it in the end."

"The babe cried like a bat in the night," Nathaniel said. "There seemed nothing wrong with her once she was born. Lissie, however, seems flushed."

"Some red to the cheeks is good. The blood is flowing correctly." The midwife inclined her head toward Nathaniel. "The child seems perfectly healthy for being a little small. She's eating? And soiling herself?"

Felicia hid a yawn. "Every two hours."

"Good, good. And you?"

Felicia shrugged. "I had a baby yesterday and have been in a cart all day. I don't feel well, but considering that, I don't feel so poorly either."

The midwife turned her attention from the child to Felicia, pressing lightly on her belly, checking between her legs.

"Still very soft in the middle," the midwife muttered under her breath. "Four hours to bring her forth?"

"That was just to bear down." Felicia glanced at Nathaniel and smiled softly. "He helped me through the laboring."

The midwife hummed a response. "You feel a little warm, but despite that and your complaints of a headache, I can't find much wrong. Send for me right away if anything new happens. For now, just rest easy. You need to lie in."

"I can guarantee she won't be doing much now that we've finally made it here," Nathaniel said.

The midwife hummed again, then gathered up her things and left the small bedroom. Nathaniel stood and stretched his sore back, then moved to sit next to Felicia. Her vision began to swim, and she closed her eyes, relishing in the peace of the mountain settlement.

He smoothed back her hair from her face and pressed a kiss to her forehead. "There's no reason to be worried anymore, is there?"

Felicia reached up, caught his face in her hands, and brought him close to kiss him, then whispered, "I suppose not."

"Get some sleep, Lissie." Nathaniel stood again. "And I'll join you in a while."

"Where are you going?" Felicia reached for him. "It's lonely here."

He caught her hand but shook his head. "It is a lonely sort of town. I'll only be outside for a little while. Don't you want enough wood in that fire tonight?"

"I suppose so. But you need rest first."

"Never you mind me." Nathaniel pressed another kiss to her head, then stooped low over the cradle, gazing at the child. He smiled broadly as she stretched her tiny limbs.

"You keep telling me to rest," Felicia said, "but you need to as well. Come back soon."

"I will, Lissie," Nathaniel said softly. "Don't worry for me."

NATHANIEL SWUNG the ax into logs, splintering them, sending wood chips into the air. He yanked the ax out with a grunt, and wiped his brow and sat on the stump, tossing the ax aside. He rubbed his face and exhaled slowly, slumping forward. "They said that you killed her first husband."

He glared at his brother.

"Well?" Jasper asked. "Are you on the run?"

"You could say that, though I highly doubt they'd be able to find us all the way up here," Nathaniel said.

"Did you kill her husband?"

Nathaniel growled under his breath, disgusted, then stood up and gathered the kindling in his arms. "I scarcely knew her or her husband when he was killed. He was killed in a raid when a group of rebels ambushed his regiment and died from his injuries on the way back into

Penchester. But if you ask me, Jasper, no patriot, or rebel would have known where they were at that time. Either way, they say they found the Major's rifle in my shop."

"She isn't the widow Hawkings, is she?"

"How the devil do you know out here?" Nathaniel asked, stepped back, dropping the tinder to the ground. "Taverns I could see, but you?" He crossed his arms. "Does gossip really spread so far?"

"When it concerns a convict and a regiment, it does. We have to protect our families, too. One hunter heard it from a man traveling from Penchester, and we've been on the watch since." Jasper pulled at his dark hair, letting out an exasperated groan. "Lord, Nathaniel, give us warning the next time you go and bring British soldiers our way. With a murderous convict on the loose, Colonel Moore and his men are on his way this instant. Why do you think I was sentry when you came up to the clearing?"

"You have to be convicted to be a convict, Jasper, and I killed no one. Are we in any real danger?"

Nathaniel glanced at the wood on the ground and sighed, lowing himself to the stump again. Jasper slapped his hand on his back, then picked it up for him.

"I don't know," Jasper said, his voice low. "But every home in this clearing knows Moore is coming to Mount Terre. If he doesn't raid the town near Devil's Run first, he'll be here in a day."

"And if he's not here within a day? Jasper, I'm innocent. I had to get out with Felicia lest I made her a widow again."

"I have no doubt of your innocence." He set the firewood on the stack against the house, then came back to Nathaniel, and took his shoulders. Nathaniel wavered, blinking aching, burning eyes up at his brother. "But we'll need to be on the ready, since the convict we're told about is *you*."

"Semantics," Nathaniel said with a click of his tongue. He rubbed his eyes and heaved a yawn. "I'm not actually convicted."

His brother glared at him. "We have no time to argue semantics."

Nathaniel pressed his lips together. "I didn't come here to idly hide away," he said. "I will protect my wife, her child, and my family from Moore."

"I know you will." Jasper softened his tone and took some of the kindling from Nathaniel's arms. "But you're going to owe us a lifetime in free barrels, nonetheless."

Nathaniel quirked a side grin. "Small price for bringing Moore and his men up to Mount Terre."

30

The sky grew threatening, the clouds billowing over with a frigid rain. William surveyed as his men searched the old barn, pushing bales of hay and straw aside with their bayonets, the tavern keep wringing the towel in her hands as she followed them.

"Oh, please don't hurt the animals." the keep pleaded. "There's nothing in here that you'd need. You're going to disturb my chickens, and they'll never lay an egg again!"

"You said that you had people stay in here." William glowered down at her, teeth bared. "What did they look like?"

"I told you, sir, she gave birth in here. I could scarcely see her face since for her being bent over in pain half the time or bundled up on her way out. She was a tiny, frail thing. A bit like an orchid. He was tall and tan, long dark hair. Pale blue eyes."

"Nathaniel Poe," one of the officers said.

"You harbored my convict." William kept his voice even, but the beginnings of a growl rumbled in his throat. He stalked toward the woman.

She backed up into a stall. "Sir, I couldn't have known they were on

the run. She needed a place to lie down! Last I knew, they were headed
for Mount Terre!"

"We already know that." He plucked the towel from her hands with
the edge of his bayonet and flung it to the side.

"That's all I know. Lor, if I had known he's a murderer, I would-
n't've—I would have held them here longer! It would've taken a day to
fetch a midwife for the girl. They started toward Mount Terre before
the child was a day old."

William studied the woman's face, then held his rifle and bayonet
upright against his chest. "We continue on," he said to his men.
"They've had to have made it to that town by now."

"But Colonel Moore, sir, we've been on the road for over half a day
straight. The horses are tired," a young officer said, his cheeks
reddening as William eyed him. "We need to give the beasts some rest,
or we'll never make it to Mount Terre by nightfall."

"We go on now." William tapped his gloved fingers together. "The
horses have rested enough."

The men filed out of the barn and to their horses. William swung
himself onto his horse, but the keep came up to him and grabbed onto
the stirrup.

"Colonel Moore, won't you—"

"Won't I what?" William asked, and spun around so fiercely, the
woman stumbled backwards. "You harbored a criminal, then let him
and the woman escape. You should be glad I don't burn down your
tavern."

The keep blanched. She held her hands up and shook her head, her
eyes welling up with tears. "Oh, no, Colonel! Please! I could not be
more apologetic! I'm—"

"It's too late for apologies now, woman," William jerked the reins to
his horse. "Count your blessings. You won't have any more."

He kicked his heels into the horse's flanks, spurring it into a gallop.
His men followed, thundering down the road.

∾

FELICIA WOKE to the sound of the rain on the heavy glass windows. It was like music, a relaxing symphony from nature herself. She snuggled deep into the mattress next to Nathaniel, breathing in the scents of woodsmoke and cooked game.

She enjoyed the cozy warmth, lying beside her husband, with her baby in the cradle. Reaching over, Felicia ran her fingers over the infant's tiny hand, then leaned back in the bed and rolled over to face Nathaniel, opting to play with his long hair braiding, and unbraiding it till it became quite soft.

His eyes still closed, he muttered, "Felicia, what are you doing?"

"Your hair is just so long," she whispered. "Am I a bother to you?"

"No... what time is it?"

"Probably close to noon by now."

Nathaniel groaned and pushed himself upright, swinging his legs over the side of the bed and wiping the sleep from his eyes. "I suppose there's still no word about Moore and his men."

Felicia shook her head, but a dizziness overtook her, and she pressed into the pillows. "I would like to think that somebody would come and tell us if he's close. Do they know here, too?"

"Aye." Nathaniel slipped on a fresh weskit and a pair of breeches, then leaned forward and pressed a kiss to her head. "And they know why. I can't say my brother is very happy that I'm the reason why they're coming. If they come here... Lord knows what's going to happen."

"But they don't know where exactly we are, right? And how big is Mount Terre anyhow? Certainly, bigger than home?"

"The area's a bigger, but not by much, and it's mostly unsettled. More sheep than people. More settlements further down the way."

Felicia closed her eyes, every thought in her mind swimming about in the swirling sea of dizziness. She brought her hand up to her forehead and exhaled slowly.

"Perhaps he won't find us all the way in the woods."

The baby yawned, stretching her hands above her head.

"Perhaps." Nathaniel crouched low next to the cradle and scooped up the child, resting her in the crook of his arm. "I hope so, not merely for my sake, but for hers. And for every child here."

"Oh..." Felicia bit at her lip, a tightness filling her chest. "I hadn't thought—Good G-d, Nathaniel! How many children are here?"

Nathaniel shrugged as he swayed back and forth. "My brother has four, three under ten years of age. I didn't ask about every other house in this clearing."

Felicia winced and he sat by her side. He ran his fingers through her hair, humming under his breath.

She held out her arms, and Nathaniel gave her the child. She smoothed the baby's wispy, downy hair and whispered, "Oh, what have we done?"

"The best we could do," Nathaniel said. "I have my musket."

"It's quite archaic."

"It gets the job done." He smirked, a small glint sparkling in his eyes. "We can't all have British military weapons."

Felicia paused, gently running her finger along her daughter's puffy cheeks. "We have Thomas's rifle."

Nathaniel shook his head. "It's not mine, and I have no right to it."

"I'm sure if you avenged him with it, he'd be quite happy. Besides, he doesn't really have a say anymore, does he?"

The window shutters banged shut and opened again. Felicia jumped and Nathaniel rose to check outside.

"What is it? A storm?"

Nathaniel grimaced. "No, nothing that I could see. Perhaps he doesn't like that idea. He seems to be very perturbed at the fact you want me to use his musket."

Felicia became silent and turned her gaze from the windows to her daughter. A guilty pang built up in her chest and the corners of her eyes stung with tears she thought had dried.

"Thomas is not a petulant ghost. He's a kind sort."

Nathaniel returned to Felicia's side and took the baby from her to set in the cradle, then sat beside her and gently massaged her shoulders. "Ghosts don't exist, no matter what my father said."

"I do," Felicia murmured and a tear trickled down her cheek.

Nathaniel nodded. "Perhaps then there is something that could be said for the spirits of the departed still being on earth. But I haven't heard of anything in the Holy Writ to say they exist."

Felicia wiped her eyes with the back of her hand. "What he used to say too."

Nathaniel scratched at the top of Felicia's head, sending tingles down her spine. She hummed and brought the blanket further up under her chin. Nathaniel leaned over, looking at the sleeping babe. "She has your lips."

"The only thing she did inherit from me. Hand her to me." Felicia's voice turned to a ringing laughter as she lowered the neckline of her chemise and brought the baby to her breast "Everything else of her is Thomas. Thomas all over. Perhaps I should name her after him, after all."

"Thomasina?"

"No. I think that's too feline. His middle name is Theodore. Theodosia has a beautiful sound to it."

"Well, there is plenty of time to think of her name." Nathaniel pulled on his boots and slapped his hat on his head. "I have to go see about setting up shop in the barn. Your father packed me enough to start again very well."

Felicia winced as the babe unlatched from her breast. She raised her neckline and handed her daughter back to Nathaniel. "How long do I have to stay in this room anyway? I'm already tired of being cooped up."

"Already?" Nathaniel laughed, taking the baby from Felicia. He grinned as he set her back down to sleep. "Midwife said about a month. You'll probably be happier for it after the ordeal you went through."

Felicia let out a groan and slipped low against the pillows with a sigh.

"Nobody told me I was to be shut away like a plague after giving birth," she said, pouting at him.

"It's to help you avoid plagues. I'll be back in a few hours, Lissie."

Felicia peeked out from the blankets and wrinkled her nose at him, then hid back under the bedclothes, and Nathaniel left with ringing laugh. She grinned sleepily under the covers.

Nathaniel sent his sister-in-law up, and when Dorcas arrived, she busied herself with cleaning the baby and switching out the old water in the basin for fresh. She was at least ten years Felicia's senior, with ruddy-brown hair and a soft face with freckles about her nose. She was careworn, soft, and thick, with strong hands and a gentle demeanor. With her came twin toddlers, a little younger than Myles from home. They were too impressed with the smaller human in the cradle to be of much help.

"Truth and Verity, don't you poke that baby." Dorcas swatted at them while she straightened up room. "Get your little fingers away from that cradle and—oh, Felicia, I'm so sorry."

Felicia grinned sleepily as the twins scampered about the room. She yawned, covering her mouth.

"Why is she so small?" Verity asked, her dark curls bouncing as she peered into the cradle.

"Is she sleeping? Can't she play?" Truth asked, tugging her sister away to peek at the new baby.

"She's just born a day and a few hours ago, that's why she's tiny," Felicia answered, a tender smile on her lips. She nodded at Dorcas, who seemed relieved that Felicia was at ease with the pestering twins. "And she can't play because she's so tiny. Give her a couple of years. She'll be able to play with you then."

"Years? That's no fun." Verity tugged on her mother's skirts. "Mama? Can't we go play?"

Dorcas picked her mobcap off her head and smoothed out her hair. "By all means. Go find your older brother."

The twins darted out of the room faster than they had come in, leaving Dorcas, Felicia, and the sleeping baby, in peace.

Felicia clapped her hands with a quiet merriment. "Is that what I have to look forward to?" Felicia asked, pointing in the direction of the girls' scampering feet.

Dorcas handed Felicia the cup of caudle she had set on the mantle when she came in. Felicia breathed in the rich warm scent of sweet red wine and fresh boiled milk while her brother-in-law's wife heaved another sigh. "Yes. Joys and pains." She sat down on the foot of the bed. "I didn't know that Nathaniel had settled down, although he should have a long time ago."

"We've only been married since October," Felicia said. "I don't know if he's truly settled down."

Dorcas' eyes flickered from the cradle to Felicia.

"She's not his," Felicia said, biting her lip. "I was married before him. I lost Thomas—"

Dorcas let out a sigh, then paused. "I know... I heard... and now with Colonel Moore—"

"Don't speak of the Moores." Felicia's voice wavered as she set the caudle down. "It's a name I despise."

Dorcas's forehead wrinkled. "An unfathomable sorry to go through." She shook her head. "And you are so young."

"I was a soldier's wife, and I suppose I am again. Nothing is certain, and I suppose marriage to a soldier is like that—either I'd die having his children or he'd die in battle. Thomas... he died before he could see his child. It happens. Surprise raids happen. I'm sure he fought valiantly."

"Felicia... you may have been a soldier's wife, but you don't need to keep such a stiff upper lip... You have been through a lot, and you need to rest."

Felicia closed her eyes, breathing in deeply. "I'm trying..."

Dorcas smoothed the blankets around Felicia. "I'll be back in to check on you. But you are feeling fine?"

"I'm feeling as fine as one can get being forced to lie-in."

Dorcas's frown turned up into a soft smile as she smoothed the blankets around Felicia. "Oh, my dear. After you've had a few, you'll learn to relish the peace you get from lying-in."

Her footsteps followed her daughters', leaving Felicia alone with the child, the only sound the rain against the windows.

NATHANIEL SET the wooden box of tools beside his musket and the barrel he had unpacked from the cart. Chickens clucked, and horses snuffled around him, and Jasper's children shouted in the distance. He paused to breathe in the scent of mountain and pine trees mingling with the musty hay and old wood. It filled his lungs and chest with a hope for the future, even if he had to start his business over from scratch.

Jasper's barn wasn't large with barely enough space for a couple of horses and some chickens. It certainly could not be mistaken for a cooper's shop. There were no shelves of ready-to-purchase items, no space to welcome customers only one small space near the front where Nathaniel could make a rough workspace, just to produce items for shipping. He wasn't thrilled with the prospect of doing his business in such a small space, but he was grateful his brother was willing to share the barn, and he was thankful for the tools that his father-in-law saved. He'd be better settled when he could build his own home and workshop. Goodness knew how long that would take to put together. The barn was a temporary business space, and as long as it stayed temporary, both of them were all right with it.

Jasper dusted off his hands, sliding a box to the side of the barn with his boot. "That should be the last one."

"I'm surprised you kept my old tools." Nathaniel began sorting through his coopering materials. "Glad of it though. We couldn't bring the bigger equipment. Doubt it would have fit on the cart anyway. Definitely couldn't fit next to her damn teapot." A smile formed on his lips, then he shook his head. "How is one so invested in tea? It's puzzling."

"She packed a teapot during an escape?" Jasper asked, moving a workbench out of Nathaniel's way.

Nathaniel shrugged and rolled out some old hoops he had kept packed away in the loft. "There really is no getting between that woman and her tea."

"She does realize that it's near impossible to find up here, right?"

"If she hasn't, she'll find out soon." Nathaniel playfully rolled his eyes. "Goodness knows she might have had us stop in Philadelphia to buy some before coming up here. Although, tea was hard to find in town."

"No matter. Perhaps she'll be fine with dandelion tea," Jasper said, and his strong square face softened as he grinned. "Dorcas doesn't seem to mind it."

"We can hope for the best when it comes to that." A sinking feeling pitted in Nathaniel's stomach. He set his jaw and cleared his throat. "But we need to pray for what's to come."

"Yes." Jasper sat on a box, resting his elbows on his knees. "The reason you're hiding here."

"I didn't come here to hide. I'll fight if I have to," Nathaniel said grimly, motioning to his musket. "I'll have my musket ready. If you are with me, you have yours."

Jasper snorted. "Of course I am."

"If worse comes to worse, we'll drive them down the pass to Devil's Run and 'round that wicked bend."

Jasper leaned back against the workbench as Nathaniel set up a barrel form. "I'll gather the men and let them know of this plan. Shoot first and don't ask questions?"

"Only if you see the redcoat." Nathaniel gripped a block of wood so hard splinters dug under his nails. He set the wood down and grimaced as he picked them out. "We don't need any civilians getting killed over one man's vendetta."

Jasper leaned forward, narrowing his eyes. His lips parted. "Why does he have such a vendetta against you?"

"I don't know." Nathaniel tossed his arms into the air. "Ask him yourself when he arrives. For all I know, it's just because I married Felicia before his brother could."

"Didn't you train the minute men in your town?"

"More or less. Why?"

Jasper tapped his knuckles to his chin and hummed. "Wouldn't that be a reason to need you gone?"

"Gabriel Barnet is just as good as I. He's training them now. Besides, if Moore thinks that one man keeps that ragtag team of boys together, he's in for a surprise. Even if he wanted me gone for some deeper reason, they're stronger than I think he gives them credit for." Nathaniel surveyed the tools before him and frowned. "This will have to wait till all dust is cleared."

"We'll see what can be done." Jasper stood with a grunt and paced to his brother, then clasped his shoulder. He smiled. "If we are on the right side of this, and we are, we'll make it out of this."

Nathaniel stepped out of the barn. The roiling gray clouds overhead drew his attention to the sky. He held out his hand and the light mist dampened it.

"I'm sure." Jasper followed Nathaniel out of the barn. "But on the bright side, maybe you won't need to stay up here."

Nathaniel clicked his tongue. "As long as Moore is around, we'll never be able to go back."

What a shame. He'd grown to love and call Penchester home. But he'd go where he was guided, and at the moment, it was back in Mount Terre. Despite his longing to be back by the Schuylkill, he had to go where he was needed.

Together, Nathaniel and Jasper started headed back to the house for dinner, but a small child darted up toward them from the woods, his face as gray as the sky, tears streaming down his face. He ran up to Jasper, and clung to his legs, burying his face in Jasper's coat.

"Papa!"

"James!" Jasper bent low, taking his son's streaky red face in his strong hands, and brushed away his tears. "What're you doing in the woods? What is the matter? You look as if you've you seen a ghost."

"I did," the boy cried. "Riding a horse! He's dead! It's a dead man riding a horse!"

Jasper glanced to Nathaniel, then back at his son, smoothing his hair, shushing him gently. "Dead men don't ride horses, James."

"I saw him! He's slumped over on his horse! He's coming this way!"

There was a rustling in the woods behind James. Nathaniel and Jasper straightened at the sound, eyes set on the forest, muscles tightening.

Jasper pulled his attention back to his son and took his arms. "Get to the house and stay there. I'm sure all you saw just a traveler. But stay with your mother."

"Yes, Papa." James took off running, his shoes squelching in the damp earth.

Nathaniel and Jasper picked up their muskets, then slowly made their way up to the forest's edge.

"Do you think it's Moore or his men?" Jasper asked in a hushed growl.

"They have too much decorum to slump." Nathaniel made a

disgusted click of his tongue but kept his musket pointed forward. "But that could be what he'd want us to think, if he's already been down to the main settlements."

"Shoot first?"

"Once you see the redcoat."

Nathaniel and Jasper crouched in the bushes and waited silently, quietly. The muffled sound of hoofs on dead leaves sent a shiver down Nathaniel's spine. He set his jaw, gripping his weapon close.

A horse stepped out of the forest, its rider slumped forward—exhausted, or dead, Nathaniel couldn't tell. But the rider wore no redcoat. He wore emerald green.

Nathaniel lowered his musket. "Hold, Jasper."

He stepped over to the horse and grabbed hold of the reins. He reached up and shook the rider's arm, garnering a tired moan from the man.

"He's alive," Nathaniel said as Jasper joined him.

Nathaniel peered at the unarmed rider. Though he wore no redcoat uniform, the rider wasn't a colonial. His clothes, though stained with the dirt and dust of travel, and soaked in rain, were far too fine for any colonist of Mount Terre. His tricorn hat and hair ribbon were missing, and his hair loose, hanging over his shoulders and obscuring his face.

Nathaniel handed his musket to Jasper, then reached up to sit the rider back upright in the saddle, then stepped back, his eyes widening. "Henry?"

Henry Moore's head bobbed as he moaned in response.

"Is he another Brit?" Jasper curled his lip as Henry slumped forward again. "You brought another one here? Nathaniel, this has got to end."

"This one is not welcome, either." Nathaniel narrowed his eyes and grabbed Henry's arm, dragging him back upright. "Henry, what in G-d's good name are you doing here?"

Henry leaned forward again, but this time, he swung himself down from the horse. His knees gave as he hit the ground, but he held onto the pommel and pulled himself to stand. The horse turned its head, nuzzling him in the chest, and he sagged into its side. He winced, running his hands through his unbound hair.

Nathaniel shook Henry's shoulders, staring into the man's exhausted eyes. "Answer me, Moore. What are you doing so far from the Schuylkill?"

"Moore?" Jasper's eyes flashed, and he gripped his weapon.

Henry held up his hands. "No, don't shoot. I'm not here as an enemy," he rasped, then cleared his throat.

"Pray tell," Jasper muttered, his musket aimed at Henry's chest.

Henry only shook his head. "Important business." He swallowed. "Is Felicia safe?"

"As safe as she can be." Nathaniel crossed his arms.

Henry relaxed his shoulders, blinked, and rubbed his eyes. "William is nearly here."

"We know," Nathaniel snapped.

"But there's more you don't know..." Henry pulled an envelope from his coat pocket and handed it to Nathaniel. "Now please, for the love of God, could I sit on something that doesn't move?"

Nathaniel glanced down at the envelope and narrowed his eyes. The vellum weighed heavily in his hands and the blue wax seal jabbed his palm.

Bach Trust Philadelphia Branch

He pressed his lips tightly with every muscle in his body stiff and on edge.

31

Nathaniel and Jasper brought Henry into the cabin, and Dorcas ushered the children outside. Henry sat at the table, a cup of black coffee in his hands, and Jasper, his musket beside him, kept a close watch on the exhausted man, thrumming his long fingers over the weapon's stock.

Nathaniel examined the broken wax seal, then glared at Henry Moore. "If what's in this letter is detrimental to Felicia or the baby—"

"No, the opposite." Henry held up his free hand. His face softened. "Is she well? She's had the child?"

"She's lying-in." Nathaniel narrowed his eyes at Henry as he opened the envelope. "The child is fine."

But before Henry could ask another question, Nathaniel gripped the letter in his fist. Calmly, he stood, and strode to Henry, looming over him. "What are you doing with Thomas's will?"

Henry flinched. His inky eyes flashed uncertainty, and Nathaniel backed off, standing beside his brother.

The bedraggled man gulped. "The better question is what was William doing with it. It was on his desk—did she have a son or daughter?"

Nathaniel eased further back, crossing his arms. He eyed Henry, and he felt the tension leave his face. His shoulders slackened and he pulled up a chair. "Why should you care?"

Henry pressed his lips together, exhaling slowly through his nose. He looked at Nathaniel, a pitiful yearning glowing like a dying ember in his eyes, then turned aside.

"My G-d," Nathaniel whispered. "You do love her..."

Henry stared at the log walls but held his head high.

Nathaniel pulled over a chair and plunked down on it, leaning over the back. "Why else would you travel from town to Mount Terre, just to warn us of something we knew?"

"I didn't know you knew. But you don't know it all..." Henry said, resigned, his voice low. He gestured toward the paper in Nathaniel's hand. "It's all there in the letter."

Anger churned in his gut, and Nathaniel shook the letter in his hand. He glanced toward Henry, studying the man, and he nodded. The man did ride to warn them, rather like Paul Revere. He slowly exhaled, and let his shoulders loosen and stretched his neck. "Why was he holding onto this? The stipulations are clearly spelled out. He's going to get half of the estate and Felicia will get the other half as soon as she responds to the letter."

"This goes far deeper than some missing payments," Henry said. "Not only has my brother decided to seize any payment Felicia might receive, but he staged the raid..."

"What?" Nathaniel's lips twisted while he deciphered what Henry meant. He bared his teeth. "What are you talking about? There was a raid—how else would Thomas have been killed?"

"A staged raid." Henry shifted uncomfortably in his seat. "There were no colonist minutemen in that area, and you know it. William staged the entire thing for a plan of his own. I think he killed—"

"There's so much racket down here"—Felicia called from upstairs, and all three men turned to the stairwell— "that you're going to wake the baby."

"Felicia, you shouldn't be up." Nathaniel stood, then swiveled back to Jasper and Henry, the former keeping a watch on the latter, while the latter hid his face. Nathaniel held out his arms, torn between gentleness and exasperation. "You're going to make yourself sick, Lissie. Go back upstairs."

"I've rested enough, and I need to move." Felicia's voice became clearer as she descended the steep wooden steps. "I don't like lying-in, and I won't do it any long—oh! What the devil are *you* doing here?"

She stood in the doorway, staring wide-eyed at Henry, her jaw set, fingers flexing and unflexing.

Henry lowered his hand from his face. "I came here to warn you."

When Henry stood up, Jasper shoved the nose of his musket into Henry's chest, forcing him to sit down again. Nathaniel motioned for Jasper to stand down, and he did, setting the musket aside. Henry slumped backward with a sigh.

"Warn me about what?" Felicia's voice was taut, and her usually pale face burned bright red. Nathaniel reached out and held her shoulders, running his hands over her arms, but she continued. "Henry, you're not somebody—"

"No... I know. I'm not somebody you want to see. You made that clear a few days ago." Henry drew in a deep breath, and he closed his eyes, then bowed his head. "But you must listen to me. Thomas wasn't killed in a raid."

Felicia shrugged Nathaniel off her arms and stalked over to Henry.

"My husband died on his way to Boston. Things like that happen—"

"Felicia... I think we need to trust him," Nathaniel said, chewing over his words, eyeing Henry and nodded curtly. He handed her the letter. "He has learned more about Thomas's death than we thought possible..."

"What's this?" Turning the paper over in her hands, her fingers traced the broken wax seal. Her brow furrowed, and she glanced expectantly between Nathaniel and Henry.

"Thomas's will," Nathaniel and Henry said at once.

Jasper's his dark eyes flashed toward Henry. "Is this man safe?"

"Yes..." Nathaniel said slowly. "I believe he can be trusted."

Felicia gaped up at him from the letter, shock written on her features. Nathaniel cupped her face in his palm, gently running his thumb over her cheek, then pointed to the letter. She bowed her head to read it.

Jasper nodded. "If you've got him under control, I'll keep watch for Moore." He rolled his shoulders, then walked outside to join his family.

"I've been waiting on this for months." Felicia eased herself into the wooden chair next to Henry, before reading the legalities concerning Thomas's estate. "When did it come in?"

"A few months ago." Henry cleared his throat. "It was on William's desk. You came in those months ago asking for it when you caught—" Henry's eyes flickered to Nathaniel then back to Felicia. "When I played the violin for you. I think it was there even then."

"I don't understand," Felicia said, the anger and shock visibly melting into confusion. Her lips parted, and she cocked her head. "Then why didn't I receive it earlier?"

"I believe my brother was holding onto your half of the estate." Henry tapped his fingers together, then reached out to her, but Nathaniel cleared his throat. Henry brought his hands to his lap. "Felicia, it goes deeper. If it were only that he was stealing your money, letting you have small pieces of it to keep you quiet..."

Nathaniel tapped his fist to his mouth, pacing about the room. He glanced out the window, squinting for movement, then directed his attention back at Henry. Repentant was a word he'd use to describe him. Remorseful and repentant. Nathaniel admired a man who admitted his wrongs. He nodded to himself, then squeezed Felicia's shoulder.

"One thing at a time." Felicia held her hand up. "You're telling me that your brother has taken—*stolen*! —my half of the estate."

Henry looked tentatively over to Nathaniel, who motioned for him to go on. Henry turned back to Felicia.

"I suppose it could be traced, though I didn't waste time trying to find out. But Victoria has noted an influx of money, and now with this info, yes, I believe William has been embezzling." Henry reached out again, this time picking up Felicia's hand, encasing it in his. "But that's not all. He's covering Thomas's murder."

Felicia pulled her hand away from Henry. Nathaniel stepped behind her, resting his hands on her shoulders to keep her from shaking.

"Henry! Stop!" Felicia's face scrunched, but tears trickled down her cheeks. "It was a raid."

"It was a 'calculated loss,'" Henry said gently. "William himself told me, while threatening my deportation to Australia, that he staged it all for some plan of his own concoction. Australia seems like a nice place this time of year anyway..." He smiled mirthlessly. "So I might as well tell you all I know. First, I was drunk—so drunk—that night that the plan unfolded."

Nathaniel crossed his arms. "So you're the town drunk who found John..."

Henry's face flushed. "Aye... he's mending at home." He paused as Felicia let out a relieved squeaking sigh and covered her face in her hands, then continued. "Drinking is one of my vices." Henry stood up and paced about the room. "I knew you loved Nathaniel. I needed a way to win you back. I—" He broke off, his gaze darting to them, then away. "I... wanted you—your estate, and I gambled the one thing I shouldn't have. Your trust. Your love."

"Oh, yes. That's gone," Felicia lowered her hands from her face, and glared. Henry winced. But her face softened, and she exhaled slowly, then steepled her fingers under her chin. "What does *your story* have to do with Thomas, or why my parents can't meet their grandchild?"

Henry shook his head. "William did most of the talking. He said that if we could pin Thomas's death on Nathaniel and have him hanged; the rebel stronghold would fall. He'd have an easy in into Philadelphia. I am sure he wants to attack the Continental Congress."

Natty's lips parted. Moore wanted to destroy the patriot stronghold and for what? A scheme to kill the Congress? He wracked his brain to figure out just what Moore planned to do, but he kept his back straight and chin squared.

"Your intents may have only been for your own heart, but how on earth could Moore scheme such a thing?" Nathaniel flexed his fingers, anger, pity, and disgust battling for primacy. The more Henry spoke, the more Nathaniel realized the man was caught in a scheme far out of his control. How could Henry be so pitifully minded?

"I cannot condone the actions of a drunk Henry Moore," Henry said. "I do know that my sole role in this was to win Felicia's heart. I failed miserably."

Felicia sat, wide-eyed and yet expressionless, her lips slightly parted, and the sight of her, like a wounded deer, drove Nathaniel to ask, "What's this have to do with Thomas? Surely, William realizes more than just a simple cooper kept the militia together."

"I don't know what he was thinking." Henry raised his hands. "I only know he staged that raid so the patriots in town would be ostracized for attacking a peaceable regiment, one that wanted no quarrel with the townsfolk. And in a raid, people must be killed, if it is to be believable... if he could have garnered sympathy from the loyalists of Philadelphia and around Penchester—" He grimaced. "It's disgusting to say aloud... Now, I can only guess that when he read the will, his plan became two-fold. I believe he wanted your estate more than I did..."

Felicia and Nathaniel's eyes met. He crossed to her seat and set his hands on her shoulders. She grabbed his, her tiny fingers curling around his.

"And if I married you," Felicia said, "that would further cover up the murder William committed."

Henry turned to face the window. "If you married me means nothing. As much as I would rather... it means nothing. Oh, it might have delayed his plan, but because you married Nathaniel, one of the leaders of the patriots in town, William knew how to cover it up. William knew he could pin—"

A single shot rang out, and the window shattered, sending shards of glass to the floor and table.

Henry froze.

Felicia stifled a scream.

Henry staggered backward, his hands covering his weskit, and red seeped through his fingers. He blinked up at Felicia and Nathaniel, then slipped to his knee. Blood dripped from his hands to the woven rug beneath him. He squeezed his eyes shut and gritted his teeth with a weak grunt.

"*Henry!*" Felicia pushed herself off the chair and to his side.

Nathaniel rushed to Felicia and Henry, keeping them low beneath the windowpane, then crept over and peered outside. A flash of red moved out of the bushes near the front porch. He growled and grabbed his musket.

"Jasper! He's here!" he called.

"Nathaniel, call Dorcas—get someone!"

A few more shots rang through the clearing, and Jasper shouted for his wife and children to run to the barn.

"Stay down." Nathaniel crouched low and touched Felicia's tear-stained cheek. "Do what you can. I'll take care of this."

Crouching low, he crept to the front door and slipped outside, leaving Henry and Felicia in the den.

Henry Moore's act of love

HENRY DREW in a breath but focused on Felicia's pale face. She gently lifted his hand away from his belly and gasped, pressing her own hand over his and the growing red seeping through his weskit's brocade.

"I'm so sorry—" he said, wavering on his knee.

Somehow, Felicia caught him as he toppled to his side, bracing him against her chest as his breathing grew hoarse. Something tickled at his lip, running down his neck. He brought up a shaking hand and wiped at the blood trickling from the corner of his mouth.

She lowered him to the floor and set his head on her lap. "Henry? I need you to hold on, dear. Please? Nathaniel is going to go find a doctor, and we'll be here, and you can just... you can..."

"I love you, Felicia," Henry whispered. "I wish I could have let you know before."

Felicia gently brushed back loose tendrils of his hair from his face. She pressed her lips together and drew in a shaky breath. "I wish you could have as well."

"It would have made little difference." He gasped, and his limbs shook. Felicia took his hands, trying keep him steady. Henry bit back a moan. "Felicia, listen to me. William killed Thomas. William killed me."

"William may have killed Thomas, but he didn't kill you yet," Felicia shushed, gently cupping his face in her hands.

He blinked, focusing on her tiny face. Her face almost glowed... so ethereal and perfect. And finally, she was looking at him with every ounce of love and affection he'd ever hoped for. The way her eyes glimmered, the way her lips parted... he could stare at her face for the rest of his life.

"And if he did kill my husband—no, no!" She gasped as his eyes slipped shut. "Henry, stay awake."

It took effort to open them, but if he did, he could see her... Henry looked up through half-lidded eyes, but the world began to lose its color. He focused on her lips, and his head lolled against her arm. "I'm tired, Felicia, let me sleep."

"I can't lose you, Henry," she whispered, gently cupping his face in her palm. "I valued our friendship. I did—I do. I—I am sorry for how I've acted. And you've risked everything to warn me today. Please, don't leave now."

"Henry..."

Henry blinked slowly and tilted his head. Beyond Felicia, a figure flickered. He reached out his hand.

"Henry, I need you to stay with me." Felicia craned her neck to look behind her, her loose hair whipping in front of her face as she turned.

Her beautiful, brown hair... He reached up and twirled a bloody finger through a curl, a soft smile on his lips. Felicia took his hand from her hair, intertwining her fingers with his.

"Nathaniel will be back soon, dear." She shifted a little, and Henry's pain spiked, then lessened. "He'll find a proper surgeon to—Henry! You've got to stay awake!"

"I'm trying." Henry coughed, praying blood sprayed onto his chin and cravat. He frowned, furrowing his brows, then rasped, "Oh, it's the better of the cravats."

Felicia wiggled her sleeve down, took its hem, and carefully wiped Henry's face of the blood and sweat. "I'll get you a new one."

He shook his head and tried to blink back the tears that welled up in his eyes, but they spilled down his cheeks all the same. A small cry escaped Felicia's lips, and she dried his eyes with an unstained part of her sleeve.

"No use." He took in a rasping breath, gritted his teeth, and squeezed his eyes shut.

Felicia held him a little tighter, keeping him still. Her voice as soft as a lark, she asked, "What can I do?"

"The pain...explodes. It burns something fierce." He grimaced, then flexed and unflexed his hands. "Ah! Make the pain go away..."

Felicia stroked his face and hummed a vaguely familiar song, though neither Vivaldi, nor Bach. The notes bounced in his head, fading in and out, but still, while she hummed, they resonated in his mind.

"My song," Henry murmured. He coughed and fresh blood spilled onto his chin.

Felicia wiped it away, still humming, still holding him close.

"You've read it..."

She nodded, her lips flickering into a small smile.

The promise he had made to Victoria—he needed to play her whatever broadsheet she had chosen. He started to lean up, panic settling into his chest. He couldn't break his promise to his sunflower.

"Victoria!" A burble of blood rose in his throat and he groaned. "I have to get back to—"

"Shhhh."

Felicia continued humming, rocking him a little. Perhaps she whispered something about Nathaniel, perhaps about a surgeon, and his chest twisted in a sharp pain. He gasped and ground his heels into the cool, wood floor, but then she resumed humming, and he eased back into her arms.

Henry's eyelids drooped. The burning in his belly abated to no more than a buzzing throb.

"Oh, Henry! No, please don't sleep!"

Henry took in a staggering breath and forced his eyes open. He drew in another labored breath. "I'm cold... tired... grant me five minutes of sleep."

"It starts to lose the sting, doesn't it?"

Henry nodded wordlessly.

"Yes, you need to sleep, but after the surgeon sees you."

"Thomas?" Henry asked, eyes half closed, voice slurred and low.

"You know, I never believed you'd go like this. I thought you'd drink yourself into oblivion. This is much worse."

There he was, standing behind Felicia, quipping with his dry wit. Henry almost smiled, but a shudder shook him as the pain spiked again.

"Is he here?" Felicia's voice was soft and low, like music on the breeze. As she dabbed at Henry's face with her sleeve, he took her wrist. He barely saw her face, and blinked, but couldn't focus on her lips, her eyes, anything. Instead, he concentrated on the peacefulness of her breathing.

"He said he'd thought I'd drink myself to death," he said, his breaths becoming more labored.

Thomas stepped beside Felicia, smiling sadly at Henry. He reached a gloved hand to him.

"Oh, come on and just take my hand, man. I'll lead you to a place where it won't hurt anymore. I promise."

"But Felicia—" Henry whispered.

Thomas seemed to draw a deep breath and let it out slowly, but he nodded, a resigned sadness in his pale eyes. *"Is in good hands with the cooper. I know, she's a hard one to leave, isn't she?"*

Henry's focus flickered between Felicia and Thomas behind her. The ghost became clearer while he became colder. He drew in a shuddering breath, then let it out slowly. Felicia, the table and chair, the window, the home were all shrouded in a white haze while Thomas stood clear as day, extending his hand.

"Felicia?" Henry's breaths grew shallow, and she tightened her hold on him, pressing her hand against his weskit. He smiled lightly, resting his hand atop hers. She was still trying to stop the bleeding. It was far too late, but the pressure of her hand against his wound was comforting.

"Yes? Henry?"

"Right my wrongs—" He shuddered. "Forgive me."

"You've made up for your wrongs. There's nothing more to be done." Felicia pressed a kiss to his cheek. "You're forgiven."

Henry tried to smile, but only a soft moan escaped his throat.

His head lolled against her shoulder, and his eyes fluttered closed.

❦ 32 ❦

"You're forgiven." Felicia stroked Henry's still face. His cheeks had gone gray, and his inky-blue eyes remained closed. She gently shook his shoulders. "You need to wake up. I said you're forgiven, Henry." Her voice trembled. "Please, wake up."

The front door swung open. Musket in hand, Nathaniel rushed back in, but though Felicia rocked Henry back and forth, she kept her focus on her husband. Her tears fell, mingling with the blood on his face. Her chest constricted as she fought the desire to retch. The man who once had ten acres in New Jersey, a disposable income, and unassailable confidence, could not have foreseen this, no matter how well-planned he kept his future. She gripped him, coughing ragged sobs.

"Natty, he's... gone. Like—"

"God in heaven," Nathaniel murmured.

"It was William... William shot him. Just like he shot Thomas." Her voice broke, but the injustice of it all hit her. Henry had been killed for the same reason Thomas was killed, for some warped sense of heroism. She clenched her teeth, grinding out her words. "Where is he? Where is that *vile* devil who killed my husband and his own brother? *Where is he?*"

"Heading down to the main settlements." Nathaniel set the musket aside. He stooped low, reaching toward Henry, but Felicia pulled his body closer to her chest.

"Don't you take him!" She broke completely, bowing over Henry's body convulsing as she wept. "I don't—want—to say—goodbye—"

"Felicia... he's gone." He placed a tender hand on Felicia's shoulder, but she shook it off. "He's gone."

His words finally penetrated through her heart. With a relenting whimper, Felicia relaxed her grip on Henry, and with a grunt, Nathaniel stooped and lifted Henry from her arms. Nathaniel him down in the wooden armchair by the table, where it seemed as if, he had only fallen asleep while sitting, despite the bloodstain over his belly.

Anger churned in her chest. How dare that William Moore—scoundrel, beast, *devil*—enter her life, act as a friend, only to tear away her first love. Her chest tightened, the burning in his face traveling throughout her body, pulsing in her limbs, saturating her core. He had lied. That was all he ever had done. All his well-wishes, his smiles, his laughter—all counterfeits. She felt used, betrayed, like a disposable pawn.

And now Henry was dead. Henry, a man for whom she tried to feel affection, tried to love, was gone. She felt betrayed on his behalf, for he had been a chess piece. She fumed and her heart ached.

She lurched to her feet and clutched Nathaniel's shirt. "Where is that... that... *vile beast*? Will they know he killed my husband? Will they know he killed his brother?"

"I'll find him." Nathaniel's nostrils flared. "I'll make sure they know. They'll know everything Moore's done. They'll know his schemes. And we'll drag his name across the colonies. He won't get away with what he's done to our home, to your husband, to Henry, to Mount Terre, to the name of the army which he fights."

Felicia gritted her teeth. She squeezed her eyes shut and whispered, "Would you kill him if it came to that?"

"I'll do what I must. But for now"—his voice softened—"you need to go back upstairs and clean up. We have to lay Henry in the cellar until... I must go tell Dorcas..." his voice trailed off, and he furrowed his dark brow. "A stronger man than I gave him credit..."

Felicia stood silently, balling her hands into fists, her chest heaving, her face burning but Nathaniel stood there in solemn solidarity, as if to give her the time to process the emotions that bubbled up to the surface. He was an anchor.

Finally, Felicia leaned against Nathaniel and buried her face in his shirt. He held her upright, hugging her against his side as they stood in the silent cabin. She pressed her head against his chest, and his breath atop her head.

"This shouldn't have happened." Felicia shuddered. "It's my fault. It's all my fault."

"No, it isn't, Lissie. You couldn't have stopped William. Not from shooting his brother, nor from killing Thomas. But, love, you are exhausted. You need to rest."

Felicia slipped out of his arms to the wooden floor and hid her face in her hands. She stiffened, the aches from her ordeal building up in her body once more. "I shouldn't have married you, Natty."

Nathaniel knelt next to her and pulled her close. His fingers combed through her hair, and she shivered. His heart beat against her cheek. "Why not?"

"I just... none of this would have happened! If I had been able... if I could have—"

"No." Nathaniel took Felicia's face in his hands, tilting her head up to meet her eyes. "This is what happens when a bloodthirsty colonel covers up a murder. He'd have his scheme no matter who stood in his way. None of this is your doing, love."

Sobs wracked Felicia as she wrapped her arms around Nathaniel's waist, pressing close to him, resting her face in the crook of his neck. "I love you! I love you so—but I just want to go back to the beginning," she gasped between tears. "Back and fix it all."

"It's impossible to change time, Felicia." Nathaniel's voice cracked. "As much as we want to, we can't."

"I just want to be normal again," Felicia said through her tears. But then, the tears stopped. She drew in a trembling breath and stared forward, her eyes becoming glassy.

"Maybe, in time, we can return to Penchester. It'll be normal again, though normal will never be the same, as much as we want it to be. But we can go back to a sense of normalcy."

Felicia wobbled as Nathaniel stood her up. She braced herself on his arm as he helped her to the stairs.

"You're shaking, my love," he murmured.

Felicia said nothing, staring ahead as they walked up to the second floor. Though her muscles ached all over, she was numb. Everything she knew and loved was gone. She was a stranger to her mind and to her lodgings.

He continued. "You need to lie down. Stay here with the baby till I come for you. There's work to be done concerning that devil who called himself a member of King George's army."

Nathaniel opened the bedroom door. The baby fussed in her cradle, snapping Felicia out of her thoughts. But when Felicia rushed to her side, Nathaniel held her back.

"The baby!" she cried.

"The blood."

Felicia glanced down at her gown and froze. The blood... Henry's blood...

Nathaniel dodged around her and pulled a fresh nightgown out of the trunk at the foot of the bed. She allowed Nathaniel to slide her chemise off and replace it with the clean one. Silently, he dipped a rag into the basin of water and wiped Felicia's face and arms.

"Settle back," he said, and while she scooted onto the bed, he scooped up the baby and handed her to Felicia, who lowered the collar of her gown and situated her daughter at her breast, cradling her neck and head, wincing as the baby latched on.

Nathaniel lowered himself to sit next to her, watching her feed her daughter, and said, quietly, "Felicia... I wish we could go back too."

Pressing her lips together, squeezing her eyes shut, she leaned her head on his shoulder, and forced back fresh tears.

"I wish we could go back. To my business. To little Myles. To Henry being alive. I'd even wish we could go back to Thomas still being alive, even though that would mean I wouldn't have you." He kissed her head. "I wish we could go back to the beginning and start all over again. But we can only start over from now. We can right wrongs and avenge the deaths. It won't be the same. But it can be normal."

They sat in silence, while the wind picked up and howled outside, rattling the windows. Felicia focused on the baby, watching her nurse. The babe was part in all this but was blissfully unaware of what had happened downstairs, what had happened the past nine months.

Felicia lowered the baby from her breast, and propped her up on her shoulder, rubbing at her back.

"I bet you wish we could go back in time just so you could have given birth in a bed rather than in some barn with chickens," Nathaniel said, a small smile on his face. He massaged the back of her neck, and she hissed a sigh of relief.

She held the baby up, looking deeply into her tiny face, then wiped it with sleeve of her gown. She laid the child on her lap, then inclined her head toward Nathaniel. He pressed a kiss to her temple, and the hint of a smile played on her lips.

"But you wouldn't have been there to help me."

Felicia laid the baby back in her cradle, and Nathaniel tucked her back into bed.

"Do you promise to stay in here?" he murmured.

"Only if you promise to take Thomas's rifle." Nathaniel started to shake his head, but Felicia grasped him, digging her fingers into his arms. "Take the musket, Nathaniel. It'll do you better."

Nathaniel bowed his head. "If that is what you wish. And I'll come back to you. I promise."

"Will you come back as you left me?"

Nathaniel set his jaw, gently cupping her face in his hands. He pressed a kiss to her mouth. "I will."

And with that, Nathaniel left Felicia and the baby alone in the room, but Felicia couldn't rest. The room was too quiet. The wind had died down. No children scurried downstairs or in the halls. Alone with her thoughts and the memories of the man who lost his life to warn her of his brother's evil.

Every time she closed her eyes, she could see Henry's face, and his pained eyes when he collapsed to his knees. She pulled the pillow over her head, as visions of Henry's soul leaving with Thomas played in her mind, images of Henry falling asleep in her arms, never to waken again. She gripped her hands into fists, her nails digging into her palms.

Was William to take everything she loved from her? Would she lose Natty too? Would he come for the baby next? Felicia balled her hands into fists, trying to eschew the thoughts that crept into her head.

"Thomas, why aren't you here for me anymore?" she whimpered. "Why can't I see you as I once did?"

"Because you don't look, Lissie."

She sat up in bed, her eyes still closed, and reached out to him. "Oh, you did take him with you," she said, her lashes damp. "Is he here? Are you really here?"

"His blood is innocent." Thomas heaved a sigh. *"I'm really here, but not as you knew me."* He tapped his ghostly fingers together and peeked over into the cradle, a broad smile creasing his cold face. *"My son?"*

Felicia reached out, almost surprised when she caught his icy sleeve. Thomas's gray features softened as he gazed at his daughter, then at Felicia. His lips smiled, but it was as if his eyes could not. She clasped his stone-cold hand in hers, intertwining her fingers with his. "Your daughter."

An inkling of joy sparkled in his eyes for but a moment, then he pulled his hand from hers and sat at the edge of the bed, just out of Felicia's grasp.

"He said you were there, Thomas. Where is he?"

"I think he's on his way to haunt his brother." The ghost's dry humor cut sharp to the point of mirthlessness.

Felicia's head lolled against the pillows, as exhaustion overtook her. "I'm serious," she murmured.

"So am I..."

Thomas reached toward her, the tips of his fingers grazing her face, but the touch brought her no comfort. It was as if a sepulcher had come to life and touched her with its marble carved features. She shuddered, and drew away from him, eyes snapping open. But Thomas was still there, even as she opened her eyes, and she gasped.

He seemed so tired, so weary and worn. She remembered the day in his office, all those months ago, when she looked into his eyes. He had lost his vitality, his shine, but he was there before her, in a tangible form.

"Why are you here?" Her eyes widened and she trembled. "Has your soul been refused entry to heaven? Has Henry been denied as well?"

He held a finger to his lips, then brushed a stray lock of hair away from her face.

"Don't worry for us, Felicia. Our souls will be called to heaven in the end of time when the trumpets blow. I may never know why, but for now, please don't worry."

"I can't help but worry. I'll never see you again."

"No, not yet." He smiled gently, then touched a finger to her nose. *"You have married a man who will protect you and no longer need me to watch over you. But as for me and Henry Moore, we'll be around... just not as you knew us. Never fear for us now. It'll be well."*

And with that, Thomas vanished, and Felicia wondered if it was for good.

She drifted off into an uneasy sleep, despite Thomas's phantom words. How could she find peace knowing Colonel Moore was on the prowl?

WILLIAM MOORE SAT astride his horse, peering through his spyglass at the rustic wooden houses that made up the settlement of Mount Terre, and contempt curled his lip, and settled into his eyes. Most people upon seeing their brother breathing his last would be in terrified shock, but William was calm and complacent all in the name of his own heroism.

The rain had abated, and clouds had disappeared, showing the sun high in its orbit, but there was no wind. Still, frigid air settling around the soldiers their breaths circled in front of them in icy mist, and the wet sound of mud squelching under boots and hooves penetrated the air.

"Look at them all." He glanced at the officer beside him. "Provincial colonials. They could benefit from having us here."

"Did you see the cooper?" Westall asked.

William sniffed at the officer and grinned.

"I smoked him out and killed a weasel while at it."

"Are we just to kill him on sight?"

"Of course not," William said. "First, we take him into custody."

And if they just so happened to be ambushed on their way back down toward the Schuylkill, Nathaniel Poe might unfortunately be killed by Natives. A smirk crept onto William's lips, and he let out a low rumbling laugh.

Westall frowned, his brow furrowing. "With all due respect, I do not think this is a laughing matter."

William grinned broader. "Perhaps I do not find it as amusing as I find it a joy to bring the man to justice. I know a great many things concerning Thomas's murder and the implications it brings. Perhaps, if you knew too, you'd laugh with me."

The officer opened his mouth to speak, but a shout from the woods before them covered his words. William leaned up in his saddle as the scout staggered toward them.

"Sir!" the scout gasped. "There's at least ten men coming down from the settlements above the lake, all armed."

William dropped his spyglass around his neck and laughed so hard bent over, holding his sides. "You think ten, miserable rebel wretches are cause for alarm? That *ten* rebels can take on my regiment?"

"There may be more coming down, but I saw only the ten."

His voice echoed in the still air. "We'll pick them off just as they did at Bunker Hill. They are no match for us, man. To your post." He motioned broadly, spreading his arms out wide, a smirk on his lips. "Men! Stand your ground. We have Yankees coming toward us. But hold your fire. Don't shoot till I say so."

The scout slipped away, and William moved to the front where his men lined up. He wanted a better look at the forest line, waiting to see the colonials coming down from their mountain settlement.

The sun sat high above the trees as they waited with their attention focused on the unmoving woods. William peered through his spyglass again. The settlements grew silent as the residents disappeared into their houses. Only an occasional snap of a twig or call of a distant bird of prey disturbed the quiet. No wind blew, no visible life made itself known around them. The air went stagnant.

Then, a cold breeze blew over the back of Moore's neck. He shivered, swiping at his collar. The icy wind blew again, just over the tip of his ears.

A voice, posh and refined, deep, and melodic like a well-tuned violin, whispered on William's right. *"Don't think you can get away with what you've done."*

"Who said that?" William asked, glancing back to his men. "Who is talking?"

"Not a soul, sir," Westall said. "We're waiting on your command."

Another voice, genteel, clear, and elegant, rang on William's left. *"Don't think you can get away with what you've done."*

The voices echoed around William's head, and the chill blew down the back of his jacket and shirt and made the hairs on the back of his neck stand up.

"Stop your nonsense," William barked.

"God as our witness, we're not saying anything," Westall repeated. His squinted through his spectacles at William, his brows furrowed.

"Don't think you can get away with what you've done."

The voices grew louder, and William looked around. His men were silent on their saddles. An icy finger pressed into William's back, between his shoulder blades, while another jabbed into his front. William fidgeted on his horse, swatting the air around him.

"I won't hesitate to kill the prankster!"

"Don't think you can get away with what you've done."

One of the men startled. "What was that?"

Subdued murmuring rippled among the officers, till Westall called over them.

"We are not at fault. We hear it, too, Colonel."

"Then who is saying it?" William roared, while the cold breeze blew over his neck and ears, and the icy fingers jabbed into his back and sternum. "Who is saying these lies?"

"What lie is said? Perhaps a colonial is heckling us," another officer offered.

"Don't think you can get away with what you've done." The voices

echoed the words over and over, till even the horses snuffled and snorted. Cold blasts of wind blew over their heads toward William. The soldiers murmured, casting uneasy and frightened glances at each other. The words grew louder and louder, till they rang out over the regiment.

William stopped fidgeting in the saddle, sitting rigid against the icy jabs and winds. He set his jaw, trying hard to ignore the voices echoing about him.

The familiar voices.

The blood rushed from his face and a thick pit formed in his stomach.

"Henry?" he whispered.

A low, rumbling laugh echoed in his ears. A jab to the stomach made him wince.

"Thomas?"

A phantom violin note played. A stab in his shoulder blades made him shudder.

"This town has to be haunted," William muttered. He shook himself, swallowing back the heavy feeling, but it turned into a slithering snake that wound its way up around his throat, coiling tighter till he felt he couldn't breathe.

Fear. Fear entered his heart, rendering him unable to move. He couldn't remember a time in his life where he was so frightened to the point of paralysis...

No. He needed to stay strong. He couldn't let the winding, coiling dread strangle him, but his heart beat faster and faster, and his breath stuck in his throat. He clenched his jaw. Narrowing his eyes, he sat up straighter in the saddle, and with trembling hands, smoothed his hair back, tightening the ribbon holding his queue.

"Specter or prankster, I'll have none of it," William growled, gritting his teeth till he heard them grind in his own ears.

Thomas and Henry's voices laughed.

"Sir, more men are coming up from the settlements," the scout said, returning to the regiment. "I saw them leave their houses."

William cleared his throat, shook his hands, and tugged on his gloves, then brought his spyglass up.

Indeed, men filed from the houses, from behind the settlements, up the dirt path that led to the forest edge, perhaps fifty or so from the lower settlements. William lowered the spyglass slowly, staring forward, lips parting in silent awe. He gulped, then sniffed in. Nathaniel's men nearly matched his regiment. The fear twisted tighter about his neck, and he loosened his necktie.

The icy wind blew, and eerie, uncanny violin chords echoing through the settlement, matching the sound of Henry's rumbling laughter.

"When do we fire?" an officer asked.

William took his flintlock pistol from its holster on his hip, running his fingers over the engraved design on the handle. He brandished it toward the disembodied music, trying in vain to silence it.

"At will," he seethed. He brought the weapon in close, poising his finger on the trigger, forcing the fear out of his heart, and replacing it with burning hatred. "But if you see the cooper, leave him for me."

33

Nathaniel and the nine men from the upper lake settlements neared the bottom of the forest, and the clearing showed through the bare trees. The sun had dipped below the tree-line, and a cold breeze blew from over Emerald Rock Lake. The Only Sounds were nature and a crackling distant bonfire, which brought with it the smell of smoke and burning oak and cedar. The wall of red appeared before them, with Colonel Moore on his horse in the front. The colonials stayed off the dirt path and moved cautiously through the bramble.

Nathaniel gripped tightly at the guns in his hands. In one, he held his worn musket that served him for years, provided meals, and trained young patriots when the need arose. In his other, he held the sleek mahogany rifle with the name of a dead British major engraved on its side. The weapon weighed heavily in his hand, and he wrapped his fingers tightly around the stock. It would be used against its own.

The men reached the forest edge and crouched amongst the bushes.

"What are we to do?" one of the men asked. "There's more of them then there are of us."

Nathaniel held a finger to his mouth, then pointed to the lower settlements, where more men trekked up their way. "We have them matched, at the least," he said, his voice low and hushed. "I'll go first. I'm the one the Colonel wants, and for the good of Mount Terre, we need to avoid a battle."

"A battle may be inevitable," Jasper said. "We need to keep them from the settlements. Keep them here."

"We'll do what we have to." Nathaniel peered through the trees at the redcoats. They were nearly twenty yards away, and Moore stared dead ahead into the forest-line, while his men poised and aimed their rifles. He prayed that he could only see the trees and not his hidden men, but regardless, his eyes burned and he gritted his teeth, glaring at the man who had ruined the lives of so many people for his own cause. Nathaniel rasped over his shoulder, "Stay low. They're ready for us."

Bringing the muskets in close to his chest, Nathaniel stepped out of the confinement of the woods, out into the waning evening light, the wind chilling him. An unearthly sudden silence greeted him, then Moore spoke.

"Ah, so the cooper has finally shown his face at last," the Colonel sneered. "How long did you think you could run?"

"You know just as well as anyone that I had nothing to do with Thomas Hawkings's death," Nathaniel said. "You have no quarrel with this town. Have your men stand down."

Moore glared at Nathaniel and let out a loud snort. "I wasn't born yesterday, Poe. Whose is the gun in your left hand? Why do you wield that weapon?"

Nathaniel glanced down at the mahogany rifle. "This belonged to Major Thomas Theodore Hawkings, the man you killed to ruin the reputation of a patriot town. You planted it in my shop. His widow, my wife, gave me this, and I'll use it if I must."

A muffled murmur grew behind the Colonel, but Moore held his hand up. "If you come with us now"—Moore quickly swatted and pushed the air in front of him, then shifted in the saddle— "there will be no cause for cause for more bloodshed."

"Bloodshed that *you've* caused," Nathaniel spat. He held his head high and addressed the soldiers behind Moore. "Would you follow the orders of a man who killed his own brother?"

A hush fell over Moore's men, then quiet murmurs swelled in the clearing. The officer standing closest to Moore lowered his weapon, but the Colonel shot him a glare.

"If you won't come with us, then use it," Moore growled. He pointed his flintlock pistol toward Nathaniel. "Go on, use the Major's musket."

"No. Not unless you tell me why you followed me and my wife miles and miles away from home? What is one man to you? Justi—"

"I said use the musket!" William pulled the trigger on his pistol, sending a ball hurtling toward Nathaniel. It missed his arm by a hair, flying into the woods fifty yards behind him.

A cry came from the woods, then the ringing peal of musket fire. An officer standing near Moore fell without uttering a sound. The color drained from William Moore's face for only a second.

"*Hold your fire!*" Nathaniel spun around as the militia erupted from the trees, firing muskets and pistols.

The sound of gunfire filled the town of Mount Terre. Shot after shot rang out from both sides.

Men fell, patriots and redcoats alike.

"Stop!" Nathaniel cried, though he found himself being drawn closer to the regiment. "This isn't your battle!"

"It's our battle now, Nat!" Jasper shouted back, gritting his teeth as an unhorsed officer lunged toward him, bayonet flashing in the waning evening sun.

Nathaniel stuck his foot out and tripped the soldier, who lost his footing and stumbled, falling to his knees. Another militiaman grabbed him by his collar and bound his hands together.

Nathaniel shot a glance over to his brother, keeping his musket aimed at Moore. He groaned internally, muscles tightening. Rage filled his head. It burned against himself, for bringing his family into a battle. But not only that, a growing fury toward Moore, who only seemed pleased that a confrontation had begun.

A young officer, no more than eighteen, charged at him. Nathaniel braced his forearms against an officer's rifle, forcing the soldier to hold it parallel. Both of Nathaniel's weapons crossed awkwardly at their noses. He grunted and tossed the old musket aside, gripping the rich, mahogany rifle in both hands. Freed of the extra weapon, Nathaniel brought his full weight down on the boy's weapon. He stumbled back under Nathaniel's weight, giving Nathaniel time to push him aside. The boy's hands were bound just as his compatriots were.

"Poe!" The Colonel's voice bellowed over the conflict. "If you want a full battle, I'll give you one." He fired his pistol into the crowd of colonials.

"Moore, your fight is with me!" Nathaniel shouted, forcing his way through the melee toward the Colonel. "Fight me, not this town!"

Colonel Moore swung himself off his horse, and in one fluid motion, pointed his pistol at Nathaniel, who dove out of the way just as the Colonel fired. The ball hit one of Moore's own men in the shoulder.

"This has to stop before more people are killed!" Nathaniel advanced toward the Colonel. "Your brother is dead. Your men are being killed and for what? To cover up Thomas's murder?"

Bayonet pointed, Moore lunged for him. It slashed Nathaniel's shoulder, drawing blood, and he brought up his own weapon and reeled away from the Colonel, who pressed closer until only their clashing muskets separated them. Moore ground his teeth and pushed his weight against Nathaniel, forcing him back a pace.

The Colonel snarled, his eyes flashing a murderous rage. "I'll cover what I must to carry out the plan."

Nathaniel screwed up his strength, and with a shout, pushed Moore back, pointing the bayonet of Thomas's musket at his chest.

"FELICIA, my dear, you must lie down," Dorcas pleaded, as she followed Felicia around the small bedroom. The baby slept soundly in her cradle, freshly fed, and cleaned.

The sun had nearly vanished from the sky, darkness covering the land, a stillness over the lake settlement, but Felicia paced back and forth, alternately shivering and perspiring, and avoiding Dorcas' outstretched hands. She paused at the window, her breath fogging the glass, and peered out toward the expanse of field that merged with the forest line. She shook her head, then rested her hands against the cold glass and pressed her forehead to the window.

The familiar snake tightened around her stomach, squeezing till the pain reached her throat. Dry heaving coughs shook her, and she doubled over, hiding her face amidst her fit of coughing.

"Who else has to die?" Her voice cracked. "I didn't bargain for this."

"Nobody bargains for death, my dear." Dorcas placed a steadying hand on Felicia's back. "Did you know Henry well?"

Felicia's throat chafed from coughing, and her knees wobbled, but she managed, "Henry... he proposed to me. I, I hadn't realized he was sincere. And now he's gone from me. He's gone with Thomas. I can't lose Nathaniel. I can't. I can't go on if I lose one more person I hold so dear."

Dorcas gently led Felicia back to bed.

Felicia peered up through her ratted hair at Dorcas and whispered, "Can't you hear the gunfire? Can't you hear it? It's deafening! It's maddening!"

Dorcas hushed her, smoothing her hair back.

"Nathaniel told me he'd be safe. He told me he wouldn't be like Thomas, called to war to die. But he's in that fight—he's in it!"

Felicia's vision faded as she struggled to breathe, and she swayed against Dorcas, who laid her down against the pillows in one motion and pulled the blankets over her chest.

"I know he's out there," Dorcas said as she tucked the blanket around Felicia, "but Nathaniel is a strong, brave man."

"So was Thomas. So was Henry. Even my father has been injured. Where are they now?"

Dorcas swiped Felicia's bangs from her forehead, and a deep frown creased her face. "You're burning up."

Felicia moaned and pushed Dorcas's hand away, then coughed again.

"I told you, silly girl, to keep in bed. Now look at you, gone and given yourself a fever." Dorcas gnawed her lower lip and trailed her fingers down the side of Felicia's face. "I'll be back with a compress."

Though Dorcas rushed from the room, the evening was far from quiet. The wind carried the low rumble of gunfire and faint shouts of men. Felicia squeezed her eyes shut and plugged her ears with her fingers. She scarcely heard Dorcas return or felt the cold, damp cloth on her forehead.

"Felicia..." Dorcas's voice was garbled in Felicia's ears, so she dropped her hands. The woman felt her forehead again and murmured, "Felicia, I need to leave you and fetch the midwife."

Felicia hummed a small response but kept her eyes closed. Unaware of how long it had been, even after Dorcas and the midwife returned, Felicia barely opened her eyes, and their figures were dim and shadowy. Their voices, though, pounded down on her ears.

"It's the puerperal." Cool hands pressed against Felicia's face and arms. "She's burning up."

"She's been refusing to lie in." It must have been Dorcas's voice though it was faded.

"Am I to die too? I can't leave my baby," Felicia moaned. "Don't let me leave her."

Another cool compress patted Felicia's brow. Someone clicked their tongue. "She caught it from her stubbornness not to lie in. It's going to have to run its course at this point. Keep the baby far from her. We can't let the child catch it, too. You don't need me to say it, Dorcas, but keep the cold cloths coming. We can't let her burn herself to death."

Someone—Dorcas?—took the baby from the cradle, and Felicia groaned in protest. She couldn't be without her baby. It was the only living memory of Thomas she had. An unfamiliar woman gave her a worried frown but followed Dorcas, carrying the cradle, as well. The stranger returned, and when she refreshed the cloth and bent over Felicia, Felicia realized she was the midwife.

"Rest and heal, dear. You may be worried for your husband," the midwife said, taking hold of Felicia's flushed hand, "but don't give him reason to worry for you."

"Tell me what's happening." Felicia drew in shaky shallow breaths, licked her lips, and whispered, "I'm frightened."

The only thoughts able to break through Felicia's feverish mind were of her baby and violin music. She needed both. She craved both. She'd die without them. She was sure of it.

"You'll be fine." The midwife set another cool rag on her forehead. "We're just going to keep the compresses coming. You just rest and—"

"The gunfire. I miss the violin. Why can't I hear *Winter*? I miss *Winter*! I can't stand the gunfire. Give me *Winter*!"

"It'll be winter in a few weeks." the woman soothed. She massaged Felicia's hand in her weathered one. "Don't rush the seasons."

"I need the violin." Felicia tossed back and forth on the bed. "Please, just play it for me. Just play the strains. Anything but the gunfire. Anything but the death!"

"I don't know how to play, dear. When your husband comes back, I'll see if he'll play for you. I promise." Her voice rose as she called, "Dorcas!"

The door opened with a gentle click.

"Thomas! Just play me *Winter*!" Felicia cried. "Why won't you play for me anymore?"

The midwife's voice lowered. "Who is Thomas?"

"Her dead husband," Dorcas murmured. "I suppose he played for her in the winter?"

"Just one strain! Oh, Thomas, please!" Felicia's eyes snapped open, and she reached out frantically, but there was nothing to grasp. The midwife gently held her back, running cold cloths over Felicia's arms, but she pushed the woman's hands aside. "Drown out the gunfire! Drown it out! Henry, you play! Play for me!"

"Henry?" the midwife asked.

But they couldn't see. For Thomas stood, nearly clear as day to her, just in front of the door, his arms folded close across his chest, and Henry stood just behind him, the look of pain still in his eyes.

"Please—" Felicia grasped toward them, flexing her hands, beckoning them to come forward.

"I can't do that now, Lissie." Thomas reached to her, but stopped himself and clasped his hands behind his back. He kept his face toward her, his mouth trembling. He squeezed his eyes shut. *"And don't tell Henry to play. You don't want us to come to you now, Felicia. If we do, you will leave the baby."*

Tears crept down her cheeks as Felicia shook her head back and forth, and the compress fell to the pillow. "But if you just drown out the gunfire, please!" she implored. "Just drown it out forever. Please, just one song. Thomas, only one refrain!"

"Keep me away, Felicia. Keep us away. Stop calling for us," Thomas begged, and tears ran down his cheeks. He grimaced. *"You need to live, Felicia."*

"Just one song!"

"No, Lissie! You need to go to sleep." Thomas glanced back to Henry, who only shook his head. *"It's not your time. Go to sleep. You don't want to join us. Not yet. Forget we're here!"*

Felicia covered her face in her hands again, falling deeper into the pillows, but still she saw them both. "Not even a note?"

Thomas shook his head, frowning.

"Please, Felicia," Henry leaned against the door frame, rubbing his hand over his face. He lowered his hand. Knitting his brows, his inky blue eyes, now sullen, beseeched her. *"For your daughter's sake, go to sleep."*

Felicia drew in a sobbing breath. She turned her gaze from them to the midwife and Dorcas. "Can't you see them?"

"No one else is here, Felicia," Dorcas said tenderly.

The midwife bowed her head, then pressed a fresh cold cloth to Felicia's neck and forehead.

Felicia's tears escaped the corners of her eyes to drip onto her pillow. "If you can't come to my side, at least stay with me. Don't leave me till I'm well."

Thomas and Henry heaved a sigh.

Thomas's arms relaxed at his sides. *"That we can do."*

"But we must leave soon after..." Henry turned his face away from her, and he held his arms close.

She rolled onto her side, hiding her face in the pillows, which kept the cloth on her forehead in place.

"I think she's falling asleep." The floorboards creaked. "She nearly left us there, I believe. Seeing visions is not a good sign."

"Is she... in the clear?"

"No. Keep watching her, and I'll check on the baby. There's no telling if she'll start to see things again."

"Aye," Dorcas said, and the midwife left the room.

Felicia glanced past her to the doorway one last time. Thomas and Henry disappeared down the hallway. She heard their boots echoing down stairwell and hugged the pillow close, soaking it in tears and sweat.

"Oh, you dear," Dorcas whispered, gently running the cold cloth over Felicia's flushed bare arm. "Try to sleep. When you wake, be better. Be better, my dear. They'll come back soon."

"No," Felicia murmured as sleep overtook her. "They must move on from me."

34

William's plan was defiled, and unholy, unbridled passion filled every nerve of his body. He and the cooper circled each other, musket and pistol cocked and ready to fire. Pale stars twinkled above them, their light bouncing off the sliver of the moon, providing the only light on the field, and the night air was frigid, biting at skin and stinging throats. Their men backed away while they glared each other down, each ready but unwilling to shoot first. Poe jabbed forward, and Thomas's bayonet pricked through the layers of William's uniform. William pushed the blade aside, slicing the back of his hand, and drew his pistol, ignoring the blood darkening the ivory handle.

"You wanted to play hero." Poe threw his hair over his shoulder, showing his dark face clearly in the night sky. "You killed Major Hawkings and Henry Moore. You used my wife's money to pad your life. Now you endanger your men to carry out your schemes. Murderer and common thief. You're a rotten man and a sorry excuse for an officer."

Blood trickled in icy droplets down William's wrist. "I'll do what it takes to stop this insurrection."

"Killing your own men?" Poe kept his voice even and his square chin held high. "Your own kin? Men who have nothing to do with your schemes? If that's what it takes to work for His Majesty, then the colonies need to be rid of you *and* your ruler. You dishonor the names of men like Thomas Hawkings and Henry Moore. You dishonor the name of your king and country."

"And what do you do?" William sneered. "You profit from what my king and country has given you. You profit from your business—this land, this soil that you've been given—without so much of a thought to repay us for saving your people time and time again. Your taxes are high, so you shoot a few soldiers to get your way. And now, your people started a war because you couldn't bear to repay your king and country for their service."

"We are sovereign colonies," Nathaniel ground out. "You took the land from my father's people. You feud with other nations on this dirt and make us pay damages without giving us the slightest representation in your courts. You bully and molest us, sending soldiers to watch over our harbors, blocking our trade till you get what you think you deserve. Now you think you can blame me for this battle you wrought? No, sir, but I'll damn well end it."

"Then end it," William growled.

Nathaniel Poe fired Thomas's rifle, and the ball tore through William's shoulder. His pistol flew from his hand. He reeled back, stumbling, and clutching his arm. An officer rushed to his side, but William gritted his teeth and wrenched the rifle from the young soldier's hands. He pointed it toward the cooper with shaky aim and fired. The recoil knocked him backward. One of his men caught him, tried to steady him, but William tore himself away and faced his opponent, blinking against the cold and throbbing pain.

The ball had pierced Poe's side, and a dark stain seeped through his jacket. The cooper staggered back a pace then slipped to one knee. One of the Yankees darted forward toward him.

"Stay back." Grimacing, the cooper raised his hand, then his head. "It's not your fight, Jasper. Let me finish it."

"It'll only get worse from here," William managed before he dropped the musket. He gasped and pressed his hand into his shoulder. He hissed as he fought through the searing pain tearing through his shoulder and arm. He could still succeed.

Colonel Moore and Nathaniel Poe meet face-to-face

He contorted his face, and his hand shook as he pulled out his gilded dueling pistol. "Give up, Poe."

"Never," Poe murmured. Leaning to his side, his fingers curled around the stock of his mediocre, backwoods musket, staring dead square at William, and he raised it. "I promised Felicia I'd avenge Thomas."

William aimed the pistol.

Both men fired.

Silence.

Blazing pain built above William's belt-buckle. He glanced down, then fell to his knees, dropping the pistol and grabbing his stomach, as the taste of iron welled up in his mouth, blood spilling over his lips. He spat it out. "I will still be a hero."

The cooper hunched over his old musket, head bowed.

On his knees, William inched his way toward Poe. He let go of his stomach biting his tongue against the agony in his belly, and grabbed the man's hair, forcing him to look up at his face. Despite the searing pain, William smirked and reached for his knife.

Poe winced and pressed a hand to his side at the sudden movement. His eyes flashing, he glared up at the William and rasped, "No hero acts like you."

William's face fell, and his limbs grew cold. He blinked, the cooper's words hitting him harder than the musket ball to his stomach. He would die unremembered. His muscles slacked and he loosened his grip on the man's hair.

Poe dropped his musket and pushed away from William, then clambered to his feet, and staggered backwards. He wiped his mouth with the back of his hand. "Your time is up, Colonel Moore."

William crumbled to his side. His useless arm lay stretched over his head, but he pressed his left hand to his stomach again. Blood seeped through his gloved fingers, staining the white with what should have been crimson, but merely looked black.

"No matter the outcome of the war, those you killed are avenged," Poe stated coolly.

Squeezing his eyes closed, William balled his hand into a fist.

And there, flickering slowly in his vision, was Henry—whole and just as he remembered seeing him in Penchester—sitting on a stump near the forest edge. William sucked in an icy breath and opened his eyes a crack.

"Henry?"

Silently observing William with sorrow engraved in his eyes, Henry shook his head. He braced his hands on his knees, stood, and covered his face with his hand. Then, he turned on his heel, shoulders back, head held high, and strode into the forest.

Cold terror convulsed through William. He called his brother's name one last time and reached out. Henry paused but a moment a blood stain forming over his weskit, and William trembled. His younger brother turned his back and kept walking.

As Henry disappeared, so also William's vision faded, and the world blackened around him.

∽

A BARN OWL'S screech tore through the forest's eerie silence after Colonel Moore called for his murdered brother then grew still, his arm outstretched to the forest.

Nathaniel shuddered as he looked down at the lifeless Colonel at his feet. Though no longer searing, the wound in his side still pulsed, but despite the pain, he drew in a deep breath.

It was done.

A redcoat approached to kneel beside his fallen commander and turned his face up to Nathaniel. "What now?"

"We call it over." Nathaniel stepped toward the soldier, offering his hand. The man took it and stood, then let go. Nathaniel motioned to the dirt road beyond the clearing. "Just go home."

The soldier nodded curtly then stepped back to join his comrades.

"And what of us?" one of the town's men asked.

"We go home too. Moore's scheming is over."

Jasper strode his side and rested a hand on his shoulder. "Natty?"

Nathaniel winced. Jasper followed his gaze to Moore, then moved from Nathaniel to the body and picked up both the red-stained pistol and the young redcoat's rifle. He handed the weapon to the young man, who stood there, pale even in the moonlight, his attention on his fallen colonel. Then, Jasper crossed the clearing to the officer holding the Colonel's bay's reins and held out the ivory-handed pistol, butt first.

The man took the weapon with steady hands. He glanced from Moore to Jasper Nathaniel. He gripped the pistol in his fist and shook his head. "This has been a tragedy. We had no clue of the severity of damage he wrought."

Nathaniel exhaled slowly, but the wound in his side made his breath hitch. "It was not your doing."

"And what of our captured men?"

Nathaniel breathed out a long, exhausted breath. "They will be returned to you within the hour."

"Thank you." The officer turned to his fellow redcoats. "We set up camp on the outskirts of town."

He barked a command, and two soldiers moved forward to collect Moore's body. The officer extended his hand to Nathaniel, who shook, then swung up onto his horse. The wall of red marched slowly away from Mount Terre.

The townsfolk slowly headed back to their homes, and Jasper returned to Nathaniel's side.

"Are you all right?"

"I will be." Nathaniel heaved a sigh, and the pain flared again. "I want to see my wife."

※ 35 ※

Thomas sat in Poe's brother's home, watching the twins play with a Jacob's ladder and ball and cup with their older brother.

What would it be like to watch the little girl in the cradle upstairs grow up, strong like he had been and beautiful like her mother?

But he couldn't linger around the life he once knew. If he was to find any peace, just within himself, he needed to leave.

Felicia had fallen into a quiet sleep a few hours ago, and relative peace filled the house. Dorcas had ceased running up and down the narrow stairs to freshen Felicia's compress. Tall, thin candles on the table flickered, warming the space with orange light. A wooden ball rolled away from the children, knocking into his boot. The hint of a smile played on his lips as he kicked it back toward them.

The twin girls stared wide-eyed when the ball rolled their way.

The eldest daughter waved her hand in his direction as the twins rolled the ball back. "Once I'm old enough, I'll move to Philadelphia. The houses there won't be quite so drafty as this one."

Thomas smirked and kicked the ball toward her. She clicked her tongue, then handed the ball to her brother.

"And I'll bring you all with me," she added, moving a twin to her lap.

The little girl squirmed out of her lap. "But, Charity, this draft is fun."

Thomas grinned as the children repeatedly rolled the ball to him and he rolled it back. He debated on picking the ball up and tossing it around but decided it best to stick kicking it. A draft couldn't lift anything, after all, and there'd be no fun in scaring the children.

The door opened with a burst of cold air, and Thomas looked up as Henry stepped into the house and closed the door behind him.

"Far too drafty!" Charity gasped and darted to check the door.

"You'll let them know we're here," Thomas said as Henry sat at the table.

"Perhaps in a house like the manor..." Henry propped his elbows up on the table, then rested his face in his hands. *"I got away with it just now, didn't I?"*

Thomas shrugged. *"What happened?"*

"They're coming back up the mountain now." Henry rubbed at his face, then let his body sag. *"It's over."*

Thomas tapped his hands on his knees. *"Who would have though all of this would happen."*

"Certainly, not I." Henry pushed himself to his feet and stepped around the children toward the staircase. *"How is she?"*

"Soundly sleeping. Best not accidentally wake her. She's sensitive to our presence."

Henry nodded solemnly, glanced up the stairs, then started for the door. *"Then shall we leave?"*

"Let's just wait until Poe gets back... then I'll know Felicia will be safe." Thomas glanced toward the stairwell. *"She's been through a lot... too much."*

Henry followed Thomas's gaze. *"Yes, God bless her."*

Thomas smiled and finally, after months, the familiar feeling of fondness buzzed in his non-beating heart. *"God bless both my girls..."*

～

THE PAIN in Nathaniel's side had turned to a dull, throbbing ache as he climbed the path with his brother. The cold no lunger stung. He was numb to the air, only hissing when a wind kicked up over the lake. The light from the cabin windows was a welcome sight. Nathaniel leaned wearily against his brother's arm as they slogged up to the front door and Jasper threw it open.

The twins rushed to their father. "Papa's home!"

Nathaniel pushed away from Jasper, who smiled as he scooped them up in his arms and spun them around. Nathaniel fell back against the door, breathing deeply.

"Jas!" Dorcas ran down the stairs and wrapped Jasper in a tight embrace. "Is it over? Please tell me everything is over."

Jasper grinned broadly. "Moore is gone."

Nathaniel pushed himself off the door and winced. "For good, too. Is Felicia in bed?"

A frown creased Dorcas's face when she saw the stain on Nathaniel's coat. "You shouldn't see her in your state. You're bleeding."

"Only a little compared to Moore." Nathaniel offered her a small smirk. "Where's my wife?"

"She's... sleeping." Dorcas twisted her lips into a frown. "She spiked a fever, and I think—"

Felicia—

No way, by heaven, he would lose Felicia. No way at all, after what they had weathered together.

Nathaniel tore away from Jasper and Dorcas, and thundered up the stairs, his brother and sister-in-law on his heels. His heart pounded in his chest, and he gritted his teeth against the throbbing pain in his side, each step hurting more than the last, the movements pulling on his wound.

He reached the bedroom and threw open the door. With a ragged gasp, he slumped against the doorframe.

Felicia slept peaceably in the bed, her chest rising and falling softly.

He took a step in, but Dorcas grabbed his arm. "I was just trying to tell you that her fever just broke."

"I need to see her," Nathaniel took another step, then froze—*the cradle was gone.* Panic seized his chest. "Where's the baby?"

"The baby is very well. The midwife didn't want her to catch anything should Felicia be contagious." Dorcas gently pulled Nathaniel away from the doorway. "Let's get you cleaned up first. You can't see her the way you are. What if she wakes up and sees you thus?"

Jasper led Nathaniel back down the stairs to the table and lowered him to a chair. Dorcas shooed the children away, then procured a basin of water.

"You'll feel much better once you're patched up," Dorcas murmured.

Nathaniel slumped back in the chair while the rush from the battle wore off and his limbs grew heavy. Dorcas moved about him, fussing, washing the dirt, sweat, and blood of the battle from his face, hands, and hair. He hissed when she dabbed at the gouge in his side—the lye soap stung as it cleaned the damaged flesh—and bound old strips of linen around Nathaniel's waist.

Jasper brought him a new shirt and pair of breeches, and Dorcas slipped out to check on the children and let him change. As soon as Nathaniel had tied back his hair and pulled on clean clothes, he took the stairs two at a time, though he was breathing heavily by the time he reached Felicia's side. He held her warm hand and watched her sleep. The deep feeling longing ate at his soul as he studied her face and he sagged as he bent over her. He had kept his promise to her, and she was finally safe.

"Felicia," he whispered.

She moaned and turned her face away from him.

Nathaniel gently massaged her hand, then kissed it lightly and placed it on her chest. He crossed the room to the crate in the corner and picked up the violin and bow. She needed the security of the regular and the violin, he knew, would be recognizable. He sat back down beside her, plucked at the strings, and turned the pegs at on its neck. The rich maple instrument weighed far more than any musket ever could. One killed with a musket but saved with music. And that instrument's previous owner had given more than Nathaniel felt he could be grateful for. He studied it for a moment, then closed his eyes and drew in the deepest breath his wounded muscles would allow. The scent of rosin recalled the memory of his father playing in the evenings by firelight, and Nathaniel knew what he needed to play. It reminded Nathaniel of Felicia. Hoping he could do his father's melody and the violin's previous owner justice, Nathaniel settled on the edge of the bed, set the violin on his shoulder and his chin on the rest, and raised the. Light notes trickled into the air as his fingers traipsed over the black fingerboard.

Her lashes flickered, and she turned her face to the music, her lips lightly parted, her brows knitted together. She blinked and a soft moan escaped. He smiled down at her but continued to play. She shifted on the pillows but did not smile back. Instead, she pressed her lips together while Nathaniel kept the music flowing.

"Thomas played this for me," she whispered, her voice hoarse.

"My father played it, as well," Nathaniel murmured, lowering the violin slightly, but never ceasing the music.

The notes flowed freely from between his fingers and the strings, the melancholic melody drifting through the room and escaping into the halls. The music spoke of longing and loss, but also of the purest reunion. He swayed with the bow strokes, ignoring the biting pain in his side. When he glanced down at Felicia, a single tear was gliding down her left cheek, glistening in the candlelight.

He drew the bow across the violin one last time, elongating the note.

"This piece reminds me of you. I imagine Thomas thought the same." Nathaniel laid the violin on the bed. He took up her hands, pressing a kiss to her fingers. "It's over, my love."

Felicia blinked slowly and let out a tired sigh. "All over?"

She seemed so small and frail, bundled under the quilted comforter. He ran cupped her face and leaned over her, hiding a wince, and kissed her forehead.

"Moore will never bother us again. His scheming is over. Both his brother and Thomas are avenged."

Felicia hid her beautiful eyes, but her lips trembled. She took in a shaky breath and let it out slowly. "You... William Moore... he was a friend. He was one of Thomas's closest friends, but all he ever did was lie and cheat. He stole my world from me. How can a man who smiles and give me well wishes kill Thomas and his own brother?"

Nathaniel brushed her brown curls away from her face, trailing his fingers over her jaw. "I don't know, but he's gone."

"Natty, I... don't' know how to feel. I should feel happy, and maybe I am, but—"

She sat up and reached out to him. He wrapped his arms around her, holding her tightly against his chest. She kissed his cheek and buried her face against the crook of his neck.

"It's over," she said again, and he hummed under his breath, combing his fingers through her hair. She gripped at Nathaniel's shirt, balling it up in her hands.

He let out a small groan when her hand brushed against his side.

Felicia pulled away from him. Her eyes widened, a look of sudden terror filling her face. "Were you hurt?"

He shrugged and murmured, "Only a graze."

Felicia whispered, "There's been too much death."

Nathaniel kissed the top of her head again.

Her face softened, as she relaxed in his arms. "Play for me?"

He grinned. As Felicia settled back down against the pillows, Nathaniel picked up the violin. "What do you want to hear?"

"Do you know anything by Vivaldi?"

Nathaniel picked at one of the strings. "I might."

"Do you know *Winter?*"

"I know a little." His furrowed while he settled his chin against the rest and played the frantic notes that sounded as if somebody stood shivering in the snow, stamping off their shoes on a mat. Nathaniel thought hard while he played, trying to get the timing of the notes and the bow strokes all in sync. A folk tune, even an English one, was one thing, but hadn't heard Vivaldi's music in ages. Still, he hammered the out the notes with as much ferocity as he could, though at the end of the segment, he gave Felicia a sad smile. "That's all I know."

Felicia beamed up at him. "That's my favorite part," she whispered. "Thank you."

Nathaniel tucked the violin and bow under his arm on his good side and leaned stiffly forward to kiss to Felicia's forehead. "You're not running a fever anymore, but go back to sleep all the same."

"I don't think I can." Felicia pouted.

"Whether you can or not doesn't matter. You should." Nathaniel straightened. "You go back to bed and this time, stay in bed, hmm? Dorcas told me you had gotten yourself the fever all because you won't lie-in."

Felicia's pout melted into a tired but mischievous grin. "Oh, all right."

"I'll check the baby and be back in a moment."

Felicia rolled onto her side and pulled the quilt over her shoulder. He felt her eyes on him while he put the violin and bow back in their case, blew out one of the candles on the bedside table, and took the other, out of the room with him.

"I love you," she called.

Nathaniel paused a moment, warmth filling his chest and spreading through his body, from the tips of his fingers to the center of his core. "I love you too, Lissie."

He closed the door and stepped quietly down the hallway and opened the door to the other bedroom. It was quiet, save the tiny breaths coming from the cradle in the corner. Nathaniel set the candle on the toilette and lowered himself on the bed beside the cradle.

The baby slept contentedly, blissfully unaware of the of events in her short life outside her mother. He let out a small hum, and gently scooped the infant up, keeping her head steady in the crook of his arm, and smiled. This child could sleep through anything, be it hell or high water, or the death of her father's murderer, though his smile faltered at that final thought.

He gazed into the baby's tiny face. Through all the bad that had happened to his new wife, the loss of her first husband, the sudden move from the town she had known and loved for years of her life, she had the child as a reminder of all the good things as well.

The baby opened her eyes, peeping around for a moment before she fixated her gaze on Nathaniel. He grinned down at her and set his finger in her tiny palm. Her tiny fingers curled around his nail, and he wriggled his finger from the child's surprisingly tight grip.

Of all the things that could have happened to Felicia, the child was probably the best of all.

"Your mother says you look exactly like your father, you know,"

Nathaniel said, his voice soft and low. "But I think you have your mother's beauty."

She closed her eyes again, stretching her limbs, giving a squeaky little yawn.

"Theodosia does have a very nice ring to it," Nathaniel said.

Still, while Nathaniel studied the child's tiny features, a tight pang of guilt constricted his chest. Before he had fully met Felicia, before he realized he loved her, he never could have known he would love a child that wasn't his own.

Certainly, he had let Myles cling to his legs and annoy him endlessly, but he never considered himself a father figure to the boy. And most assuredly, when he promised to protect the child growing in Felicia, he had meant it with all his heart.

But he hadn't counting on loving her already.

Even as he had fought Moore hours earlier, he had one goal in mind: to protect that new child and to make it home to his wife and child. *His* child.

He had thought of Felicia's daughter as his own and it hurt him, building a heavy guilt in his chest. Telling Felicia he'd treat her child as his own and thinking of the child as his own were different things entirely, but they had become one and the same.

"I just don't deserve someone as sweet as Felicia," he said under his breath. "Or something as sweet as this child."

"Master Cooper." The voice echoed faintly in the room.

Nathaniel tilted his head up, glancing about. He took the candle and moved it, lighting the corners of the room.

"You stood by your word to protect my wife and daughter. You avenged me for their sake. If you don't think you deserve them, then you're mistaken. I wouldn't have any other take my place. Just tell my daughter of me, will you?"

He closed his eyes and exhaled slowly. The words played in his mind but didn't sound of his own voice. He reflected on them. If Thomas Hawkings were there to tell him thus, then perhaps he had some modicum of worthiness. Nathaniel shook his head. He was weary, indeed, if he was hearing voices. He gently laid the sleeping child in the cradle.

"We'll let your mother sleep, just a bit, before bringing you to join us, little one." He stroked her soft cheek. "And as soon as you can understand, you'll know what has happened these past few months. I'll make sure you know of your father's bravery and of the bravery of the man who died to protect you."

Nathaniel quietly left the room, closing the door behind him.

F elicia loved it when her husband played the violin. She loved the way his long, tan fingers traipsed over the neck of the instrument, the way his dark brows furrowed in concentration, the way he swayed to the music that came from his hands. She sat and listened to him with a sigh, and he gave her a small smile, chin against the rest.

After Nathaniel closed his shop in the center of Mount Terre, they shared a simple meal, he picked up the violin and asked Felicia what song he should play, and then the music began.

Even though a war had begun, there was always time for a tune or two.

Little Deliverance Theodosia danced around her father's feet as he played the maple instrument, twirling about in circles, her dark blonde hair whipping about her face. It only took so many twirls, though, before the toddler fell on her bottom in a fit of giggles, and Felicia scooped Deliverance up into the air before cuddling the little girl on her lap.

Nathaniel bowed low after the final bow stroke, and Deliverance clapped her tiny hands. "Papa! More songs! More!"

"I think that it's far past time you were in bed," Nathaniel said, setting the violin in its case.

Deliverance pouted and turned her big pale blue eyes to Felicia.

"Oh, don't look at me, little orchid." She stood and set Deliverance on her hip. "I'm quite inclined to agree with him."

Deliverance's pout intensified, but Felicia relentlessly carried her upstairs to her bedroom. She unpinned her daughter's dress, slipping it off her shoulders, and hung up the little floral gown in the wardrobe. Felicia turned as Deliverance attempted to pry off her buckled shoes. She knelt in front of her, unfastening the buckles. Before she could slide them off, Deliverance promptly flung her shoes across the room, where they landed on the windowsill. Deliverance giggled, and Felicia shook her head and slipped off her stockings. Deliverance scrambled up into her bed and burrowed under the blankets.

Felicia lowered herself to her daughter's side. "Time for prayers."

Deliverance cleared her throat, steepled her hands together, and bowed her head. "God bless Mama and Papa," she said. "And help Papa get the splinter from his finger. Also tell my first Papa hello and Uncle Henry too. Um... God bless Grandmama and Grandpapa, and please let me get a dog, the end."

"Amen."

"That, too."

"That's a good girl." Felicia pressed a kiss to her daughter's forehead and stood. "We'll see about the dog."

Deliverance squirmed as Felicia took up the candle from the bedside table. She leaned over, flexing her little fingers. "G'night, baby."

Felicia stepped forward and Deliverance patted Felicia's stomacher, then intertwined her fingers in the lacing.

Felicia smiled and took Deliverance's hand, kissing her palm. "Goodnight, my little love."

"G'night, Mama."

Felicia closed the door quietly and went down the stairs, candle in hand.

Nathaniel sat in the armchair by the fire, picking at the stubborn splinter in his right forefinger.

"She went to bed easily tonight," Felicia said, holding out her hand, palm up.

Nathaniel hummed and let her take his afflicted hand. She squinted at his finger in the candlelight, then slipped a pin from her dress and pricked out the splinter, catching it on the edge of the pin. She wiped it onto her apron and stuck the pin back into her dress.

"When does she not get to bed easily enough?" Nathaniel asked.

"When you've played one too many songs for her," Felicia said, but squealed as Nathaniel pulled her down onto his lap. He pressed a tender kiss onto the back of her neck.

"I don't think there really can be one too many songs, now, do you?" Nathaniel murmured into her hair.

Felicia laughed. "Oh, not really."

Nathaniel wrapped his hands around her waist, sliding them over her belly. "Then shall I play one more just for us?"

"Yes." She retrieved the violin case. She handed it over, sitting at his feet as if she were a little girl, resting her head upon his knee. He stroked her cheek, then picked up the violin.

Nathaniel played the song he played the day that they married, the piece that swelled with the fervor of the backwoods till it soared high, only to come back down to the mountain's peak. It wasn't Vivaldi, and even in the four years since they've been married, he only could play that one, small portion of *Winter*. Someday she'd bring him to a concert in Philadelphia so he could hear the full piece. But the song he played was just as rich and full as something from Vivaldi's quill.

Nathaniel took the violin from the shoulder and set it in the case, but the music lingered in her mind.

She sighed. "Natty, who wrote that piece?"

He sat back in his seat, closing his eyes. "I did. But I would hardly venture to say I wrote it. It's just in here," he said, pointing to his head. "I might not know what a G looks like, but I *do* know what it sounds like."

Felicia gasped. "Natty! I didn't know you composed."

"I didn't either." He peered down at her through half-lidded eyes. "I play what comes to my mind. I just can play the same tune twice."

Felicia reached up, cupping his face in her hands, and kissed him. He rested his hands over hers, and she felt him smile.

"If I'd known that you were going to react this way, I would've told you years ago that I thought up that piece."

"Hmm, well, I'm glad you told me now." She stood and put the case back in its corner "Are you quite ready for bed?"

"I think so." He stood up and stretched. "I think I have been since I got home from work. Mrs. Wadsworth ordered another butter churn."

"Another one?" Felicia took his hand in hers as they walked to the stairs. "Hasn't she got three already?"

"Yes. Each a different size. Handheld. Bigger. Bigger still. She wants this one to hold about three pounds of butter. I'm trying to figure out just what one woman could do with that much butter."

Felicia grinned. "Maybe she just keeps breaking hers to get new ones from you." She leaned up on the tips of her toes and kissed on his cheek.

He stopped and set his fists on his hips. "You walked a fine line with me that day, I'll have you know."

"It was worth it," Felicia said. "I gave you sandwiches. You love my sandwiches."

Nathaniel smothered a laugh, trying not to wake Deliverance. "I think I loved Selah's sandwiches." He rested a hand on his stomach. "Your sandwiches are not quite the same, my love."

"That's because I make them with so much love, it tends to over-power the other flavors," Felicia said. Nathaniel quirked a brow at her and crossed his arms. Felicia sighed and stepped close, resting her head against his chest. "I've gotten better."

"Indeed, you have," Nathaniel said, leading her to their bedroom. "Though I have to say the first year was rough."

"I had never cooked before." Felicia wrinkled her nose, unpinning her overdress and stomacher from her stays. "But at least we suffered together."

"Deliverance got the best end of the deal. Most of the year, she had milk to eat and after that? Mashed baked apples." He grinned. "How on earth did we survive that year?"

"Willpower, my love. *You* got a stronger stomach, and *I* learned to cook better."

"That I do. That you did." Nathaniel flopped back onto the bed. He hissed as his muscles relaxed after the long day of being hunched over forms. "Are you joining me?"

"I have more layers than you could ever wish to wear, and you best believe I have to let my hair all down. I'm not wearing it to bed all up like this," Felicia said from her toilette against the side wall of the bedroom.

"Shall I brush your hair for you?" Nathaniel asked, and Felicia swiveled in her chair to look at him, nodding vigorously.

She took her hair down from its coiled mass and it tumbled down her back as she shook it out. Nathanial took her brush, running it through her hair. The brush strokes sent shivers down Felicia's spine. She leaned back in the wooden chair, tilting her head up to see Nathaniel. He smiled down at her and scratched his fingers on her head.

"Have you gotten any letters recently?" He set the brush down then ran his fingers through her hair.

"I have!" Felicia rummaged through a drawer in the toilette. She held up a piece of parchment and waved it in the air. "Dorcas brought it over this afternoon—it's from Mother. She said Victoria is marrying Officer Westall in the spring."

"The girl deserves some happiness," Nathaniel murmured.

"Aye. And she seems to be finally at some peace with it. We're invited to go to the wedding." Felicia rested her hands on her belly. "I surmise I won't be due for another couple months or so."

"We'll make the trip." Nathaniel stood Felicia up, playing with the hair that framed her face. "Gives your parents the chance to see Deliverance again."

"And perhaps Deliverance can sit for a portrait to send to Thomas's parents. They adore her so."

The only light in the bedroom came from the little bit of moonlight streaming in through the shutters as they made their way to bed. Nathaniel shifted on the mattress and placed his hand over her belly.

"Felicia..."

"Hmm?"

"About the child... if he is to be a boy..."

"A son," Felicia murmured with a smile. "Another Nathaniel Poe."

A solemn look crossed Nathaniel's face, and he shook his head. "What about John Henry?"

Felicia drew in a deep breath, then let it out slowly. "For my father and..." Her voice broke off, and tears pricked the corners of her eyes.

"And for the man who risked—and lost—everything for us."

Felicia turned her face toward Nathaniel and whispered, "I think that's a wonderful name."

She glanced up to the ceiling and mouthed a silent prayer. Both of her children would be named for men had their lives stolen. She thanked God for those men, then praised Him for the one lying beside her that moment.

Felicia slipped down against the pillows, pulled the covers over them, then wrapped her arm over Nathaniel's waist. She moved a lock of his hair, kissing the shell of his ear.

"Goodnight, Natty," she whispered.

Nathaniel tilted his head toward her, giving her a sleepy grin, and nuzzled her hair.

She breathed in his scent of cedar and rosin and relaxed into his arms, listening to the nightingales outside, feeling his heartbeat against her cheek. Its rhythm conveyed a different melody than before, but it was the glorious new music of her life—of their life. The new babe fluttered within her. She closed her eyes and smiled, pondering all that had happened in her heart.

MOORE FAMILY

WINTHROP/
HAWKINGS/POE FAMILY

COLONEL WILLIAM
MOORE

HENRY MOORE

ABIGAIL
WINTHROP

JOHN
WINTHROP

VICTORIA
MOORE

MAJOR THOMAS
HAWKINGS

FELICIA HAWKINGS
POE

NATHANIEL POE

DELIVERANCE
THEODOSIA HAWKINGS
POE

JOHN HENRY POE

ACKNOWLEDGMENTS

To begin this acknowledgement section, stating how this book came to be is in order. *Pondered* began in 2014, when I was far too young for this project. I was fresh from my first year of college when my aunt sent me a clipping from a magazine that had a contest for Christian women's fiction.

My deadline was pressed, but the minimum word limit was only ten-thousand words. Which, I suppose to somebody who doesn't write seems like the longest thing to ever pen. (Somewhere, Victor Hugo is laughing.) But as I had been given bad information from the world's leading novel-writing website, the one where they have you write fifty-thousand words in a month, I was under the assumption that novels were far shorter than they actually are. I'd aim for the gold but wouldn't be upset if I only got thirty or twenty thousand.

I got to ten-thousand words and called it quits on that awful draft.

Yet without it, *Pondered* would not exist. I did salvage some of the skeleton. In fact, there's a passage describing Nathaniel's workspace that I was able to copy over and edit into this one.

I had checked out hundreds of books on the 1770s, so my foundation was fairly firm.

I had the basic plot.

Man takes on widowed, expectant wife of a redcoat major. Man is patriot.

That was about it. I scrapped nearly everything and stopped trying to write "Christian Fiction."

Over the next few years, I had shoved it aside, but it lingered in my brain. The title never left my mind. *Pondered in her Heart.* Even after graduating college and writing four novels before this one, it remained.

So I had to write it. And I did in July of 2019. The first draft was completed after the much-needed scrap and revise. New characters were added. Higher stakes. A new villain—would you believe Felicia's mother used to be the main villain? Abigail Winthrop would never have tolerated such nonsense.

Finally, after many drafts and edits, I have the book that you hopefully have just enjoyed.

And now, I can actually thank people for helping this book become what it is.

I'm going to acknowledge my Aunt Cathy. She gave me the clipping to jumpstart the original idea.

My mother, with whom I discussed the original plot details. She also was forced to listen to the updated ideas on long car rides. So thanks for that.

However, I do NOT thank you for laughing hysterically at me when I was sobbing over edits of Chapter 31. That was uncalled for.

Every girl in The Enchanted Lair. Without you guys, I would not be where I am today in my writing and publishing journey.

Tori. Without your three-am conversations, Chapter 31 wouldn't exist. I suppose it does need to exist even if I rather it not. Also for providing the inspiration for William's daughter. Thanks, dude.

Jess. My illustrator. I'm acknowledging you for sending me unprompted extra art of Henry Moore at seven in the morning my time, sending me from my bed to run around the house without my glasses on, blindly trying to show my family the art. She's also acknowledged for sending me art of Les Miserables characters to calm me down after sobbing at Chapter 31 after my mom laughed hysterically at me.

So once again, Mom, that was uncalled for.

My editor, Cathy Hinkle, who has taken this book from one to one hundred, despite tragedy and Covid-19. She's also started the hashtag #hugsforHenry. You have been invaluable and a treasure. Thank you so much.

The face-claims and works that have inspired me when drafting this novel. The first reader to pick up on the "Cool, Cool Considerate Men" reference in this book, should contact me and I will give you a tin of tea based on one of the characters in the book.

Reeses Orme, who was the bestest girl in the world, who comforted me during the original writing of Chapter 31.

Petitaire Orme, who kept jumping on his mother's lap and pressing keys with his paws, adding his own thoughts to the book. Thank you, baby boy, but "+39432309-," really doesn't mean much for this novel. Maybe next time.

C.S. Lewis, for writing *The Problem of Pain* and *A Grief Observed* which were referenced in this novel. Also for writing *The Chronicles of Narnia*. Without that series, I wouldn't be an author.

Finally, to my father, who brought home the 1979 cartoon version of *The Lion, The Witch, and the Wardrobe* when I was twelve. That sounds like it doesn't matter in the slightest, but without it, I wouldn't have jumped deep into my love for Narnia and then for writing. Without this, ultimately, I would have no knight to protect me from the dragons that would breathe fire later on me in the coming years. I shudder to think of where I'd be if you didn't come home with that movie just because you happened upon it. Must have been God telling you to pick that up, because honestly that's what started all of this. Thank you from the bottom of my heart.

Thank you all.